INTERNATIONAL ACCLAIM FOR

JONATHAN COE'S

THE TERRIBLE PRIVACY OF

MAXWELL SIM

JONATHAN COE

THE TERRIBLE PRIVACY OF
MAXWELL SIM

Jonathan Coe's awards include the John Llewellyn
Rhys Prize, the Prix du Meilleur Livre Étranger, the
Prix Médicis Étranger, and, for *The Rotters' Club*,
the Bollinger Everyman Wodehouse Prize. He lives
in London with his wife and their two daughters.

www.jonathancoewriter.com

THE TERRIBLE PRIVACY OF

MAXWELL SIM

JONATHAN COE

Vintage Contemporaries
Vintage Books
A Division of Random House, Inc.
New York

FIRST VINTAGE CONTEMPORARIES EDITION, MARCH 2012

The Library of Congress has cataloged the Knopf edition as follows:
Coe, Jonathan.
The terrible privacy of Maxwell Sim / by Jonathan Coe.—1st U.S. ed.
p.   cm.
1. Losers—Fiction.   2. Divorced men—Fiction.
3. Middle-aged men—Fiction.   4. Failure (Psychology)—Fiction.
5. Interpersonal relations—Fiction. 6. Automobile travel—Fiction.
7. Self-actualization (Psychology)—Fiction.
8. Psychological fiction.   I. Title.
PR6053.026T47 2011
823'.914—dc22 2010035997

Vintage ISBN: 978-0-307-74215-5

Book design by Soonyoung Kwon

www.vintagebooks.com

Printed in the United States of America
10 9 8 7 6 5 3 2 1

Man is a lever whose ultimate length and strength he must determine for himself.

—Donald Crowhurst,
quoted in *The Strange Voyage of Donald Crowhurst*,
by Nicholas Tomalin and Ron Hall

Geography no longer matters because there is no near or far, the monetary sheath enclosing the globe has destroyed the geography of distances.

—Alasdair Gray, *1982, Janine*

One day I will die, and on my grave it will say, "Here lies Reginald Iolanthe Perrin; he didn't know the names of the flowers and the trees, but he knew the rhubarb crumble sales for Schleswig-Holstein."

—David Nobbs, *The Fall and Rise of Reginald Perrin*

Through words, she offers us her shaming revelations. Through words, she gives us her terrible privacy.

—James Wood,
writing about Toni Morrison
in the *Guardian*, 18 April 1992

CONTENTS

Salesman found naked in car

Grampian Police patrolling the snowbound stretch of the A93 between Braemar and Spittal of Glenshee on Thursday night spotted a car apparently abandoned at the side of the road just below the Glenshee Ski Centre.

On closer inspection it became clear that the unconscious driver was still inside the car. Clothes belonging to the middle-aged man, who was almost naked, were found scattered throughout the vehicle. On the passenger seat beside him were two empty whisky bottles.

The mystery deepened as the policemen inspected the boot of the car and found two cardboard boxes containing more than 400 toothbrushes, as well as a large black bin liner filled with picture postcards of the Far East.

The man was suffering from severe hypothermia and was flown to Aberdeen Royal Infirmary by air ambulance. He was later identified as Mr. Maxwell Sim, aged 48, of Watford, England.

Mr. Sim was a salesman employed on a freelance basis by Guest Toothbrushes of Reading, a company specialising in ecologically friendly oral hygiene products. The company had gone into liquidation that morning.

Mr. Sim has made a full recovery and is believed to have returned to his home in Watford. Police have not yet confirmed whether they will press charges for drink driving.

Aberdeenshire Press and Journal
MONDAY, 9 MARCH 2009

SYDNEY-WATFORD

When I saw the Chinese woman and her daughter playing cards together at their restaurant table, the water and the lights of Sydney Harbour shimmering behind them, it set me thinking about Stuart, and the reason he had to give up driving his car.

I was going to say "my friend Stuart," but I suppose he's not a friend anymore. I seem to have lost a number of friends in the last few years. I don't mean that I've fallen out with them, in any dramatic way. We've just decided not to stay in touch. And that's what it's been: a decision, a conscious decision, because it's not difficult to stay in touch with people nowadays, there are so many different ways of doing it. But as you get older, I think that some friendships start to feel increasingly redundant. You just find yourself asking, "What's the point?" And then you stop.

Anyway, about Stuart and his driving. He had to stop because of the panic attacks. He was a good driver, a careful and conscientious driver, and he had never been involved in an accident. But occasionally, when he got behind the wheel of a car, he would experience these panic attacks, and after a while they started to get worse, and they started to happen more often. I can remember when he first started telling me about all this: it was lunchtime and we were in the canteen of the department store in Ealing, where we worked together for a year or two. I don't think I can have listened very carefully, though, because Caroline was sitting at the same table, and things between us were just starting to get interesting, so the last thing I wanted to hear about was Stuart and his neuroses about driving. That must be why I never really thought about it again until years later, at the restaurant on Sydney Harbour, when it all came back. His problem, as far as I can remember, was this: Whereas most people, as they watched the coming and going of cars on a busy road, would see a normal, properly functioning traffic system, Stuart could only perceive it as an endless succession of narrowly averted accidents. He saw cars hurtling towards each other at considerable speeds, and missing each other by inches—time and time again, every few seconds, repeated constantly throughout the day. "All those cars," he said to me, "only *just* managing not to crash into each other. How can people stand it?" In the end it became too much for him to contemplate, and he had to stop driving.

Why had this conversation just come back to me, tonight of all nights? It was 14 February 2009. The second Saturday in February. Valentine's Day, in case you hadn't noticed. The water and the lights of Sydney Harbour were shimmering behind me, and I was dining alone since my father had, for various weird reasons of his own, refused to come out with me, even though this was my last evening in Australia, and the only reason for my visiting Australia in the first place had been to see him and try to rebuild my relationship with him. Right now, in fact, I was probably feeling more alone than I had ever felt in my life, and what really brought it home to me was the sight of the Chinese woman and her daughter playing cards together at their restaurant table. They looked so happy in each other's company. There was such a connection between them. They weren't talking very much, and when they did talk, it was about their card game, as far as I could tell, but that didn't matter. It was all in their eyes, their smiles, the way they kept laughing, the way they kept leaning in to each other. By comparison, none of the diners at the other tables seemed to be having any fun. Sure, they were all laughing and talking too. But they didn't seem to be entirely *absorbed* in each other, the way the Chinese woman and her daughter did. There was a couple sitting opposite me, out on a Valentine's Day date by the looks of it: he kept checking his watch, she kept checking her mobile for text messages. Behind me there was a family of four: the two little boys were playing on their Nintendo DSs, and the husband and wife hadn't spoken to each other for about ten minutes. To the left of me, slightly blocking my view of the waterfront, was a group of six friends: two of them were involved in this big argument which had started out as a discussion of global warming, and now seemed to have more to do with economics; neither of them was giving any ground, while the other four sat there in bored silence, looking on. An elderly couple on the other side of me had chosen to sit side by side at their table, rather than opposite each other, so that they could both look at the view instead of talking. None of this depressed me, exactly. I daresay that all of these people would go home thinking they'd had a perfectly enjoyable night out. But it was only the Chinese woman and her daughter who I really envied. It was clear they had something precious: something I wanted badly. Something I wanted to share in.

How could I be sure that she was Chinese? Well, I couldn't. But she looked Chinese to me. She had long black hair, slightly wild and unkempt. A thin face, with prominent cheekbones. (Sorry, I am just not very good at describing people.) Bright red lipstick, which struck me as an odd touch. A lovely smile, slightly tight-lipped but all the brighter for that, somehow. She was expensively dressed, with some sort of black chiffon scarf

(I am not very good at describing clothes either—are you looking forward to the next few hundred pages?) held in place by a
large golden brooch. So she was well-off. Elegant—that would
be a good word to describe her. Very elegant. Her daughter
was well dressed too, and also had black hair (well, you don't
get many Chinese blondes), and seemed to be about eight or
nine years old. She had a beautiful laugh: it started as a throaty
chuckle and then bubbled up into a series of giggles which cas-
caded and finally died away like a stream tumbling down a hillside into a series of pools. (Just like the ones Mum and I used to
walk past whenever she took me for a walk on the Lickey Hills,
all those years ago, at the back of the Rose and Crown pub, on
the edge of the municipal golf course. I suppose that's what
her laugh reminded me of, and perhaps that's another of the
reasons the Chinese girl and her mother made such an impression on me that evening.) I don't know what was making her
laugh so much: something to do with the card game, which
wasn't a really silly, childish one like snap, but didn't seem to
be very serious or grown-up either. Perhaps they were playing knockout whist or something like that. Whatever it was,
it was making the little girl laugh, and her mother was playing
along with her laughter, encouraging it, joining in, surfing on
its waves. It was such a pleasure to look at them, but I had to
ration my glances, in case they noticed I was looking and the
Chinese woman decided I was some kind of creep. Once or
twice she had noticed me looking at her and had held my gaze
for a couple of seconds, but it wasn't long enough, I couldn't
read any kind of invitation into it, and after those couple of
seconds she looked away and she and her daughter would start
talking and laughing again, quickly rebuilding that wall of intimacy, that protective screen.

Right at that moment, I would have liked to text Stuart,

but I didn't have his mobile number anymore. I would have liked to text him to say that I understood, now, what it was he'd been trying to tell me about cars. Cars are like people. We mill around every day, we rush here and there, we come within inches of touching each other, but very little real contact goes on. All those near misses. All those might-have-beens. It's frightening, when you think about it. Probably best not to think about it at all.

Can you remember where you were the day John Smith died? I suspect that most people can't. In fact I suspect that many people can't even remember who John Smith was. Well, there have been a lot of John Smiths, of course, over the years, but the one I'm thinking of was the leader of the British Labour Party, who died of a heart attack in 1994. I realise his death doesn't have the global resonance of a JFK or a Princess Diana, but I can still remember where I was, with absolute clarity. I was in the canteen of that department store in Ealing, having my lunch. Stuart was with me, and two or three other guys including one called Dave, who was an absolute pain in the arse. He worked in electrical goods and was just the kind of man I can't stand. Loud and boring and much too sure of himself. And sitting at the table next to ours, all by herself, was this lovely woman in her early twenties with shoulder-length, light-brown hair, who looked lonely and out of place and kept glancing in our direction. Her name (as I was to find out, soon enough) was Caroline.

I'd only been working at the department store for a month or two. Before then I'd spent two or three years on the road selling toys for a company based in St. Albans. It was a nice enough job, in a way. I became good friends with the other south-eastern rep, Trevor Paige, and we had some great times together, in those two or three years, but I never enjoyed being on the road as much as he did, and it wasn't long before the novelty of all that travelling had well and truly worn off. I started looking for a chance to settle down. I'd recently put down the deposit on a nice little terraced house in Watford (not far from Trevor's, as it happened) and was keeping my eyes open for a new job opportunity. The store in Ealing had always been one of my regular calling points, and I'd also made it my business to become friendly with Stuart, who ran the toy department. There's always something rather artificial, I suppose, about friendships formed for business reasons, but Stuart and I did genuinely grow to like each other, and after a while I tried to make sure that Ealing would be my last call of the day, so we could go out for a quick drink together after we'd had our meeting. And then one evening Stuart called me at home, outside work hours, and told me that he was being promoted to a job in the office upstairs, and he invited me to apply for his job running the toy department. Well, I hesitated at first, worrying how Trevor was going to react; but in the event, he was fine about it. He knew it was just what I'd been looking for. So a couple of months later, I found myself working in Ealing fulltime, and having lunch every day in the canteen with Stuart and his colleagues, and that was when I started to notice this lovely woman in her early twenties with light-brown hair who always seemed to be eating lunch by herself at the next table.

It all seems like such a long time ago, now. Anything seemed possible, in those days. Anything at all. I wonder if that feeling ever comes back?

Best not to go down that path.

OK, then: the death of John Smith. There was a bunch of us guys in the canteen that day, sitting at one of the Formica-

topped tables having our lunch. It was early in the summer of
1994. Don't ask me if it was sunny or rainy, though, because no
sense of the weather outside ever managed to filter through to
that dimly lit space. We took our lunches in a sort of perpetual
twilight. What was different about that day, however, was that
Dave—that's the obnoxious guy from electrical goods, the one
I couldn't stand—had asked Caroline to join us. Clearly, his
plan was to try chatting her up, but it was all rather painful
to witness because he kept making all the wrong moves. After
failing to impress her with a description of his sports car and
the state-of-the-art stereo system at his fancy bachelor pad
in Hammersmith, he turned to the subject of John Smith's
death—which had been announced on the radio that morning—and started using it as an excuse for a series of bad-taste
jokes about heart attacks. Things like this: apparently, following Smith's first heart attack in the late 1980s, the doctors had
been able to revive his heart but not his brain—so was it any
wonder that they'd made him leader of the Labour Party? Caroline's response to this attempt at humour was to persist with
the contemptuous silence she had maintained throughout the
meal; and apart from some tepid waves of laughter there was
no reaction from anyone until I heard myself saying—slightly
to my own astonishment—"That's not funny, Dave. Not funny
at all." Most of the guys had finished their lunches by now, and
it wasn't long before people started getting up and leaving, but
not me and Caroline: neither of us said anything, but we both
decided to stay behind and linger over our puddings, as if by
some unspoken agreement. And so for a minute or two we sat
there in awkward, expectant silence, until I made an embarrassed comment about sensitivity not being Dave's strong
point, and then, for the very first time, Caroline spoke.

That was the same moment, I believe, that I fell in love

with her. It was her voice, you see. I had been expecting something clipped and ultra-refined to go with her looks, but instead
she came out with this really broad, down-to-earth Lancastrian
accent. It took me so much by surprise—I was so enthralled by
it—that at first I forgot to listen to what she was actually saying
and just let her voice play over me, almost as if she was talking
in some mellifluous foreign language. Quickly, though, before
I made too disastrous an impression, I pulled myself together
and started to concentrate and realised that she was asking me
why I hadn't joined in with the jokes. She wanted to know if
it was because I was a Labour supporter and I said no, it was
nothing to do with that at all. I just told her I didn't think it was
right to make jokes about someone so soon after he had died,
especially when he had always seemed to be a decent man and
was leaving a wife and a family behind. Caroline agreed with
me about that but she also seemed to be sorry about his death
for a different reason: she thought it had come at a terrible time
for British politics and said that John Smith would probably
have won the next election and might have turned out to be a
great prime minister.

Well, I admit it was not the sort of conversation you usually heard in the canteen of the department store, let alone the
sort that I very often took part in myself. I've never been very
interested in politics. (In fact, I didn't even vote in the last two
elections, although I did eventually vote for Tony Blair in 1997,
mainly because I thought it was what Caroline wanted me to
do.) And when I found out, as I soon did, that Caroline was
working in the maternity section of the department store only
as a temporary measure, while she began her first novel, I felt
even more out of my depth. I hardly ever read novels, never
mind trying to write one. But in a way this only fuelled my
curiosity. I couldn't work Caroline out, you see. After spend-

ing all those years on the road, cold-calling people and trying to sell them stuff, I was fairly satisfied with my ability to size people up and decide, in the space of a few seconds, what it was that made them tick. But I hadn't met many people like Caroline. I'd never been to university (she was a history graduate from Manchester) and had spent most of my adult life in the company of men—businessmen, at that. The kind of people who never gave away much about themselves when they talked and tended to take the status quo for granted. Compared to them, Caroline was an unknown quantity. I couldn't even begin to guess what had brought her to this job.

She gave me the explanation for that on our first date, and a very sad story it turned out to be. We were in a branch of Spaghetti House (one of my favourite chains, back in those days, though you don't see so many of them anymore) and while Caroline picked at her tagliatelle carbonara she told me that, when she was at university in Manchester, she'd got quite deeply involved with a man who was studying English in the same year as her. Then he'd got a job in London, working in a TV production company, so they'd both moved down and found themselves a flat in Ealing. Caroline's real ambition was to write books—novels and short stories—so she took the job in the department store as a temporary thing, trying to get on with her writing in the evening and at weekends. Meanwhile, her boyfriend started an affair with someone he'd met at the production company, and fell madly in love with her, and within a couple of weeks he'd dumped Caroline and moved out, and she was left all by herself, living somewhere where she had no friends and doing a job in which she had no interest.

Well, the truth is obvious enough now, isn't it? There's a phrase, a cliché, for the state Caroline was in back then: *on the rebound*. She liked me because I was being kind to her, and because I'd caught her at a low ebb, and because I probably wasn't quite as crass and insensitive as the other guys in the canteen. But there's no denying, in retrospect, that I was out of her league. In a way it's amazing we lasted as long as we did. But of course, you can't see into the future. I usually have trouble seeing a couple of weeks ahead, never mind fifteen years. Back then we were young and naive, and at the end of that evening in the Spaghetti House, when I asked her if she'd like to drive out into the country with me at the weekend, neither of us had the slightest idea where it would lead, and all I can remember now is the shining light of gratitude in her eyes as she said yes.

Fifteen years ago. Is fifteen years a long time, or a short time? I suppose everything is relative. Set against the history of man-kind, fifteen years is just the blink of an eye, but it also seemed that I had travelled a long way, an unimaginably long way, from the hope and excitement of that faraway first date in the Spa-ghetti House to the evening a few months ago, 14 February 2009, when (at the age of forty-eight) I found myself sitting alone at a restaurant in Australia, the water and the lights of Sydney Harbour shimmering behind me, and I couldn't stop staring at the beautiful Chinese woman and her little daughter who were playing cards together at their table. Caroline had left home by then. Walked out, I mean. She had been gone six months and had taken our daughter, Lucy, with her. They had moved up north, to Kendal in the Lake District. What was it, finally, that drove her away? Just a long-standing build-up of frustration, I suppose. Apart from the birth of Lucy, it seemed that the last fifteen years hadn't brought Caroline any of the things she'd been hoping for. The great novel remained unwrit-ten. She hadn't even managed to finish a short story, so far as

I knew. Lucy's arrival had put paid to a lot of that. Mother-hood is pretty demanding, after all. I certainly couldn't see why being married to me should stop her from writing anything, if that's what she really wanted to do. Another thing that occurs to me is that, deep down (and this is painful to admit), Caroline might have been a little bit ashamed of me. Of my job, to be more precise. I'd moved on, by now, to one of the biggest and most prestigious department stores in central London, where I was employed as an After-Sales Customer Liaison Officer. It was an excellent job, as far as I could see. But maybe there was a part of her that thought the husband of an aspiring writer should do something a bit more . . . I don't know—artistic? intellectual? You'd think we might have discussed some of these issues, but the saddest thing about our marriage, during the last few years, had been the almost complete lack of com-munication. We seemed to have forgotten the art of talking to each other, except in the form of screaming rows accompanied by the swapping of painful insults and the hurling of household objects. I won't rehearse all the details but I do remember one of our exchanges, from the penultimate squabble or perhaps the one before that. We had begun by arguing over whether to use an abrasive scourer or a soft sponge to clean off the stainless-steel surface of our cooker, and within about thirty seconds I heard myself telling Caroline that it was clear she didn't love me anymore. When she failed to deny it, I said, "Sometimes I don't even think you *like* me that much," and do you know what she said to that? She said, "How can anybody like a man who doesn't even like himself?"

Well, if she was going to talk in riddles, we would never get anywhere.

———

The Chinese woman and her daughter stayed at the restaurant for a long time. Considering how young the daughter was, it was surprising that they were still there at about ten-thirty. They'd finished eating ages ago and all that was keeping them there now was the card game. Most of the tables were empty, and soon it would be time for me to go back to Dad's flat as well. There were some things we needed to talk about before I caught my flight home the next afternoon. I needed a pee before leaving, though, so I stood up from my table and made my way to the gents' in the basement.

I don't like to pee standing up. Don't ask me why. As far as I know, there was no traumatic incident when I was a child, getting molested in a public toilet or anything like that. In fact I don't like to pee standing up even when there is no one else in the gents', in case someone walks in when I'm halfway through, causing me to stop in mid-flow and turn myself off like a tap, and then have to walk out in a fury of frustration and embarrassment, with my bladder still half-full. So I sat down in one of the cubicles—after making the usual preparations, wiping the seat and so on—and that was when it really hit me. The loneliness. I was sitting in a tiny little box, underground, tens of thousands of miles from home. If I were to have a sudden heart attack sitting on that toilet, what would be the consequence? Some member of the restaurant staff would probably find me just before they locked up. The police would be called and they would look at my passport and credit cards and somehow, I suppose, through the use of some international database, they would work out my connections to Dad and to Caroline, and they would phone them up and tell them. How would Caroline take the news? She'd be pretty upset, at first, but I'm not sure how deep that would go. I didn't play much part in her life anymore. It would be worse for Lucy, of course, but even she was growing steadily more distant: it was more than a month since I'd heard anything from her. And who else was there? There might be one or two passing tremors of feeling from friends or work colleagues, maybe, but nothing major. Chris, my old schoolfriend, might feel . . . well, something, some spasm of regret that we'd become estranged and hadn't seen each other for so long. Trevor Paige would be sorry, genuinely sorry. So would Janice, his wife. But beyond that, my passing wouldn't send out many ripples. A Facebook account gone inactive— but would any of my Facebook friends really notice? I doubted it. I was alone in the world, now, terribly alone. I would be flying home the next day, and pretty much all that would be waiting for me when I got there was an unlived-in flat full of Ikea furniture and three weeks' worth of bills, bank statements and pizza-delivery adverts. And now I was sitting by myself in a little wooden box in the basement of a restaurant beside Sydney Harbour while upstairs, just a few feet above my head, were two people who—however much they might in other ways be alone in the world—at least had each other; at least were bonded to each other, with a strength and an intensity that was obvious to anyone who so much as glanced at them. I envied them for that, fiercely. The thought of it filled me with a sudden, overwhelming need to get to know this beautiful Chinese woman and her beautiful daughter, who loved each other so much. The prospect of walking away from this restaurant without attempting to introduce myself—to make them aware, somehow, that I existed—seemed intolerable.

And the amazing thing was that the more I thought about it, the more I realised there was no reason why I shouldn't actually do it. Why was I even hesitating? This was the very thing I was supposed to be good at. Before Caroline and Lucy left me, knocking me for six and turning me into a sort of involuntary hermit, I had built an entire career on my ability to get on with people. What else do you think an After-Sales Customer Liaison Officer does, after all? It's more or less the very definition of the job. I could be charming when I wanted to be. I knew how to put a woman at her ease. I knew that politeness, good manners and an unthreatening tone of voice would usually disarm even the wariest stranger.

And so that night—for the very first time since Caroline had walked out on me, six months earlier—I finally came to a decision: a strong one. Without even bothering to work out what I was going to say, I left the cubicle, gave my hands a cursory rinse and climbed back upstairs with quick, resolute steps. I was breathing heavily and tense with nervousness but also a sense of freedom and relief.

But the Chinese woman and her daughter had paid their bill and were gone.

2

My father was asleep when I got back from the restaurant, so we had to wait until the morning, over breakfast, to resume our argument about his flat in Lichfield.

Actually "argument" is too strong a word for the kind of confrontations I have with my father. So is "confrontations," for that matter. My father and I have never raised our voices to each other. If either of us disagrees with the other, or takes offence, we simply retreat into a wounded silence—which has been known to last, in some instances, for several years. This method has always worked for us, after a fashion, although I know that other people find it peculiar. Caroline, for instance, was forever taking me to task on this subject. "Why do you and your father never talk to each other properly?" she used to ask me. "When was the last time you had a real conversation with him?" I would remind her that this was an easy thing for her to say. She didn't know what a difficult man my father was. In fact she barely knew him at all, having only met him once, the time we took Lucy out to Australia when she was about two. (My father had not come back to England for my wedding, or for the birth of his only grandchild.) As it happened, both he and Caroline were aspiring writers—although my father's preferred form of expression has always been poetry, if you please—so she'd been hoping that this shared interest would provide some common ground; but even she had to concede, after a few days, that he wasn't the easiest person to understand or talk to. All the same, it remained a bone of contention between me and Caroline, during the next few years, that my relationship with my father was so badly damaged. I was an only child, and my mother had died when I was twenty-four, so he was really all that I had in the way of family. And when Caroline finally left me, her parting gift (if you can call it that) was this trip to Australia, which she paid for without telling me anything about it: the first I knew being an e-mail from Expedia one day just before Christmas, reminding me to apply for an online tourist visa. She had booked me on a flight which left Heathrow exactly six months to the day after her departure—sensing, perhaps, that I would not be ready for the journey before then, and that this was the earliest I could expect to have climbed out of the trough of depression to which she knew she was condemning me. And in this respect, her calculation (the word seems appropriate, somehow) proved to be accurate. Just goes to show, I suppose, that after all those years she really did know me inside out.

Well, Caroline, it was a charming thought. Cheer up your abandoned husband by sending him off to see his estranged father for three weeks and get them talking to each other again. The trouble is, it takes more than a bit of goodwill and a cut-price airfare to engineer a miracle like that. The next morning, as we ate our last breakfast together in near-silence, I realised that my father and I were as distant as we'd ever been. If the Chinese woman and her daughter were at one end of the scale of human intimacy, we were right at the other. In fact we were almost off the scale. Looking back, there were any number of things we could have bonded over. The fact that our partners had a habit of walking out on us, for instance. Since moving to Australia more than twenty years ago, my father had drifted in and out of any number of half-hearted relationships: I had met only one of the women involved, and she had given up on him five or six years ago. Since then he had been living with a retired pharmacist in the suburb of Mosman, but they'd split up just a few weeks earlier, and he'd now been obliged to find a new apartment, which at the moment was barely decorated or furnished. So we could have talked about that sort of thing; but we didn't. Instead, we returned to the subject of his flat in Lichfield. He'd bought it back in the mid-1980s, just after Mum died—in response to some unspoken impulse, I imagine, to return to the city of his birth—and I'd always assumed that he'd sold it again before moving to Australia. But apparently not. Apparently it had been sitting empty for the last twenty years. Now, I realise that most sons would have got angry with their fathers when they learned that a potentially valuable family property had been allowed to sit empty for twenty years, falling into disrepair. But all I said was, "That seems a bit of a waste." And all he said was, "Yes, I should probably do something about it." Then he asked if I would go and look at the flat when I went back to England. I thought he meant that he wanted me to start the process of putting it on the market, and I began telling him that it wasn't a good time to try selling property in the UK right now, the credit crunch was starting to bite, people were losing their jobs and their savings, everyone was in a state of financial uncertainty, and house prices were falling every month. To which my father answered that he had no intention of selling the flat. He said that he just wanted me to go there and look for a blue ring binder on one of the bookshelves, with the words *Two Duets* written on the spine, and send it back to him. I asked him what was so significant about this blue ring binder and he said it contained some "important" poems and other bits of writing, and he wanted it now because the only other copy had been thrown away by his former partner (the pharmacist from Mosman) a few weeks ago when they'd split up. Also, he said that I should read it before sending it to him because among other things it explained how I came to be born; and then he launched into a long and rather bizarre digression about how I would never have been born if there hadn't been two pubs close to each other in London, both called the Rising Sun, back in the late 1950s. Again, other sons would probably have pressed their fathers on this point, but I suppose I just thought, "Oh God, there goes Dad again—rambling away, off on some strange tangent of his own," and instead I started asking him exactly where the ring binder could be found and precisely what shade of blue it was. So, given an opportunity to delve into a potentially interesting byway of our shared history, we instead ended up discussing stationery. The usual situation, in other words. And after that I went into the spare bedroom to pack.

In the taxi on the way to the airport, I didn't think about my father. I found myself thinking about the Chinese woman and her daughter, and what a shame it was they'd left the restaurant before I'd had the chance to speak to them. All was not entirely lost, it's true, because I had managed to corner the waiter after I came back upstairs, and he told me something about them that was potentially useful. He didn't know who they were, or where they came from, but he did know this: that they came to the restaurant regularly, on the second Saturday evening of every month, without fail; and that they were always alone and never brought a man with them. And for some reason—although I know it sounds crazy—I was comforted by both of these things. That restaurant may have been ten thousand miles from where I lived, but the world is a small place these days, and getting smaller all the time, and at least I knew I could get on a plane whenever I wanted to and fly to Sydney and go to that restaurant on the second Saturday of any month, and there they'd be, playing cards and laughing together. Waiting for me. (I know that sounds fanciful, but that was how I'd already started to think of it.) And what's more, they would be alone. There was no one else, no rival for their attention. I'd guessed as much, actually, from the way they behaved towards each other. There was no room for another person in that relationship. The presence of a man would have polluted it. Unless, of course, that man happened to be me.

OK, so I was letting my imagination run away with me. I was surrendering to fantasies. But maybe that in itself was a good sign. For six months now I had barely spoken to anybody. I had been off work for nearly all of that time, and had spent most of it alone at home, mainly in bed, occasionally in front of the television or the computer. As for human contact, I'd lost all appetite for it. Mankind, as you may have noticed, has become very inventive about devising new ways for people to avoid talking to each other, and I'd been taking full advantage of the most recent ones. I would always send a text message rather than speak to someone on the phone. Instead of meeting with any of my friends, I would post cheerful, ironically worded status updates on Facebook, to show them all what a busy life I was leading. And presumably people had been enjoying them, because I'd got more than seventy friends on Facebook now, most of them complete strangers. But actual, face-to-face, let's-meet-for-a-coffee-and-catch-up sort of contact? I seemed to have forgotten what that was all about. Forgotten, at least, until the Chinese woman and her daughter had reminded me. It may sound like a strange thing to say, but their closeness, their intimacy, had been the first thing I'd seen in six months which had given me hope. Had made me feel, even, that my luck might be about to turn.

And then, that very next day at the airport, something else

happened that gave me exactly the same feeling. I was standing in the queue, waiting to check in, and hoping that I would be checked in at a particular desk, which was being staffed by a friendly-looking woman, a brunette with hazel eyes and an unforced smile. I wanted it to be her because she looked like the kind of person who might—just possibly—offer you an upgrade if you asked nicely enough. Anyway, I didn't get her. Instead I found myself dealing with a grey-haired, overtanned guy of about my own age, or perhaps even older, who had no interest in making small talk and rarely looked up from his work to make eye contact. It seemed pretty clear that I was on a hiding to nothing here. But I couldn't stop myself from trying, all the same.

"Busy flight?" I heard myself ask.

"Pretty busy," he answered.

"No chance of an upgrade, then?" I said, and he grunted with laughter.

"If I had a dollar for everybody who asked me that . . ."

"Happens a lot, does it?"

"All the time, mate. All the time."

"So how do you decide?"

"What?" he said, looking up.

"How do you decide who gets an upgrade, and who doesn't?"

"I guess," he said, staring at me directly and appraisingly before lowering his eyes again, "I have to like the look of whoever's doing the asking."

He said nothing more, and I felt crushed into silence. It wasn't until I had finished checking in, watched my suitcase sway off into oblivion and walked a few yards away from the desk that I thought to check my two boarding cards (one for each leg of the journey) and realised that he *had* upgraded me—to something called Premium Economy class. I looked back at the man to show my gratitude. He was busy with the next passenger, but he still found time to glance across at me. His expression remained blank—even surly—and yet he winked at me before returning his gaze to the computer screen in front of him.

Two hours later, at about four-thirty in the afternoon, Sydney time, I was sipping my second glass of champagne, waiting for takeoff, and contemplating the delights of the journey ahead.

I had a seat on the aisle; the one next to mine, a window seat, was currently empty. The seats were wide and well-padded, and I had plenty of leg room. I felt an almost sensual glow of pleasure at the thought of the pampering I could look forward to. Thirteen hours to Singapore, which would include dinner, a few more glasses of champagne to wash it down, a choice of more than five hundred movies and TV shows on the entertainment console in the seat-back, and perhaps a light snooze somewhere along the way. Then a couple of hours' stopover at Singapore airport, back on to a plane, a large whisky, some sleeping pills, and I would be out like a light until we reached Heathrow the following morning. Couldn't be better.

At least that's how it should have been. The trouble was, as I said, that seeing the Chinese woman and her daughter had unexpectedly reawakened my need for human contact. I wanted to talk. I was desperate to talk.

No surprise, then, that when a pale, overweight businessman in a light-grey suit squeezed past me, with the most cursory nod of apology, and settled into the adjacent window seat, I felt an overwhelming urge to engage him in conversation. It was a misguided urge, I have to say. If my experience in sales had taught me anything over the years, it was how to read people's faces, so it really should have been pretty obvious that this aloof and weary-looking stranger had little interest in talking to me, and would have much preferred to be left alone with his newspapers and his laptop. But I suppose the truth is that I did notice it, and purposely chose to ignore the fact.

The businessman took a minute or two to settle into his chair and get comfortable. Once settled, he realised he'd left his computer in a bag in the overhead locker, so then he had to get up again and there was some more slightly breathless tugging and manipulating to be done before we were both back in our places. Then he flipped open the laptop and almost at once started typing furiously. After about five minutes he stopped, glanced quickly over the words on the screen, pressed a final button with a firm, almost theatrical gesture, then sighed and sat back in his chair, panting a little bit as the computer shut itself down. He turned his head towards me, not really looking at me; but the gesture was enough. I took it as my doorway into conversation, even if he hadn't meant it that way.

"All done?" I said.

He looked blankly at me, obviously not expecting to be addressed. For a moment I thought he wasn't going to say anything, but then he managed: "Uh-huh."

"Last-minute e-mails?" I ventured.

"Yep."

His accent seemed to be Australian, although it was pretty hard to tell just from the words "Uh-huh" and "Yep."

"You know what I love about aeroplanes?" I asked, undaunted. "They're the last place left to us where we can be totally inaccessible. Totally free. No one can phone you or text you on an aeroplane. Once you're in the air, nobody can send you an e-mail. Just for a few hours, you're away from all of that."

"True," said the man, "but not for much longer. There are already some airlines where you can send e-mails and use the net from your own laptop. And they're talking about letting passengers use their mobiles soon. Personally, I can't wait. What you like about flying is just what I hate about it. It's dead time. Completely dead."

"Not really," I said. "It just means that if we want to communicate with someone during a flight, it has to be done directly. You know, like—talking. It's a chance to get to know other people. New people."

He glanced across at me as I said this, and something in his expression told me that the chance of getting to know me was one he might have passed up without too many spasms of regret. But the rebuff I was expecting didn't come. Instead, he held out his hand and said gruffly, "The name's Charles. Charles Hayward. Friends call me Charlie."

"Maxwell," I returned. "Max, for short. Maxwell Sim. Sim, like the actor." I always said this when introducing myself, but usually, unless I was talking to a British person of a certain age, the reference would go over their heads, and I would have to add: "Or like a SIM card."

"It's good to know you, Max," said Charlie; then he picked up his newspaper, turned away from me, and began reading it, starting at the financial pages.

Well, that wouldn't do. You can't sit right next to someone for thirteen hours and ignore them completely, can you? In fact, not just thirteen, but twenty-four hours—because I noticed from the boarding card lying on his table that Charlie and I had been seated together on the second leg of the flight as well. It simply wouldn't be human to sit in silence for all that time. I was pretty sure, anyway, that, if I made a big enough effort, I would manage to draw him out. Now that we'd exchanged a few words, I realised that he didn't look unfriendly, as such, just stressed out and overworked. He must have been somewhere in his mid-fifties: over dinner he told me that he'd grown up in Brisbane and now held a fairly high-powered position in the Sydney office of a multinational corporation which was starting to experience financial difficulties. (This, I suppose, was the reason he wasn't flying Business Class.) He was on his way to London for crisis talks with some of the other senior figures: he didn't specify what the difficulties were, of course (why would he, to someone like me?), but apparently it was all to do with leverage. His company had taken out loans which were overleveraged, or underleveraged, or something like that. At one point when he was trying to explain this to me he started to look quite animated, and I thought there was a chance he might become positively chatty, but when he realised I knew nothing about leverage, and had no real understanding of any financial instrument more complicated than an overdraft or a deposit account, he seemed to lose interest in me, and from then on it became increasingly difficult to get more than a few words out of him. It didn't help that he'd drunk several glasses of champagne and a number of beers with his lunch, and was beginning to look even more tired than he had before. The other problem was that, as he grew more and more taciturn, I did the opposite and—as if terrified by the possibility of silence between us—started to turn garrulous, and began pouring out confessions and confidences which I'm sure this new acquaintance must have found boring, if not a little embarrassing.

It all began when I told him: "You're so lucky, you know—living in Sydney. What an amazing city. So different to where I live . . ."

I left a short silence, which he finally broke with the dutiful question: "Don't you live in London, then?"

"No, not London exactly. Watford."

"Ah, Watford," he repeated. It was hard to tell whether

he was investing the word with curiosity, disdain, sympathy or anything else.

"Have you been to Watford?"

He shook his head. "I don't believe I have. I've been to some great cities. Paris. New York. Buenos Aires. Rome. Moscow. Never Watford, for some reason."

"There's a lot to be said for Watford," I insisted, with a defensive edge to my voice. "Not many people know that it's twinned with Pesaro, an extremely attractive Italian town on the Adriatic coast."

"I'm sure it's a marriage made in heaven."

"Sometimes," I continued, "I do ask myself why I ended up living in Watford. I'm from Birmingham originally, you see. I suppose it came about because I got this job a few years ago with a toy company based in St. Albans, and Watford's pretty close to there, as you probably know. Or perhaps you don't. Anyway, they're right next to each other. Couldn't be handier, really, if for any reason you wanted to go from one to the other. Mind you, I stopped working for that company pretty soon after moving to Watford, which is ironic, when you think about it, because after that I started working at a department store in Ealing, which is actually further from Watford than St. Albans is. Not *much* further, you understand, just another . . . well, ten or fifteen minutes, if you're driving. Which I usually was, because it's quite hard to get from Watford to Ealing by public transport. Surprisingly hard, as a matter of fact. But I certainly don't regret taking that job—the job in Ealing, I mean—because that was how I met my wife, Caroline. Well, my ex-wife, I suppose she will soon be, because we separated a few months ago. I say separated, but what happened, really, was that she told me she didn't want to be with me anymore. Which is fine, you know, that's her prerogative, you've got to respect that kind of decision, haven't you? And she's . . . you know, she's very happy now, she's with our daughter, Lucy, they've moved back up north, and that seems to suit them, because for some reason, I don't know why, Caroline never really seemed to take to Watford, she never seemed entirely happy there, which I think is a shame, because, you know, there's something good to be found everywhere, isn't there? Which isn't to say that, living in Watford, you wake up every morning and think to yourself, Well, life may be a bit shit, but look on the bright side, at least I'm in Watford. I mean, it's not as if Watford is the sort of place where the very fact that you're living there gives you a reason to go *on* living, that would be overegging the pudding a bit, Watford just isn't that sort of place, but it does have an excellent public library, for instance, and it does have the Harlequin, which is a big new shopping centre with some . . . terrific retail outlets, actually, really terrific, and it does also—now I come to think of it, and this will amuse you, actually—well . . ." (noticing his frozen expression, I wasn't so sure) ". . . it might amuse you, anyway, it does also have Walkabout, which is a big, sort of themed bar, which has a big sign outside it offering to give you 'The Awesome Spirit of Australia,' although, thinking about it, when you're in there, it never really feels as though you're *in* Australia, you never *really* forget that you're in Watford, to be perfectly honest, but then if you're like me, and you like living in Watford anyway, what's wrong with that? I mean, some people are just happy with what they're given, aren't they, and I don't see anything wrong with that, I mean, I wouldn't say it had ever been my *ambition* to live in Watford, I don't ever recall my father sitting me down on his knee and asking me, Son, have you ever thought about what you want to do when you grow up, and me saying back to him, Well, Dad, I don't really mind, just as long as I end up living in Watford—

I don't remember any occasions like that, it's true, but then, for one thing, my father just wasn't that sort of person, he never did sit me down on his knee, as far as I can remember, he was never very tactile, or affectionate, or very . . . *present*, really, in my life, in any meaningful way, from the age of about—well, for about as long as I can remember, I suppose—but anyway, my point is that just because Watford isn't the sort of place you dream of moving to all your life, that doesn't make it the sort of place you can't wait to move out of, in fact I had a conversation along these lines a few years ago with my friend Trevor, Trevor Paige, who is one of my oldest friends, actually, we go right back to the 1990s, right back to when I used to be a sales rep for this toy company that I was telling you about, he used to cover Essex and the East Coast, and I was doing London and the Home Counties, but I left that job after a year or two, as I said, to go to this department store in Ealing, but Trevor stayed on, you see, and we carried on being friends, mainly because he only lived a couple of streets from me in Watford, until about two years ago, that is, because about two years ago we were having a drink together in Yates's Wine Lodge in the precinct, and suddenly he said, You know what, Max, I'm fed up, I am, I'm really pissed off, and I said, Pissed off? What are you pissed off with? and he said, Watford, and I said, Watford? and he said, Yes, I am, I am well and truly pissed off with Watford, I've had it up to here with Watford, I've lived in Watford for eighteen years now and to be perfectly frank I really think I've seen everything that Watford has to offer and it can truly be said that Watford holds no further delights or surprises in store, and I'll go further than that and say that if I don't get out of Watford soon I shall probably kill myself or die of boredom or frustration or something, which was a huge surprise to me, I must say, because I'd always thought that Watford suited

Trevor and Janice—that's his wife's name, Janice—down to the ground, and in fact that was one of the things that Trevor and I had always had in common, really, the fact that we were both quite partial to Watford and more than partial, actually, we were both quite *fond* of Watford, you know, a lot of our best memories and the most treasured . . . shared moments in our friendship were associated with Watford, like for instance the fact that we'd got married in Watford and our children had been born in Watford, and to be honest I thought that Trevor had really just lost it that night and it was the alcohol talking, and I can remember thinking to myself, No, Trevor will never leave Watford, he can talk the walk but he can't walk the . . . talk, or take the walk or something, anyway, I thought he'd never go through with it, but credit where it's due, there was more to Trevor than I thought, and it hadn't all been bluster, he wanted a clean break with Watford and a clean break with Watford was what he got, and six months later he and Janice moved to Reading, where he got this new job—a very good new job, by the sound of it—with a company that makes toothbrushes, or imports them anyway, I think they import them from overseas, but they distribute them all over the UK, and not just regular toothbrushes but specialist toothbrushes with quite, you know, innovative designs, and also dental floss and mouthwash and a number of other oral-hygiene products, which is actually quite a fast-growing . . . erm, excuse me?"

I'd become aware that somebody was tapping me on the shoulder. I turned round and saw it was one of the stewardesses.

"Sir?" she said. "Sir, we need to have a word with you, about your friend."

"My friend?"

I didn't know who they meant at first. Then I realised she must be talking about Charlie Hayward. There was another stewardess standing beside her, and a male flight attendant. They didn't look happy. I remembered there'd been a bit of fuss a few minutes earlier, when one of them had come to take his tray away, but I'd been busy talking and hadn't taken much notice. Anyway, as they now informed me, it was impossible to be sure of the exact timing—not until they'd found out if there was a doctor on the plane—but apparently he'd been dead for at least five or ten minutes.

It was a heart attack, of course. It usually is.

The airline handled it all very delicately, I must say. They sent me a letter a week after I'd got home, letting me know a few extra details which I have to say were comforting, very comforting. They told me that Charlie Hayward had suffered from heart problems for some time—this was his third attack, they said, in the last ten years—so the news hadn't come as a complete shock to his wife, although of course she was devastated. He had two daughters, both in their twenties. The body was flown back home from Singapore and he was cremated in Sydney. On the way out to Singapore, though, they'd had no choice but to keep him in the same seat, right next to me. They put a blanket over him and said I could come and sit with them if I liked, on one of the staff seats by the galley, but I said no thanks, it was OK. Somehow I thought that would have been rude, disrespectful. Call me fanciful, if you like, but I felt he would have appreciated the company.

Poor old Charlie Hayward. He was the first person I'd really managed to speak to, after taking my decision to reconnect with the world. Not a very auspicious start.

However, things were about to get better.

3

I was the last person to leave the plane after it landed at Singapore. While they lifted Charlie's body out and carried it off, I moved over to another seat, and sat there for a while after the other passengers had gone. Depression came over me. I could feel it. I was used to it by now, and knew how to recognise it. It reminded me of a horror film I saw on TV when I was a little boy. This man was trapped in a secret chamber in a big old castle, and the villain of the story pulled a lever which made the roof of the chamber start coming slowly down on top of him. Closer and closer, until it threatened to crush him. That's what it felt like. It never quite crushed me, of course, but it got close enough that I could feel it, weighing down on my spine, cutting off my freedom of movement, paralysing me. Whenever this happened, I would for some time be physically unable to raise myself, to will myself into motion. You could never really tell what was going to bring it on, either. It could be anything. In this case I suppose it was a sort of relapse: having said so much to Charlie, having unburdened myself so shamelessly of so many words, a tidal wave of words finally breaking through the floodgates, after months and months of withdrawal from the world, months made long by silence, by lack of human contact (contact, that is, unmediated by technology)—after all that, and the disaster it had just led to, indirectly or otherwise, I was already suffering something like a nervous reaction. I lapsed into immovable stillness and had no awareness, none at all, of what was going on around me. Finally, I noticed that a stewardess was once again—it was even the same stewardess, I believe—shaking me gently by the shoulder. "Sir?" she was saying, in a kindly undertone. "Sir, we must ask you to leave the plane now. The cleaning staff are waiting to come on board."

Sleepily I tilted my head towards her and, without a word, rose to my feet in a slow and I suppose trancelike movement. I made my way down the aisle, through Business Class and then out along the walkway towards the arrivals lounge. For some of the time I think the stewardess must have been walking alongside me. She said something like, "Are you OK, sir? Would you like someone to come with you?" but the reply I gave must have been reassuring enough for her to trust me to my own devices.

A few minutes passed. I can't say for certain where I would have spent them, but after a while I became aware that I was sitting at a café table, conscious of an oppressive, sticky heat and surrounded by shops bearing the names of familiar global brands, through which crowds of jetlagged passengers wandered in their own kind of daze, their eyes glazed and sightless, each one threading between the racks and stands and revolving displays with the thoughtless tread of a sleepwalker. I looked down at the liquid in my coffee cup and saw that it appeared to be some sort of cappuccino. Presumably I had ordered it and paid for it. I inserted a finger between my neck and the collar of my shirt in order to wipe away a ring of sweat that had gathered there. As I did so my eyes were drawn to one figure in particular amidst the crowd of somnambulant shoppers. She was a young woman of about twenty-five, and my first impression of her was curious. I am not a particularly spiritual person but the first thing I noticed about this woman—or thought I noticed—was that she was wearing a very colourful blouse. In fact it was probably this burst of colour, making her stand out like a fiercely burning beacon, that had first caught my attention and startled me out of my latest trough of depression. But actually, when I looked at her more closely, her clothes were of quite an ordinary colour and what I must have sensed, instead, was something else about her that was colourful, something internal, some kind of bright and luminous aura. Does that make any sense? As I continued to watch her this aura slowly flickered out and faded away, but there was still something compelling and irresistible about her. For one thing, while the surrounding crowds seemed to be drifting ever more slowly, as if in a state of deep hypnosis, this woman had a sense of purpose. A rather furtive sense of purpose, admittedly. She wandered from shop doorway to shop doorway, trying to appear nonchalant but unable to stop herself from looking around her so frequently and so warily that I wondered if she might be a shoplifter. Since she never actually went into any of the shops, however, I had to discount this theory. She was dressed in a rather masculine fashion, with a blue denim jacket which seemed quite unnecessary in this kind of heat, and had the sort of short hair and boyish looks I've always found particularly sexy. (For instance, Alison used to have the same looks—Chris's sister, Alison Byrne—although the last time I saw her, about fifteen years ago, she had started to wear her hair long.) I suppose you would call this woman's hair reddish, or perhaps strawberry blonde. It looked as though she might have used henna on it. Anyway, the jacket is the important thing, because after a while I began to suspect that she might only be wearing this jacket in order to conceal something underneath. I came to this conclusion after watching her, I suppose quite brazenly, for a minute or more, during which time she noticed me and flashed me one or two anxious and irritated glances. Embarrassed, I averted my gaze, turned it towards my now empty coffee cup, and tried to concentrate on something else—in this case, an announcement over the PA system: *Welcome to Singapore. Passengers in transit are respectfully reminded that it is forbidden to smoke anywhere inside the terminal building. We thank you for your cooperation and wish you a pleasant onward journey.* Then, the next time I looked at her she caught my eye again, and this time she came over, weaving through the drifting swarms of passengers until she reached my table and was standing over me.

"Are you a policeman or something?" she asked.

She had an English accent. Quite posh, but with that hint of Mockney that posh young people these days seem compelled to affect.

"No," I said. "No, I'm not a policeman." She said nothing in response to that, just continued to stand over me, glaring down suspiciously, so I added: "Why would you think I was a policeman?"

"You were staring at me."

"That's true," I admitted, after a moment's reflection. "I apologise. I'm very tired, and I'm halfway through a stressful journey. I didn't mean anything by it."

She thought about this before saying, "OK," in an uncertain tone of voice. "And you don't work . . . for the airport, or anything like that?"

"No," I said. "I don't work for the airport."

She nodded, apparently satisfied. Then, just before turning away, she added: "I'm not doing anything illegal, you know."

Again her tone was tentative, as if she didn't really know whether this was true or not. I tried to reassure her by saying, "That had never occurred to me." I was trying to see what she had hidden beneath her jacket, where I could see a distinct bulge, but it was impossible to tell. She was on the point of turning away again, but something still seemed to be holding her back. It occurred to me that she was tired and might like to sit down.

"Can I get you a coffee?" I asked.

Immediately she thudded down into the seat beside me. "That would be great," she said. "I'm bushed."

"What sort?"

She asked for a skinny latte with a shot of maple syrup, and I went to buy it for her. When I got back to the table with our coffees her jacket was no longer bulging. Whatever had been under there she had now transferred to her handbag, which was a loose, roomy affair she was just in the process of zipping up—again, with that slightly furtive air which seemed to characterise all her movements.

I decided not to reveal my curiosity, in any case, and to confine our conversation to small talk. "My name's Max," I said. "Maxwell Sim. Sim, like the"—I glanced at her, and hesitated—"like the card you put in a mobile phone."

She finished zipping up her bag and held out her hand. "Poppy," she said. "Where are you headed?"

"Back to London," I said. "Just a quick stopover here. Couple of hours. Should be at Heathrow first thing in the morning. On my way back from Australia."

"Long trip, then. Business? Pleasure?"

"Pleasure. Theoretically." I took a sip of coffee, and muttered, "Best-laid plans, and all that," into the froth. "How about you?"

"No, this is a working trip for me."

"Really?" I tried not to sound surprised. Now that we had started talking, she seemed even younger than I'd first thought—not much more than student age—and I found it hard to imagine her as a business traveller. She didn't look the part at all.

"Sure," she said. "I travel a lot in my line of work. In fact that's pretty much what it consists of. Travelling."

"Were you . . . working just now?" I asked, for some reason. I suppose it was an impertinent question, but she didn't seem to take it that way.

"While you were watching me?"

I nodded.

"Well, yes. I was, as a matter of fact."

It seemed as if she wasn't going to tell me any more.

"Of course," I said, "it's none of my business what you do for a living."

"It certainly isn't," said Poppy. "After all, we've only just met. I don't know anything about you."

"Well," I began, "I work—"

"Don't tell me." Poppy held up her hand. "Give me three guesses."

"OK."

She sat back, arms folded, and looked at me with an appraising but also mischievous gleam in her eye. "You write software for a computer-game company with a reputation for horrific misogynistic violence."

"No, not at all. You're miles off."

"All right, then. You breed organic chickens on a small-holding in the Cotswolds."

"Not that."

"You're a celebrity hairdresser. You do Keira Knightley's highlights."

" 'Fraid not."

"You work in a gentlemen's outfitters in Cheltenham.

Bespoke three-piece suits and frighteningly accurate leg measurements."

"No, and that's four guesses. But you're getting closer."

"One more, then?"

"OK."

"Well, how about . . . Senior Lecturer in Contemporary Fashion at the University of Ashby-de-la-Zouch."

Actually, I do consider myself quite a smart dresser, and since she made this suggestion with a lingering glance at my Lacoste shirt and Hugo Boss jeans, I was rather flattered. Even so, I shook my head. "So, do you give up?"

"I suppose so."

I told her the truth: that I was the After-Sales Customer Liaison Officer for a department store in central London.

To which her immediate response was: "What on earth does that mean?"

Now, I decided, was not the time to go into a huge amount of detail. "I'm there to assist the customers," I explained, "when there's been a problem with their purchase. A toaster that doesn't work. A pair of curtains that doesn't hang properly."

"I see," said Poppy. "So you work in the returns department."

"More or less," I conceded, and was about to add, "*Used* to, at any rate," and start explaining that I hadn't actually been to work for the best part of six months, but something stopped me. I had overburdened Charlie with my confidences, after all, and that hadn't panned out too well. "So, is it my turn now?"

She smiled. "It wouldn't really be fair. You'll never guess what I do. Not if I gave you a thousand guesses."

It was a nice smile, revealing her white, neat but slightly uneven teeth. I realised that perhaps I was staring at her more intently, and for longer, than was strictly polite. How old *was* this woman, exactly? Already I felt more comfortable talking to her than I'd felt talking to anyone for a long time, and yet she must have been at least twenty years younger than me. The realisation gave me a curious feeling: half-uneasy, half-exhilarated.

Meanwhile, Poppy was unzipping her handbag, and then she opened it up just far enough for me to see something unexpected inside: a digital recording device of some sort (professional quality, by the looks of it, at least the size of a hardback book) and a large microphone (again, the sort that professionals use, robust, chunky and sheathed in a grey polyester windscreen). As soon as I had peered over and had a good look at this equipment, she zipped the bag shut again.

"There you are," she said. "A clue."

"Well, then . . . You must be some sort of sound recordist."

She shook her head. "That's only part of what I do."

I pursed my lips, unable to come up with another guess.

"You say it involves a lot of travelling?" I prompted.

"Yes. All over the world. Last week I was in São Paolo."

"And this week Singapore?"

"Correct. Although—and this is another clue—I didn't leave the airport on either occasion."

"I see . . . So you make sound recordings of airports?"

"Also correct."

Try as I might, I couldn't see what she was driving at. "But why?" I had to ask, eventually.

Poppy placed her coffee cup carefully on the table and leaned forward, her chin cradled in both hands. "Put it this way. I'm part of an organisation that provides a valuable and discreet service to an exclusive clientele."

"What sort of service?"

"Well, I don't really have a name for my job, because I

don't normally tell people what it is. But since I'm making an exception for you, let's just say that I'm a . . . junior adultery facilitator."

A sort of wicked thrill went through me when she spoke these words. "Adultery facilitator?" I said. It was exciting just to repeat the phrase.

"OK," said Poppy, "I'll explain. My employer—whose name I'm not supposed to tell anyone—has set up this agency. He's set it up for people who are having affairs—mainly men, but not always, by any means—and want things to go smoothly and safely. Things are very difficult for the modern adulterer. Technology has made everything much more complicated. There are more and more ways of being in touch with someone, but everything leaves a trail. In the old days you might have written someone a love letter and the only witness would be the person who saw you popping it into the postbox. Nowadays you send someone a couple of text messages and the next thing you know, there they are on an itemised phone bill. You can delete as many e-mails from your computer as you like, but they'll still be stored, somewhere or other, on some big mainframe in the middle of nowhere. More and more elaborate strategies are required if you don't want to get caught out. "This"—she patted her handbag—"is just one of them."

"So how does it work?" I asked.

"It's quite simple. First of all, I travel all over the place, to a number of different airports, and make some recordings, and when I get home I compile them all into a CD. A CD which we then sell on to our clients, as part of their package. Now suppose that you're one of these clients (although I have to say, you don't look much like an adulterer). You're away on a business trip in the Far East. But you decide to cut the business trip short, and spend a night or two in Paris with your mistress instead. Obviously your wife mustn't find out about it. Well, here's a good way of putting her mind at rest. Just before you come home, you phone her from your hotel suite in Paris. Your loved one has slipped into the bathroom for a shower, so you put the CD onto the stereo system, call your wife, and what does she hear in the background while you're talking to her?" Opening the bag, she pressed the recorder's "Play" button, and from the internal speaker I could hear a recording of the announcement that I'd found myself listening to a few minutes earlier: *Welcome to Singapore. Passengers in transit are respectfully reminded that it is forbidden to smoke anywhere inside the terminal building. We thank you for your cooperation and wish you a pleasant onward journey.* Poppy smiled at me, triumphant. "So there's your alibi. After hearing that, who's going to think twice about where you might be calling from?"

I nodded slowly, to show that I was impressed. "And people pay for this?"

"Oh, yes," said Poppy. "Big money." She stretched out the word "big." "Honestly, you'd be surprised."

"What sorts of people?"

"All sorts. Unhappily married people are everywhere. But still, the fees are rather steep, so we tend to attract a certain sort of clientele in particular. Investment bankers, professional footballers, that kind of thing."

I was struck by the insouciance with which she was telling me all this. Titillating though I found the idea of an "adultery facilitator," I also thought it rather shocking. "What about . . ." I said, trying to choose my words with care, "what about the moral dimension?"

"The what?" said Poppy.

"I just wondered if you had any qualms about it. You

know . . . the fact that you're helping people to cheat on other people. Does it bother your—your conscience, at all?"

"Oh, that." Poppy stirred up the froth at the bottom of her coffee cup and sucked nonchalantly on her plastic spoon. "I've gone past the stage where I bother about that kind of thing. I got a First in History from Oxford, you know. And do you know what kind of jobs I've been doing since? The shittiest of the shitty. The best was PA to the director of a lap-dancing club. The worst was . . . well, you don't want to hear about the worst. And that's without the months of unemployment in between. This job gives me easy money, and it's regular work, and it allows me plenty of time to sit around reading, and watching films, and going to galleries, which is what I really like doing."

"Yes, I know things are . . . difficult out there at the moment. I just thought—"

"You know, you're starting to sound just like Clive. This is exactly what he said to me when I told him about this job. And do you know what I said back to him?"

Of course I didn't. I didn't even know who Clive was. But my first—and indeed, only—thought at this point was that I wasn't happy another man's name had been introduced into the conversation already.

"Well, I lost my temper," Poppy said, "which I very rarely do with Clive. I said to him, Do you realise that, if there's one thing people of my age cannot stand hearing, it's people of your age giving us lectures on morality? Look at the world around you. The world *you've* bequeathed to us. D'you think it allows us any scope to do things on principle? I'm sick of hearing·about how my generation has no values. How materialist we are. How lacking in any political sense. Do you know why that is? Take a wild guess. That's right—because that's how you brought us up! We may be Mrs. Thatcher's children, as far as you're concerned, but *you* were the ones who voted for her, again and again, and then carried on voting for all the people who came after her, and followed exactly in her footsteps. You're the ones who brought us up to be these consumerist zombies. You chucked all the other values out of the window, didn't you? Christianity? Don't need that. Collective responsibility? Where's that ever got us. Manufacturing? Making things? That's for losers. Yeah, let's get those losers over in the Far East to make everything for us and we can just sit on our backsides in front of the TV, watching the world go to hell in a handcart—in widescreen and HD, of course." She sat back, looking faintly embarrassed for having spoken so passionately. "So, anyway—that's what I said to Clive, when he told me I shouldn't be doing this job."

Well, it was certainly all very interesting. Poppy had raised a lot of issues there, and given me plenty to think about. In fact, she had touched on so many important subjects that it was hard to know where to begin. "Who's Clive?" I asked.

"Clive? Clive's my uncle. My mother's brother."

I breathed a sigh of relief and said, "I'm so glad to hear that." It came out before I could stop it.

"Glad?" said Poppy, bemused. "What are you glad about? You're glad that my mother has a brother?"

"Well . . . yes," I said, fumbling hopelessly. "It's not good to be an only child. I mean, I'm an only child, and I wouldn't recommend the experience . . ." This was ridiculous. I would have to change the subject as quickly as possible. "Your agency's fees must be very expensive," I said, "if they have to cover the cost of you flying all over the world on a weekly basis."

"They are expensive," said Poppy. "But that's not the reason. Actually, it doesn't cost that much for me to fly out here and back. I do it on standby, you see. It's slightly unpredictable, because you never know if there's going to be a seat available—sometimes you end up having to sleep in the airport, which isn't so great—but usually it works out."

"And were you lucky this time?"

"Well, it was a close thing. I'd got my eye on a BA flight—"

"7371?" I asked, hopefully.

"That's the one. Is that your flight?"

"Yes. Did you get on it?"

"I didn't think I was going to. At first they told me it was full up. But apparently a seat's become available, for some reason."

A beautiful certainty suddenly took hold of me.

"Did they put you in Premium Economy?"

"That's right. Why?"

"I think you're going to be sitting next to me."

"What makes you think that?"

Should I explain to her the circumstances of Charlie Hayward's recent demise? That would mean telling her she would be taking the place of a dead man. Did she look the squeamish type? I wasn't going to risk it—wasn't about to do anything that might throw a shadow over the journey home the two of us would soon enjoy, side by side. Out of nowhere, after all, fate had dropped this lovely young woman into my lap, and now it seemed we were going to be bound even more closely together. Not to mince words, for the next twelve hours we were going to be sleeping together. And on our first date!

4

For the second and final leg of the journey, Charlie was supposed to have had the aisle seat, and I should have had the window. Poppy said that she didn't mind where she sat, but I didn't
really believe her. Everybody prefers a window seat, don't they?
So I insisted she take the seat by the window. I was determined
to make the journey as comfortable for her as could be. I was
determined to do everything in my power to make the best possible impression on her. I was determined to make her like me.

"By the way, I suffer from clinical depression," I said, as
soon as we were settled.

Poppy seemed completely unfazed, to my relief. She just
looked at me for a few seconds and said, "Yes, well, I guessed it
was something like that."

"Really?" I said. "It's that obvious?"

"Let's just say I have a nose for these things."

And after that, at least, the information was out there; it
was something understood between us. She was the first person
(I mean apart from my employers, and my GP, and my Occupational Health Officer—the first friend, I suppose is what I'm
trying to say) with whom I had felt brave enough to share this
shameful secret. And if I had been expecting her to edge away,
retreat into wary silence, ask a stewardess if she could be moved
to another seat, or anything like that, I would have been wrong.
It seemed to make no difference to how she thought of me.
I felt intensely grateful for that, and immediately it seemed
to establish an odd sort of intimacy—a settled, comfortable

sort of intimacy—which meant that conversation between us, which I had thought would be nervous and forced, seemed from then on to unfold with a rhythm that was entirely natural. To be honest, in the next few hours we did not talk nearly as much as I'd assumed we would. We sat for much of the time in the sort of companionable silence you would expect from an elderly couple who had been married for thirty years—just like that couple I'd seen at the restaurant in Sydney Harbour, sitting together on the same side of the table so that they could share in the view rather than talk to each other. A couple of hours into the flight (about two a.m., Singapore time, it would have been) that's how we were: me flicking through the different movies on the little seat-back screen in front of me, sometimes commenting on them to her, not really able to settle on anything, while Poppy, having spent a few minutes writing up a brief report on her laptop, was now using it to pass the time with what seemed to be some kind of incredibly complicated three-dimensional Sudoku.

More importantly, though, in the idle moments between these activities, we would talk.

"What about jet lag?" I asked her at one point.

"Mmn?"

"In this job of yours. Surely your body clock must be all over the place. Is it ever a problem?"

Poppy shrugged. "Doesn't seem to be. Sometimes when I'm at home I wake up a bit early. Sometimes a bit late. It's not a big deal."

I sighed enviously. "What it must be like to be young."

"You're not in your bath chair yet, Grandad."

"Well, it's going to take me a day or two to recover from this trip, I know that. And I have to get over it as quickly as possible because later this week I've got a decision to make."

"Really?"

"Really. It'll be six months since I've been off work. I have to go into the department store and see their Occupational Health person, and tell her whether or not I want to come back. And even if I say that I do, she might decide I'm not well enough, which will probably give them an excuse to"—it took me a while to remember the euphemism—"let me go. Which might well be what they're hoping for anyway."

"And do you?"

"Do I? Do I what?"

"Want to go back."

I thought about this for a few moments, but it was too hard a question to answer directly. My thoughts raced ahead, instead, to everything that would be waiting for me when I got home: the bleak, chafing February weather, the empty flat, the pile of junk mail on the other side of the door. Oh yes, it was going to be bad. Just then, it didn't even feel as though I could face that lonely homecoming, let alone the decision that would have to follow it.

"You know, I still have this fantasy," I said eventually, "that I'll get home, and she'll be there waiting for me. Caroline. She's still got a key, you see, so it could happen. I open the door, and as soon as I open it, I know that she's back. I don't see her at first, but I can tell someone's in there—the radio's on, there's a smell of fresh coffee in the kitchen. The place is warm, and tidy. And then I see her sitting on the sofa, waiting for me, reading a book . . ." I turned towards Poppy again. "It's not going to happen, is it?"

All she said was: "You know, I'm sure you've been seeing a therapist, but is there anyone else you can talk to about these things? Someone in your family, say?"

I shook my head. "Mum's dead. She died young—more than twenty years ago. Dad's a lost cause. We've never been able to talk much. I don't have any brothers or sisters."

"Friends?"

I thought about my seventy friends on Facebook. Honesty compelled me to admit: "Not really. I've got this friend called Trevor. He used to live nearby, but he's moved away now. Apart from that . . ." I tailed off, suddenly wanting to change the subject, or at least the focus of attention. "What about you? Do you have any siblings?"

"Nope. I've got my mother, but she's a bit . . . self-absorbed, shall we say. She doesn't really 'do' other people's problems. And Dad ran off some time ago, when she caught him having an affair." Another laugh—more rueful this time. "He could have done with the services of a good adultery facilitator, now I think of it. What a pity we weren't in business then."

"So you're like me, then?" I said, perhaps a little too eagerly. "You don't really have anyone you can talk to."

"It's not quite like that," said Poppy. "You see, I have my uncle. Uncle Clive."

She abandoned the Sudoku then, and closed down the programme, so all I could see on her laptop was her desktop wallpaper—which appeared, rather bizarrely, to be a photograph of some sort of catamaran, a very old one, half-decayed, a ruin of shattered plyboard and flaking paint, lying abandoned somewhere on a tropical beach. My eyes rested curiously on this for a while, as she told me more about her uncle and why she liked him so much. She told me how her mother had sent her to this posh boarding school in Surrey at the age of thirteen; how she was supposed to be just a weekly boarder and come home every Friday evening, but since her mother was often out of the country she would go and stay with her uncle instead; how she came to cherish and look forward to these visits; how Clive (who lived in Kew) would take her almost every weekend to the cinema, or the theatre, to concerts and art galleries, introducing her to worlds which before then had been closed to her; and how, if he wasn't seeing her at the weekend, he would write long letters to her, letters full of news, full of humour, full of fun and information and anecdote and, above all, full of love.

"And you know what?" she told me. "I still read those letters. I still take them with me everywhere."

"Everywhere?"

"Yes. Even on these trips. I've got them right here." She tapped her forefinger against the laptop. "I scanned them all in. And all the photos he used to send me. This one, for instance—this is one of Clive's." She was pointing to the photograph of the washed-up boat. "Well, he didn't take it or anything like that," she explained. "It was taken by an artist called Tacita Dean. The boat's called the *Teignmouth Electron*."

"Teignmouth?" I said. "That's in Devon, isn't it?"

"That's right. Where Clive and my mum grew up."

"So why do you have it on your desktop?"

"Because there's an amazing story associated with it. The story of a man called Donald Crowhurst." She gave a yawn, protracted and involuntary, before remembering to cover it with her hand. "Sorry—I'm really sleepy all of a sudden. Have you heard of him?"

I shook my head.

"He was the man who sailed round the world in the late sixties. Or at least said he did, but actually he didn't."

"I see," I said, totally confused.

"I'm not explaining this very well, am I?"

"You're tired. You should go to sleep."

"No, but it's a great story. I think you should hear it."

"I'm fine. I'll just watch a movie. You're too tired to talk. Tell me the story in the morning."

"I wasn't going to tell you the story. I was just going to read you what Clive wrote to me about it."

"That can wait."

"Tell you what." Poppy tapped a few keys on her laptop before passing it over to my table, then reached beneath her own seat where she'd stashed her pillow and blankets. "You can read his letter. There it is. It's a bit long, sorry—but you've got plenty of time, and it'll do you more good than watching some terrible rom-com for a couple of hours."

"Are you sure that's OK? I mean, I don't want to look at anything that's . . . too private."

But Poppy assured me it was OK. So while she snuggled down under the blankets, I placed her computer on my lap and looked at the first page of her uncle's letter. It had opened up in Windows Picture and Fax Viewer, so I could still see the creamy yellow of the notepaper on which he had written it, and even make out the faint swirling watermark behind the handwriting. The writing itself was crisp, angular and easily legible. I guessed that he had been using a fountain pen. The ink was navy blue, shading almost into black. As I started reading the first sentences I felt a slight pressure against my left shoulder, and looked down to see that Poppy had placed her pillow next to it and settled her head there. She looked up at me, just briefly, as if to ask permission with her eyes, but at the same instant her eyelids flickered and closed as she slipped into a deep, unshakeable sleep. After a few seconds, when I felt it was safe to do so, I breathed a goodnight kiss into her hair, and could feel my own body tingle with happiness.

WATER

12 March 2001

Dear Poppy,

I was sorry not to see you this weekend. Weekends are always a bit lonely here when you're not around. You missed a glorious display in the Gardens—the crocus carpet is in full bloom already, very early this year—and to stroll along Cherry Walk, one's eyes taking in swathe upon swathe of these white and purple beauties, their heads bobbing in the breeze, is to realise that spring has come again—finally! Anyway, I hope you had a good time with your mother. Did she take you anywhere, do anything interesting with you? The NFT were showing *The Magnificent Ambersons* on Saturday evening and I would also have liked to take you along to that. I went by myself in the end, but while I was there I bumped into a friend of mine, Martin Wellbourne, and his wife, Elizabeth, and they were kind enough to invite me for supper with them afterwards. So it was not such a solitary evening after all.

Now, about our plans for Saturday. I think I mentioned that there was a show at Tate Britain at the moment that you might find especially interesting? They are showing some films and photographs by a new young artist called Tacita Dean. You might possibly have heard of her already. A couple of years ago she was short-listed for the Turner Prize. If you don't like the sound of it, just say so and we shall certainly find something else to do, but I hope you will want to come.

I have to say that I have very particular and personal reasons for wanting to see this show. You see, it contains a short film inspired by the disappearance at sea of the lone yachtsman Donald Crowhurst in the summer of 1969—and even, so I am led to believe, some photographs of his ill-fated yacht, the *Teignmouth Electron*, which Ms. Dean has taken just in the last couple of years, travelling for this purpose to its final resting place at Cayman Brac in the Caribbean.

It occurs to me that you might not know what on earth I am talking about here. It also occurs to me that, if I am to tell you a little bit about my fascination with the story of Donald Crowhurst, this is going to turn into a very long letter. But, no matter. It is Monday morning, an empty day stretches ahead of me, and there is nothing I like better than writing to my niece. So, excuse me for a moment while I go and pour myself another cup of coffee, and I shall try to explain.

Well, now.

If I am to make you understand what the figure of Donald Crowhurst meant to me, when I was an eight-year-old boy, then I must take you back—back more than thirty years, to the England of 1968—a place, and a time, which already seem unimaginably remote. I'm sure that the mention of that year summons up all sorts of associations for you: the year of student radicalism, the counterculture, anti-Vietnam rallies and the Beatles' *White Album* and all of that. Well, that only tells part of the story. England was—and always has been—a more complicated place than people would have us believe. What would you say if I told you that, in my memory of things, the great hero, the defining figure of that era was not John Lennon or Che Guevara, but a conservative, old-fashioned, sixty-five-year-old vegetarian with the looks and bearing of an avuncular Latin master? Can you even guess who I might be talking about? Does his name even mean anything anymore?

I'm referring to Sir Francis Chichester.

You probably have no idea who Sir Francis Chichester was. Let me tell you, then. He was a yachtsman, a mariner—one of the most brilliant that England has ever produced. And in 1968 he was a celebrity, one of the most famous and talked-about people in the country. As famous as David Beckham is today, or Robbie Williams? Yes, I should think so. And his achievement, although it might seem pointless, I suppose, to today's younger generation, remains, in many people's eyes, much greater than simply playing football or writing pop songs. He was famous for sailing around the world, single-handed, in his boat the *Gypsy Moth*. He completed the voyage in 226 days, and most incredibly of all, during that time he made only one stop, in Australia. It was a magnificent feat of seamanship, courage and endurance, performed by the most unlikely of heroes.

I had the enormous good fortune to grow up next to the sea. I think you've visited the town where your mother and I grew up, haven't you? Shaldon, it is called, in Devon. We lived in a large Georgian house close to the water. Shaldon itself, however, is built around a relatively modest saltwater inlet, and to get to the seafront proper you have to go half a mile up the road to neighbouring Teignmouth. And here you will find everything you might want from a seaside resort: a pier, beaches, amusement arcades, miniature golf, dozens of boarding houses and, of course, down by the docks, a lively marina, where yachtsmen and boaters of every description would gather every day, and the air was always alive with the whispering noises of masts and rigging as they creaked and shifted in

the breeze. From an early age—ever since I can remember—
my mother and father used to take me down to the marina to
watch those comings and goings, the ceaseless ebb and flow
of maritime life. Although we never sailed ourselves, we knew
plenty of people who did: by the age of eight I was a veteran of
several modest ocean voyages aboard yachts belonging to my
parents' friends, and had developed a deep schoolboy fascination for all things nautical.

No wonder, then, that Francis Chichester and his accom-
plishment loomed so large in my consciousness. Although we
never actually made the pilgrimage along the coast to Plymouth to see him make his return landing in May 1967, I vividly
remember watching coverage of the event—along with millions of others—live on BBC television. If I remember rightly,
the normal schedules had even been cleared for the purpose.
Plymouth docks and the area surrounding them were covered
with swarms of well-wishers—hundreds of thousands of them.
They cheered and applauded and waved their Union Jacks in
the air as the *Gypsy Moth* glided into the harbour, surrounded
by launches carrying journalists and TV camera crews. Chichester himself stood on the deck and waved back, looking
tanned, serene and healthy—not at all like someone who had
spent the last seven and a half months enduring an extreme
form of solitary confinement. It had been an occasion which
made my heart swell with uncomplicated patriotic pride—
something I cannot remember feeling very often since. And
after that I began keeping a scrapbook full of cuttings about
Chichester's voyage and any other boating-related stories I
could cull from the newspapers my parents favoured.

Those newspapers, I seem to remember, were the *Daily
Mail* on weekdays, and on Sundays—along with at least half of
the nation, it always seemed back then—the *Sunday Times*. And

it was in the *Sunday Times*, on 17 March 1968, that I read this electrifying announcement:

£5,000

The £5,000 *Sunday Times* round-the-world race prize will be awarded to the single-handed yachtsman who completes the fastest non-stop navigation of the world, departing after 1 June and before 31 October 1968, from a port on the British mainland and rounding the three capes (Good Hope, Leeuwin and Horn).

A race! And a race that would top Chichester's achievement by subjecting the competitors to an even more extreme test of survival—a *non-stop* circumnavigation. Quite apart from the trial of seamanship involved, could anybody survive such an ordeal psychologically? As I said, I had already sailed in one or two yachts. I knew what the cabins were like: surprisingly cosy, sometimes, and surprisingly well equipped, but above all *tiny*. Even smaller than my little bedroom at home. The fact that Chichester had lived in such a confined space for so long was, to me, almost his most impressive feat. It seemed incredible that these men were prepared to live like that for so many cramped, waterlogged months.

Who were these masochists, in any case? Already, after reading a few of the *Sunday Times* reports, I had concluded for myself that the strongest contender was a French yachtsman called Bernard Moitessier. He was a fabulous seaman—lean, sinewy and totally dedicated to the life of the lone explorer. He had already sailed his thirty-nine-foot boat *Joshua* through the fearsome waters of the Southern Ocean and round Cape Horn, encountering (and surviving) terrifying storms in the process.

It appeared that he was reluctant to enter the race, but under its rules, he had no choice: the *Sunday Times* had cleverly arranged things so that any sailor who set off round the world from a British port between June and October was a contender for the prize, whether they wanted it or not. I pinned my colours to Moitessier and even persuaded my parents to buy me an expensive hardback copy of his book, *Sailing to the Reefs*, for my eighth birthday. The writing was rather too dense and poetic for me to enjoy, but I pored for hours over the black-and-white photographs of the muscular Moitessier powering his boat through the waves and swinging effortlessly from rope to rope amid the rigging of his yacht like a nautical Tarzan.

The other entrants to the race, announced one by one, failed to capture my imagination in the same way. There was Robin Knox-Johnston, a twenty-eight-year-old English merchant marine officer; Chay Blyth, a former army sergeant, one year his junior; Donald Crowhurst, aged thirty-six, a British engineer and manager of an electronics company; Nigel Tetley, a Royal Navy lieutenant commander; and four others. None of them seemed in Moitessier's league. One or two of them, from what I could gather, had barely been to sea before. But then something happened to change my mind, and my allegiance. My father came in from work one day with a copy of the *Teignmouth Post & Gazette* and showed me the front-page story—which announced, amazingly, that Donald Crowhurst had now decided not just that he was going to set sail from Teignmouth, but that he had even agreed to name his yacht the *Teignmouth Electron*. (In return, as it later emerged, for a number of local sponsorship deals.)

The name of the man who had persuaded Crowhurst to bestow these benefits on a town with which he otherwise had no connection was Rodney Hallworth: a one-time Fleet Street crime reporter, now Devon-based press agent and assiduous promoter of anything and everything that might raise the profile of Teignmouth in the eyes of the wider world. From the stories which he now began to feed to the local and national newspapers, I began to build up an image in my mind of Donald Crowhurst as a kind of yachting superhero: the dark horse of the race, and therefore its most intriguing and alluring competitor. Not only was he an accomplished seaman, apparently, he was an electronics wizard, and a designer of genius, who despite making a late entrance into the race was going to snatch it from under the noses of his rivals by setting sail in a sleek, modern, radically innovative vehicle which had been built to his own specifications—a trimaran, no less, with a unique self-righting system which would activate in case of a capsize, and which was controlled (here was the clincher— the word which, in 1968, set everybody's pulse racing) by a *computer.*

Instantly, Donald Crowhurst became the focus of all my interest and admiration. He was due to arrive in Teignmouth in only a matter of weeks—and I, for one, couldn't wait.

A support committee had now been formed, and one of my father's sailing friends was a keen member. In this way we were drip-fed pieces of information. Crowhurst's boat was finished, we were told, and he was already sailing it from a boatyard in Norfolk round to the Devon coast. He would be with us in a matter of days. As it turned out, this forecast was optimistic. Teething troubles dogged that maiden voyage, which took four times as long as it should have done, and it was mid-October by the time Crowhurst and his team made it to Teignmouth. On the Friday afternoon after his arrival, my mother picked me up from school and took me down to the harbour to catch an early glimpse of my hero and watch some of his preparations.

All children, I imagine, have a defining moment at some point in their lives, when the meaning of the word "disappointment" becomes cruelly apparent to them. A moment when they realise that the world, which they had hitherto conceived as being ripe with promise, rich with infinite possibilities, is in reality a flawed and circumscribed place. That moment can be devastating, and can linger in the mind for years afterwards, much stronger than the memory of early joys and infant excitements. And in my case, it came that grey Friday afternoon in mid-October, when I had my first sight of Donald Crowhurst.

This was the man who was going to win the *Sunday Times* round-the-world yacht race? The man who was going to defeat Moitessier, the brilliant, experienced Frenchman? And this was the *Teignmouth Electron*, the ultimate in modern boat design, which was going to skim across the massive waves of the Southern Ocean, every nuance of its fleet-footed movement tempered and adjusted by the latest in computer technology?

Frankly, both of these things seemed hard to credit. Crowhurst cut a poor, diminished figure: after all the bravado of his newspaper interviews, I had been expecting someone with an aura of confidence about him, some sense of derring-do— a *presence*, in other words. Instead, he seemed ineffectual and preoccupied. I have the impression (in retrospect, of course) that he was alarmed, even terrified, by the spotlight that had been turned upon him, and the weight of expectation that came with it. As for the much vaunted *Teignmouth Electron*, not only did it look puny and fragile, but the preparations around it were shambolic. The boat itself seemed to be still under construction, with a succession of workmen trooping on and off it every day, performing endless repairs, while on the quayside bewildering numbers of supplies were steadily accumulating in messy piles—everything from carpenter's tools to radio equipment to tins of soup and corned beef. In and around all this chaos, Crowhurst himself pottered aimlessly, posing for the omnipresent camera crew, quarrelling with his boat-builders, popping into telephone kiosks to remonstrate with would-be suppliers, and every day looking more and more obviously sick with apprehension.

Well, the great day came at last: 31 October 1968. A drizzly, overcast and altogether dismal Thursday afternoon. There wasn't a great throng at the quayside, nothing to compare with the crowds who had gone to Plymouth to welcome Chichester the year before, that's for sure—maybe about sixty or seventy of us. Our teacher had given the whole class permission to leave early if we wanted to go and watch, and of course most of the children had taken advantage of this, but wherever the others went, it wasn't to wave goodbye to Donald Crowhurst on his round-the-world voyage. I was the only child of school age who made the effort, of that I'm fairly certain. My mother was with me, my father must still have been at work, and as for your mother—I don't know where she was. You would have to ask her. I remember the mood among the crowd as being sceptical as much as it was celebratory. Crowhurst had acquired a fair number of detractors in Teignmouth over the past few weeks, and he didn't do much to assuage them when he turned up for his grand departure in a beige V-neck sweater, complete with collar and tie. Hardly the outfit Moitessier would have chosen for his send-off, I couldn't help thinking. And things got worse after that: Crowhurst set off at three o'clock exactly, but almost immediately got into difficulties, was unable to raise his sails and had to be towed back to shore. The crowd became even more derisive at this point, and many of them went home. My mother and I stayed to watch. The problem took nearly two hours to put right, by which time dusk was falling. Finally, he set sail again just before five: and this time it was for real. Three launches went with him—one of them containing his wife and four children, wrapped up tightly in the duffel coats that were considered essential fashion items for youngsters at the time. Despite the fact that Crowhurst was cutting such an unimpressive figure, I can remember envying them for having him as their father: being at the centre of attention, being made to feel so special. Their launch followed his yacht for about a mile, after which they waved goodbye to him and turned back. Crowhurst sailed on, into the distance and over the horizon, heading for months of solitude and danger. My mother took me by the hand and together we walked home, looking forward to warmth, tea and Thursday-night television.

What were the forces operating upon Donald Crowhurst during the next few months? What was it that made him act as he did?

Most of what I know about the Crowhurst story—apart from my early memory of seeing him off from the harbour, that is—comes from the excellent book written by two *Sunday Times* journalists, Nicholas Tomalin and Ron Hall, who had access to his logbooks and tape recordings in the months after he died at sea. They called their book *The Strange Voyage of Donald Crowhurst*, and in it they quote something that he said into his portable tape recorder not long after leaving home: "The thing about single-handing is it puts a great deal of pressure on the man, it explores his weaknesses with a penetration that very few other occupations can manage."

In Crowhurst's case, there were the obvious pressures of living alone at sea—the cramped conditions, the constant noise, motion and dampness, the terrible privacy of his tiny cabin—but there was also pressure coming from other sources. Two other sources, to be precise. One was his press agent, Rodney Hallworth; the other was his sponsor, a local businessman called Stanley Best, who had financed the building of the trimaran and was now its owner, but in return had insisted upon a contract stipulating that, if anything went wrong with the voyage, Crowhurst would have to buy the boat back off him. This meant, in effect, that he had no option but to complete the circumnavigation: anything else would reduce him to bankruptcy.

The pressure coming from Hallworth was slightly more subtle, but no less insistent. Hallworth had spent the last few months building Crowhurst up into a hero. A man who was essentially little more than a "weekend sailor" had now been chosen to take on, in the eyes of the newspaper-reading public, the role of the lone, audacious challenger—the embodiment of Middle English backbone and resilience, a plucky David battling it out with the yachting Goliaths. Hallworth had done (and continued to do) a brilliant if totally unscrupulous job. It's hard not to see him as a prototype "spin doctor," well before that term came to be so prevalent. In any case, Crowhurst had certainly been made to feel that he could not let this public down, and he could not let his press agent down after all the work he had put in. There could be no turning back.

He was not long into his voyage, however, before something became all too painfully obvious: there could be no going forward either. It took little more than two weeks for his attempt at a solo circumnavigation to be revealed as a complete fantasy.

"Racked by the growing awareness," he wrote on Friday, 15 November, "that I must soon decide whether or not I can go on in the face of the actual situation. What a bloody awful decision—to chuck it in at this stage—what a bloody awful decision!" The *Teignmouth Electron*'s electrics had failed; her hatches were leaking (the port forward float hatch had let in 120 gallons in five days); Crowhurst had left vital lengths of pipe behind in Teignmouth, making pumping out water almost impossible; his sails were chafing; there were screws constantly coming loose from his steering system; and as for the "computer" which was supposed to self-steer the yacht and respond to its every motion with exquisite sensitivity—well, he had never even got around to designing or installing it. The cat's cradles of multi-coloured wires running so visibly all over the cabin were connected to nothing at all. In other words, the *Teignmouth Electron* was barely seaworthy—and yet this was the vessel in which he proposed to sail across the Southern Ocean, the most dangerous sea passage on earth! "With the boat in its present state," he wrote in his logbook, "my chances of survival would not, I think, be better than 50-50." Most people would have said that even this assessment was optimistic.

So, there was no going forward, and no turning back. Deadlock. What, in these circumstances, could Donald Crowhurst possibly do?

Well, this is what he did: he hit upon a solution worthy, you might say, of our very own prime minister. For—just like Mr. Blair, faced with the twin undesirables of free-market capitalism and state-heavy socialism—Donald Crowhurst decided that there was another possibility: a "Third Way," no less. And it was, even his critics would have to admit, an extremely daring and ingenious one. He decided, in fact, that if he could not *make* a voyage around the world, single-handed and non-stop, he would do the next best thing and *fake* one.

Remember, Poppy, that these were the 1960s. All the technologies which are now becoming available to us—the e-mail, the mobile phones, the Global Positioning Systems—were yet to be invented. Once Donald Crowhurst set sail from Teignmouth Harbour and drifted into the high seas he was about as alone as it's possible to imagine a human being could be. His only means of communication with the wider world was a hopelessly unreliable radio system. For weeks, even months at a time, it was quite likely that he would not have the slightest contact with the rest of humanity. And during that time, it was equally likely that the rest of humanity would not have the slightest idea where he was to be found. The only record of his route would be the one that he himself made in his logbooks, in his own handwriting, taking positions using his own equipment. So, what was to stop him giving a completely false account of his voyage? He didn't need to go round the three capes at all. He could wander down the coast of Africa, then tack over to the west, hang about in the mid-Atlantic for a few months, and tuck in quietly behind the genuine racers after they had rounded Cape Horn and were heading back towards Great Britain. He would come in a decent fourth or fifth—in which case no one would be interested in scrutinising his logbooks too carefully, and honour would have been saved.

Keeping two entirely different sets of logbooks—one recording his real journey, one containing the fake records— would require considerable skill and ingenuity, but Crowhurst was capable of it. At any rate, he obviously found this idea preferable to the prospect of humiliation and bankruptcy. So he made up his mind, and the great deception began.

Back in Shaldon, I had not been giving Donald Crowhurst an enormous amount of thought. The ramshackle, undignified nature of his departure had somewhat shaken my faith in my hero. What's more, he had barely been mentioned in any of the newspaper reports covering the first few weeks of the race. Several of the competitors had already dropped out and, of those that remained, it seemed to be Robin Knox-Johnston, Bernard Moitessier and Nigel Tetley who were capturing the journalists' imaginations. I can remember getting very excited, though, one day in December when Crowhurst was suddenly back in the news—and, indeed, dominating that weekend's sporting headlines—with a *Sunday Times* story reporting that he had claimed a world record for the furthest distance travelled by a single-handed yachtsman in one day—something in the region of 240 miles, I think. This, of course, would have been just after he had made his decision to start keeping false records of his progress.

After that, I kept following the race as best I could, cutting out the latest reports from the newspaper every Sunday and pasting them into the new scrapbook which my mother had bought me for this purpose from the Teignmouth post office; but again, things began to go pretty quiet on the Crowhurst front. That spring was when I was selected as goalkeeper for the school team, and an obsession with football began to supplant my obsession with yachts. Also, my mother and father bought their first caravan, and we took it on a trip to the New Forest during the Easter holidays. I remember being upset because *your* mother (who would have been almost ten) spent the whole week reading Mallory Towers stories and wouldn't play with me. I remember the Move playing "Blackberry Way" on *Top of the Pops*, and Peter Sarstedt with his interminable "Where Do You Go to My Lovely." These are the things that survive, in my mind, from the early months of 1969. Family life, ordinary life. A life spent surrounded by other people.

Meanwhile, somewhere in the mid-Atlantic, Donald Crowhurst was going slowly mad.

Chillingly, the encroaching madness was chronicled in his logbooks. I suppose with no human company whatsoever, and no opportunity to communicate with his wife and children by radio in case it gave his position away, it's not surprising that he attempted to find solace during those long, lonely months in the silent communion with pen and paper. At first, alongside the details of his position—real and fake—he would just write rambling assessments of his current situation, reflections on the nautical life, even the occasional poem. This one, for instance, was written after a bedraggled, shivering owl had perched for a while on Crowhurst's rigging, prompting him to think that this might perhaps be the weakling of a migrating flight, "a misfit, in all probability destined like the spirit of many of his human counterparts to die alone and anonymously, unseen by any of his species":

> *Save some pity for the Misfit, fighting on with bursting heart;*
> *Not a trace of common sense, his is no common flight.*
> *Save, save him some pity. But save the greater part*
> *For him that sees no glimmer of the Misfit's guiding light.*

But later, as the horror of his predicament began to bear down on him more heavily, Crowhurst's logbook entries became still more peculiar. Quite apart from the intense isolation to which he was subjecting himself—months of absolute solitude, with nothing but the rolling immensity of the ocean on every side to distract his eye—there would also be the dawning awareness that, if he carried this hoax off, he was going to have to live an enormous lie for the rest of his life. It would be one thing to tell lies to journalists or even saloon-bar yachting friends—thrilling tales of bravado on the high seas, the horrors of the Southern Ocean, the exhilaration of rounding Cape

Horn, these Crowhurst could spin by the dozen—but what was he going to tell his wife, for instance? Could he lie next to her, night after night, knowing that her love and admiration for him were based, in part, on acts of heroism which he had shown himself far from capable of performing? Could he keep that truth hidden from her for the next forty or fifty years? I have written of the "terrible privacy" of his cabin. Could Crowhurst's lies survive the even more terrible privacy of family life?

And then, a few months later, towards the very end of the race, his situation grew even more desperate. He found himself destroyed, in effect, by the very success of his own fabrications and exaggerations. For when he had rejoined the race and telegraphed his position to an astonished Rodney Hallworth who had assumed, not having heard from Crowhurst for months, that he must probably be dead, the news of his supposed progress was radioed on to Nigel Tetley, now the only other yachtsman, apart from Robin Knox-Johnston, who was still in the running. (Moitessier, remarkably, had rounded Cape Horn in good time but had then turned his back on the race altogether, protesting that the cash prize and attendant publicity were an affront to his spiritual values.) Knox-Johnston, then, was certain to win the prize for first man home; but the problem was that he had set out months before the others, so he was not going to win the £5,000 prize for *fastest* circumnavigation. That now seemed to be a toss-up between Tetley and Crowhurst. Tetley was in the lead but Crowhurst—apparently—was gaining on him fast. Tetley, deciding that he could take no chances, began to push his own trimaran (the ironically named *Victress*) harder and harder on the home stretch. But it had already suffered badly in the Southern Ocean, and it was coming apart. Late one night—while he was sleeping—the port bow came away and smashed a hole in the bow of the main hull. Water was pouring into the boat. He could immediately see that there was nothing for it but to send a Mayday message and abandon ship. He took his camera film, logbooks and emergency radio transmitter with him into the inflatable life raft, and then spent the best part of a day drifting anxiously in the Atlantic before an American rescue plane appeared in the late afternoon to pick him up. For Tetley, the race was over and his dream was shattered.

But for Crowhurst, too, this was the worst thing that could possibly have happened. As the clear winner of the prize for fastest voyage, he would come under intense media scrutiny. Already Rodney Hallworth was telegraphing him with news of the hero's welcome that awaited him: the circling helicopters, the TV camera crews, the boatloads of newspaper reporters. His logbooks would soon be examined in the minutest detail— and he must have known, in his heart, that they would not pass muster. Unmasked as a fraud, how would he survive? Stanley Best would want his money back. Hallworth himself would be a laughing stock. His own marriage might even crumble under the strain . . .

Faced with the impossibility of his position—realising that his audacious "Third Way" had turned out to be just another cul-de-sac—Crowhurst simply gave up. Instead of racing, he began to coast. He drifted into the Doldrums and allowed the yacht to plod its way through those stagnant, seaweed-infested waters untended while he sat below deck, naked in the steaming heat, methodically trying to repair his broken radio transmitter—a task which involved rebuilding it from scratch, at some risk of severe electrical shocks and injuries from his soldering iron, and which took almost two weeks to complete. But at least this project kept him, for a while, from too much introspection. When it was finished, in the hot, lonely days that followed, Crowhurst blocked off all thoughts of the reception waiting for him at home and retreated into a fantasy world of pseudo-philosophical speculation. Inspired by the only book he had thought to bring along on the voyage (Einstein's *Theory of Relativity*), he began to pour out words on to the pages of his logbooks, scoring the letters so deeply with his pencil that he frequently tore the paper. Thousands and thousands of words. Viewed now, they show in stark detail the process of a mind quickly unravelling under pressure. He began by addressing one of the greatest riddles of mathematics: the impossible number, the square root of minus one.

> *I introduce this idea* $\sqrt{-1}$ *because it leads directly to the dark tunnel of the space-time continuum, and once technology emerges from this tunnel the "world" will "end" (I believe about the year 2000, as often prophesied) in the sense that we will have access to the means of "extra physical" existence, making the need for physical existence superfluous.*

Continuing this theme, but descending further into fantasy, he started to believe that the human race was on the verge of an enormous change—that a chosen few, like him, would soon be mutating into "second-generation cosmic beings," who would exist outside the material world altogether, thinking and communicating in a way that was entirely abstract and ethereal, breaking through the boundaries of space, so that there would no longer be any need to exist in a physical, bodily relationship with other people at all. As the bearer of this momentous news he began to see himself as a personality of huge importance, a kind of Messiah, while remaining aware that to the rest of the world he would always appear much less than that: he was resigned to being viewed as a "Misfit"—"the Misfit excluded from the system—the freedom to leave the system." Finally, on the last day of his life, his scrawls became even more incoherent and abstract ("there can only be one perfect beauty/that is the great beauty of truth"), and his sense of having sinned, having lied, having let everybody down, became overwhelming:

> *I am what I am and I*
> *see the nature of my offence*

In his last writings, Crowhurst had also become obsessed with time—months of notating his real and fake positions on the earth's surface having made him weary, perhaps, of thinking in terms of the space dimension any more. He had begun to preface many of his sentences with exact notes of the time at which he was writing them. And so we know that at some moment between 10:29 and 11:15 on 1 July 1969 he wrote what were almost his final words:

> *It is finished—*
> *It is finished—*
> *IT IS THE MERCY*

And then, after scribbling a few more tortured phrases, he took his chronometer, and the logbook containing his false record, climbed on to the stern of the *Teignmouth Electron* and disappeared, never to be seen again.

We were not short of real heroes, in the summer of 1969. The news that Crowhurst's yacht had been discovered in mid-ocean, that he was missing and believed dead, appeared in the Sunday newspapers on 13 July. Two weeks later, on the 27th, he dominated the front pages again, but by this time his logbooks had been read, his fraud unmasked, and all the stories were of his attempt to perpetrate a remarkable hoax on the *Sunday Times* and the British public. I read these stories with bewilderment, I remember, and perhaps a certain sense of youthful betrayal. But then, sandwiched neatly between those two Sundays, on 20 July 1969, came another story, not unrelated to man's hunger for exploration, for feats of heroic achievement, for redefining his own position in the dimension of space: Neil Armstrong became the first human being to walk on the moon.

It was a summer of wonders, in other words. But strangely, the wonder of my erstwhile hero, Donald Crowhurst, and his tragic downfall, is the one which has stayed with me and haunted me most insistently over the years. Which is why I am fascinated, now, to see that other people—including Tacita Dean—have been haunted by it, too. Where does its resonance lie, I wonder? Crowhurst is hardly an admirable figure, after all. The men who emerge with the greatest stature from the Golden Globe saga are Knox-Johnston and Moitessier. The most heartbreaking story, in a way, is that of Nigel Tetley, the "forgotten man" of the race, who so nearly bagged that £5,000 prize, and who quietly—leaving no messages or any trail of newspaper headlines—died in a wood near Dover three years later.

So . . . why Donald Crowhurst? Or, to put it another way, what does it say about our own time, the time we are now living in, that we find it easier to identify not with Robin Knox-Johnston—an almost comically stubborn, courageous, patriotic sportsman—but with a lesser figure entirely: a man who lied to himself and those around him, a little man in the throes of a desperate existential crisis, a tormented cheat?

Well, Poppy, I have no doubt that we will not find the

answer to these questions during our visit to the show on Saturday. And I'm sorry to have written at such length on a subject which, although it has always been very important to me, can hardly strike the same chord with you, or perhaps with anyone of your generation. But I think we will have an interesting morning anyway, and I hope a good lunch afterwards. Temperatures are due to go down at the end of the week, though, so we'll not be dining *al fresco*—and remember to bring your scarf and gloves!

Looking forward to seeing you again.

Your always loving Uncle,

Clive

5

When I finished reading this letter, my left shoulder was numb from the weight of Poppy's head leaning against it. I gently eased her off, and instinctively she shifted her weight, leaning over to the other side of her seat, away from me. I took her pillow and, carefully raising the back of her head, slid the pillow behind it. Her mouth was half-open and there was a little bubble of saliva at one corner. I rearranged her blanket, making sure that both of her shoulders were covered, and tucked it in around the edges of her body. She gave a little sigh and slipped even deeper into untroubled sleep.

I sat up, rubbed my eyes and listened for a while to the steady drone of the engines. Most of the passengers were asleep, and the cabin lights were giving out a strange, muted sort of twilight glow. On the screen in front of me, a perpetually shifting map showed the plane's progress towards London: it told me that we were, at that moment, somewhere over the Arabian Sea, a few hundred miles west of Bangalore. As with anything technological, I had no idea how this miraculous device worked. Forty years ago, it seemed Donald Crowhurst could drift for months in the mid-Atlantic, a speck in the ocean, surrounded by limitless miles of open sea but somehow hidden from everyone else on the planet. Nowadays, any number of orbiting satellites were trained on us every minute of the day, pinpointing our locations with unimaginable speed and accuracy. There was no such thing as privacy anymore. We were never really alone. That actually should have been a comforting thought—I'd had enough of loneliness, more than enough, over the last few months—but somehow it wasn't. After all, even when he'd been thousands of miles out to sea, even when there had been whole oceans lying between them, Crowhurst had still been bound to his wife, by invisible cords of feeling. He could have been certain, at almost any time of the day or night, that she would have been thinking of him. Yet here I was, with a kind, affectionate young woman sleeping right by my side (the most trusting and intimate thing you can do with another person, I sometimes think), and the sad truth was that any closeness I felt between us was likely to be temporary. At the end of the flight, it would probably be gone.

I read the letter from Poppy's uncle again, during those wakeful hours, and then a third time. It left me with far more questions than answers. Had Donald Crowhurst been a coward to do what he did? I found it hard to see it that way. He'd been only thirty-six when he set out on his voyage, and for my own part I still felt like a child by comparison, even though I was now forty-eight (having celebrated my birthday in Australia two weeks earlier, at a budget-priced Greek restaurant in Sydney, struggling as usual to keep a conversation going with my father). To be the master of a boat like that—let alone to convince yourself, and others, that you could pilot it single-handed around the globe, through the most dangerous seas on earth—suggested . . . what? Self-delusion? No, I didn't think that Crowhurst had been deluded. Quite the opposite. By today's standards he seemed almost inconceivably mature and self-confident. Thirty-six years old! In my mid-thirties, like most of my friends, I was still agonising over whether I was ready to have kids or not. Crowhurst had tackled that much earlier in his life: he had already had four. What was it about my generation? Why were we so slow to grow up? Our infancy seemed to stretch into our mid-twenties. At the age of forty we were still adolescents. Why did it take us so long to assume responsibility for ourselves—let alone for our children?

I yawned and felt my eyelids beginning to weigh heavy. The battery on Poppy's computer was almost exhausted too—about eight minutes to go, the meter said. I pressed the forward button in Picture and Fax Viewer and looked for one last time at the pictures of Donald Crowhurst she had scanned in. I couldn't put my finger on it, but something about them bothered me, gave me a little shiver of unrest. Besides the photo of the abandoned yacht, there were three others: Crowhurst in his weatherproofs and setting sail from Teignmouth, the scene Poppy's uncle had witnessed himself; Crowhurst towards the end of his voyage, a self-portrait, with moustache and a new, sun-hardened look to his face; and a startlingly younger-looking Crowhurst on dry land, in front of the BBC cameras, being interviewed prior to his departure.

This last one, a close-up, was the most unsettling. His face was turned partly away from the camera, looking downwards, lost in anxious thought; he was chewing nervously on the knuckle of his thumb. Here, already, he looked like a man in torment, as if all too aware that the image he was presenting to the world was fraudulent, that the truth behind it was darker, more dangerous, too painful to confront. But why did I find it so disturbing?

Then it dawned on me. Of course—it was obvious, now that I'd noticed it. He was the spitting image of my father.

WATFORD–READING

6

I missed her.

Already I missed her.

Poppy had been gone only fifteen minutes, and already I missed her dreadfully.

Should I read anything into the fact that she hadn't wanted to come and have a coffee with me? Of course not. She'd had a long flight, and she was tired, and she wanted to get home. We'd said goodbye in baggage reclaim, a bad place to say goodbye—noisy, chaotic, oppressive. But she only had hand luggage and I had to wait for my case to come up on the carousel, so that was where it had to be, our goodbye. After that, I collected my case, wheeled it outside, saw the queue for taxis—at least fifty-strong—and wheeled it back in again.

I took the escalator up to the departures lounge and bought myself a cappuccino. I think it was the hottest drink I had ever been served in my life. Twenty minutes passed before I even dared to put my lips to it. In the meantime I watched the comings and goings of the other passengers. Nobody, apart from me, seemed to be travelling alone. This can't have been true, objectively speaking, but it was how things appeared that morning. After about ten minutes a man sat at the table next to mine. He looked roughly my age, apart from the fact that his hair was grey, almost white; and *he* was alone, so I was almost on the point of saying something to him, just for the relief of talking to someone again, but then his wife and two daughters turned up. The two daughters were very pretty. I guessed that the younger one was about eight, the older one twelve or thirteen—close to Lucy's age. His daughters were very pale; in fact the whole family was very pale. I listened in on their conversation for a little while. He was going to Moscow for a few days, and his family had come to see him off. He sounded quite nervous about this trip, for some reason, but his wife was trying to be reassuring about it, and kept saying things like, "You've done this sort of thing dozens of times before." He mentioned that he was going to have to give lots of interviews, and I wondered if he might be famous, but I didn't recognise him. They left after another ten minutes or so.

My cappuccino was still too hot to drink. I picked up my mobile phone and retrieved Poppy's number from the memory and looked at it. I wished I'd been able to take a picture of her before she left, but I knew that would have felt like a weird favour to ask. It would have put her off. So all I had was her mobile number. A face, a personality, a pair of lively eyes, a body, a human being, all reduced to eleven digits on a screen. All somehow contained in that magical combination of numbers. Better than nothing, at any rate. At least I had a means of contacting her. At least Poppy was in my life now.

I took a tentative sip of my cappuccino, which had been served to me twenty-five minutes earlier, recoiled as the still-scalding liquid sent scorching needles of pain through my lips, tongue and the roof of my mouth, and gave it up as a bad job. I dragged my suitcase out from under the table and went to try my luck with the taxi queue again.

It was about nine o'clock in the morning as I approached home. I was slumped in the back of a taxi, looking out at the monochrome grimness of urban Hertfordshire through sleepy eyes. It was the third week of February, the morning skies were thick with cloud, and to me the world had never looked greyer, or felt chillier. I thought about the country I had left behind, so full of warmth, colour, vitality: the rich blue of the summer skies over Sydney; the dazzling play of light on the harbour waters. And now this. Watford, windswept and rainy.

"Just drop me here, will you?" I said to the driver.

He looked at me in some puzzlement as I hauled my suit-case out of the front of the cab and paid him his fare (fifty pounds, plus tip). But I knew—even though it was just putting off the evil moment—that I couldn't go home just yet. I still needed a little more time to gather my strength. So I wheeled my case behind me again as I turned left off the Lower High Street and walked up Watford Field Road. When I reached the field itself, I sank down on to a bench. The wooden slats were wet and I could feel the dampness seeping through my trousers and underpants and into my skin. It didn't matter. My house was only about half a mile's walk from here, and I would go there in a few minutes; but in the meantime, I just wanted to sit, and think, and watch the people walking by on their way to work—to check, I suppose, that I still felt some kind of bond with these people: my fellow humans, my fellow Britons, my fellow Watfordians.

It was tough going.

Someone must have passed by my bench every thirty seconds or so, but nobody said hello, or nodded, or made eye-contact. In fact, every time *I* tried to make eye-contact, or looked as though I might be about to speak to them, they would look away, hurriedly and pointedly, and quicken their step. You might have thought this would be especially true of the women, but it wasn't; the men looked just as alarmed at the prospect that a stranger might be trying to engage with them, even fleetingly. It was sobering to see how even the little spark of common humanity I was trying to ignite between us made them panic, turn tail and flee.

For those who don't know Watford Field, it's a scrap of parkland, probably no more than two hundred yards on either side, and not far from the main thoroughfares of Waterfields Way and Wiggenhall Road, so the traffic noise is pretty much constant. It's not exactly an oasis but I suppose that any green space to which you can beat a retreat is to be valued these days. After a while I began to feel oddly settled there, that morning, and despite the cold and damp I sat there for much longer than I'd intended. As it got later, of course, fewer and fewer people passed by. Soon it got to the point where I hadn't seen a soul for ten minutes. And it was more than an hour since I'd spoken to anyone—if you can count my mumbled farewells to the taxi driver as speaking, in any meaningful sense. It was probably time to give up and face the forbidding emptiness of my house.

Then a man appeared, rounding the corner from Farthing Close and coming towards me. And there was something in the uncertainty of his progress, the hesitancy of his bearing, that made me think that this might be the one. He was probably in his early twenties, wearing a navy-blue fleece and stone-washed drainpipe jeans. He had a shock of thick, curly black hair and what seemed to be the beginnings of a moustache—tentative, like everything else about him. He was looking around in apparent bewilderment, and twice, before he reached my bench, he stopped and turned to look into the distance, as if checking out alternative roads he might have taken. Obviously he was lost. Yes, that was it—he was lost! And what did people do when they were lost? They stopped to ask for directions. That was what he was going to do. He was probably trying to get to the railway station on the High Street. Or maybe the General Hospital. Both were nearby. He was going to ask me how to get there, and we would have a conversation. I could even imagine how the conversation might go. Even before he had spoken to me, I was rehearsing it in my head. "Where are you trying to get to, mate? The station? Well, High Street station is just round the corner, but if you're heading for London you'll be better off going to Watford Junction. About ten, fifteen minutes from here. Keep going straight down this road— back towards the Lower High Street—then hang a left and keep straight on till you get to the big junction with the ring road . . ."

I could hear his footsteps now, accelerating rapidly, and also his breathing, which was irregular and urgent. I saw that he had nearly reached me. And that he wasn't looking quite as friendly as I thought he would.

"Then you cross the ring road," I silently continued, none-theless, "and you go past the entrance to the Harlequin on your right, and the big Waterstone's . . ."

"Give me your phone."

The voice in my head ceased abruptly. "What?" I looked up and saw him glaring down at me, his face a compound of malevolence and panic.

"Give me your fucking phone. Right now."

Without another word I stuffed my hand into my trouser pocket and tried to extricate my mobile. The trousers were tight and it wasn't easy. "Sorry about this," I said, wriggling and struggling. "It doesn't seem to want to come."

"Don't look at me!" the man shouted. Actually, he seemed more like a boy. "Don't look at my face!"

I'd almost managed to extract the phone from my pocket. It was ironic: my last model had been a super slimline Nokia which would have slipped out easily. I'd gone for this more chunky Sony Ericsson because it was better for playing MP3s. I didn't think it was appropriate to explain this right now, though.

"Here you are," I said, and handed him the mobile. He snatched it off me violently. "Was there anything else you wanted—I mean like . . . cash, credit cards?"

"Fuck you!" he shouted, and ran off down Farthing Way, in the same direction from which he'd come.

It had all happened in a few seconds. I flopped back down on the bench and watched his receding figure. I was shaking slightly, though soon became calm again. My first instinct was to dial 999 and call for the police, but then I realised I no longer had a phone to do it on. My second instinct was to start wheeling my suitcase back towards my house, stopping at the convenience store so I could buy some milk and make myself a cup of tea when I got there. Strangely, instead of worrying too much about the loss of my phone—which was insured against theft, at any rate—I was more disappointed that my long-awaited moment of human contact hadn't quite panned out the way I'd been hoping.

Just then I heard footsteps approaching again. Running, this time. And the same panting, irregular breath. It was my mugger. He ran straight past my bench, ignoring me, stopped suddenly, looked this way and that, then ran a hand through his hair.

"Shit," he was saying. "Shit!"

"What's the matter?" I asked.

He wheeled round. "Uh?" He looked at me more closely and registered, I think, for the first time, that I was the same person whose phone he had just stolen.

"What's the matter?" I repeated.

It took him another few seconds to assess the situation and

to decide that I wasn't just trying to wind him up. Then he said: "I'm lost, man. I'm completely fucking lost. Which way's the station from here?"

My heart swelled when I heard these words. "Well, there are two stations. Where are you trying to get to?"

"Central London, man. I've got to get back to London pronto."

"Then your best bet is Watford Junction. It's about ten, fifteen minutes from here. Keep going straight down this road— back towards the Lower High Street—then hang a left and keep straight on till you get to the big junction with the ring road—"

"The ring road, yeah? Where all the traffic lights are."

"That's right. Then you cross the ring road, and you go past the entrance to the Harlequin on your right, and the big Waterstone's—"

"OK, OK, I know the Harlequin, I know my way from there. That's fine, man. That's great. I'm sorted."

"Pleased to be of help," I said, smiling at him directly now.

But this was a mistake, because it just made him scream, "And don't look at my face, man, don't you *dare* look at my fucking face!" before turning and running at an athlete's sprint towards the edge of the field and the road that led down to Lower High Street.

I must have been seriously jet-lagged, because I wasn't thinking straight. As I trudged over to the convenience store, all I could think about the mugging was that it would make a good story to tell to Poppy, and in fact I was so pleased to have this story to tell her, so pleased to have a ready excuse for contacting her this morning, that I spent the time quite happily composing a quirky, downbeat text message about the episode in my head. It wasn't until I reached the store and rested my suitcase outside that I realised I couldn't send her a text message, because I no longer had my phone, and also, because I no longer had my phone, I no longer had her number, or any means of contacting her.

So, that was that.

I went inside to buy the milk.

7

As I pushed open the front door of my house, I expected to feel the dead weight of piles of junk mail behind it. But there wasn't that much. Maybe a dozen envelopes. To be honest, after an absence of three weeks I would have expected more than that.

Leaving my suitcase in the hall, I scooped up the letters and carried them into the sitting room. It was freezing in there. Needless to say, there was no sound of a radio drifting in from the kitchen, no smell of freshly brewed coffee wafting through the hall. Caroline and Lucy were—as I'd known they would be—more than two hundred miles away. All the same, maybe they'd written one of these letters. When they first went away, Lucy used to write to me quite often, every couple of weeks or so, usually enclosing some drawing or collage or piece of writing that she'd done at school. But the letters had been slowing down lately. I think the last time I'd received one had been in November. Let me see . . . I skimmed through the envelopes and quickly saw there was nothing from her. Three credit-card bills. Letters from gas and electricity suppliers touting for business. Bank statements, mobile-phone bills. The usual crap. Nothing of interest there at all.

I went into the kitchen to turn the heating on and boil the kettle, and while I was there I glanced at the answering machine mounted on the wall. It blinked the number 5 back at me. *Five* phone messages, while I'd been away for almost a month? This was ridiculous. Did I dare listen to them?

While I was plucking up courage, I went upstairs and into the back bedroom to boot up my computer. The trick, as always, was to walk into the room and do whatever I had to do there without looking around. I'd become quite good at it by now. It was how it had to be done, because this bedroom used to be Lucy's. The sensible thing would have been to redecorate it after she and Caroline had moved out, but I hadn't been able to face doing that—not just yet. It still had the pink girly wallpaper she used to like, and the Blu-Tack marks on the wall where she used to stick all the posters from her animal magazines—big close-ups of sleeping hamsters and impossibly cute wombats and things like that. Luckily the posters themselves were gone. But the wallpaper was a painful reminder. Maybe this was the week I should do something about it. There was no need to strip it off, I could just paint over it—three or four coats of brilliant white emulsion ought to be enough to hide the flowery pattern. In the meantime, I just looked straight ahead of me, limiting my field of vision to the things I was meant to be concentrating on. It was easier that way.

Back in the kitchen, I made a mug of strong tea and took a couple of sips before pressing the "play" button on the answering machine. But my mood of trembling anticipation was short-lived. A message from my employer reminded me to come in for a final meeting with the Occupational Health Officer in a few days' time. There were two messages from my dentist: an automated one confirming my appointment two weeks ago (which I had forgotten all about) and one from a real person, left the following day, asking me why I'd failed to turn up and noting I would have to pay for the check-up anyway. Then there were two blank messages, consisting simply of long electronic beeps followed by the noise of somebody hanging up. One of these might have been from Caroline, of course, but

I couldn't dial 1471 to find out, because both of these calls pre-dated the messages from my dentist.

So much for the telephone.

Well, maybe Facebook would cheer me up. I had more than seventy friends on Facebook, after all. Surely that must have created some activity while I'd been away. I took my tea upstairs, settled down in front of the computer and logged in to my home page.

Nothing.

I stared at the screen in shock. Not a single friend had sent me a message or posted anything on my wall in the last month. If the evidence was to be believed, in other words, not one of those seventy people had thought of me once during my absence.

My stomach felt suddenly hollow. My eyes started to sting: I could feel tears coming. This was worse than I could possibly have imagined.

There was only one thing left: e-mail. Could I bear to open Outlook Express? What if my inbox told the same story?

My fingers moved mechanically, robotically, across the key-board. I clutched the mouse in my right hand and never took my eyes off the screen as it filled first with the programme's welcome message, and then with the subject headers of e-mails previously received. Slowly, my heart thumping, a pit of dread opening up in my abdomen, I moved the cursor across the screen and clicked on the fateful button: "send/receive."

The dialogue box appeared. The progress messages flashed up: Finding Host. Connecting. Authorising. Connected. Then a few seconds' pause while the computer seemed to be teasing me, relishing my torment, until—*Yes*, oh, joy!—"Receiving list of messages from server," and—I could hardly believe this—the first message came flagged with the astonishing announce-ment, "Receiving Message 1 of 137."

One hundred and thirty-seven messages! How was that, then? Who said that nobody cared about Maxwell Sim anymore? Who said I didn't have any real friends?

Next to my inbox icon, the numbers quickly started to mount up. Twenty messages, sixty, seventy-five—they were piling in. It was going to take me all day to read these. Who might they be from—Chris, Lucy, Caroline? Or perhaps even my father, trying to make amends for the way my visit to Australia had fizzled out?

I closed my eyes for a moment, took a deep breath and then got started on the first few messages, which read:

> Your manhood is under construction? Try the blue magic pill.
> The vigor in your pants will be unbreakable
> When your tool is big, the rest of the world seems so little
> for you
> Your powerful uprise will excite women
> The things are really bad when your male friend is dead
> Rock hard erect monster
> The fastest way to success is to restore your manliness
> A fabulous instrument will give you a fabulous reputation
> Give yourself the edge over the other guys
> Push your banger inside lady

Well, never mind, that was only the first ten. It looked like the spam filter must have been turned off, for some reason. But there were bound to be some proper messages in there somewhere. What was next?

> The friend in your pants will be dancing like at a party
> Here to help you leave the pain of smallness
> Your gun stands to attention—everybody shocked!
> Wind joystick round leg!

You can renew and restore your youth condition
The truth behind 9 inches
Never disappoint her again!
Make your stick voluminous
You'll call it Peter the Great
Take part in a sexual marathon with our qualified help
The hard friend in your pants will look up into the sky
Upgrade your apparatus
Give your rocket best fuel

Oh God. There couldn't be many more of these—could there?

Life with a small tool is pathetic and miserable

That was a bit harsh, surely. Amidst all the other problems in my life, it had never really occurred to me that I might have "a small tool" before. I'd always considered myself pretty average in that department, I suppose. And yet now, in the face of this onslaught, my "male friend"—as I would henceforth think of it—was beginning to feel as puny and wizened as a button mushroom.

Tired of your little friend staring at the floor?
Tired of ending the night with just a kiss?
Fornicate like a macho!
Now you don't have to turn off the lights when you take off your pants
Women will give you stars from the sky to sleep with you
Know her from the sexual side how is she inside completely
Women want to be penetrated hard
Only huge boners can reach g-spot
You must be The Real Man with huge dignity

Get the longest banana
Help her find happiness! Rid her of pain!

Rid her of pain? That was an interesting one. As these headers scrolled by in a kind of blur, as it became obvious that these were the only messages anyone had sent me in the last three weeks, my mind began to wander and I started wondering if these really *were* strangers writing to me, if in fact I was just the random recipient of advertising from drug companies and porn sites. Some of these phrases were beginning to sound philosophical. Might there even be a kind of wisdom buried within them—a wisdom intended for me, personally?

Recapture a bit of your youth again

Yes, I would certainly like to do that.

What else do you need to be a perfect man?

That was a question I had asked myself many times. Did these people have the answer?

Learn how to be really inside her

That was something I'd never learned, certainly not with Caroline. How true. How much better if I'd learned to be really inside her.

Give her concrete firmness

Again, was that where I'd gone wrong? Was that why I'd allowed her to walk away from me? Not enough concrete firmness? I was up to about a hundred, now. And still they kept coming.

Your rigid friend will keep his head straight up
Women will be singing odes to the majestic monster in your pants
Finally get the attention you deserve!
Forget the past and focus on the future—get bigger today
No woman will dare turn her back on you
Nobody can be blamed for your pitiful member but you can
change it
Hello Max
Flaccidity won't be your rod's trouble
Enlarging your male tool means winning a war
Size matters in this real world

Wait a moment, though—"Hello Max"? That didn't sound like spam.

I frantically scrolled back up to the rogue message and looked at it again. It was from Trevor—Trevor Paige. It was a real e-mail, from a real person. I clicked on it and, with a surge of relief and happiness, read the words which to me, at that moment, seemed as eloquent, as moving, as pregnant with grace and meaning as anything Shakespeare or any other poet had ever written.

hi max will be in watford this wed how about a beer regards trev

And after reading this message over and over until it was burned on to my memory, I laid my arms across the computer keyboard, rested my head on them and sighed with heartfelt gratitude.

8

A few minutes later, I went to bed. I'd been planning to fight the jet lag, if I could, but I was far too tired. I fell asleep straight-away but the sleep itself was fitful, disturbed.

Do you know the kind of dream that's halfway between being a dream and being something else? As if your waking mind refuses to lie still, and despite being exhausted it won't quite allow your unconscious to take over? Well, it was like that at first. I kept seeing images of my old schoolfriend, Chris Byrne, and his sister, Alison, but I couldn't tell if these images were from a dream or a memory. We were teenagers, and I was with them both in a place I didn't recognise, somewhere in the country, surrounded by woodland. Chris had long hair, 1970s-style, and looked as though he had already reached shaving age: there were the beginnings of a beard growing in wisps round his face. He was sitting cross-legged on a carpet of leaves, playing his guitar and not taking any notice of Alison or me. There was an expanse of sparkling water at the edge of the wood and Alison was walking towards it. As she walked, with her back towards me, she took hold of the bottom of her T-shirt and pulled it off over her head slowly, seductively, with a teasing glance back in my direction. Underneath she was wearing an orange bikini top. Her skin was smooth, flawless and tawny brown.

My next-door neighbour took some rubbish out to her dustbin and the clanging of the lid woke me up sharply. I sat up in bed and looked at the clock: two-thirty in the afternoon. I sank down against the pillows and gazed at the ceiling, feeling suddenly wakeful. Why had I been dreaming—or thinking— about Chris and Alison? Presumably it was because for the last three weeks, along with all the other annoying things he had been doing, my father kept asking me how Chris was doing and whether I was seeing much of him these days. How typical of him to insist on this, how typical of him to seize (unknow- ingly?) on one of my sorest points and tweak it until I was on the verge of losing my temper every time he mentioned it. By the way, I should have explained this before now, but Chris was my oldest friend, from back in primary school in Birmingham. I'd kept in touch with him pretty consistently ever since then until five years ago, when Caroline, Lucy and I had gone on holiday with Chris and his family to Cahirciveen, in County Kerry. It had been a disastrous holiday—disastrous because of an accident that happened to his son, Joe, who had ended up with quite nasty injuries. A lot of blame was flung around in the wake of this accident, in various directions, a lot of things were said that shouldn't have been, and the upshot had been that Chris and his family had left early and flown back to En- gland. Since then, he hadn't contacted me once. Presumably he was waiting for me to contact him, but I didn't feel able to do that, because . . . well, now is probably not the time to explain. It all gets very complicated. As for why the ins and outs of my friendship with Chris should be of any interest to my father ("How is he?" he kept asking, "When did you last see him? Who did he get married to?"), it seemed this would remain one of life's unsolved mysteries.

I lay in bed a little while longer, thinking about that image of the three of us together in the woods. Then I realised where it came from: in the long, hot summer of 1976 (the summer of the drought, as it will always be remembered by people of my age) our two families had gone camping together in the woods near Coniston Water, up in the Lake District. I couldn't remember much else about it, except that my father had taken a lot of photographs that week, and I still had them in an album somewhere. Yes, in the dreaded back bedroom, unless I was much mistaken.

I fetched the album and got back into bed with it, turning the bedside lamp on and propping myself up against the pillows. The album was bound in dark-blue imitation leather, and the prints inside had seen better days, their once vivid colours now badly faded. Also, I'd forgotten what a lousy photographer my father was. That's to say, I'm sure his pictures were good if you liked nature photography, or extreme close-ups of weird pieces of rock whose exposed textures happened to have caught his fancy, but if you wanted to be reminded of what your family holiday had been like, you were wasting your time looking at them. I flicked through the pages impatiently, wondering why on earth he had not seen fit to take a single picture of me or my mother. Or any other human being, for that matter. But I knew there was at least one picture of Chris and Alison in here—a picture I had once known well, although I hadn't looked at it for at least ten years—and when I eventually found it, on the very last page of the album, I realised the images that had been coming to me in bed that morning had been strange hybrids: half-memory, half-dream. In the photograph, Chris and his sister were standing up to their knees in the water on a grey, sunless afternoon. Their hair was wet from swimming and Alison in particular looked extremely cold. She was wearing that orange bikini, and her young, evenly tanned body was topped off by auburn hair cut into a boyish short-back-and-sides.

I yawned loudly and let the album drop on to the bedspread. When I did this, and the light from my bedside lamp caught the picture of Chris and Alison at a new angle, I noticed something odd: if you looked at it closely, you could see that the photograph had once been folded in half: there was a faint crease, running in a vertical line exactly down the middle. Why would that have been? I yawned again, turned away from the album, and reached out to turn off the lamp. It was no good trying to think straight while I was feeling like this. I could tell that I still needed lots more sleep. My last waking thought was not of my broken friendship with Chris Byrne, or my once-complicated feelings towards his sister, but of Poppy. I couldn't believe that I didn't have her number anymore. And she had never even told me her second name.

I woke up again just before seven, and shortly afterwards did something I'm rather ashamed of, involving my computer and the Internet. I wasn't going to talk about it here but, well, I suppose the idea is that I tell you the whole story, warts and all, so I can't very well leave it out.

How shall I explain this?

It's to do with Caroline. It's to do with Caroline and how much I still missed her.

The thing is that—besides e-mail and the telephone—I did have another means of contacting Caroline, one I only used very occasionally, though, because it made me feel a bit cheap, a bit dirty, a bit angry with myself. Nevertheless, there were still times—times when I missed her really badly, and wanted more than a polite, quickly curtailed chat or a couple of functional sentences about Lucy's progress at school—when using this method seemed like my only option.

It began like this.

When we were married and Lucy was, I suppose, about five or six, Caroline started using the Internet a lot more than she had been. I think it happened when Lucy developed a nasty rash around the base of her neck one time and Caroline went online to see what she could find out about it. Sooner or later this led her to a site called Mumsnet, which was full of mothers discussing just this kind of problem, comparing experiences and offering solutions. Anyway, the rash came and went but clearly they were discussing a whole lot of other things on Mumsnet because soon Caroline was spending half of the day on there. After a while I seem to remember asking her something sarcastic like how many hours a day could you spend having online conversations about MMR injections and breast pumps, and she told me that actually she was contributing to threads about books and politics and music and economics and all sorts of other things, and that she'd made a lot of friends online already. "How can they be your friends," I asked, "if you've never met them?" and she told me this was a very old-fashioned thing to say, and that if I was going to come to terms with the twenty-first century I was going to have to keep up with how the concept of friendship was evolving in the light of new technologies. I couldn't think of an answer to that one, I have to admit.

Well, maybe Caroline had a point after all. That's to say, looking back I can understand why she needed to go online to find all these friends and have all these discussions. She certainly wasn't finding them at home. She'd tried making friends with the other mothers at Lucy's school, and had even tried, at one point, to get a local writers' group started, but somehow none of this ever seemed to quite work out. Thinking about it, she was probably really lonely. I always hoped that she'd become best friends with Trevor's wife, Trevor's wife, Janice, but I suppose you can't force these things. It would have been good if we could have done things together as a foursome, but Caroline was never especially keen. And I was no help, to be honest. I know perfectly well that I wasn't in Caroline's league, intellectually. I never read as many books as she did, for instance. She was always reading. Don't get me wrong, though—I like books as much as the next man. When you're on holiday, for instance, down by the swimming pool and baking yourself in the sun, there's nothing I like better than putting my nose into a book. But with Caroline, it was more than that. Reading seemed to become her obsession. She would regularly get through two or three books a week. Novels, most of them. "Literary" or "serious" novels, as I believe they're called. "Don't they all start to seem the same after a while?" I asked her once. "Don't they all kind of blend into one?" But she said I didn't understand what I was talking about. "You're the kind of person," she used to say, "who will never have his life changed by a book." "Why should a *book* change your life, anyway?" I said. "The things that change your life are things that are real. Like getting married, or having children." "I'm talking about having your horizons expanded," she said. "Your consciousness raised." It was something we were never going to agree about. Once or twice I tried to make a bit more of an effort, but I could never really see what she was getting at. I remember asking her for some pointers about books I should read: ones that might potentially change my life. She told me to try some contemporary American fiction. "Like what?" I asked. "Try getting one of the Rabbit books," she told me, and when I came back from the bookshop a few hours later and showed her what I'd bought, she said, "Is this meant to be some sort of joke?" It was *Watership Down.*

(Bloody good book, actually, if you ask me. Didn't change my life, though.)

I'm digressing so much, I suppose, in order to put off telling you the really shameful thing, which is this: after we'd split up, and after Caroline and Lucy had moved up to Cumbria, I joined Mumsnet myself. I logged on with the user name South-CoastLizzie and pretended to be a single mother from Brighton with her own little business making items of jewellery and suchlike. Of course I knew what Caroline's user name was, and I made a special point of following the threads where I could see that she was taking part in the discussion. Gradually I made it my business, whenever she made a post, to be the next poster in the thread: I would follow up her point, sometimes adding a little qualification or correction just for form's sake, but usually agreeing with her. Sometimes this was difficult, especially if the thread (as it often was) concerned a particular book or writer, but in those cases I would basically confine myself to generalities and try to bluff my way through. After I'd been doing this for a few weeks—when Caroline was definitely aware of the existence of SouthCoastLizzie and might even be curious about her—I sent her a PM saying that my real name was Liz Hammond, that I really liked her posts and felt we had a lot of interests in common, so how would she feel if we started writing to each other a bit more directly, by e-mail? I wasn't sure I'd even get a reply: but I did. And when it came, it really astonished me.

Caroline and I were together for about fourteen years. In all that time, I can honestly say that she never, *ever* wrote to me—or even spoke to me—with the kind of affection she showed to Liz Hammond in that first e-mail. I won't quote it—even though I can remember most of it by heart—but I can promise you that you would not believe the warmth, the friendliness, the *love* she put into those words, those words addressed to a complete stranger—a complete stranger *who didn't even exist*, for Christ's sake! Why had she never written or talked to me like that? I was just so shocked, so *wounded*, that I couldn't even respond for a few days. And when, finally, I did manage to write back, I have to admit I was a little scared. Clearly I was going to see another side of Caroline if I carried on with this correspondence—a side I'd never been allowed access to during our marriage. That would take some getting used to. Anyway, I decided not to rush things. If Caroline and the non-existent Liz Hammond got too close too quickly, then everything would soon become very complicated. I didn't want to turn into her best friend or anything, I just wanted to be kept up to date with the sort of day-to-day stuff I was never going to learn in my guise as her ex-husband. And that was more or less what happened. I learned to ignore the jealousy I felt every time she sent a message—the sense that it was me, the man who'd been married to her for twelve years, who had always been the real stranger as far as she was concerned—and instead just concentrated on the bits of news I'd learned this way: the fact that Lucy had taken up the clarinet, or was turning out to be good at geography, those kinds of things. In return I drip-fed Caroline pieces of information about my fictional self, while half-regretting that I'd ever started the whole business. We swapped photographs a few times, and in return for the picture of her and Lucy standing in front of their Christmas tree (which I've framed, as it happens, and put on the mantelpiece) I plucked a random photo of somebody's children from the Internet and told her they were my son and daughter. There was no reason why she shouldn't believe me.

All sounds very sad, put like that, doesn't it? But—to be fair to myself—I only ever did it when I was feeling especially desperate: and tonight was one of those times. Getting to know Poppy and then losing touch with her so quickly, swapping

Sydney for Watford, realising that I was no closer to my father than I'd ever been, bearing witness to the death of poor old Charlie Hayward—all of these things had upset me, and combined to make me feel, that jet-lagged evening, about as low as I'd ever felt. I needed contact with someone again, and that someone had to be Caroline, and it had to be more than the brush-off she would give me if I just phoned her up to ask how things were.

Anyway, I didn't make it a long e-mail. I apologised for my three weeks' silence, saying that my computer had crashed and the repair had taken ages. I told her that the bespoke jewellery business in Brighton was beginning to fall off a little as the credit crunch started to bite. I went on to the *Daily Telegraph* website to get a quick look at the news and asked if she thought the government really meant it when they said they were going to ban executive bank bonuses. All of that added up to about three paragraphs, which was all I could manage for the moment. I signed off—"Take care and keep in touch, Liz"— and added a little yellow smiley face.

Caroline replied about an hour later. It was the usual sort of e-mail: warm and open, full of news, the odd touch of humour, lots of heartfelt questions about how Liz was doing, whether she thought her business was going to be OK, and so on. When I printed it out it went on for about two pages. This was Lucy's second term at her new secondary school and it seemed she was settling in well. Her new science teacher was "eminently fanciable," apparently. Caroline finished by talking about herself a little in the last paragraph: she said her writing was starting to gather momentum at last, that she'd found a good writers' group to attend every Tuesday evening in Kendal, that she'd achieved a breakthrough because she'd begun drawing on her own experience—mainly episodes from her marriage—but was writing it up in the third person, to give it a kind of "distance and objectivity." As it happened, she'd just finished a short story in the last couple of days—would Liz maybe like to read it, and offer some helpful criticism?

It gave me a sick feeling in my stomach to be doing this, I must admit. I felt as though I was rifling through Caroline's underwear drawer or laundry basket. Even so, there was a kind of ugly fascination to it that kept drawing me back. It intrigued me she could feel so much for an imaginary person (Liz) and so little for a real one (me). My memory darted back to Poppy's uncle's letter, and the point at which it chronicled Donald Crowhurst's descent into madness. What was it that he had written in his logbooks? He'd started by trying to work out the square root of minus one, and this had led him into some crazy speculation about people mutating into "second-generation cosmic beings," relating to one another in a way that was entirely non-physical, non-material. Well, perhaps he hadn't been going mad after all. Round about the year 2000, he'd predicted, hadn't he? Pretty much when everybody started using the Internet, in other words. An invention which now allowed someone like Caroline to have her closest relationship with someone who was just a figment of my imagination.

I put her e-mail away, rubbed my eyes and shook my head vigorously. This was an absurd line of thought. I didn't want to follow Donald Crowhurst into that dark tunnel, thank you very much. I would go downstairs to make myself a cup of tea. And stop this ridiculous charade about Liz Hammond in its tracks while I could. That had been my last e-mail. No more subterfuge. No more pretence.

All the same, I was curious to read that story.

9

"Now, I know what you're thinking," said Trevor. "You're thinking that, potentially, we're standing on the brink of an economic catastrophe. Right on the edge of the precipice."

Actually, that was not what I'd been thinking. I was thinking how good it was to see Trevor again. I was thinking that his energy and enthusiasm were just as infectious as ever. I was thinking how nice it was to be sitting next to Lindsay Ashworth, the unexpected third member of our party, who had been introduced to me as his "colleague." And I was also thinking that I would not have thought it possible for anybody—not even Trevor—to discourse at such length, with such animation and single-mindedness, about toothbrushes: a subject from which he had not deviated once in the half hour since we'd taken our seats in the hotel bar.

"Well, we're all nervous about the economic situation," he continued. "Small businesses are going to the wall left, right and centre. But Guest Toothbrushes, I have to say, are pretty well placed. Capitalisation is good. Liquidity is excellent. We're confident we can ride this recession out. Not complacent, mind you. I never said that we were complacent. I said confident—quietly confident. Isn't that right, Lindsay?"

"Absolutely," said Lindsay, in her gentle, measured Scottish brogue. "Actually, Max, Trevor made a very good point in our strategy meeting earlier today. Do you mind if I paraphrase, Trevor?"

"Paraphrase away."

"Well, Trevor's point was this. And it actually takes the form of a question. Well, three questions, in fact. We're heading into a major global recession, Max. So let me ask you something: will you be replacing your car this year?"

"I doubt it. I'm barely using it at the moment, actually."

"Fair enough. And are you planning to take your family abroad this summer, Max?"

"Well, the rest of my family sort of . . . don't live with me anymore. I expect they'll be taking their own holiday."

"Point taken. But would you be taking them abroad, if they still lived with you?"

"No, I doubt it."

"Exactly. So in the light of the current economic problems, you're not going to be replacing your car, and you're not going to be taking a foreign holiday this year. Tell me this, though, Max." She leaned forward, as if to deliver the killer blow. *"Are you planning to cut down on cleaning your teeth?"*

I had to admit that I had no plans of this sort.

"Exactly!" she said. "People will always clean their teeth and will always need toothbrushes. That's the beauty of the humble toothbrush. It's a recession-proof product."

"But," said Trevor, holding up his forefinger, "as I said before, this does *not* give us cause to be complacent. Oral hygiene is a very competitive market."

"Highly competitive," Lindsay agreed.

"Intensely competitive. Full of some extremely big players. You've got Oral-B, you've got Colgate, you've got GlaxoSmithKline."

"Names to reckon with," said Lindsay.

"Gigantic names," said Trevor. "These are the Goliaths of the toothbrush business."

"Good image, Trevor."

"It's Alan's, actually."

"Who's Alan?" I asked.

"Alan Guest," Trevor explained, "is the founder, owner and managing director of Guest Toothbrushes. The whole thing is his baby. He used to work for one of the majors but after a while he decided, 'Enough's enough. There has to be an alternative.' He didn't want anything more to do with the giants, or their business models. He wanted to be David."

"David who?" asked Lindsay.

"David the little guy who had the fight with Goliath," Trevor said, slightly irritated by the interruption. "I don't know his second name. History doesn't record his second name."

"Ah. Now I get you."

"Alan realised," Trevor continued, "that he couldn't take on the majors on their own turf. It wasn't a level playing field. So he decided to move the goalposts instead. He had a vision, and he saw the future. Like Lazarus on the road to Damascus."

"He rose from the dead," said Lindsay.

"What?"

"Lazarus rose from the dead. It was someone else on the road to Damascus. Lazarus never went to Damascus, as far as I know."

"Are you sure about that?"

"Well, he might have done—who knows? Maybe he popped into Damascus now and again. Probably had relatives there or something."

"No, I mean are you sure it wasn't Lazarus who had the vision?"

"Ninety per cent sure. Maybe ninety-five."

"Well, it doesn't matter. Like I said, Alan saw what the majors were doing wrong. He saw where the future lies: green toothbrushes."

"Green?" I said, puzzled.

"I don't mean the colour. We're talking about the environment, Max. We're talking about sustainable energy, renewable sources. Let me ask you—where do you think most toothbrushes are made?"

"China?"

"Correct. And what are they made of?"

"Plastic?"

"Right again. And what are the bristles made of?"

I could never answer questions like this. "I don't know . . . Something synthetic?"

"Exactly. Nylon, to be precise. Now, what does that sound like to you? To me it sounds like a recipe for environmental disaster. Dentists recommend that we change toothbrushes every three months. Four times a year. That means you're going to get through about three hundred toothbrushes in your lifetime. Worse than that, it means that in the UK alone, we probably throw away about two hundred million toothbrushes every year. Good for the big corporations, of course—it means people have to keep buying new ones. But that's old-style thinking, Max. You can't put sales ahead of the environment anymore. For the sake of humanity, we've all got to change our tune. The profit motive has to play second fiddle. It's no use the band just playing on while the *Titanic* sinks. Somebody's got to start rearranging the deck chairs."

I nodded wisely, doing my best to keep up.

"Now, Alan knew the solutions weren't difficult to find. They were right there on his doorstep, staring him in the face. He knew we were standing at a crossroads. There were two obvious roads to go down, both leading in the same direction, and the signposts were pretty clear." He reached into the inside pocket of his jacket and pulled out something I thought was going to be a pen, but in fact was a toothbrush. "Option number one," he said, "a wooden toothbrush. Beautiful, isn't it? This is one of our leading models. Handmade by a company in Market Rasen, Lincolnshire. Made from sustainable wood, of course—one hundred per cent European pine. No damage to the rainforests, here. And when you've finished with it, you can throw it on the fire, or shred it and put it in the compost."

I took the toothbrush, weighed it in my hand appraisingly and ran my finger along its elegant curves. It was a handsome object, there was no denying that. "What are the bristles made of?" I asked.

"Boar's hair," said Trevor. He noticed that I recoiled slightly. "Interesting reaction, Max. And by no means uncommon. What's the problem, exactly? Much better than nylon. Very good for the environment, using boar's hair."

"Unless you happen to be a boar," Lindsay pointed out.

"I don't know," I said. "There's just something a bit weird about putting pig's hairs in your mouth when you're cleaning your teeth. Something a bit . . . unclean?"

"Lots of people would agree with you," said Trevor. "And you can't expect them to change their attitudes overnight. If you're going to preach to people, you've got to convert them first. It's a gradual process. All roads lead to Rome, but it wasn't built in a day. And so, for the more conservatively inclined, we have . . . this." He produced another toothbrush from the same pocket. It was pale red, almost transparent. "Good old-fashioned plastic handle. Good old-fashioned nylon bristles. *But*"—he twisted the top of the toothbrush, and the head came away neatly—"completely detachable, you see? Throw away the head after you've used it, and the handle will still last you a lifetime. Minimal damage to the environment."

"And minimal profits," I said.

Trevor gave a pitying laugh and shook his head. "The thing is, Max, we don't think like that at Guest. That's short-term thinking. That's thinking *inside* the box. We're *outside* the box. In fact, we're so far outside the box that the box is actually in another room, and we've forgotten where that room is, and even if we could remember, we've given the keys back ages ago and for all we know the locks might have been changed since then anyway. None of that matters, do you see?"

"Yes," I said. "Yes, I'm beginning to."

"We're not saying that profitability isn't an issue," Lindsay put in. "Profitability is very much an issue. We have to stay ahead of the competition."

"Lindsay's right. The fact is, we don't have the field to ourselves."

"Really?"

"You see, when you're like Alan, and you have truly original ideas," said Trevor, "it's inevitable that other people are going to have them as well. There are plenty of wooden toothbrushes on the market. Plenty of toothbrushes with detachable heads, too. But *this*, we think, is the killer. Nobody else has one of these."

From his pocket he drew a third toothbrush. It was the most unusual one yet. Yes, it was wooden, but the head—which seemed to be detachable—featured an extraordinarily long, thin, synthetic brush which swivelled when you twisted it. It was a thing of beauty and wonder.

"I can see you're impressed," said Trevor, with a smile of satisfaction. "I shall leave you to contemplate that for a few minutes. Same again, for both of you?"

While Trevor was away at the bar, Lindsay and I seemed to reach an unspoken agreement that we would not talk about toothbrushes. Unfortunately, since we knew so little about each other, it was hard to think of anything else to talk about. A situation like this would normally have embarrassed me, but today I was feeling far too cheery to be discomfited by it. My thoughts, you see, were full of Poppy, who had made contact with me again that very afternoon. My mobile phone had already been replaced—without having to change the number—and this meant that Poppy had been able to call and invite me to dinner: dinner on Friday evening, at her mother's house, no less, where I would have the chance to meet (among other people, I assumed) the famous Uncle Clive. All day the world had been seeming a better, friendlier, more hopeful place as a result—which was why I now found myself smiling at Lindsay with what looked (I hope) like genuine warmth. She was in her late thirties, I guessed, with platinum blonde hair cut into a Louise Brooks–style bob. By now she had taken off her businesslike grey pinstriped jacket to reveal a white sleeveless top which showed off her pale, slender arms. I wondered if Trevor had told her much about me: anything about our long-standing friendship; the many years we had been neighbours in Watford; what a fine, upstanding, reliable, sociable chap I was. That sort of thing.

"Trevor tells me that you've been suffering from clinical depression," she said, draining the remains of her gin and tonic.

"Oh, did he mention that? Well, yes—it's true. I've been off work for a few months."

"That's what I heard. I must say I was surprised. You don't look to me like someone who's very depressed."

This was good news, at any rate. "I think I'm over the worst of it now. In fact I have to go in to work on Friday, to see the Occupational Health Officer. They want to know if I'm going back, or if they can, you know . . . let me go."

Lindsay took the slice of lemon out of her glass and bit into it. "And . . . ?"

"And?"

"Are you going back?"

"I'm not sure," I said, truthfully. Then: "I don't really want to. I feel like starting afresh, doing something totally different. Not really the right time to do that, though, is it? Not with the job market the way it is."

"You never know," said Lindsay. "Something might fall into your lap."

"I don't believe in miracles."

"Neither do I. But people get lucky breaks sometimes." She bit off the flesh from the other half of her lemon slice and put the rind back in her glass. "Did Trevor not tell you I was coming along tonight?"

"No. I suppose I should have guessed something was up when he said we were meeting here. Normally we go to the pub."

I was glad that we hadn't, I must say. This place was much nicer. We were in the lounge bar of the Park Inn Hotel, where the seats were soft and deep, the décor was calming, there were no crowds, and smooth, jazzy music oozed out of the speaker system at a volume almost outside the range of human hearing. It was characterless and impersonal here, but pleasantly so, if you see what I mean.

"What makes you think that something's up?" said Lindsay.

"I don't know. Maybe I'm wrong," I said, "but I just get the feeling that all this is leading up to something, and I don't quite know what."

"What it's leading to," said Lindsay, leaning forward slightly and lowering her voice to a near-whisper, "is almost certainly up to you."

Her gaze met mine for a brief, charged moment. I was still trying to think of a suitable reply when her mobile rang. She glanced at the screen.

"My husband," she said. "Excuse me for a minute, will you?"

She stood up to take the call and wandered over to the other side of the room. I heard her say, "Hello, honey, how's tricks?" and then Trevor came over with the drinks.

"One pint of Carlsberg for your good self," he said. "They serve it good and cold here, I must say. Cheers." We both took long draughts, and then he asked me about my Australian trip, and we talked about that for a while. "It's done you good, I reckon," Trevor told me. "You're looking much better than I thought you would."

I was grateful to him for saying this, but before I'd had a chance to thank him he changed the subject.

"What do you think of Lindsay, then?" he asked.

"She seems very nice."

"She's more than that. She's fantastic. The best in the business."

I nodded, but after a moment or two felt compelled to ask: "The best *what* in the business, exactly?"

"Didn't I tell you? Lindsay's our PR Officer. She reports to me, as Head of Marketing and Strategy, and runs all our campaigns. And her latest"—Trevor put down his glass of lager and looked to the left and right, as if industrial spies from a rival company might be seated at the adjacent tables—"her latest is an absolute beauty. A copper-bottomed, one hundred per cent corker. It's going to send us . . . up there." He raised his hand towards the ceiling, apparently meaning to signify an ascent into the stratosphere.

"Sorry about that, chaps," Lindsay now said, returning to our table. "Spot of bother with the other half. Pissed off that I'm not there to cook his dinner for him, even though I already told him I was coming here tonight. Haven't managed to drag him beyond the caveman stage yet, unfortunately."

"I was just telling Max," Trevor said, "that you have come up with an absolute peach of a campaign for the IP 009."

"The IP 009?" I queried.

Trevor picked up the toothbrush from the table. "This gorgeous specimen here," he cooed, regarding it lovingly. "Number nine in our interproximal range, and the undisputed jewel in the crown of the Guest catalogue."

The design of the handle and the texture of the wood reminded me of the first brush Trevor had shown me, although this was clearly a superior version. "Is it made by the same people?" I asked.

"Actually, no," he said. "This is an import from Switzerland. Unfortunately this is beyond the range of any British manufacturer at the moment. They could probably manage the handle, but this"—he indicated the detachable head—"is where the real genius lies. You can put on three different brushes: one for ordinary cleaning, one for routine interdental work, and this one, which we are claiming is the longest and most far-reaching interproximal brush currently available in the UK. *Fifteen millimetres* of flexible but hard-wearing nylon-polyester blend, engineered by Swiss craftsmen with such incredible skill that it can rotate on three different fulcrums to any angle you care to mention. This brush will reach anywhere in your mouth—absolutely *anywhere*—without you having to contort and gurn in front of the mirror. It will even get plaque out from the gingival crevice between the second and third upper molars, which as anyone involved in dentistry will tell you is the Holy Grail of oral hygiene. We are *hugely* proud of this product, and this is why we're going to launch it next month, with a massive fanfare, at the British Dental Trade Association Showcase at the NEC. For which purpose, Lindsay here has come up with a wonderful new slogan, which sums up not only this product but the whole ethos of Guest Tooth-brushes, in a phrase which is simple, elegant and to the point. Lindsay?" He glanced across at her expectantly, and jerked his head. "Go on. Tell him."

Lindsay smiled modestly. "It's nothing special, really. Only Trevor seems to be quite taken with it. OK, here goes." She closed her eyes, then took a breath. "*WE REACH FURTHEST.*"

There was a short silence, while this phrase was allowed to hang in the air. We all sat there for a while, savouring it, as if it were a fine wine which released its secrets on to our palettes only gradually.

"That's . . . *good*," I said at last. "I like that. That has a certain . . . Well, I don't quite know what."

"*Je ne sais quoi?*" suggested Trevor.

"Yes—that's it."

"There's more," Trevor said. "You don't know the half of it yet. Lindsay's playing her cards far too close to her chest. Come on, Lindsay, tell him about the campaign. Tell him about your masterstroke."

"OK."

She reached into her handbag and took out an impossibly compact and glossy white notebook computer. Within seconds of her touching the spacebar it had shimmered into life, and she was on the first page of a PowerPoint presentation. The illustration appeared to show a map of the British Isles.

"Now, the thing is, Max, we already have a great product here, and we already have a powerful slogan. In a slightly more relaxed economic environment, that would usually be enough. But given how things are at the moment, we have to try a bit harder. That's my job, essentially: that's what a PR person does. You've got to get hold of the package, which could be as dull as an old tin box, and you've got to dress it up, make it a bit Christmassy, so that it appears attractive."

"Find a gimmick, you mean."

"Well . . ." Lindsay looked doubtful. "I don't really care for that word."

"Me neither," said Trevor.

"What I was looking for," said Lindsay, "was a way of taking that phrase—*'We Reach Furthest'*—and getting even more mileage out of it. Pushing it as far as it would go. Let's face it, oral hygiene is a hard sell. What we have here is an amazing toothbrush—a revolutionary toothbrush—but it's not easy to get people to understand that. For most people, a toothbrush is a toothbrush is a toothbrush. It's an object. A useful object, definitely. But still, people just aren't all that interested in objects. If you want to sell something, you have to *dramatise* it. You have to turn it into a story. What's more, if what you're trying to sell is the best of its kind, you have to give it the best kind of story. You have to do it justice. Now, what do *you* think is the best kind of story, Max?"

I wasn't expecting this. "Boy meets girl?" I said, hopefully.

"Not bad. That's certainly one of the best. But try to think of something a bit more archetypal than that. Think of the *Odyssey*. Think of King Arthur and the Holy Grail. Think of *Lord of the Rings*."

Now I was stuck. I hadn't read the *Odyssey* or *Lord of the Rings* or even seen the film, and King Arthur and the Holy Grail made me think of Monty Python.

"The *quest*," Lindsay said at last, when it became clear that I didn't know the answer. "The journey. The voyage of discovery." She pointed at the screen of her laptop, indicating, in turn, four red crosses that had been marked at various points on the edges of her map. "Do you know what these are, Max?

These are the four extreme inhabited points of the United Kingdom, settlements that are further north, south, east and west than any others. Here we are—look! Unst, in the Shetland Islands, to the north of Scotland. St. Agnes, one of the Scilly Isles, off the coast of Cornwall. Manger Beg, in County Fermanagh, Northern Ireland. And Lowestoft, at the very eastern tip of Suffolk in England. We've done research which establishes that none of our rivals, none of the big corporations, have managed to get a foothold in those places. Some of them, yes—but not all four. But supposing we did? Supposing we were able to claim, at next month's showcase, that we were the only company whose products were on sale in each of those locations? Do you know what that would give us the right to say?"

Trevor and Lindsay both looked at me, leaning forward in their chairs, breathless with anticipation. I glanced from one to the other. Simultaneously, their mouths started to form the first word, the beginning of the slogan they were willing me to pronounce. It looked like a "w" sound.

"'*W . . . W . . . We . . . ?'*" I began, interrogatively, and when they both responded with an eager nod, my confidence mounted and I was able to complete the phrase: "*We reach furthest!*"

Trevor sat back and spread his hands, with the proudest of smiles beaming from his fleshy, good-natured face. "Simple, isn't it? Simple, but beautiful. The IP 009 reaches furthest, and *the company itself* reaches furthest. Product and distributor working together in perfect synergy."

He began to tell me more about the campaign they had in mind. A team of four salesmen would set off in their cars, at noon on the same Monday, from the company's office in Reading. They would each take with them a box full of samples, and a digital video camera so they could keep video diaries of their journeys. They would set off in four different directions, each heading for one of the extreme points of the United Kingdom. There would be a prize for the first salesman to arrive back at the office from his destination (although this was really a foregone conclusion, since Lowestoft was so much closer than the others) but essentially they would be encouraged to take as long as they wanted, within reason. The company had allowed for five nights' hotel expenses, and the real object was to make the video diaries as interesting as possible: when the sales team returned, their footage would be cut together in time for the Dental Trade Association fair and made into a twenty-minute film to be looped continuously on a video monitor at the Guest Toothbrushes stand.

"Sounds fantastic," I agreed.

"It will be," said Trevor. "It's going to blow people away. Can you imagine the impact of that film? A radical break-through in toothbrush design, coupled with breathtaking shots of the British countryside at its wildest and most remote. I'm creaming my trousers just thinking about it. The only thing is, we still have one problem. We're a man short."

He looked at me, and at last the penny started to drop.

"Guest Toothbrushes," Lindsay explained, "is a small organisation. That's Alan's vision, and that's how he wants to keep it. There are just ten of us, and only one man on the sales team."

"David Webster's his name," said Trevor. "Excellent guy. First-rate rep. He's going to do the Northern Ireland leg for us."

"What about the others?"

"Well, a couple of us are going to muck in. I'll be going down to the Scillies, and our accounts honcho will be head-ing off to Lowestoft for a couple of days. But as far as Shetland is concerned, we need to bring someone in for the week. Someone with sales experience, obviously, and someone who isn't working at the moment. Which is why, Maxwell, my old chum"—he laid a friendly hand on my knee—"my thoughts turned immediately to you."

I looked from Trevor to Lindsay, and back again to Trevor. His eyes were eager and appealing, like a spaniel puppy begging to be taken for a walk. Lindsay's eyes, cobalt blue, were trained on me more steadily; behind their unmoving lucidity I felt I could detect something else, something keener and more urgent—a real hunger, it seemed, for my agreement and cooperation. I could not unravel the complex of motives behind this gaze, but still, there was something fearsomely compelling about it.

"I don't have a very reliable car," I said.

Trevor laughed. A relaxed laugh, as if relieved that this was the only obstacle. "We're hiring four cars, especially for the occasion. Four identical black Toyota Priuses. Have you ever driven one?"

I shook my head.

"Beautiful cars, Max. Beautiful. A pleasure to drive."

"The Toyota Prius," Lindsay added, more earnestly, "sits perfectly with the ethos we're trying to promote at Guest. It's a hybrid vehicle, which means that it runs on a combination of unleaded petrol and electric power, and the two power sources are permanently kept in the most efficient relationship by an onboard computer. It's sleek, modern and radically innovative. And fantastic for the environment, of course."

"Just like our toothbrushes," said Trevor. "In fact you could say that the Prius is almost a sort of . . . toothbrush on wheels. Don't you think, Lindsay?"

Lindsay thought about this. "No," she said, shaking her head.

"No, you're right. Scrub that idea." He laid his hand on my knee again. "So, Max, what do you think?"

"I don't know, Trev . . . It's been so long since I went on the road. When were you thinking of?"

"We kick off a week on Monday. And we'll pay you a flat fee of 1K, which when you look at it *pro rata* is pretty bloody generous. You're not working at the shop these days, are you?"

"I haven't been in for a few months, no."

"Well, then! What's to stop you?"

What, indeed, was to stop me? I told Trevor and Lindsay I would sleep on it, but really there was no need for that. In any case, I hadn't got over the jet lag yet, and wasn't sleeping much at night anyway. That night I lay awake and thought about Poppy, and the fact that I would be seeing her again in a couple of days' time, but I also found myself thinking about Lindsay Ashworth's pale-blue eyes and slender arms, and then I started thinking about random things like her description of the Toyota Prius as sleek, modern and radically innovative, and I wondered why that phrase sounded curiously familiar. I didn't think too much about the proposal itself, though, because my mind was already made up. The next morning, I called Trevor from Starbucks on my mobile and told him I was in. The delight and relief in his voice were a pleasure to hear. And even I couldn't suppress a little shiver of excitement at the thought that, two weeks from now, I would be on a ferry to the Shetland Isles.

10

Friday began on a note of high spirits and rare optimism. It ended in bitter disappointment.

I had arranged to meet the Occupational Health Officer at 10:30. I took the train from Watford Junction at 8:19 and arrived at London Euston seven minutes late, at 8:49. I took this train because Trevor was coming into central London today as well, and had suggested meeting for breakfast.

We met at a branch of Caffè Nero on Wigmore Street. I had a breakfast panini filled with eggs, bacon and mushroom. When I ordered this panini, the guy behind the counter, an Italian, told me that "panini" was a plural word and if I was only going to ask for one, I should ask for a "panino." He seemed very insistent about this but I thought there was something slightly disturbed about him so I took no notice.

While we were eating our paninis, Trevor told me something interesting, which had a direct bearing on my meeting with the Occupational Health Officer.

There was something I should know, he said, about the current situation at Guest Toothbrushes. He had just learned that David Webster would shortly be handing in his notice, having been headhunted by GlaxoSmithKline. This meant that they would soon be advertising for a new rep, and if I did a good job on the Shetland trip, Trevor didn't see why the post shouldn't be mine for the taking. The final decision, it seemed, would be taken jointly by himself and Alan Guest, so basically, as long as I made a favourable impression on Alan, it was in the bag.

Everything was just getting better and better.

I mulled over this news as I walked the few hundred yards towards the department store which had, until six months ago, been my regular place of work. The sun had finally put in an appearance, and today it didn't seem too fanciful to hope that spring might be around the corner. I could feel a new lightness in my step, which I did not associate with this part of the world at all. Not that I particularly minded seeing the Occupational Health Officer, a pleasant, mild-mannered lady who never treated me with anything other than sympathy and kindness. We'd had three meetings before this, the first one being some time in mid-August last year, a few weeks after Caroline had left home, taking Lucy with her. It had been coming for a long time, I suppose, but still—the shock of it, the awful knowledge that my worst fear, the one thing I'd been dreading most in all the world, had actually come to pass . . . Well, before very long, it flattened me completely. I struggled on for a week or two and then, one morning, I woke up and thought about getting out of bed and going into work and my body literally refused to move. It was that same feeling I described to you before: like that horror film I'd seen when I was a child, with the man trapped in a room and the ceiling bearing down on him relentlessly. I spent the whole day in bed, not getting up till about seven in the evening, if I remember rightly, when I was desperate to relieve myself and have something to eat. And then I stayed home for most of that week, mainly in bed, sometimes slumped in front of the TV, and didn't drag myself into work until Friday afternoon, when my supervisor called me into her office and asked what was going on and sent me straight down to see Helen, the Occupational Health Officer, for the first time. Not long after that I was also seeing my GP and by the early autumn I was on all sorts of pills, but none of it did anything to help. I couldn't see the point anymore, couldn't see any way forward. Of course it was the departure of Caroline and Lucy that had triggered it, but it soon reached the stage where everything depressed me. Absolutely everything. The world seemed to be on the point of economic collapse and the newspapers were full of apocalyptic headlines saying the banks were about to crumble, that we would all lose our money and it would be the end of Western civilisation as we knew it. I had no idea whether this was true or not, or what I should do about it. Like everybody else I knew, I had a big mortgage, massive credit card debts and no savings. Was this a good thing, or a bad thing? Nobody seemed able to tell me. So I just stared all day at the TV news, not understanding any of it except for the prevailing mood of anxiety and despair which everyone seemed to be trying to put across, and gradually fell prey to a sort of unfocused panic which fitted in all too easily with my general inertia. The prospect of returning to work receded further and further into the distance. Helen, the Occupational Health Officer, referred me to a psychiatrist, who interviewed me for a couple of hours and then came up with his diagnosis: I was depressed. I thanked him for his opinion, he sent his bill in to the department store, and went back home. Weeks passed, then months. I didn't start to come out of it until I checked my e-mails one day and saw that there was one from Expedia reminding me that my trip to Sydney was only a few weeks away. I hadn't even known that I was supposed to be going. As I said, Caroline had booked the trip for me just before leaving. In my current state I must say that the prospect of flying to Australia held precious little appeal; but Helen was convinced that it would do me good, and encouraged me to go through with it. So I flew to Sydney and saw my father, and everything else you know. Or at least everything that I've chosen to tell you.

My meeting with Helen lasted for twenty minutes.

She reminded me that I was coming up to the end of the six months' fully paid leave that I was allowed on medical grounds, and asked me what I had decided to do next. Was I ready to come back to work? I told her that I didn't want to come back to work. I didn't mention anything about the new life I was proposing for myself as a toothbrush salesman. It seemed more prudent, somehow, to keep that to myself. Helen looked genuinely upset that I didn't wish to return to the department store. She explained that my supervisor had told her, in a written memo, that I had been widely regarded as a first-class After-Sales Customer Liaison Officer. I would be a great loss to the company, she said. I told her that my mind was made up, and my decision was final. We shook hands. She promised to set the necessary paperwork in motion.

I thought about visiting my old department on the fourth floor and saying goodbye to my former colleagues; but I decided, in the end, that if I did that there would be too many embarrassing moments to get through, too many awkward explanations to make. It was better to have a clean break. So I took the escalator down to the ground floor, and left the department store through the front doors, rather than the staff exit. To tell the truth, I couldn't wait to get out of the place.

Poppy's mother lived in a wealthy part of London. Her postcode was SW7. I had the whole afternoon ahead of me, so I took my time and spent an hour or two wandering through those rampantly posh, absurdly prosperous streets. Looking at the grand, aloof, imperturbable façades of those solid Georgian terraces, I could tell that it would be years—decades, even—before this recession had any impact round here. These people had built a solid wall of money around them, and it wasn't about to fall down any time soon.

A mile away, in High Street Kensington, where I spent much of the afternoon, things weren't so comfortable. I counted half a dozen shops which had closed for business and boarded up their windows. The ones that were left were usually part of big national or global chains. People didn't seem to want to buy shoes or stationery anymore, although they seemed to have an inexhaustible appetite for mobile phones and were happy to spend £3.50 on a cup of coffee. So was I, for that matter. I went to Starbucks and ordered a tall peppermint mocha and—by way of a late lunch—a toasted panini with tomato and mozzarella. The barista who served me was from the Far East and didn't correct me when I asked for the panini. While I ate the panini and drank my coffee, I thought about the decision I had made today. Was I doing something foolish? These were uncertain times. Trevor assured me that Guest Toothbrushes was on a secure footing, but small companies were going to the wall every day. The department store, on the other hand, was a long-established business, commanding huge customer loyalty with a name that was recognised all over the UK. And here I was, giving all that up on the basis of a potential offer (no more than that) of a permanent job with a company I knew almost nothing about. But I did trust Trevor. And the salary he had mentioned was better than the one I'd been getting. It was so hard to know what was the right thing to do. Too many unknown quantities.

Unable to resolve these difficulties, I thought instead about the journey I would be making in just over a week's time. The retail outlet I would be visiting was a chemist's shop in the village of Norwick, at the northernmost end of Unst. Trevor had already made contact with them, and they were prepared for my visit. Apparently, getting them to buy some of the company's products was more or less a formality. That had been arranged over the telephone, so there would be very little actual selling involved. He told me that my main task was simply to relax, enjoy the journey and make my video diary as interesting as possible. The ferry for Shetland left Aberdeen every day at five in the afternoon, giving me plenty of options. If I wanted to do it quickly, I should arrange only one overnight stop, on the Monday night, somewhere between Reading and Aberdeen. The obvious place, from my point of view, was Cumbria. It gave me the perfect excuse to call on Caroline, possibly even take Lucy out for a meal. (I doubted Caroline herself would want to come.) I should start thinking about buying her a present, something nice to take up with me . . .

   Thinking of this made me realise that I really ought to buy a gift for my hosts tonight. I left Starbucks and went into a shop selling outrageously priced bars of chocolate, cut into elegant slimline blocks and wrapped up in minimalist packaging; it was as if the designers at Apple had started making confectionery. I bought one for Poppy—a sheet of milk chocolate, subtly marbled with whiter and darker blends—and then decided to get something similar for her mother as well. I emerged from the shop feeling well pleased with my purchases. It was only later, on my way back to SW7, that I started to feel a bit foolish. I had just exchanged twenty-five pounds for two bars of chocolate. Had I started to forget the value of things, like everybody else?

———

"In any case," Clive said, "one of the things we're all starting to realise is that the value of any object, be it a house or"—glancing in my direction—"a toothbrush, for instance, is in fact . . . nothing! Just the amalgam of different valuations which different members of society put upon it at any one time. It's entirely abstract, entirely immaterial. And yet these completely non-existent entities—we call them *prices*—are what we base our whole society on. An entire civilisation built on . . . well, on air, really. That's all it is. Air."

There was a short silence.

"That's hardly an original observation," Richard said, reaching for another olive.

"Of course not," said Clive. "I never said it was. But until now, most people have never really appreciated it. Most people have gone about their daily business on the comfortable assumption that something real and solid underpins everything they do. Now, it's no longer possible to assume that. And as that realisation sinks in, we're going to have to adjust our whole way of thinking." He smiled a combative smile at Richard. "Naturally, I realise that in your line of business this is old news. You've known for years what the rest of us have only just begun to work out. And done very nicely out of it into the bargain, I might say."

Richard's line of business was investment banking, of one sort or another. I hadn't really been concentrating when it was explained to me. I'd taken an instinctive dislike to him the moment we were introduced, and suspected the feeling was mutual. He was there, it seemed, because his girlfriend, Jocasta, was Poppy's oldest friend from university. She seemed perfectly nice but it was clear she intended to monopolise Poppy for most of the evening. Name cards had been laid out on the dinner table, and we had been split up,

I realised, along generational lines. I was stuck with the old-ies at one end of the table—Poppy's mother, Charlotte, and her uncle Clive—and had this obnoxious bloke Richard sit-ting next to me, Jocasta opposite him, with Poppy at the far end, almost as far away from me as it was possible to be. I was sitting opposite Clive, who I must say seemed every bit as friendly and engaging as Poppy had made him out to be. Her mother struck me as being inscrutable. She was what I sup-pose proper writers describe as a "handsome" woman, mean-ing that she might well have been quite a beauty, ten or fifteen years ago. It sounded as if she didn't have a job and subsisted on independent means of some sort; but it was hard to find out any more than that, because she didn't talk about herself much, just pumped me for information about how I had met her daughter and (without asking me this directly) what my intentions towards her were. It was hard going, sitting next to Charlotte. I noticed she was hitting the red wine fairly heavily even before the first course was served, and I must say that I felt like joining her. The evening wasn't going to be as much fun as I'd hoped.

"Come on, Clive," said Jocasta, bridling at his last com-ment. "That's well below the belt. You shouldn't kick a man when he's down, you know."

"Down?"

"Richard lost his job a couple of weeks ago," said Poppy. "Didn't anybody tell you?"

"Oh," Clive said. "No, I didn't know that. I'm sorry."

"Unceremoniously booted out of the office," said Rich-ard. "Cardboard box full of belongings and all that. No sur-prise, really. It's been coming for weeks. I was one of the last to go in my department, in fact."

"Which department was that?" Charlotte asked.

"Research."

"Really? How odd to think that banks need a research department."

"Not at all. This particular bank has one of the largest of its kind."

"And what sort of people work there?" Clive asked. "Mainly economics graduates, I suppose?"

"No, not economics usually. Quite a number of pure mathematicians. Some of them had a background in physics, usually at the more theoretical end. There were quite a few engineers, like me. A Ph.D. was the minimum requirement."

I was struggling to make a contribution to this discussion, and trying to think how a department of physicists and engineers could ever be of much use to a bank.

"So they were getting you to do . . . what, exactly? I suppose you were designing new ATM machines, and that sort of thing."

Jocasta laughed wildly when she heard this.

Richard just said, "Hardly," and gave me one of the most condescending smiles I had ever seen. I felt suitably crushed, but Clive rather gallantly tried to back me up.

"Well, what were you doing, then? We're not all banking specialists, you know."

Richard took a sip of wine, and seemed to deliberate for a moment as to whether answering this question was worth his while. Eventually he said: "We were being paid to devise new financial instruments. Extremely complex and elaborate financial instruments. Have you heard of Crispin Lambert?"

"Of course," said Clive. (Certainly I hadn't.) "Sir Crispin, I believe he's become, since retiring. I was reading an article just the other day where his opinion was quoted."

"Oh, what was he saying?"

"Well, as far as I can remember he was saying that the good times were obviously over but it wasn't really anybody's fault—least of all *his* fault or the fault of people like him—and everybody was just going to have to get used to tightening their belts and forgetting about this year's plasma TV or holiday in Ibiza. I believe he was speaking from the drawing room of one of his many country properties at the time."

"Make fun of him if you like," said Richard, "but anybody who knows anything about the history of investment banking in this country knows that Crispin was a genius."

"I don't doubt it," said Clive, "but isn't it geniuses like him who've got us into the current mess?"

"What's your connection with him, Richard?" Charlotte asked.

"Our bank bought up his jobbing firm back in the 1980s," Richard explained, "and from then on you can see his influence on more or less everything we did. Of course he'd been gone some time before I arrived, but he was still a legendary figure. He basically set up the research department. Built it up from scratch."

"And these financial instruments you were devising," said Clive. "They form the basis of most of our mortgages and investments, is that right?"

"Putting it crudely, yes."

"So would we mere mortals understand anything about them if you were to explain them to us?"

"Probably not."

"Well, give it a try anyway."

"There's no point. It's a very specialised area. I mean, would you be any the wiser if I told you that a Logic Note is a hybrid note paying a coupon rate that's the lower of the geared annual inflation rates and the geared spread between two CMS rates?" There was a stupefied silence around the table. "Or that an MtM Capped Dual Power Discount Swap combines an inverse floater fixed-rate range-accrual swap with a ratchet feature?" Richard allowed himself a terse, triumphant smile. "There you are, you see. These things are best left to the people who understand them."

"And does that include the people whose job it was to sell these products?"

"The sales team? Well, they were supposed to understand them, obviously, but I suspect they rarely did. But still, that was never really our problem."

"Maybe it wasn't your problem," I said, "but surely any-body could see it was going to be a recipe for disaster. A sales-man can't possibly sell something that he doesn't understand. And not just understand, but believe in."

There was a slightly shocked pause after I'd said this; in order to break it—and perhaps to justify my intervention—Poppy explained: "Max has worked in sales quite extensively in the past."

"In the financial sector?" asked Jocasta.

"That's odd," said Richard. "I thought I heard you telling Clive that you were involved in toothbrushes."

"No, not the financial sector," I admitted—wishing, at that moment, that I was far, far away from this dinner table. "I used to sell . . . leisure products, for children. And now, yes, I am . . . moving into toothbrushes. That's true." From the look on her face I thought that Jocasta was going to burst out laughing again. Richard said nothing, although the disdain around the corners of his mouth was clear. Clear enough, at any rate, for me to add: "I'm really excited about it, actually. You know, it's not going to earn me three hundred K a year and a five-hundred-thousand-pound bonus, but at least I know I'm selling a bloody good product. Well designed, not just churned out, made with a bit of care, and a bit of thought for the future . . ." I tailed off, conscious that everybody was looking at me. "After all," I concluded, a bit lamely, "we all need toothbrushes, don't we?"

Clive rose to his feet and started clearing away the plates. "Quite," he said. "And arguably, we need them more than we need Dual Power Discount Swaps."

After he had left the room, Charlotte asked Richard: "So, are you looking for something else now?"

"Not just at the moment. Need to find my feet again first. We should be all right for a year or two anyway. If push comes to shove, we can always sell the Porsche."

Jocasta looked across at him sharply, as if he had just casually raised the possibility that she might prostitute herself.

Poppy laughed. "But you never drive it anyway. That car hasn't moved from outside your flat for three months."

"We're afraid we'll lose our parking space," hissed Jocasta, without a trace of self-mockery. She got up to go to the toilet.

After that, Richard quite obviously turned his back on me and began a long, animated conversation with Poppy. In fact, from what I could overhear, he was openly flirting with her. I'd noticed that he and Jocasta hadn't had much to say to each other all evening, and it now began to occur to me that, with his loss of job and status, their relationship was probably under strain. But what on earth could Poppy find to like about this self-satisfied oaf? I strained to hear as much as I could, but it was difficult, with Clive trying to engage me in a dialogue about Donald Crowhurst ("Poppy tells me his story has captured your imagination") and her mother making ferocious small talk about a family friend who had just bought a cottage on one of the Shetland Isles. For the next hour and a half,

Poppy and I didn't get the chance to exchange a single word. Finally, I looked at my watch and realised I would have to leave if I was going to catch the 11:34 to Watford. There were other, later trains, but I didn't want to travel home in the middle of the night; and let's face it, this evening had been a write-off.

"Come next door for a minute," said Clive. "There were some things I wanted to give you before you go."

We went into the next room, a sort of sitting-room-cum-study. Charlotte's flat was on the third floor of a mansion block overlooking a serene and leafy garden square, and perhaps this used to be one of the bedrooms. It struck me that it was a large flat for a woman to be living in all by herself.

"Here, I brought you the book," said Clive, proudly. "And the DVD."

He handed me an old hardback copy of Ron Hall and Nicholas Tomalin's book, *The Strange Voyage of Donald Crowhurst*, and a DVD of *Deep Water*, the feature-length documentary that had recently been made about his journey.

"You'll enjoy these," he predicted, happily. "The whole story just gets more fascinating the more you find out about it."

"Thanks," I said. "Let me know how I can get them back to you. Through Poppy, maybe."

"Or directly, if you prefer," he said, and handed me his card. It gave his business address as Lincoln's Inn Fields. I hadn't even known that he was a lawyer. "Send me an e-mail or something anyway—let me know what you think of the film."

"Yes," I said, for form's sake. "I'll do that."

Clive hesitated; he was clearly on the point of saying something more personal.

"Poppy told me . . ." he began, and left a pause—during which I wondered exactly what Poppy *had* told him about me. Maybe that she was hugely attracted to me but embarrassed to admit it because of the age difference? "Poppy told me you've been off work with depression."

"Ah," I said. "That." Curious how this piece of information seemed to be following me everywhere I went. "Yes, but I think . . . I think I'm over it now."

"That's good to know," said Clive. His smile was kind. "All the same, you know, these things take time. I was just thinking about your trip to Shetland."

"Just what I need, probably. Take me out of myself."

"Probably. But it'll be lonely up there. And you'll be a long way from anyone you know."

"No, I'll be fine. I'm really looking forward to it."

"Good. I'm glad to hear it." He patted me gently on the back and said, rather unexpectedly, "Take care, Max." But I was far more interested to see that Poppy had just appeared by his side, with her coat on.

"Thought I'd walk you to the station," she said. "We didn't really get the chance to talk much, did we?"

I was glowing with happiness as we walked side by side to South Kensington tube. The fact she had gone to the trouble of keeping me company; the fact that our bodies kept almost colliding, because we were walking so close together—there seemed a perfect logic to these things. It felt as though everything that had happened to me in the days since meeting Poppy was leading up to one charged, pivotal moment that was now very nearly upon us. Just a few more steps until we reached the arcade at the entrance to the tube station, and then it would be time: time to do what I'd been hoping to all evening.

"Well," said Poppy breezily, when we had arrived. "Good to see you, Max. I'm off to Tokyo tomorrow, assuming I can get onto the flight, but . . . well, good luck with your Shetland trip, if I don't see you before then. And thanks for the chocolate."

She reached up and offered me her cheek. I took both her cheeks between the palms of my hands, tilted her face firmly towards mine, and kissed her on the lips. The kiss lasted for perhaps a couple of seconds before I felt her mouth tauten and disengage itself, and Poppy pulled violently away.

"Erm . . . excuse me?" she said, rubbing her mouth. "What was that about, exactly?"

At this point I became aware that passers-by were looking at us, with curiosity and amusement. Or looking at me, rather. I suddenly felt very stupid, and very old.

"Was that . . . not what you were expecting?" I said.

She didn't answer at first, just took a few steps back, giving me a slightly incredulous glance. "I think I'd better go," she said.

"Poppy—" I began; but words failed me.

"Look, Max." She came a little closer: that was something, at any rate. "Do you not get it?"

"Get it? Get what?"

"What tonight was about? What it was for?"

I frowned. What was she talking about?

"Max . . ." She gave a little sigh of despair. "You're twenty years older than me. You and I could never be . . . a *couple*. You're old enough to be my . . ."

She tailed off, but it wasn't the hardest sentence in the world to complete, even for a dimwit like me. "OK. I see. I get it. Goodnight, Poppy. Thanks for walking me to the station."

"Max, I'm sorry."

"No need to be sorry. Don't worry. I get it now. It was a kind thought. And your mother's a very attractive woman. Lovely, in fact. Just not my . . . not my type, I'm afraid."

She may have tried to answer me, I don't know. I turned away and without looking back walked down the stairs towards the ticket barriers. My face was burning and I could feel tears of humiliation pricking my eyes. I brushed them away with the sleeve of my jacket as I fumbled in my pocket for my travel card.

You might have thought that things couldn't have got any worse that night. But they did. Out of some weird masochistic impulse I checked the e-mails on my Liz Hammond account and saw that Caroline had written her a message, attaching—as requested—a copy of her latest short story. It was called "The Nettle Pit."

I swear to you that my heart stopped beating for a few seconds when I saw this title. She *couldn't* have done that, could she? She couldn't have written about *that* episode?

While the story was printing out, I went to fetch myself a drink. There wasn't much in the house, so I had to make do with vodka. My hands were shaking. Why put myself through this, after that dreadful parting from Poppy? Wasn't it enough that an evening on which I'd been pinning so many (false) hopes had already ended in catastrophe?

It was no use. I was powerless in the face of a morbid curiosity that made me drag my steps into the sitting room, vodka in one hand, ten printed sheets of A4 in the other. I flopped down on to the charcoal-coloured Ikea sofa and glared at the framed photograph of Caroline, Lucy and the Christmas tree which looked back at me mockingly from the mantelpiece, then began to read. Began to read *her* account—written in the third person, to give it "objectivity" and "distance," if you please!— of what had happened five years ago on that family holiday in Ireland.

EARTH

THE NETTLE PIT

" 'Cheating' is an interesting concept, don't you think?" said Chris.

"How do you mean?" said Max.

Caroline stood against the kitchen sink and watched the two men talking. Even from this seemingly insignificant exchange, she could detect a world of difference between them. Chris was a skilled and attractive conversationalist; however small the subject, he would approach it enquiringly, quizzically, endeavouring always to penetrate to the truth and confident that he would get there. Max was perpetually nervous and uncertain—nervous even now, in conversation with the man who was (or so he liked to tell everyone, including himself) his oldest and closest friend. It made her wonder—not for the first time, on this holiday—exactly why the fondness between these two men had endured for so long.

"What I mean is, as adults, we don't talk about cheating much, do we?"

"You can cheat on your wife," said Max, perhaps a touch too wistfully.

"That's the obvious exception," Chris conceded. "But otherwise the concept seems to disappear, doesn't it, some time around teenagerhood? I mean, in football, you talk of players fouling each other, but not cheating. Athletes take performance-enhancing drugs, but when it's reported on the news the newsreader doesn't say that so and so's been caught *cheating*. And yet, for little kids, it's an incredibly important concept."

"Look, I'm sorry—" Max began.

"No, I'm not talking about today," said Chris. "Forget about it. It's no big deal."

Earlier that afternoon Max's daughter, Lucy, had been involved in a fierce and tearful argument with Chris's youngest, Sara, over alleged cheating during a game of French cricket. They had been playing on the huge expanse of lawn at the front of the house and their screams of reprimand and denial had been heard all over the farm, bringing members of both families running from every direction. The two girls had not spoken to each other since. Even now they were sitting at opposite ends of the farmhouse, one of them frowning over her Nintendo DS, the other flicking through the TV channels, struggling to find anything acceptable to watch on Irish television.

Chris continued: "Is Lucy curious about money yet?"

"Not really. We give her a pound every week. She puts it in a piggy bank."

"Yes, but does she ever ask you where the money comes from in the first place? How banks work, and that sort of thing."

"She's only seven," said Max.

"Mmm. Well, Joe's getting pretty interested in all that stuff. He was asking me for a crash course in economics today."

Yes, he *would* be, Max thought. At the age of eight and a half, Joe was already starting to manifest his father's omnivorous, bright-eyed curiosity, while Lucy, only a year younger, seemed content to exist in a world of her own, composed almost entirely of fantasy elements: a world of dolls and pixies, kittens and hamsters, cuddly toys and benign enchantments. He was trying not to worry about it too much, or resent it.

"So I told him a little bit about investment banking. You know, just the basics. These days, I told him, when you said that someone was a banker, it doesn't mean that he sits behind a counter and cashes cheques for customers all day. I told him a real banker never comes into contact with money at all. I told him that most of the money in the world nowadays doesn't exist in any tangible form anyway, not even as bits of paper with promises written on them. So he said to me, 'But what does a banker *do*, Dad?' So I explained that a lot of modern banking is based on physics. That's where the concept of leverage comes from. Gears, ratchets and so on—you find terms like this coming up in modern theories of banking all the time. Anyway, you must know all about that."

Max nodded, even though he didn't, in fact, know any such thing. Caroline, who knew her husband well (too well) after all this time, saw the nod and recognised it for the bluff it was. The little private smile she offered to the kitchen floor was tinged with sadness.

"I told him that a lot of modern banking consists of borrowing money—money that isn't your own—and finding somewhere to reinvest it at a higher rate of return than you're giving to the person you're borrowing it from. Joe thought about that for a while, and said this very interesting thing: 'So bankers,' he said, 'are really just people who make a lot of money by cheating.'"

Max smiled appraisingly. "Not a bad definition."

"It isn't, is it? Because it brings a different moral perspective to bear on things. A child's perspective. What the banking community does isn't *illegal*—at least most of the time. But it does stick in people's throats, and that's why. At the back of our minds we still have unspoken rules about what's fair and what isn't. And what they do isn't *fair.* It's what children would call cheating."

Max was still thinking about this conversation later that night, when he and Caroline were lying in bed together, up in the attic bedroom, both on the point of falling asleep.

"I didn't think Chris would have gone for all that 'out of the mouths of babes' stuff," he said. "Bit too cute for him, I would've thought."

"Maybe," said Caroline, non-committally.

Max waited for her to say more, but there was only silence between them; part of a larger, magical near-silence which hung over the whole of this coastline. If he listened closely, he could just about hear the waves, about half a mile away, breaking gently on the strand.

"Close, aren't they?" he prompted.

"Who?" Caroline murmured through her encroaching cloud of sleep.

"Chris and Joe. They spend a lot of time together."

"Mmm. Well, I suppose that's what fathers and sons do."

She rolled over slowly and lay flat on her back. Max knew this meant that she was almost asleep now, the conversation over. He reached out and took her hand. He held on to her hand and looked up at the restless clouds through the bedroom skylight until he heard her breathing become slower and more regular. When she was fully asleep he gently let go and turned away from her. They had not made love since Lucy was conceived, almost eight years ago.

When they prepared for their walk the next morning, the skies were grey and the estuary tide was low.

The two wives would be staying behind to prepare lunch. Pointedly sporting a plastic apron as her badge of domestic drudgery, Caroline came out onto the lawn to wave the party off; but before they all struck off through the fields and down the path towards the water's edge, Lucy took her parents to one side.

"Come and see this," she said.

She clasped Max's hand and led him across the lawn towards the hedgerow which marked the boundary of the farmland. Out of the hedge grew a young yew tree, with a single, gnarled branch stretching out back towards the lawn. A piece of knotted rope hung from the branch, and the earth underneath had been scooped out to form a deep basin, now choked and brimming with a dense thicket of stinging nettles.

"Wow," said Max. "That looks nasty."

"If you fell in there," said Lucy, "would you have to be taken to hospital?"

"Probably not," said Max. "But it would really hurt."

Caroline said: "Not a very good place to put a rope, really. I don't think you'd better do any swinging on that."

"But that's our game," said a boy's breathless voice behind them.

They turned round to see that Joe had run over to join them, his father trailing behind.

"What game would that be?" Caroline asked.

"It's a dare game," Lucy explained. "You have to get on the rope and then the others push you and then you have to swing across like ten times."

"I see," said Chris, in a tone of resigned understanding. "Somehow this sounds like one of your ideas, Joe."

"It was, but everybody wants to do it," his son insisted.

"Well, I don't think you'd better."

"What would you do," Caroline asked, "if one of you fell in there? The stinging would be terrible. It would be all over your body."

"That's the point of the game," said Joe, with the triumph of one stating the obvious.

"There are lots of dock leaves," said Lucy. "So if you fell in, you could make yourself better."

"Five words," said Caroline. "No, no, no, no, no."

Joe let out a sigh of resignation and turned away. But he was not given to brooding on life's disappointments, and his enquiring mind was never at rest for long. As they headed down towards the estuary path, Caroline could hear him asking his father why it was that dock leaves always grew in proximity to stinging nettles, and she could hear his father replying—as always—with a concise, informed explanation. Her eyes followed them as their figures receded and Joe's two sisters ran to catch up with them: the bodies of father and son, so alike already in shape and bearing despite the years between them, and the eager, thronging daughters—all three children clustered around their father, drawn together into an inseparable group by blood and mutual affection and above all their unflinching regard for him. And she watched Max and Lucy following them down the same path: hand in hand, yes, but somehow sundered—some force intervening, holding them apart—and sundered in a way that she herself recognised, from personal experience. For an instant, in the odd paradox of their closeness and separation, she saw an emblem of her own relationship with Max. A shaft of keen, indefinable regret pierced her.

Now she could hear the two of them talking as they walked away.

"So why *do* dock leaves always grow next to stinging nettles?" Lucy was asking.

"Well," Max answered. "Nature is very clever . . ."

But whether he managed to tell her any more than that she couldn't say, their voices being carried off by the sea breeze.

How did he do it, Max found himself wondering on that walk. Just how did Chris get to be so bloody knowledgeable?

He could have understood it if he was just talking about things which fell within his own area of academic expertise. But it wasn't only that. The fact was that he knew everything. Not in an offensive, I'm-cleverer-than-you sort of way. It was merely that he'd been alive for forty-three years and in that time had taken notice of the world around him, absorbed a lot of information and retained it. But why couldn't Max have done that? Why couldn't he remember the simplest things about physics, biology or geography? How could he have lived for so long in the physical world and not learned anything about its laws and principles? It was embarrassing. It made him realise he was drifting through life in a dream: a dream from which he would maybe awaken one day, probably in about thirty years, only to realise that his time on this earth was almost over, before he had got even the slightest handle on it.

Max looked up from these gloomy reflections as he felt Lucy's hand slip from his grasp and watched her run away to catch up with Chris and his three children. The genial, ramshackle, ivy-covered outline of Ballycarberry Castle rose up before them, and she was running towards the point where the river curved, where it was sometimes possible to cross at low tide. Chris was explaining to Joe and his daughters about the tides and the gravitational pull of the moon, another subject about which Max had never achieved anything approaching mastery. He began to half-listen but then, feeling self-conscious, picked up a flat stone and attempted to skim it across the river's surface. After a couple of skips, it sank. Turning to catch up with the others, he found that Chris had now gathered all four children around him beside an exposed cross-section of the river bank. Even Lucy seemed to be paying attention.

"Now, when a great chunk of the earth is exposed like this," Chris was saying, "the brilliant thing is that it tells you all sorts of stuff about the history of the area. Can anyone remember what these different layers of soil are called?"

"Horizons!" said Joe, keenly.

"That's right. They're called soil horizons. Now, normally the top layer—this thin, dark layer here—is known as the 'O' horizon, but this one would be classified as a 'P' horizon, because this part of the countryside is so watery. Do you know what 'P' stands for—something that you find a lot in Ireland?"

"Peat?"

"Peat, exactly! Then we have the topsoil, and the subsoil. Notice how the different horizons get lighter and lighter as you get farther down. Even here, though, the subsoil is still quite dark. That's because Ireland has a very rainy climate and rain is very effective in breaking down rock to form soil, and also in distributing nutrients through the soil. But the soil here is also quite sandy, because we're at the mouth of an estuary."

"What's an estuary, Dad?"

"An estuary is any coastal area where freshwater from rivers and streams mixes with salt water from the ocean. So, estuaries form the boundaries between terrestrial systems and marine systems. They tend to have very rich soil because it's full of decaying plants and animals. Look here in the subsoil, for instance . . ."

Oh, it was impressive stuff, Max had to admit. But then, you'd expect Chris to know about soil. He had been teaching geology at university level for fifteen years, and was now a senior lecturer. Max wondered if his daughter realised this. Probably not. She was starting to stare at him with the same starry-eyed adoration as his own children.

Soon Chris, his daughters and Joe moved on, chatting away happily, making for the three stone steps which had been cut roughly into the wall, allowing people to climb up onto the walkway and thence along the grassy path to the castle itself. Lucy, meanwhile, lingered uncertainly. She took her father's hand again and looked up into his eyes. It wasn't at all clear that she had understood the finer points of this little lecture, but she had definitely understood something: she had understood the bonds of faith and admiration that connected Chris's children to their father; she had understood the cheerful reverence with which they had listened to him. She had understood all of this; and Max knew she was now wondering why the same feelings did not bind her to her own father. Or, rather, she was now groping for those feelings, with a kind of forlorn hope. She wanted to be talked to like that. She wanted her father to explain the world to her, with the same confidence and authority that Chris beamed out to his children with every word. As they, too, began to walk on, she looked around her, and Max knew she was taking in her surroundings with a new kind of curiosity; knew that she would soon have questions of her own to ask him and that he would be expected to have the answers.

It happened sooner than he had been anticipating.

"Daddy," she began, innocently enough.

"Mmm?" said Max, stiffening himself for the impending curve ball.

"Daddy, why is the grass green?"

Max laughed, as though this was the simplest and most innocuous question in the world; he opened his mouth to allow the answer to fall almost carelessly from his lips, then stopped, realising that he didn't have the faintest idea of what to say.

Why is the grass green? What kind of question was that? It just *was* green. Everybody knew that. It was one of those things you took for granted. Had anybody ever explained to *him* why the grass was green? At school, maybe? What would that have come under—biology, geography? That was ages ago. Of course Chris would know, yes. He'd been to a posh school and would have learned that it was something to do with . . . was it chromosomething, some word like that? Didn't "chromo" mean "colour" in Greek, or Latin? Chromosomes, was it something to do with chromosomes? Or that other thing that sunlight did to plants—photo . . . photo . . . photosynthesis. Was that what made things go green?

He glanced down at Lucy. She was looking up at him patiently, trustingly. She seemed very young, for a moment, younger even than her seven years.

It was no use. Silence would be the worst response of all. He was going to have to tell her *something*.

"Well," he began, "every night the fairies come out, with their little paint brushes and their pots of green paint . . ."

God, he hated himself sometimes.

Caroline and Miranda had finished preparing lunch some time ago and were relaxing at the kitchen table, a bottle of red wine sitting between them, already half-emptied.

"You see," Caroline was saying, "the trouble with Max is . . ."

But there lay the problem. What *was* the trouble with Max? And even if she knew, should she really be confiding in this woman, the wife of her husband's best friend, a woman she barely knew? (Although she was already getting to know and like her pretty well on this holiday.) Wouldn't that in itself be a kind of betrayal?

She sighed, giving up—as usual—the struggle to put her finger on it. "I don't know . . . He just doesn't seem very happy, that's all. There's something about his life, about himself . . . Something that he doesn't like."

"He's very quiet," Miranda conceded. "But I assumed he was always like that."

"He's always been quiet," said Caroline. "But it's been getting worse lately. Sometimes I can't seem to get a word out of him. I suppose he talks all day at work." Changing tack, she said, "I wonder what he and Chris have in common. They're such different people, yet they've been friends for so long."

"Well, that counts for a lot in itself, doesn't it? Shared history and so on." Miranda could sense something bearing down upon Caroline, some weight of apprehension. "Lots of couples go through difficult times," she said. "And Lucy seems very close to her father."

"You think so?" Caroline shook her head. "They *want* to be close. But they don't know how to do it. *He* doesn't know how to do it." Finding her wine glass empty when she attempted to drain it off, she said, "What Lucy would really like is a brother or sister. Your Joe looks in seventh heaven, with a big sister and a little sister to play with. It's so great, seeing the three of them together like that. How families should be . . ."

"It's not too late, is it?"

Caroline smiled. "I'm not too old, if that's what you mean. But it's probably too late in other ways." She reached for the bottle, refilled their glasses, and took what was more than a sip. "Ah, well. *Would've, should've, could've.* The most painful words in the language."

How much further this conversation might have progressed, how much more dangerously confiding Caroline might have become, they would never know. At that moment the back door of the farmhouse was flung open. They could hear the distressed voices of children and adults from the garden, and now Chris rushed purposefully into the kitchen, looking harassed and short of breath.

"Quick," he said. "Where's the first aid box?"

Miranda jumped to her feet. "What's happened? Who's hurt?"

"It's Joe, mainly. Lucy a bit as well. Baking soda—that's what we need. Do we have any baking soda?"

"But what *happened*?"

Without waiting to hear the answer, Caroline ran outside onto the lawn, where a scene of chaos was awaiting her. Joe lay stretched out on the grass, motionless: at first she thought that he was unconscious. Max was kneeling beside him, a hand laid tenderly on his brow. Lucy came running to meet her mother and flung herself at her, clasping her fiercely with bare arms which, Caroline couldn't help noticing, were mottled and livid with angry crimson blotches.

"What have you done to yourself, love? What happened?"

"It was the nettle game," Lucy told her, between sobs. "The dare. We came back from the castle and then started playing it and Daddy was pushing Joe on the rope. He was swinging really hard and then he fell off and landed right in the middle of the pit. I climbed in and tried to help him out."

"That was brave of you."

"It really, really hurts."

"I bet it does. Don't worry. Chris and Miranda will be out here any second now. They're finding some stuff to put on it."

"What about Joe? He was wearing shorts and everything. His legs . . ."

Caroline turned to look at Joe, stretched out on the lawn, and her husband at his side. In just a few seconds Joe's father and mother would have reached their son, tending to him, ministering to his needs. But in years to come, it would not be those next few minutes' confusion and frantic activity that Caroline would remember. It would be this one moment of stillness: the tableau (as she would always recall it) laid out before her as she turned. The prostrate body of Joe, lying so still and so reposeful that one might even imagine him to have died. And kneeling beside him—crying, unless Caroline was mistaken—her husband, fixated by the pain and distress not of his own daughter but of another man's child. And the strange thing about it was that after watching Max so closely, and with so much bewilderment, during the last few days, after torment-ing herself with the riddle of his unhappiness, his maladjust-ment, his sense of being forever ill at ease in the world, at that moment she saw him—or imagined she did—in an attitude that for once suited him, and made perfect sense. She saw him as a man surrendering to a feeling which must have come so naturally, with such a healing inevitability, that it might almost have felt like a release: a man in mourning over the death of the son he had always wanted.

11

At 11:30 on the morning of Monday, 2 March 2009, I found myself in Reading, sitting in Alan Guest's office. All ten full-time staff members of Guest Toothbrushes were present, including Trevor, Lindsay, David Webster and chief accountant Tony Harris-Jones. The weather outside was grey but moderate, with no immediate threat of rain. Beneath us on the forecourt I could see four black Toyota Priuses, ranged neatly in a line; sitting on a bollard next to them, a bored-looking press photographer was chatting with his colleague, a local journalist, who stood leaning against one of the cars and smoking a cigarette. The offices of Guest Toothbrushes were part of an industrial estate in the south-western suburbs. Beyond the forecourt I could see rows of warehouses and low-lying office buildings, the province of firms specialising in bathroom fittings, computer components and sports and leisure wear. A network of little roads and mini-roundabouts criss-crossed the estate, but I couldn't see any cars using them. It was almost eerily quiet.

As for the mood in Alan Guest's office, I could best describe it as tense. Today was a big day in the history of Guest Toothbrushes—there were three bottles of non-alcoholic champagne on the table, along with eleven glasses—but for some reason nobody seemed to be feeling particularly celebratory. Alan himself, a thin, ascetic-looking, silver-haired man in his mid-fifties, had a distracted air about him. It was falling to Trevor to do most of the talking.

"Now, gentlemen, we've been monitoring the forecasts on the BBC Weather site, and I have to say that the news isn't too bad, for most of you . . ."

I should really have been listening to this, but wasn't able to concentrate. My mind kept going back to Caroline's story. For the first few days after reading it I'd been able to think of nothing else. I was so outraged, so furious with her, that every inch of mental space (can you measure mental spaces in inches? I've no idea) had been colonised by thoughts of how I was going to respond. I drafted dozens of e-mails in my head—some of them from me, some of them from Liz Hammond. I picked up the phone a dozen times, thought about calling and then put it down again. In the end, as you probably guessed, I hadn't responded at all. How could I? What was I supposed to say? My sense of betrayal at what she had written was beyond words. And although I'd managed to calm down about it since then—to a certain extent, at least—there were still moments when my sense of injustice reared up again. I couldn't help it. It was a completely involuntary thing. And it was happening now.

"So we're not anticipating any major meteorological upsets," Trevor continued. "Certainly not in the first half of the week. Things might get a little choppy on the crossing from Aberdeen, Max, if you leave it till Wednesday or Thursday, but I can't see you having to do that . . ."

At the same time, I had to concede my grudging admiration for what Caroline had done. I'm no literary critic (God forbid), but as a piece of writing it struck me as . . . well, competent, at any rate. No worse than many of the turgid yawn-fests she'd thrust under my nose during our marriage, in her attempt to get me to read "serious" novels.

"Now, as you know, we've allowed in our expenses for

five nights' accommodation, but clearly most of us won't be needing that. After all, there's a competition for the first man there and back, but I think we all know who's going to win that one." Laughter, and glances in the direction of Tony Harris-Jones, whose journey would be taking him no farther than Lowestoft. "But if the rest of us can manage it in four days, or even three, all such savings would be much appreciated by our Supreme Leader, I'm sure. We are in the midst of a nasty recession and times are tough out there, as everybody is all too aware." The glances were directed at Alan Guest this time, with no laughter to accompany them. He stared ahead, expressionless. "And please, might I add, be reasonable when choosing your accommodation. No five-star establishments, please. No Scottish castles or country-house hotels. Think Travelodges, or Best Westerns, if you feel like pushing the boat out. Try to keep it under fifty quid a night, if at all possible."

And the other thing was—how had she done it, exactly? Was she a mind-reader or something? Caroline and I had barely spoken to each other in the final years of our marriage, it seemed to me now. I'd spent most of that time sitting in silence beside her, either in front of the television or at the wheel of our car, or opposite her at the breakfast or dinner table, neither of us speaking a word, and I can honestly say that I never had the faintest idea what was going on inside her head. But in writing that story she had more or less transcribed my thoughts, and transcribed them, I would say, about 85 per cent accurately. It was frightening. Was I really so transparent, or was she simply blessed with amazing powers of perception that I had never suspected or noticed before?

"As for the competitive element of this trip, Lindsay has been doing some more brainstorming over the weekend—she never stops, this woman, *never* stops—and has come up with another absolute gem of an idea. Lindsay, I'll hand the floor over to you for a moment, if I may."

But there was an ironic side to this as well. Caroline would never realise it, but she'd fallen at the last fence. Those powers had failed her at the most crucial point. Because she was wrong—totally, fatally wrong—about what I'd been thinking that day, after Joe had been pulled out of the nettle pit and she saw me kneeling over him on the grass. "In mourning over the death of the son he had always wanted"—is that what you reckoned, Caroline? Was that the spin you'd decided to put on it? Well, listen to this: you were miles off. Not even close. And neither you nor anybody else was ever going to find out the truth, either. Not if I had anything to do with it.

Lindsay, meanwhile, had started to tell us something about the onboard computer system on our Priuses. I really ought to be paying attention.

"So what happens is, when you press the 'info' button on the fascia, you get a choice of two screens. One of them is the energy monitor screen, which tells you where the power is coming from at any given time, and the other screen gives you detailed information about how much petrol you've consumed since the trip counter was last reset. Those trip counters have been set to zero on all four vehicles, by the way, so please don't touch them until you're safely back here . . ."

Another nasty thought had occurred to me, too. A lot of the information which had formed the basis of her story could have been obtained only from Lucy. Especially that stuff about me not knowing why the grass was green. (Which was all perfectly true—and still is.) So, Caroline and Lucy must have had a right old laugh, at some time or other, about how silly old Daddy knew fuck-all about the important things in life, always trying to bullshit himself out of difficult questions and awkward situations. Obviously, these days my comical ignorance about matters of general knowledge formed the basis of many of their cosy mother-and-daughter chats. Well, I suppose I should be glad that I gave them something to bond over . . .

"So what we're offering you, gentlemen, is the opportunity to win not just one but *two* highly desirable prizes. The first man there and back gets one of these handsome signed certificates—a beautiful addition to any office wall, I think you'll agree. But there will also be a cash prize of *five hundred pounds*"—there were cheers, whoops and loud intakes of breath, again, from everybody except Alan Guest, whose face remained inscrutable—"for the driver who does the most to demonstrate the green credentials of Guest Toothbrushes, by returning home with the *lowest average figure for petrol consumption* on his information screen. In other words, drive carefully, folks, *and* economically!"

Lindsay sat down to widespread applause, and at this point the wine bottles were opened and the meeting dissolved into informality. I heard Alan take Trevor aside and say, "Don't let everyone hang about—remember, we've got that newspaper man waiting outside," so after just a few minutes we drained our glasses, left the office en masse and trooped down the echoing concrete staircase that led to the forecourt, Trevor, David, Tony and I lugging our overnight bags with us.

Without really meaning to, I found myself at the back of the group, walking alongside Lindsay Ashworth. Sometimes these things just happen, I've noticed, when there's an unspoken chemistry between two people. It's like invisible choreography: you don't plan to fall into step with the other person, but somehow everyone else moves aside and you realise you've found each other, without even meaning to. That's how it had been with Caroline, the first time we spoke to each other over the Formica-topped tables in that gloomy staff canteen all those years ago, and that's how it was that morning, with me and Lindsay. When she saw I was walking beside her, she turned and smiled at me. Her smile was full of warmth and encouragement, but also with something more troubling behind it: a certain nervousness, perhaps.

"So," she said, "are you ready for this?"

"Ready for what?" I asked.

"Ready to take the IP 009 to places it's never been before."

I nodded. "Don't worry. I won't let you down."

"Good."

Something in the way she said this prompted me to remark: "Funny atmosphere in there this morning. Everybody seemed a little bit on edge."

"Oh, you noticed that, did you?"

"Is everything OK?"

We'd already been talking in undertones, but now Lindsay brought her face even closer to mine. "Keep it to yourself, but Alan had a meeting with the bank today. It didn't go well." She stopped walking so that the others could get farther ahead—we were on the staircase between the first and second floors. "They're refusing to offer him any more credit. And he's furious about it, because he only switched the account to these guys a few weeks ago."

"Which guys?" I asked, and when Lindsay told me the name of the bank, I recognised it at once. It was the same one that Poppy's obnoxious friend Richard used to work for. "But . . . the firm itself is all right, yes? I mean, everything's solid and secure?"

"I don't think there are any long-term problems," said Lindsay. "I think it's more of a short-term cash-flow thing." She added: "That's why Alan's mad at me as well."

"At you? Why would he be mad at you?"

"I sprang this idea of the prize for petrol consumption on him this morning. He said we couldn't afford it."

"It's only five hundred quid, though."

"Exactly. That's what I thought. Anyway, at the moment we can't even stretch to that, apparently. So he's making a big deal of putting up the money himself."

"His own money?"

"Yep."

We started to walk on again.

"All this," I said, "puts a bit of pressure on you, I suppose."

"You could say that. I think he's started to feel that this whole stunt is a bad idea. So if it goes wrong . . ."

"You'll get the blame?" She nodded, and I said, "Don't worry. It won't go wrong. It's a brilliant idea, anyway."

Lindsay gave me a brief smile of gratitude. We had reached the ground floor, and she held the heavy door open for me as we left the draughty staircase behind and stepped out into the grey, feeble sunlight. Everyone else was already halfway across the car park, heading towards the row of black Priuses. Once we were outside, Lindsay stopped to light a cigarette.

"You know, this is the first month," she said, "that we've not been able to pay our mortgage. Martin hasn't worked so far this year."

Trevor had told me that Lindsay's husband worked in the building trade. That was all I knew about him, and I didn't enquire further.

"Tough times, Max," she said. "Nasty times. Somebody's screwed up, haven't they? Somebody near the top. But no one's going to admit it." She glanced across at the little crowd gathered around the four black cars. "Come on, anyway. The paparazzi are waiting to meet you. You don't want to miss out on your fifteen minutes of fame."

It turned out to be rather less than that. The photographer took a picture of the four of us standing in front of one of the cars, and the journalist asked us some vague questions about what sort of toothbrushes were most useful to people who lived in remote parts of the country: he didn't seem to have quite grasped the point of the exercise. Their work was done in just a couple of minutes, but instead of leaving they hung around to watch our departures, all the time maintaining a slightly amused and disdainful air which I think the rest of us found off-putting, to say the least.

It was all very confused and hectic. Alan Guest presented us with the video cameras on which we were to record our diaries. (Lindsay had one as well and was wandering around from car to car, already shooting footage at random.) The instruction manuals, he told us, were in our glove compartments—along with the instruction manuals for the cars themselves, which seemed to come in two volumes and to total more than five hundred pages. He told us not to be alarmed, assuring us that we didn't need to look at these manuals immediately and that we would find the cars very simple to drive. I wasn't entirely convinced by this, because I not only couldn't get my car to start but didn't even know where to insert the little cuboid of plastic I'd been presented with in lieu of what in days gone by would have been a set of keys. Finally Trevor came over and explained to me that there was a button you had to press while holding down the brake pedal with your foot. It all seemed very complicated, and there was no satisfying throaty response from the engine when I followed his instructions. But when I put the car into drive mode it did indeed start to move—so unexpectedly, in fact, that it shifted forward a couple of yards and ran into one of the bollards at the edge of the car park. It was only a gentle nudge—didn't do any damage to the bumper, or anything like that—but I suppose in retrospect it wasn't too auspicious. Alan Guest did not look especially pleased.

Finally, on the stroke of midday, we drove off in convoy. Behind the fleet of four intrepid salesmen, Lindsay and Alan followed in his BMW, with Lindsay still filming us. When we reached the largest of the mini-roundabouts on the periphery of the trading estate, we all pulled over: this was our official starting-point. The roundabout had four exits, and we were each to peel off on a different one. Lindsay and Alan got out of their car and stood in the centre of the roundabout. A keen March wind was blowing, and rain had started to drizzle down. Alan, well wrapped up in his coat and scarf, put his hands together to make a kind of megaphone, and shouted: "This is it, chaps! Good luck!" Lindsay was still capturing everything on camera.

Tony Harris-Jones went first, taking the eastern exit. Then it was Trevor: he performed a 360-degree turn on the round-about, doubling back the way he had come and heading south. David Webster took the western exit. And then it was my turn. All I had to do was head straight on, taking the second exit, which led north. I had my window open to say goodbye to Alan and Lindsay, and as I passed beside them he gave me a formal wave but she, I noticed, looked up from her filming (she had not done this for any of the others) and blew me a discreet kiss with her left hand as I drove by.

When I saw her gesture, my heart lifted, and I experienced a new, curious sensation: a glow of happiness spreading through my body, starting at my feet and rising up until even my scalp was tingling.

And then, as soon as she was out of sight, I felt suddenly, terribly alone.

READING–KENDAL

12

CAUTION

Drive safely, obey traffic rules.
Watching this screen while vehicle is in
motion can cause a serious accident.
Make selections only if stopped.
Some map data may be incorrect.
Read safety instructions in Nav. Manual.

I Agree

This message had been displaying on my screen for about fifteen minutes. I was on the M4, eastbound, heading back towards London but about to turn off north on to the A404(M) towards Maidenhead. Traffic was light, and I was currently doing about seventy-six miles an hour on the inside lane. I was beginning to get used to the car, but the number of buttons located on either side of the screen was intimidating. I was going to have to pull over somewhere and have a proper look at them. In the meantime, surely it would be safe to touch the "I Agree" icon? I couldn't just stare at this message for the whole journey. It was like those boxes you have to tick when buying something online, agreeing to the terms and conditions which nobody bothers to read. You have no choice but to agree. You're given the illusion of choice, but that's all. Maybe that's how things usually are.

Anyway, when I pressed the button, a map appeared. It showed the motorway I was driving on, and it showed me— or at least my car—as a little red arrow heading determinedly forward in an eastbound direction. How many satellites were trained on me at that moment, I wondered, in order to calculate this ever-changing position? I'd read somewhere that it was always about five: five pairs of eyes keeping me under constant surveillance, from their vantage point high up in the sky. Was this a reassuring thought, or a frightening one? As usual, I couldn't quite decide. There are so many new facts of life that we just don't know what to think about. All I knew for certain was that it had been different, very different, back in Donald Crowhurst's day, when he drifted unobserved for months in the mid-Atlantic and believed he could fool the world, with the help of some bogus calculations pencilled into a logbook, into thinking that he'd spent that time battling with storms in the Southern Ocean. Not much chance of pulling off a deception like that nowadays.

The motorway traffic was getting heavy, and it was a relief when I saw the exit sign for Junction 8/9 (Maidenhead and High Wycombe) up ahead. As I turned off and drove up the slip road, I soon found myself braking too sharply. The brakes on this car seemed ultra-sensitive: you only had to give them the lightest of touches. There were two lanes of traffic backed up towards the roundabout, with about ten cars in each. I came to a halt, taking advantage of this temporary stillness to press one of the other buttons alongside the screen.

The button I chose was labelled "info." When I pressed it, three green columns appeared on the screen. It took me a few moments to work out what they signified. Apparently, each one represented five minutes' driving time and told you what your petrol consumption had been during this period. During my first five minutes I had been averaging thirty-four miles to the gallon; in the second, forty-nine; and in the third, fifty-one. Not bad, but it wasn't going to win me any prizes. I had been hoping for an average of sixty-five or more. Was I doing something wrong?

After negotiating the roundabout and joining the High Wycombe road, I slowed down to forty-five miles an hour, and immediately my fuel efficiency began to rise. I seemed to be averaging between seventy-five to eighty miles to the gallon now, so I drove at this speed for another mile or so, until the driver stuck in the lane behind me started angrily flashing his lights. I speeded up, feeling obscurely guilty even though I had been engaged (looking at it from one point of view) in an environmentally friendly act. It would be difficult to drive at that speed all the way to Aberdeen, I realised, even though I was bound to win Lindsay's five-hundred-pound prize if I did.

Ten miles later, the A404 joined the M40 and I took the first exit at the roundabout, swinging onto the motorway and heading north-west. On either side of me England—or what little you could see of it from the perspective of the motorway— lay stretched out, reposeful and inviting, dressed modestly in muted greens and greys. I could feel my spirits beginning to rise. I was in the mood for adventure after all.

My plan was this: today, I would drive to Birmingham at a careful, unhurried pace, consuming as little petrol as possible. I would arrive mid-afternoon, check into a hotel, and then pay a visit on Mr. and Mrs. Byrne, the parents of my old schoolfriend Chris Byrne and his sister, Alison. They still lived in Edgbaston, in a house backing on to the reservoir, and I had already spoken to Mr. Byrne; over the weekend I'd phoned him to ask if he still possessed (as my father believed he did) a spare set of keys to the flat in Lichfield. To which Mr. Byrne had answered, Yes, we've definitely got them here somewhere. (Although he didn't seem to know where, exactly.) So I intended to pick up the keys, and visit the flat itself the next morning. All of this would mean a very slow start to my journey; but it still gave me plenty of time to reach Shetland, and in any case there was no point in driving to Kendal tonight, because Lucy wouldn't be able to see me. I'd already been in touch with Caroline about that, and she'd told me that Lucy was going round to a friend's house, for a birthday tea and sleepover. So I would have to take her out to dinner on Tuesday evening. That was fine. I could still get to Aberdeen on Wednesday afternoon in plenty of time to make the five-o'clock ferry. In the meantime, visiting Mr. and Mrs. Byrne might be a pleasantly nostalgic way to spend a couple of hours.

I settled down to a steady fifty-five miles per hour. Every other vehicle on the motorway was going faster, even the heaviest lorries. My petrol consumption was back down to seventy miles per gallon, and I began to think of all the petrol that people would save if they drove at this speed all the time. Why was everybody in such a hurry? What difference did it make if you arrived at your destination half an hour later than you could have done? Perhaps it was motorways themselves that were the problem. They allowed you to drive faster, yes, but more than that, they *made you want to drive faster*, they *obliged* you to drive faster, because driving on them was such a boring experience. I had only been on the M40 for about fifteen minutes, but already I was bored. There was absolutely nothing to see, nothing to look at, apart from the little punctuation marks that broke up the motorway itself—roadsigns, chevrons, gantries, bridges—all of which merged into one indecipherable, meaningless sequence after a while anyway. There was countryside on both sides, but it was featureless: the occasional house, the occasional reservoir, the occasional glimpse of a distant town or village, but apart from that, nothing. It occurred to me that the areas bordering our motorways must make up a huge proportion of our countryside, and yet nobody ever visits them or walks through them, or in fact has any experience of them other than the monotonous, regularly unfolding view you get through the car window. These areas are wastelands; unaccounted for.

"Welcome Break, 3 Miles," one of the signs said; so I decided to go off the motorway there and have some lunch. The next services—operated by Moto—were another twenty miles away, and the ones beyond that were more than forty miles. I didn't want to wait that long. Besides, even though I didn't fancy Kentucky Fried Chicken at the moment, the face of Colonel Sanders beaming out at me from the welcome sign was somehow reassuring. So I entered the slip road at Junction 8A, negotiated the network of mini-roundabouts, and found myself looking for a space in a car park that was, at this time of day, full almost to the bursting point. Eventually I slotted my Prius between a Ford Fiesta and a Fiat Punto, and turned off the ignition with a sense of relief.

It was 1:15, and I was hungry. All around me, people were heading for the main food hall—businesspeople like me, mainly, wearing dark suits, shirt and ties, sometimes with the jackets slung over their shoulders (although it was cold today, and I for one was going to keep mine on). I felt a surge of well-being at the thought that I was part of something again: part of a nationwide process, part of a community—the business community—that was doing its bit, day in and day out, to keep Britain ticking over. We all had a part to play. Everybody here was involved in selling something, or buying something, or servicing or checking or costing or quantifying something. I felt connected again: back in the mainstream.

The services themselves were a perfect microcosm of how a well-functioning Western society should operate. All the basic human needs were catered for here: the need to communicate (there was a shop selling mobile phones and accessories) and the need to amuse yourself (there was a gaming area full of slot machines); the need to consume food and drink, and the need to shit or piss it out again; and, of course, the eternal, fundamental need simply to buy a whole load of stuff—magazines, CDs, cuddly toys, chocolate bars, DVDs, wine gums, books, gadgets of every description. What with the Days Inn located just across the car park, with its offer of cheap beds for the night, you could theoretically move into this service station and never leave. You could spend your whole life here, if you wanted to. Even the design was good. I'm old enough to remember what service stations used to be like in the 1970s and early 1980s. Horrible, cheap plastic tables and unspeakable food outlets selling runny eggs and burgers swimming in grease. Here we had big picture windows looking out over a paved area with fountains tinkling away attractively; the tables were clean and modern-looking and some of them even had individual table lamps mounted on elegantly curved supports. Some thought had gone into all this. And the choice of food! There was Burger King, of course, and KFC, but if you were a bit more health-conscious than that, a big sign announced that "I ♥ Healthy Food" and directed you towards counters where all manner of salads and fresh-looking sandwiches were available. Not to mention an outlet called Coffee Primo, which offered latte, cappuccino, mocha, hot chocolate, espresso, americano, vanilla cream frappe, caramel cream frappe, Twinings teas, a couple of dozen other caffeine-laden options and, of course, the ubiquitous paninis.

Despite this plethora of choice, unimaginable (when you think about it) a generation ago, before Thatcher and Blair set about transforming our society, I decided to have a hamburger. Sometimes a burger is exactly what you need. No extras, no frills. What's more, at this place you didn't even have to talk to anyone to get your hamburger. You did it all on your debit card, selecting your order on a machine, putting your card into the terminal, and then taking the receipt to a collection point. Worked very well, too. My burger was ready within about thirty seconds. When I saw it, though, I felt a bit guilty for not ordering something a bit more healthy, so I went and stood in the queue at the sandwich counter and bought myself a bottle of pomegranate-and-lychee-flavoured spring water, which cost £2.75. Then I took my meal over to one of the tables next to the big picture windows.

I had brought a fair amount of reading matter with me. First of all there were the manuals for the Prius—one for the car itself and one devoted entirely to the onboard SatNav. There were also the instructions for the Bluetooth headset I had been provided with, which connected up to the car some-how and could be controlled from the steering wheel. Trevor and Lindsay had been especially keen that I should get this up and running as soon as possible, because they wanted to be able to keep in regular contact. I wondered, in fact, if it was too early to phone Lindsay right now. Perhaps it was. There was hardly an urgent need for her to know that I had reached Oxford Services after an hour and a quarter's driving. And then I had to study the manual for my video camera, which looked pretty complicated too. I would keep that for later, probably. Best to concentrate on the SatNav for the time being. I sat and read the manual for about ten minutes, until I felt reasonably sure I had grasped all of the essentials. I felt confident now that I knew enough to use it on the next stage of the journey, as far as Birmingham.

When I got back into the car, I turned on the ignition and pressed the "I Agree" icon as soon as it flashed up on the map screen. Then I pressed the "destination" button and rather laboriously entered the address of Mr. and Mrs. Byrne on the touchscreen display. Within a couple of seconds the computer had located their house and was offering me a choice of three different routes from my current position. I chose what seemed to be the quickest one, straight up the M40 and then north-bound into Birmingham along the Bristol Road. And then, as soon as I had made this selection, I heard a female voice say:

—*Please proceed to the highlighted route, and the route guidance will start.*

It wasn't so much what she said, it was the way that she said it.

Most people, I would say, are attracted to other people on the basis of their looks. And of course I'm as susceptible to that as anybody else. But the first thing I find *really* attractive in a woman, nine times out of ten, is her voice. That was what I noticed about Lindsay Ashworth the first time we met—her lovely Scottish accent. And, going back further than that, it was the first thing I'd noticed about Caroline as well—her flat Lancastrian vowels, which were completely unlike anything I was expecting to hear from someone who in every other respect seemed so elegant and posh and metropolitan. Now, this may sound ridiculous, but even those two women, Lindsay and Caroline, did not have voices as appealing as the one that came out of this machine. This was, quite simply, a beautiful voice. Breathtakingly beautiful. Probably the most beautiful I had ever heard. Don't ask me to describe it. You'll have realised by now that I'm not great at this sort of thing. It was an English voice—not classless, exactly, more what used to be called Received Pronunciation or "BBC English." There was something slightly haughty about it, I suppose. It had an undertone that might even be described as a little bit bossy. But at the same time, it was calm, measured and infinitely reassuring. It was impossible to imagine this voice sounding angry, or to imagine hearing it without feeling soothed and comforted. It was a voice that told you everything was right in the world—your world, at any rate. It was a voice without a single note of ambiguity or self-doubt: a voice you could trust. Perhaps that was what I liked about it so much. It was a voice you could trust.

I put the car in drive and pulled out of the car park. As I left the service station I passed a notice which read: *"Thank you for visiting Oxford Services. Your visit and registration number have been captured on CCTV."* More evidence, if any was needed, that I was not as alone as I'd thought.

"What do you think of that, then?" I found myself saying to the voice on the map. "Bit sinister, isn't it?"

And she answered:

—*Exit coming up. Then, two hundred yards later, straight on at the roundabout.*

For the time being, I forgot all about my desire to phone Lindsay.

I continued to drive slowly, trying to save petrol, so it was another hour and a half before I reached Junction 1 of the M42.

—*In half a mile, exit left, towards Birmingham South.*

It was the first time she had spoken to me in about ten

minutes. I had worked out, by now, that I could summon up her voice whenever I wanted by pressing the "map" button on my steering wheel. If you did that, she would usually tell you to carry on doing whatever you were doing at that moment. So every few minutes I would press the button, and she would tell me to *"Proceed on the current motorway."* I wasn't listening to the radio. I had tried a bit of Radio 2 and a bit of Radio 4 but I didn't want to listen to other people chattering away. I wanted to be left alone with my thoughts, and with Emma's voice whenever I felt like hearing it.

Oh—did I not tell you that she was called Emma? I'd spent most of the last hour trying to decide what I was going to call her. Finally I chose Emma because it had always been one of my favourite names. Partly it was a memory of having to read Jane Austen's novel for English O Level at school; I hated the book—one of Caroline's favourites, by the way—and only got a "D" in the exam, but for some reason the heroine's name had stuck in my mind as a sort of emblem of classiness and sophistication. Also, I used to have a bit of a crush on Emma Thompson, the actress—going back to the late 1980s, when she looked really boyish and did that film where she had an amazing sex scene with Jeff Goldblum. So, what with one thing and another, Emma seemed an appropriate choice.

—Exit left. Then, heading slightly right at the roundabout, take third exit.

Our relationship was going to be put to its first test now, because I had decided not to follow her instructions for the next few minutes. She wanted me to head down the A38 to the Lydiate Ash roundabout, then take a right turn towards Rubery. But I had other plans. I wanted to drive straight over the crest of the Lickey Hills and to rejoin the A38 via the B4120 at the bottom of the hill. It was a more scenic drive, and it would take me through some of the landscape of my early childhood. But how would Emma respond? Would she understand the nostalgic impulse that lay behind it?

Feeling a little nervous at my own audacity, I ignored her insistent repetition of *"Next left"* as I circled the roundabout and took the *fourth* exit rather than the third. I imagined what Caroline might have said if I'd ignored *her* directions on one of our family holidays: "No, not this one!" There would have been a sigh of exasperation, and then her voice would tense, slipping into that awful register of angry resignation at my stubbornness and stupidity. "Fine. If you think you know better than I do, just carry on. I won't bother looking at this anymore." At this point she would have thrown the road atlas into the back of the car, narrowly missing Lucy, who would be sitting up on her booster seat and listening to the argument with wide-eyed bewilderment, her little brain probably asking itself whether this was how grown-ups always spoke to each other. Yes, that's just how it would have been. I could remember countless scenarios like that.

But with Emma, it was different. She said nothing at all, at first. The only sign that she had taken any notice of my decision was a message on the screen that said *"Calculating Route."* Then, after a few seconds, her voice returned. There was no change in her tone at all. Still calm, still measured. Totally unflustered by my little act of rebellion. *"Proceed for about two miles on the current road,"* she said. And that was it. No disputes, no sarcasm, no questions asked. She accepted my authority, and responded accordingly. God—how easy life would have been if Caroline could have behaved more like that! I was already beginning to think that in Emma I had found something like the perfect partner. I pressed the "map" button, just so I could hear her say it again.

—Proceed for about two miles on the current road.

Beautiful. I loved the little pause she put in after *"miles."* She spoke it as if it were a line of poetry.

I was now driving up the Old Birmingham Road. On my left was the entrance to the primary school where Chris and I had met, becoming friends on our very first day, at the age of five. We had been inseparable after that—best friends for the next five years. And then, at the age of ten, we had been the only children from our year to sit the entrance exam for King William's School in the centre of Birmingham. Chris passed the exam. I didn't, and ended up going to Waseley Hills Comprehensive with all my other primary-school friends.

"And that was probably it, wasn't it?" I said to Emma. "That was the turning point. So many things followed from that."

—Proceed for one mile on the current road.

Chris and I continued to see each other, of course. But the real reason for that, I suspect, was that our fathers had by now become such good friends, after meeting at various school-related social occasions. Chris's dad was a lecturer at Birmingham university and my father, who liked to think of himself as an intellectual as well as a poet, was not going to let that friendship die, even after Chris started going to a much posher school and his family had moved out of Rubery and into the leafier, more middle-class enclave of Edgbaston. So Chris and I kept our own friendship going, mainly out of a genuine liking for each other but also out of our youthful intuition that it was what both of our families wanted and needed from us. And yet I'd always been conscious of the differences between us, from that point on. As I drove past the school and on towards the summit of the hill, a memory came back to me. Chris and I were eleven years old; we had been at our new schools for a few weeks. He had come round to our house and we were talking in the back garden and he was asking me about Waseley and he said, "What are the masters like?" And at first I didn't know what he was talking about. It took me a few seconds to work it out. "Is that what you call them, then, the teachers?" I said. "You call them masters?" A sudden image came to my mind and I could see a white-haired authority figure pacing up and down between the old wooden desks, wearing a gown and lecturing his attentive pupils on Latin declensions: a figure straight out of *Goodbye, Mr. Chips* or a Billy Bunter novel. And I felt a ripple of shame—inferiority—pass through me as I realised what different worlds Chris and I now inhabited.

—*At the next roundabout, take a left turn. First exit.*

I did what Emma told me at this point. But then I decided on another little detour to test her patience and, just past the Old Hare and Hounds pub, took a spontaneous left turn into Leach Green Lane. She went quiet for a few seconds while the computer tried to get its head around what I was trying to do, then she said:

—*In two hundred yards, right turn.*

"I see where you're coming from," I told her, "but we're going to deviate from the route for the time being. Hope that's OK. The thing is, we're going on a sentimental journey. And I don't believe you have a setting for that."

—*Right turn coming up*, she insisted.

I ignored her and turned left. In a few hundred yards I saw what I had been looking for: a grey, pebbledashed house, disorientatingly similar to all its neighbours, with a meagre expanse of asphalt in front of it where an ancient, green Rover 2000 had been parked. I pulled up opposite the house, on the other side of the road.

—*In two hundred yards, make a U-turn*, Emma suggested.

Without turning the engine off, I got out of the car and stood leaning for a while, against the passenger door, looking across at the house. This was where I had lived for thirteen years, starting in 1967. Me, Mum and Dad. It hadn't changed, not in the slightest. I stood looking at it for another two or three minutes, shivering slightly in the March breeze, then got back into the car and drove on.

"Well, what was I supposed to think?" I said, easing the car back on to the main A38 towards the city centre. "What was I supposed to feel? I haven't seen that house for more than twenty years. That was where I grew up. That was where my childhood took place, and to be honest I come back and look at it now and I don't feel that much. My childhood was nothing much to shout about. Like everything else about me, I suppose. Unexceptional. That's what I should have on my gravestone. 'Here lies Maxwell Sim. He was a pretty ordinary bloke, really.' What an epitaph. No wonder Caroline got bored with me after a while. No wonder Lucy doesn't want much to do with me. What did we do, the three of us, in that house for thirteen years that wasn't done by millions of other families in identical houses up and down the country? What's been the point of it all? That's all I want to know. Not too much to ask, is it? What's the point? *What is the fucking point?*"

—*In half a mile*, said Emma, *bearing slightly left at the round-about, take first exit.*

She had an answer for everything, that woman.

13

—Proceed for about two miles on the current road.

I was now driving past the old Longbridge factory. Or rather, I was driving now past the gaping hole in the landscape where the old Longbridge factory used to be. It was a weird experience: when you revisit the landscapes of your past, you expect to see maybe a few cosmetic changes, the odd new building here and there, the occasional lick of paint, but this was something else: an entire complex of factory buildings which used to dominate the whole neighbourhood, stretching over many square miles, throbbing with the noise of working machinery, alive with the figures of thousands of working men and women entering and leaving the buildings—all gone. Flattened, obliterated. Meanwhile, a big billboard erected in the midst of these swathes of urban emptiness informed us that, before too long, a phoenix would be rising from the ashes: a "major new development" of "exclusive residential units" and "retail outlets," a utopian community where the only things people would ever have to concern themselves with were eating, sleeping and shopping; there was no need to work anymore, apparently, none of that tiresome stuff about clocking in at factory gates in order to do anything as vulgar as *making* things. Had we all lost our wits in the last few years? Had we forgotten that prosperity has to be based on something, something solid and tangible? Even to someone like me, who had done nothing more than skim the papers and the news websites over the last couple of weeks, it was pretty obvious we were getting it badly wrong, that knocking down factories to put up shops wasn't turning out to be such a great idea, that it wasn't sensible to build an entire society on foundations of air.

—Proceed for about three quarters of a mile on the current road.

I noticed that it was no longer necessary to drive through Northfield: they had found the money to build a new by-pass, so new in fact that even Emma didn't seem to know about it. She became thoroughly confused as I weaved through its traffic lights and roundabouts, although once again I had to admire the way that even as she gave contradictory pieces of advice and recalculated furiously, her tone remained completely unflappable. What a woman. Selly Oak provided her with no such problems, and she guided me expertly down Harborne Lane and Norfolk Road to the Hagley Road. I arrived there not long after three o'clock and checked into the Quality Hotel Premier Inn, where the single rooms cost little more than forty pounds a night, well within Alan Guest's budget. The room wasn't very big, and it didn't have a very nice view, but it was comfortable. I was on the first floor, at the back. There was a kettle and a couple of sachets of Nescafé so I made myself a coffee and lay on the bed for thirty minutes or so, recovering from my drive. I felt a bit lonely and thought about phoning Lindsay, but decided to leave it until the evening.

Mr. and Mrs. Byrne weren't expecting me for another hour and a half. There was just enough time to drive to King's Norton and visit the churchyard there, so that's what I did. My mum's grave was in good shape. I bought some flowers from the local Tesco Express and leaned them up against the headstone. I didn't have a vase or anything like that. *Barbara Sim, 1939–1985* was all it said. Dad had wanted to keep the wording simple, or so he told me at the time. Forty-six years old. I was already older than that. I had outlived my own mother. And yet it seemed to me that it would take many more years before I ever felt as grown-up as my mother had always seemed to me. She had been twenty-two when I was born. Her final twenty-four years of life had been spent bringing me up, seeing me through into adulthood, and in that time she had devoted herself to me, selflessly. She had given me unconditional love. She may not have been that clever, she may not have had a fantastic education, she may not have understood my father's poetry (neither did I, for that matter), but emotionally she had been wise beyond her years. Perhaps circumstances had forced her to be like that, or perhaps it was just that her generation, living always in the shadow of the war, somehow managed to grow up faster than mine did. Whatever the reason, I now felt humbled (yes, that really is the word—no other will do) to think what a great mother she had been. She made my own attempts at parenthood look pathetic.

1939–1985. It wasn't enough. We should have written something else on her headstone, something more.

What, though?

"She was a lovely woman, your mum. Donald and I always thought so. Hardly a day goes by when we don't talk about her."

Mrs. Byrne finished pouring milk into my tea and added a couple of spoonfuls of sugar, as requested. I noticed that her hands were shaking slightly. The onset of Parkinson's, maybe? I picked up the tray of tea things and followed her back into the conservatory.

"This is very intriguing," said Mr. Byrne. He was examining the IP 009, holding it up to the failing afternoon light and scrutinising it from every angle. "What's your target? How many are you hoping to sell?"

"She was always a delight to talk to. Made any social occasion go with a swing," said Mrs. Byrne. She was still talking about my mother. I had noticed that it was difficult to keep a conversation going with Mr. and Mrs. Byrne, because they always talked about two completely different topics simultaneously.

"Well, that's not really the idea," I said to Mr. Byrne. "It's not about how many I manage to sell. It doesn't matter if I don't sell any at all this week."

This was true, up to a point. Guest Toothbrushes already had relationships with most of the major pharmaceutical retailers—including the supermarkets—and orders were usually taken in bulk, online or over the telephone. However, Alan had still told me that, were I to chance upon any independent outlets, I should take the opportunity to drop in and show them some of the merchandise. This was one aspect of my journey that I wasn't looking forward to. It was a long time since I had done any cold-calling.

"It's a beautiful piece of design, all right," he said. "We should really get a couple of these ourselves."

"Oh, well, in that case," I said, reaching inside my jacket pocket to produce another one, "take these as a gift. Please. With the compliments of Guest Toothbrushes."

"Are you sure?"

"Absolutely."

"Well, that's splendid. Isn't that splendid, Sue?"

Mrs. Byrne nodded abstractedly, but her mind was on other things. First of all she handed out the cups of tea and the home-made scones, and then she said, "So you have to drive all the way to Aberdeen?"

"That's right."

"Well, you should really call in on Alison. She'd love to see you."

"Oh, be quiet, Sue," Mr. Byrne said, tutting. "He doesn't have time to call on Alison. Tell me, Max, is Harold renting out the flat in Lichfield now? Because we haven't been up to check on it for a number of years, and the last time we spoke to him, that's what he said he was intending to do."

"Well, I really don't see why not," said Mrs. Byrne. "Even if he just dropped in for a cup of tea, that would be something, and surely he'll be going right through Edinburgh if he has to get to Aberdeen."

"I don't believe Dad's rented it out," I said to Mr. Byrne; and then, turning to his wife, "I think there's a ring road, so I won't actually be going through the centre."

"He's missing out on a fair bit of rental income, then," said Mr. Byrne.

"Yes, but you can easily get to Alison's from the ring road," said Mrs. Byrne.

"I'll go and get the keys, anyway."

"I'll fetch the street map and show you exactly where she is."

While they were away, I sipped my tea and munched on my scone and looked out over their back garden. It was a lovely big garden, stretching down to the edge of the reservoir in a series of falling terraces. Beyond their fence I could see the path that led around the reservoir. You could walk this path in about thirty minutes, I seemed to remember. I'd done it with Alison once. I would have been about fifteen. It was not long before our families went to the Lake District together. I'd probably come round to see Chris but somehow I'd managed to end up walking round the reservoir with Alison, who was a couple of years older than me, and with whom I'd always had an odd, not-quite-flirtatious friendship. (I somehow felt I was meant to find her more attractive than I actually did, if that makes sense.) Should I go and see her in Edinburgh? Drop in for a cup of tea? I hadn't seen her since Chris's wedding, more than fifteen years ago. It couldn't do any harm, I suppose . . .

Mr. and Mrs. Byrne returned at the same time, their minds still running on parallel tracks.

"When do you have to get to Shetland, exactly?" Mrs. Byrne asked.

"Here they are," said Mr. Byrne, handing me a set of keys. "By the way, is that your Prius outside?"

"I suppose it doesn't matter much, as long as I'm there by the end of the week," I said to Mrs. Byrne. "Yes, it is," I said to her husband. "Only for this trip, though."

"Well, then, why don't you have dinner with Alison and Philip tomorrow night?"

"How are you finding it? Is it a good drive?"

I assumed that Philip was Alison's husband. The name sounded vaguely familiar.

"That won't work, I'm afraid. I'm seeing Lucy—my daughter—tomorrow night. In Kendal. Yes, I'm loving it. Do you know I averaged sixty-five miles to the gallon coming up here? And the SatNav is amazing."

"Kendal? What's your daughter doing in Kendal?"

"Sixty-five isn't bad. Mind you, there are some small diesel cars these days which can manage almost that. How big's the engine?"

"Well . . . Caroline left me, you see. About six months ago. She and Lucy are living in Kendal now. I don't know how big the engine is—sorry. It probably says in the manual."

"Oh, Max, I had no idea. You must be devastated. Why didn't Chris tell us about it, I wonder?"

"I heard the acceleration is rather poor. Not much power if you want to overtake in a hurry."

"Yes, it's been a . . . disappointment. The biggest disappointment of my life, in fact."

Mr. Byrne stared at me in surprise, until his wife tapped him reprovingly on the knee.

"He's talking about the break-up of his marriage, not the acceleration on his car. Can't you listen?" She turned to me and said: "A lot of relationships go through a blip, Max. I'm sure it's only temporary."

"I don't think so," I said. "They've moved to the other end of the country. It feels pretty permanent to me."

"Did you try counselling, and so on?" asked Mrs. Byrne.

"Were you shagging around or anything?" asked Mr. Byrne.

"Donald!" said his wife, exasperated.

"Yes," I answered. "I mean yes, we did try counselling. And no, I wasn't shagging around."

"Max," said Mrs. Byrne. "Why don't you stay to dinner? I've made a chicken pie, and there's plenty for the three of us."

"I wasn't being rude," said Mr. Byrne. "It's just that strange things happen to men when they hit their mid-forties. For some reason they get an uncontrollable urge to have sex with twenty-year-old girls."

"That would be lovely," I said. "Staying for dinner, that is, not having sex with twenty-year-old girls. Which would also be lovely, of course, but . . . But anyway, I'm afraid I can't. Dinner, I mean. I've got . . . I've got plans for tonight."

"Oh dear. Well, I'll make another pot of tea, anyway."

She disappeared into the kitchen, leaving me and Mr. Byrne alone for a few minutes. For a horrible moment I thought he was going to attempt a heart-to-heart with me about the break-up of my marriage, but I needn't have worried. We talked about the Toyota Prius instead. He told me about an article he'd read which claimed the manufacturing process was so long and complicated that it actually cancelled out the environmental benefits of the hybrid engine. Also, apparently, there was a big question mark over whether it was possible to recycle the battery. He seemed to know an awful lot about it. But then Mr. Byrne, like his son, had always struck me as being well informed. He was another of those men blessed (unlike me) with a hungry, enquiring mind.

Mrs. Byrne was away for about twenty minutes. I wasn't sure why it should be taking her so long to make a pot of tea. When she finally reappeared, however, all was made clear.

"Sorry about that," she said. "I've been on the phone to Alison. I thought I'd call her on the off chance. She says she's at home all week, and she'd love to see you on Wednesday."

"Oh," I said, rather taken aback. "Well, that's great. Thank you."

"Philip's in Malaysia at the moment, so she's booking a restaurant in town for that evening, and the two of you can go out and have a cosy dinner. The boys are both at boarding school now, of course."

"I'm very grateful, but—"

"Ah!" Mr. Byrne jumped to his feet. "That gives me an idea."

After he left the room, I struggled to get my head around this new development. It would mean adding an extra day to my journey, catching the ferry from Aberdeen on Thursday evening and arriving in Shetland on Friday morning. Was this a problem? Not necessarily. The other three salesmen would probably have reached their destinations and gone home by then, but why should that bother me? It wasn't a race. Or, if it was, I was never going to be the first one home. I was hardly the Robin Knox-Johnston or Bernard Moitessier in this scenario, after all. And besides, I was already well on course to win the other prize—the one for petrol consumption.

"Well, that would be . . . that would be terrific, actually. Yes, why not? I'd love to see Alison again."

"And I'm sure she'd love to see you. Splendid. That's all arranged, then."

Beaming at me happily, she passed me another scone. I saw my own reflection in the glass panels of the conservatory, leaning across to take it from the offered plate. Outside it was now almost dark. A bleak evening lay ahead of me, alone in my room in the Quality Hotel Premier Inn, yet I couldn't bring myself to accept the Byrnes' offer of dinner at their house. There was still a limit on how much human company I could tolerate in one day. I ate the scone in silence while Mrs. Byrne talked to me soothingly, filling me in on news about friends of hers whom I'd either never met or couldn't remember. Then, after a few minutes, Mr. Byrne returned, huffing and puffing and carrying a big cardboard box.

"There!" he said, depositing it on the floor of the conservatory with an air of triumph.

"Oh, Donald!" said his wife. "*Now* what are you doing?"

"This is from the attic," he explained.

"I know where it's from. What's it doing down here?"

"You said you were sick of the sight of it."

"So I am. That's why I took it up to the attic. What have you brought it down again for?"

"It doesn't belong in our attic. We've got enough clutter up there. It's Alison's."

"I know it's Alison's. I keep asking her to take it away with her, and she keeps forgetting."

"She doesn't forget. She deliberately doesn't remember."

"Well, all right. No need to quibble. What of it?"

"Max can take it up to her."

"Max?"

"He's going to visit her, isn't he? Well, he can take this with him."

"Oh, don't be silly."

I looked at the box, which was so large that Mr. Byrne had had difficulty carrying it by himself, and was so full of papers that it was almost overflowing. Still, it would fit in my boot easily enough, and I could see no reason why I shouldn't take it.

"No, that won't be a problem," I said. "What's in here?"

"All of Alison's coursework. Nearly thirty years old, I should think."

"We should throw it out," said Mrs. Byrne, "that's what we should do. Burn it."

"We can't do that," her husband said. "She sweated blood over this."

"A lot of good it did her. She never even qualified."

"Sue, if you remember, she *did* qualify. She never *practised*. Not the same thing at all. And she still might, now that the children are almost grown up."

"Practised what?" I asked. It was so long ago now, I couldn't even remember what Alison had been studying.

"Psychology," said Mr. Byrne. "She always wanted to be a therapist."

This rang a distant bell. But it only served to remind me that, when all was said and done, I barely knew Alison, and had precious little shared history with her. Did I really want to spend the whole of Wednesday evening having dinner with a virtual stranger? Well, it was too late to backtrack now. Mr. and Mrs. Byrne were both completely sold on the idea—one of them, apparently, for weird sentimental reasons, and the other because he was itching to get shot of this cardboard box.

"There you are—takes up no space at all," I said a few minutes later, lifting it carefully into the boot of the Prius. My suitcase and laptop were back at the hotel, so the only other items in the boot were two small boxes of toothbrush samples. Mrs. Byrne had come out to see me off. The night was chilly and our breath steamed in the air as we stood on the front drive. I said goodbye hastily—almost rudely, perhaps—partly because I didn't want her to catch cold, but mainly because I'm not one for protracted farewells. Just as I climbed into the car and was about to start it, though, Mr. Byrne came running out of the house.

"Don't forget these!" he said, holding up the keys to my father's flat.

Somehow I had managed to leave them inside. I wound down the window and took them from him. "Thanks," I said. "That was a close one."

"Are you *sure* those are the right keys?" Mrs. Byrne asked.

"Of course they are," said Mr. Byrne.

"They don't look like the keys to Harold's flat to me."

Her husband ignored her. "Look after them," he told me. "It's the only set."

"No, it isn't," said his wife.

He turned back to her and sighed. "Pardon?"

"I said it's not the only set. Miss Erith has one."

"Miss Erith? What are you talking about? Who's Miss Erith?"

"The old lady who lives in the flat opposite. She has a set of keys. She still collects the post, doesn't she? You know—all those postcards."

"Postcards? You're talking nonsense."

"I am *not* talking nonsense. He still gets dozens of postcards every year, all from the same man." She leaned down through the window and said to me, "*I* know what I'm talking about, even if he doesn't. Ignore him. Have a lovely evening with your daughter tomorrow. And give our love to Alison, won't you?"

"Not just our love—those papers as well!" said Mr. Byrne. "Don't forget those papers! Don't let her fob you off."

"I won't."

"And thanks for the toothbrushes!"

"Not at all. Thanks for the tea."

I waved goodbye and closed the window before they had the chance to say anything else. Otherwise we could have been there all night. Talking to them was beginning to wear me out, frankly—especially Mrs. Byrne, who I was beginning to think might be getting a little eccentric. Her remark about postcards seemed very peculiar, for one thing. It seemed highly unlikely that anybody would still be sending postcards to my father in Lichfield, after he had been away for more than twenty years.

So—now where?

I drove into the centre of town first of all. I had Emma to keep me company, of course, but I hadn't given her a new destination to find so she thought we were still going to Mr. and Mrs. Byrne's house and her directions were rather confused. I didn't mind. I was happy just listening to her voice.

Birmingham had changed a lot since I'd last been there. So many new buildings had gone up—shopping malls, most of them—that I couldn't get my bearings half of the time. Eventually I found a multi-storey car park and then walked up to the new development of shops and cafés in the old canal basin. There were quite a few restaurants whose names I didn't recognise, but in the end I went to Pizza Express because it felt familiar and comforting. You always know where you are with Pizza Express.

The restaurant was busy. Everyone looked about twenty years younger than me and as usual I felt self-conscious sitting there eating by myself. I'd brought nothing to read, so I took out my mobile phone and while waiting for my pizza I sent a text message to Trevor. He called me back a few seconds later, using the hands-free set we had all been given to use in our cars—though I hadn't got around to setting mine up yet. The acoustics in the restaurant were pretty bad so it was hard to hear what he was saying, but I gathered he was only about half an hour away from Penzance already, and he seemed very amused that I'd only got as far as Birmingham. "Ah well," he said, before we lost reception altogether, "as long as you're enjoying yourself."

I'm not sure that I was enjoying myself, exactly. When I left the restaurant it was about eight-thirty, and I found a quiet corner beside one of the canals in order to make my phone call to Lindsay—the treat I had been promising myself for the last few hours. When she didn't answer, I left a message, but maybe she didn't get it because for some reason I never heard from her that evening.

Of course I could have driven up to Lichfield there and then, stayed the night in my father's flat and saved Guest Toothbrushes the price of a night's hotel accommodation. But I had a feeling that visiting my father's flat wasn't going to be the most cheering of experiences. I thought it was probably best to see it in the daylight. Meanwhile there was nothing much else to do but drive back to the Quality Hotel Premier Inn and watch TV or maybe (on my laptop) the DVD of *Deep Water* which Clive had given me.

Driving there, I must say, Emma and I got on famously. Especially when, as we approached the roundabout at Holloway Circus, I thought it would be funny if I tried to confuse her by driving round and round in a circle. What a laugh! *"Next left,"* she kept saying. *"Next left. Next left."* Over and over, at shorter and shorter intervals, as I sped up and whizzed round the roundabout one more time. I still couldn't get a rise out of her, though. However fast I went, however many circuits I completed, she never lost her cool. I must have gone round about six or seven times before I noticed a police car approaching from the direction of New Street Station, up Smallbrook Queensway. I made a hasty exit up towards Five Ways and from there I drove back to the hotel at a very sensible twenty-eight miles per hour.

Once I'd parked the car I checked in the boot, because while I'd been using Holloway Circus as a carousel I'd heard some strange noises coming from there. Sure enough, my antics on the roundabout had caused Alison's cardboard box to slide about from end to end, and most of the papers that had been sitting precariously on top were scattered all over the place. The wind was now quite strong, and as soon as I opened the boot some of these papers blew out and started flying around the car park. Swearing loudly, I ran backwards and forwards in every direction trying to catch them all, but while I was doing this another gust blew up and even more of them started to scatter. I slammed the boot shut and finally succeeded, with a great deal of effort and a certain amount of help from a rather bemused passer-by, in gathering them all together again. I scrunched them up in a bundle clutched tightly against my chest and got into the back of the car to try to straighten them out and put them in some sort of order. I was out of breath and strangely disturbed by the whole episode. As far as I knew these were just ancient college essays of Alison's, of no particular value, but at the same time I felt I had been entrusted with an important task in returning them to her and didn't want to mess it up.

However, this thought went clean out of my head when I glanced at the top sheet of paper as I laid it out on the back seat of the car. What do you think was the first word to catch my eye?

It was "Max."

Not just once, either. The word "Max" occurred four or five times on this page alone.

I seemed to be looking at the middle of an essay of some sort. I started rooting around in the random pile of papers on my lap to try to find other pages from the same essay. Most of them were still together, and still in sequence, but some appeared to be missing. I found what was obviously the last page of the essay, 18. Then I found the first page, which was headed "PRIVACY VIOLATION—Alison Byrne, 22nd February 1980." *Privacy Violation?* What was all that about? There was also a note paper-clipped to this first page. It was in different—more masculine—handwriting, and after I'd read a few lines I realised it must have been written by her tutor.

Dear Alison,

I think it is clear from the seminar on Thursday and our chat afterwards that you have a particular interest in the issue of privacy violation and the way that it impacts on relationships with the people involved. As everyone this term is required to write a "self-reflective" essay drawing on some aspect of their own experience, I wondered whether this might be something you'd like to write about? Perhaps

there is a particular incident from your own past that
might be germane to this topic.

   Please rest assured that the self-reflective essays are
NOT for marking and will not be seen by the tutors unless
you specifically request it. The idea is that we trust you to
complete them in your own time, and the value of the essays
is considered to lie in the exercise of writing them and the
opportunity for heightened self-awareness that they might
bring.

   Anyway, it is up to you what you write about, I merely
throw this out as a suggestion.

                                         Best regards,
                                          Nicholas.

After reading this, I looked at the beginning of the essay.
The first paragraph just seemed to give a few words of introduction but the second began with, "It was the long hot summer of 1976" and then, a sentence later: "Towards the end of
August that year we went on a camping holiday to the Lake
District for one week with our friends the Sim family."

The Lake District? She'd written an essay about our holiday in Coniston? Why? What had happened that week that
had anything to do with "privacy violation"?

My hands were shaking as I shuffled through the rest of
the papers. It felt like I was about to have a panic attack or
something. I had to find the missing pages and read the essay
through in its entirety, however painful it turned out to be. As
with Caroline's short story, I felt myself being driven on by an
appalling, self-destructive curiosity. Reading that story had
been difficult enough. Was this going to be even worse?

The missing pages were, it transpired, still mixed up with

Alison's other papers in the boot of the car. It took me about fifteen minutes to put the whole thing together. Then I said goodnight to Emma ("Wish me luck," I murmured), locked up the car and took the sheaf of papers with me up to my hotel room on the first floor. I made myself another cup of Nescafé, turned on the TV for company, muted the volume, then lay down on the bed and started to read.

FIRE

THE FOLDED PHOTOGRAPH

The incident I'm going to describe took place more than three years ago. However, it is still very fresh in my mind. It had a big effect on me because it put some distance between myself and someone I was thinking of getting close to.

It was the long, hot summer of 1976. "Long, hot summer" in this case is not just a cliché because throughout the UK there was bright sunshine and very little rain for almost the whole of that summer—so much so that the government appointed a special "Minister for Drought." Towards the end of August that year we went on a camping holiday to the Lake District for one week with our friends the Sim family.

The Sims had once been our neighbours in the Rubery area of Birmingham. They had one son, whose name was Max, and he had been best friends with my younger brother Chris at primary school. However, at the age of eleven the two boys were sent to different secondary schools. Chris was accepted for a place at King William's School in Birmingham (I was already going to the equivalent girls' school). This was a selective school and you had to pass an exam to get in. Max had failed the exam and so he went to the local comprehensive school. A couple of years after this happened, we moved away from Rubery into a house with a big garden backing on to Edgbaston Reservoir. Despite this, Chris and Max stayed quite good friends and our parents continued to see a lot of each other.

At the time of this incident, Chris and Max were both sixteen years old, while I was nearly eighteen. In many ways I felt too old to be going on holiday with my family, and in fact this was the last time I did so. I had already been away to France earlier in the summer with one of my girlfriends, but this camping holiday came right at the end of August and since the weather was still nice and I did not really fancy being left on my own for a whole week at home I decided to go along.

Our campsite was by the side of Coniston Water. There were caravans on the site as well as tents, and there was a modern toilet block with shower etc. My family had a big family tent with two separate "bedrooms" so we were quite comfortable really, even though I am not a great fan of living under canvas. The Sims pitched their tent (which was quite a lot smaller) a few yards from ours, but facing it, so that the space between the two tents became a sort of common area. This was the place where, every evening, we would light a fire and sit around it eating supper and talking amongst ourselves. Afterwards my brother Chris would sometimes get out his guitar but I'm pleased to say there was no singing or anything like that. He just used to strum these melancholy minor chords and stare into the distance. Both he and Max were at the age when boys get terrible crushes on girls and Chris was pining for one of the girls at my school. I had already told him he didn't stand the slightest chance but he took no notice.

As for Max, he was beginning to look slightly lovelorn as well—but, unless I'm very much mistaken, his crush was on me.

Even though I had known Max for many years, I had only

recently started to notice how grown-up he had become, and that in the process he was turning into rather a good-looking boy. The fact that he was more than two years younger than me ought to have put him strictly "off limits" but I did find it flattering that he seemed to be smitten with me, and if I am to be perfectly honest with myself, one of my reasons for coming on this holiday in the first place was the fact that Max was going to be there. But the poor boy was very unsure of himself. I adopted a sort of "treat 'em mean, keep 'em keen" approach, and pretty much ignored him for most of the week. I was hoping that this would force him to bring his intentions out into the open, but I'm afraid he interpreted my behaviour very literally and probably just thought I didn't like him very much.

One thing I quickly noticed was that the family dynamic among the Sims was quite different from the dynamic in our family. Max and his mother were extremely close. In fact she sort of babied him and was always feeding him up—giving him extra helpings of food at meal times, buying him treats such as chocolate bars and packets of Fruit Gums from the local shop, and so on. (Despite this he was extremely skinny. He was at that age when boys can stuff their faces with food all day and it doesn't seem to put an ounce of fat on them.) On the other hand Max did not appear to be close to his father at all. In fact Mr. Sim did not appear to be close to either his son or his wife. He was a quiet man, very introspective and rather difficult to talk to. He worked as a librarian at one of the local technical colleges in Birmingham, but Max once told me that his father had always really wanted to be a poet. One of the things I noticed about him that week was that he always carried a notebook with him and could often be seen writing in it. One evening when we were all sitting around the fire my father even persuaded him to read us one of his poems from the notebook.

I went stiff with embarrassment when I heard this and was expecting him to read some terrible bit of doggerel in rhyming couplets about the birds and the flowers and the sunshine and all that sort of nonsense. But instead, the poem that he read out was rather good. I don't really know very much about poetry, and this one was quite hard to understand at times, but at least it wasn't bland or banal or anything like that. I couldn't say what it was about exactly, but it conveyed this atmosphere—this atmosphere of loss and regret and something to do with the past that was somehow sinister and frightening. I remember that we all sat in slightly surprised silence when it was finished. We were all quite impressed, I think—apart from Mrs. Sim, who just looked mortified. I don't mean to be rude when I say this, but it seemed pretty obvious to me that she didn't have the faintest idea what her husband was going on about when he wrote his poetry. I don't think she had had much of an education and I don't even think she was especially bright. She worked part-time as a doctor's receptionist in Moseley, and although she was a very kind person and very down-to-earth— as well as being *extremely* pretty—it did make you wonder why on earth she and her husband had got married or what they had in common. Other people's relationships are a mystery, though, and perhaps they should stay that way.

As well as his notebook, the other thing that Mr. Sim never failed to carry with him was his camera. He had a chunky, complicated, antique-looking camera that was probably worth a lot of money and which he always stowed away carefully in its battered leather carrying-case. He mainly took photographs of landscapes, or extreme close-ups of tree trunks or fungus or stuff like that. Not holiday snaps, in other words. But of course, like his poetry-writing, his photography was very much a solitary pursuit. He never took Max with him, as far as I can remember, to give him a lesson in how to frame a picture or what exposure to use: there generally seemed to be very little flow of information from father to son. I found this difficult to relate to because my father was always talking to us, always teaching us how to do things. On the first night of the holiday, for instance, I remember him disappearing off with Chris into the woods at the side of the lake and returning with lots of twigs and branches to start building the fire. He asked me if I wanted to help but I was too busy reading a copy of *Cosmopolitan*. Max also didn't seem very interested, and in any case he was helping his mother peel the potatoes, although I seem to remember he sliced his finger open while he was doing it and had to wear a plaster for the next few days. Anyway, my dad went about building the fire with his usual thoroughness, and talked Chris through the process step by step. He said that it wasn't enough just to chuck a pile of sticks on the floor and light them with a match. You would never get a long-lasting fire that way. First of all you had to clear an area of ground and preferably enclose it with a ring of stones because that would provide insulation. Then you built a pile of kindling, using dry twigs and small pieces of wood, along with bits of old cardboard and egg boxes and suchlike if you had them. It was important, Dad said, not to pack the kindling too tightly together—there had to be room for the air to circulate. Of course there was plenty of good dry wood around to use as kindling and fuel because it had not rained in that part of the world for weeks. There were several ways you could arrange the larger pieces of wood on top of the kindling, Dad said: he and Chris experimented with different shapes during the course of the week (pyramid-shaped, star-shaped, "log cabin" style, and so on) but ended up deciding that making a kind of wooden tepee was best, because that way the kindling burned really well at the centre, and the outside logs would fall inward and feed the fire when they were ready. To get the fire started they used all sorts of things as tinder—moss, dry grass, pine needles, bark shavings—and Chris always did a good job collecting it, because for the next few days he had the responsibility of building the fire by himself and every night he only needed one match to get it started and we always had a really good blazing fire which lasted for a couple of hours or more. It was very cheering to have such a good fire going every night because, although the days were still pretty warm, the evenings were starting to grow chilly. The best thing was when the fire had been burning for quite a while and the heart of it was really hot; by then we would have had our supper and we would get out a packet of marshmallows and roast them at the centre of the fire for dessert. Delicious.

Towards the end of the week, the weather began to change. All week it had been so warm that most of us had been swimming in the lake every day. There was a little shingle beach down at one end of the campsite, but if you walked a bit farther through the woods you eventually came to another one, even smaller—in fact you could hardly call it a beach, it was so tiny, just a scrap of shingle, really, enclosed by trees, wide enough for two or three people to sit, at a pinch—and this had become our favourite spot. None of the other campers seemed to use it. And this was where we came, on the last full day of the holiday, late on Friday afternoon—my brother, Max and me. The sky had clouded over and was now hanging heavy and slate-grey over Coniston Water. The temperature must have fallen by seven or eight degrees since the day before. Every day we had swum in the lake off this beach and that's what we had come for today, but when we got there the prospect didn't seem so appealing. In fact Max immediately sat down on the grass above the beach and announced that he wasn't going to go in today. Chris called him a wimp and promptly stripped down to his swimming trunks. He waded knee-deep into the water and then came to an abrupt halt: it was clearly much colder than he'd been expecting. I wasn't sure what I was going to do, exactly, but I started to undress anyway. Underneath my T-shirt and jeans I was wearing a little orange bikini that I hadn't worn on this holiday so far. I had bought it in France earlier that summer with my girlfriend. It was rather skimpy and revealing and I knew—mainly from the effect it had had on all the French boys!—that I looked pretty good in it. The week was nearly over now and I was getting a bit tired of playing hard to get with Max so I thought if he saw me in this bikini it might spur him into action. As I slipped out of my jeans and pulled my T-shirt over my head I could feel that his eyes were on me, although when I turned to smile at him he just looked away quickly. "Are you sure you're not going to come in?" I said, but he shook his head. He was smiling back at me but, as always with Max, it was impossible to say what the smile meant or what he was thinking. I stood there for a few seconds, regarding him with enquiring eyes, my hands on my hips— making sure he got a damn good look at me in that bikini—but still he didn't respond, so I turned with a sigh and started to walk out into the water.

God, it was cold. Perhaps it was just the psychological effect of the grey skies and the lack of sunshine, but the lake felt icy compared to the previous days. Positively Arctic. What's more, as Chris and I waded in, we could feel a few slow, fat raindrops beginning to splash on the surface of the water. The first rain for weeks! "Are you sure this is a good idea?" I asked Chris, but a few seconds later he was under, and straight after that he swam over to me, grabbed me by the shoulders and pushed me under as well. I screamed and kicked at first, but then I gave in and started swimming alongside him, thinking that my body would get used to the cold in a moment or two.

It was no use, though. The water had me in its freezing grip and after five minutes or so I realised I wasn't going to warm up and that I wasn't really enjoying myself. "This is too cold," I said. "I'm freezing to death." "Don't be silly," Chris answered, but then he saw how violently I was shivering. "I'm serious," I said. "I'm going to get frostbite or something," and I started to walk back to the shore. Chris came with me, and we waded back side by side. Max was waiting on the beach with our towels but I realised now that he had been joined by his father as well. Mr. Sim was standing on the beach looking at us both, but before we'd had time to reach dry land he shouted out, "Stop!" and took his camera out of that leather carrying-case. "Hold it right there," he said. "That looks absolutely perfect." So we both remained stock still, up to our knees in freezing water, while he stood there fiddling with his lens and getting us into focus.

I felt a little bit uneasy about it, even at the time. I don't know why that should be. It was just a family friend, taking a picture of me and my brother on holiday—what could be more innocuous? But there was something about the deliberation with which he took the photo—making us stand shivering for ages while he got the composition exactly right, and something about the commanding (almost bullying) way he had shouted, "Stop!"—that gave me a nasty feeling. For one thing, he didn't normally take this kind of photograph: arty shots of dandelions and tree trunks, yes, but not people—so why me and Chris? Why now? And for another, all of a sudden I really wished that I hadn't been wearing that bikini. It was skimpy enough to start with, but with the wet and the coldness it had gone almost see-through and my nipples were probably standing out like cherries. It was all very well Max seeing me like that, but his father . . . well, that was quite creepy, in my opinion. So as soon as he'd taken the picture I dashed back on to the shore without meeting his eye and grabbed my towel from Max and wrapped myself up in it. I was shivering uncontrollably and my teeth were chattering so much I could barely talk. Meanwhile, Mr. Sim packed his camera away in a manner that was almost too casual and said, in a tone of forced joviality, "That one's going to come out really well. So, who's coming with us all to the pub tonight?"

It turned out that we weren't going to have supper round the fire that evening after all. The grown-ups had booked a table at the local pub instead. But it also turned out that the chill in my body wasn't going to go away anytime soon. I really had allowed myself to get far too cold, and nothing seemed capable of warming me up—not even the two or three cups of boiling hot tea my mum made for me when we got back to the tents. After I'd drunk the tea, I went into our tent and snuggled down into my sleeping bag and just lay there, shivering. My mum told everyone that I wouldn't be coming to the pub and there followed a short conference about what should be done. I could hear Max saying that he didn't want me to stay behind on my own and that he would stay too, to keep me company, and of course that made me feel really happy. Whatever else you might say about him, Max had always been like that—thoughtful, I mean, and considerate. One of nature's gentlemen. Then Chris said that he would stay behind too and I thought, Oh no, what a nuisance. But somehow Mr. Sim managed to talk him out of it. I remember thinking how sad it was that Mr. Sim went to such lengths to persuade Chris to come to the pub with them, when he was perfectly happy for his own son to stay behind. But I suppose that was just typical of their relationship. Anyway, I was very pleased with the outcome, as you can imagine.

After they had all gone to the pub Max popped his head around the flap of my tent and asked if I was feeling OK. I said I was fine but he could see that I was still very cold and asked if I wanted some more tea or some hot chocolate or something. I agreed that would probably be a good idea and said I would put the kettle on the Primus stove and also make a few sandwiches or something for us both to eat. "OK then," Max said, rising to his feet. "I'll get the fire started."

Well, those were famous last words if ever I heard them.

Not to put too fine a point on it, Max's attempts to light a fire that night, and keep it going, were nothing short of disastrous. Everything that could have gone wrong went wrong. The kindling was too damp (thanks to the rain earlier that afternoon) and he didn't collect enough of it. The logs he collected for fuel were far too big, and he had no tools to cut them up with. He kept trying to hold them still with his feet and break them apart with his hands, but all he succeeded in doing was injuring himself. Somehow he managed to tear half the skin off his left hand, and you should have heard the swearing when he did it! From then on he was trying to do everything with one hand wrapped up in a handkerchief, and of course that just made things even worse. I kept saying to him, Max, it really doesn't matter, sit down, drink your cocoa, eat your sandwiches, for heaven's sake relax, let's have a nice evening together while everyone is away—but it was no use. He wouldn't sit still. He'd got it into his head that I wanted a fire—the kind of fire that Chris would have built—and a fire was what I was going to get. And then, after he'd created this "thing" that to me just looked like a random pile of twigs, grass, logs and bracken, he couldn't even get a match to light. It took him at least three or four matches to get the kindling started, after which the whole thing began giving off so much smoke that within a couple of minutes our whole corner of the campsite was smothered with the stuff, and people were coming over from their tents to complain and tell us to put it out. It was at this point that I started to laugh, but actually this was the worst thing I could have done. It just made Max look more miserable than ever, and he redoubled his efforts to make the thing work by running off to find even more damp firewood. When he came back I had been planning to say something overtly flirtatious to him, like, "There are other ways we could keep warm, you know, Max," but when I saw his face the words just froze on my lips. To say that the moment for that kind of thing had passed would be an understatement. I could tell that the evening was now completely ruined, for him and for both of us. There were tears of frustration in his eyes as he threw yet more useless damp vegetation onto the smouldering pile, and started fumbling with the matchbox and the matches through his bloodstained handkerchief. I knew this had started with a generous impulse—he was worried about me, and wanted to keep me warm—but it had gone way beyond that now. Maybe this sounds silly, but I thought I could tell what was going through his head, or at least through his subconscious. This was not about building a fire anymore. This was about Max's relationship with his father. Chris had been taught how to do this. Dad had made the time, and found the patience, to pass that lesson on from one generation to another. That was how their relationship worked. But Max didn't have any of that. His father had abandoned him years ago—perhaps never even made a connection with him in the first place. And that left him clinging to this placid, benign mother who also had nothing to teach him, nothing to pass on. He was alone in the world, and already he was struggling. It became too painful, watching him throw spent match after spent match onto a fire that was never going to take. "I've had enough of this," I said, "I'm going inside. Call me when you've got it going." But when I looked outside again, about half an hour later, there was nothing but a faintly smoking heap of wood where the fire was meant to be, and Max was nowhere to be seen. He had gone off somewhere by himself.

That's not quite the end of the story. I wish it was, really, because I don't like the actual end of the story very much at all. Nevertheless, I'm aware that I haven't really addressed the essay topic yet, and in order to do that I have to briefly describe what happened round at the Sims' house a couple of weeks later.

I was feeling guilty about Max, I have to admit. That last evening had been such a fiasco, when it could have been so different, and I couldn't help blaming myself, to a certain extent. True, he had behaved like a total idiot, but I could probably have made the situation better if I hadn't lost my temper with him so quickly, and the truth of the matter was that I still felt fond of him, for all his uselessness. So I'd decided to give him one last chance.

I didn't want to ask him for a drink, or anything like that, so in order to keep things casual I thought I would simply call in at his house one Sunday afternoon and suggest going for a walk somewhere—maybe on the municipal golf course, which was just across the road from where they lived. I didn't call him on the telephone or anything. I wanted just to pretend that I was in the area anyway and had dropped by on the spur of the moment.

It was a nice sunny afternoon, in mid-September. I walked

up their little drive and rang the front doorbell. It didn't seem to be working but the door had been left on the latch and I was able to push it open.

The first thing I would normally do would be to shout, "Hello! Is anybody there?" but today I didn't, because I could tell straightaway that the house was quite empty and silent, apart from a gentle rhythmic snoring coming from one of the bedrooms upstairs. Not wishing to wake whoever was asleep, I tiptoed up the stairs and found that the noise was coming from the spare bedroom, which I remembered as being a sparsely furnished room with nothing much in it apart from a wardrobe and a single bed. Who would be in there, and why would they be sleeping?

The door was ajar. I silently pushed it further open and looked inside.

It was Mr. Sim, and I can only imagine that he must have had a heavy Sunday lunch a couple of hours earlier—perhaps washed down with some red wine—because I cannot believe that he meant to fall asleep in the attitude in which I found him. He was lying on his side, facing the door. His trousers and pants were pulled halfway down his legs and in his right hand he held a crumpled tissue. His penis lay wrinkled and flaccid between his legs, and from its purple tip a little strand of semen dribbled down onto the pale-blue bedspread. Purple and pale blue—Aston Villa colours. That was the first silly thought that came into my head. Weird how the mind works. The only other thing I could see on the bedspread was a photograph: a glossy colour print of the picture he had taken on the small shingle beach next to Coniston Water. I noticed that he had folded it neatly and carefully in half, so that the figure of Chris was hidden and the only person you could see was me, all wet and cold in my skimpy orange bikini. It was almost as if the picture had been deliberately composed—the perfect symmetry of the two of us standing there, one on either side of the frame—in order to make this possible.

I could only have glimpsed Mr. Sim in this position for a couple of seconds before I heard the front door open again and voices coming from downstairs. Quickly I withdrew—only just in time, for I could hear him waking with a start and hurriedly making himself decent.

I heard Max and his mother walking through into the kitchen. They had left the front door open so I went downstairs silently and slipped outside. I didn't want to talk to them and didn't want them to see me. And I certainly didn't want to come face to face with Mr. Sim.

After that I made it my business to keep out of the way of Max and his family for a long time. I think I even managed to avoid seeing them at Christmas, somehow or other, even though in the normal course of events we always saw each other at Christmas, usually spending most of Boxing Day together. Nobody seemed to notice that I was avoiding them, so nobody asked me for an explanation. It was hard on Max, of course, but I knew that he would probably get a crush on some other girl, sooner rather than later. Things between us could have been very different, if he hadn't been so fixated on the idea of starting a fire that last evening at the campsite. That had been our great opportunity, and once it had passed, maybe there was no going back anyway. What would I have said to him, that Sunday afternoon, if we had gone for our walk on the golf course together? I really don't know. All I know is, after I had seen his father like that—after I realised that he must have been watching me, and lusting after me, all week, and after I realised what his reasons were for taking that photograph—I could not have got myself involved with Max, however much I liked him.

In conclusion, therefore, what has writing this essay taught me? I suppose it has reinforced my conviction that the consequences of privacy violation can be very destructive and hurtful. In this case, they destroyed the possibility of my ever having a relationship with Max, despite the fact that, prior to these events, I had liked him very much, and even found myself attracted to him.

Alison Byrne, February 1980

14

—Straight on at the roundabout—take second exit.

"Well, Emma, this is just a great situation, isn't it?"

—Exit coming up.

"I now have a mental image of my father which I'm probably never going to be able to get out of my head."

—In two hundred yards, right turn.

"And just to cap it off, tomorrow night I'm going to be having dinner with the woman who put it there."

—Right turn coming up.

"I really didn't think I could get any more angry with my father. I really couldn't see how he could sink any further in my estimation. But—well done, Dad. You've managed it! Not just tossing yourself off over a picture of one of my friends, but managing to get caught doing it! Way to go, Dad. Way to *fucking* go. Are there any other ways you'd care to fuck up my life? Because you might as well finish the job off now that you've made such a good start."

I pulled furiously on the steering wheel as I made the right turn and took the curve much too fast. In the process I nearly clipped the bumper of a four-wheel-drive that was waiting to pull out from the road I was turning into. The driver tooted her horn at me. I glared back.

—Proceed for about four miles on the current road.

By now I had left Walsall behind and was heading northeast along the A461. According to Emma, I was about eight miles away from Lichfield: nineteen minutes' driving, at my current speed. It was another grey morning, slightly windy, slightly wet. The onscreen display told me that the temperature outside was 5 degrees Celsius. There was not much traffic on the roads. I had avoided the motorways so far this morning. Motorways, I realised, made you feel disconnected from the landscape around you. This morning I wanted to drive through real places, I wanted to see shops and houses and office blocks, I wanted to see old ladies pulling shopping trolleys along the street and clusters of surly teenagers gathered around bus shelters. I didn't want to be like my father anymore: hiding away from life and pleasuring himself in shameful secrecy while his wife and son were out taking a Sunday-afternoon walk. I wasn't prepared to think of myself as a pathetic figure, not just yet.

I was driving too fast. I couldn't keep my foot from pressing down on the accelerator. I had only averaged fifty-two miles to the gallon so far today.

—*Proceed for about three miles on the current road.*

What was I going to find when I opened the door to this flat, anyway? My father hadn't been there in more than twenty years. Had anybody else been inside it in that time, apart from Mr. and Mrs. Byrne? All I knew was that somewhere in there I would find a blue ring binder, with the words *Two Duets* written on the spine, containing a bunch of incomprehensible poems and a story which would apparently explain why I wouldn't have been born if it hadn't been for the proximity of two London pubs both called the Rising Sun. Did I really want to discover any more, at this stage, about the circumstances of my birth or, worse still, my conception? I wasn't sure that I did. I had already learned quite enough about my father and what he did with his bodily fluids.

—*Proceed for about two miles on the current road.*

I glanced down at the map screen. There I still was, a little red arrow pluckily making its way along the A461. Advancing upon my destination inch by inch. How insignificant it made me look, and feel. I thought of those satellites, thousands of miles up in the sky, looking down on me and millions like me, looking down on all those people rushing around here and there on their individual, everyday, ultimately pointless errands. The incomprehensibility, the horror of it, suddenly came over me and made me shiver: I felt a momentary hollowness in my stomach, as if I were standing in a lift that had started to plummet.

"Steady on there," I said—partly to Emma, partly to myself. "Don't go down that route. You can go crazy thinking about stuff like that."

I tried to concentrate on something more immediate—the landscape around me. Emma and I were entering Staffordshire now. We had left the urban dreariness of Walsall behind and entered a more restful, leafier territory. The houses occasionally dotting either side of the road were built of that distinctive Staffordshire red brick, and every so often the road would rise gently and pass over a canal, its walls built of the same brick, part of an elaborate network which testified mournfully to a now vanished industrial past. My grandparents—that is to say, my dad's mother and father—had lived in this area right up until their deaths (within a few months of each other) in the late 1970s, so I was dimly familiar with it. It was part of the lost landscape of my childhood. Not that we'd ever visited my grandparents very much. My father had never been close to his parents. He had kept them at a distance, just as he did with everyone else.

—*Heading slightly right at the roundabout, take second exit.*

I wouldn't go through Lichfield itself, not through the centre. I would skirt the city on its eastern side. In days gone

208 • THE TERRIBLE PRIVACY OF MAXWELL SIM

by, before motorways and by-passes, travelling through England must actually have involved visiting places. You would drive along high streets (or ride your horse along them, if we're going to go that far back) and stop at pubs in the town centre (or staging posts or coaching inns or whatever they used to be called). Now the entire road network seemed to be set up to prevent this from happening. The roads were there to stop you from meeting people, to ensure that you passed nowhere near any of the places where humanity congregates. A phrase came to me, then—a phrase that Caroline was fond of repeating. "Only connect." I think it was from one of the fancy writers she was always trying to get me to read. It occurred to me now that whoever designed England's roads had precisely the opposite idea in mind: "Only disconnect." Sitting here in my Toyota Prius, with only Emma for company, I was cocooned from the rest of the world. Not only did I not have to interact with other people, the roads saw to it that I didn't even have to see them if I didn't want to. Just how my father would have liked it—the sad, miserable bastard.

"Not that I give a flying fuck about him anymore," I said to Emma. "Why should I waste any more energy thinking about him? The only thing that makes me angry is that he frightened Alison off. Supposing she and I *had* gone out together that afternoon? What would that have led to? She might have been my girlfriend. We might have got engaged. We might have got married and had children. My whole life might have been different."

—*Proceed for about half a mile on the current road.*

"Still, what's the use? '*Would've, should've, could've.* The most painful words in the language.' That's another quotation, isn't it? Where did I get that one from?"

—*In two hundred yards, left turn.*

"I remember—it's from Caroline's story. Christ, now I've even started quoting my own wife's fiction back at myself. Although why I call it fiction I don't know, since all the treacherous cow did was to take something from our life together, our *shared* life—something personal, something *private*, for fuck's sake—and turn it into some nice bit of writing that all her friends at the Kendal creative writers' group can ooh and aah over before they start knocking back the Pinot Grigio."

My voice had risen to a shout. I knew it was wrong to have lost my temper like this in front of Emma, so I pressed the map button and allowed her calming voice to take over for a while, guiding me with no fuss or difficulty to the road where my father's flat was located on the outskirts of Lichfield. Occasionally, out of my passenger window, I saw distant glimpses of the famous cathedral, but otherwise there was nothing to remind me that I was skirting around one of England's more picturesque cities, the birthplace of Dr. Johnson, if I remember correctly. We had to drive for a long time down a monotonous, single-carriageway road, lined on both sides with terraced houses from the interwar years, until we reached a busy junction where Emma told me to go *"Sharp left at the roundabout—take first exit."* This took you into a quiet backwater of residential streets, dominated by three imposing, eight-storey apartment blocks overlooking the main arterial Eastern Avenue. It was hard to say when these might have been built. Postwar? They looked like council blocks, but good-quality council blocks. There were balconies on every floor and the buildings looked clean and well maintained. *"Your destination is ahead,"* Emma told me, so I thanked her and parked the car in a bay at the side of the road and turned off the ignition. Then I looked up at the middle of the three apartment blocks. This was where my father's flat was supposed to be. I felt a tightness in my whole body. I was stiff with apprehension.

Before walking over to the main entrance, I took out my video camera and filmed for about twenty seconds, panning all over the building, left and right, up and down. It was the first time I'd used the camera, but it seemed pretty easy to operate. I'm not quite sure why I did it, though: partly to calm my nerves, perhaps, and partly because I thought my father might like to see the footage the next time we met, whenever that would be. At any rate, it was hardly going to be of much use to Lindsay or Alan Guest for their promotional video. Afterwards I put the camera back in the glove compartment and locked the car.

It's odd that when I think back to that morning, and remember myself walking across the expanse of asphalt in front of the tower block, it feels as though it was all happening in complete silence. Yet obviously there's no such thing as complete silence anymore. Not in England. So there must have been the rumble of traffic from the Eastern Avenue, or the distant wail of police sirens, or the crying of a baby in a pushchair two streets away, but that's not how I remember it. All was stillness. All was mystery.

I took the lift up to the fourth level and emerged into a dark, featureless corridor with a shiny linoleum floor and walls painted an intimidating shade of deep brown. The little windows at either end of the corridor admitted just a hint of the grey, late-morning light—two feeble glows in the distance to my left and my right—as I walked over to the doorway of my father's flat, full of trepidation, my footsteps so light and measured that they barely made a sound. I took the keys that Mr. Byrne had given me and tried to fit one of them into the lock—which in itself was quite hard to locate in this gloom. The key didn't seem to fit. Nor did the other two on Mr. Byrne's key ring. I tried each of them again, one after the other, but two of them didn't fit at all, while the other one did—with a fair amount of forcing—but refused to turn.

I remembered Mrs. Byrne's comment, as we'd said good-bye yesterday evening, that she didn't think I'd been given the right keys. I'd taken no notice at the time, assuming it was simply the wittering of a confused old woman, but maybe she knew what she was talking about.

"Shit!" I said, out loud, and started trying the keys again. But it was no use. However hard I twisted the one key that seemed almost to fit, the lock refused to yield. After two or three minutes, I wrenched the key out of the recalcitrant lock and threw it on the floor in frustration.

"Shit!" I said again. Why was it that everything I tried to do, whenever it had anything to do with my father, always ended in disappointment and frustration? I thumped the locked door of his flat so hard that it hurt my fist and then stood in the darkness of the corridor for a few seconds, wondering where I could go from here. Would it be too anti-climactic just to give up, return to the car, and continue with my journey north?

Then I remembered the other thing that Mrs. Byrne had mentioned: that there was another set of keys, belonging to a woman called Miss Erith who lived in the flat opposite. That had to be worth trying, surely.

I approached the door and hesitated for a moment before ringing the bell. Suppose there was no one at home. Well, that would be the end of it, then. But no—I could hear voices, muted, coming from inside. A man's voice and a woman's.

Quickly, before I had the time to tell myself that I was doing something foolish, I rang the bell. Almost immediately I regretted it, but there was nothing I could do about that now. After a couple of seconds I could already hear footsteps coming towards the door.

The door opened and I found myself looking at a small man of Pakistani origin, who seemed to be in his late sixties.

"Yes?" he said.

"I'm sorry—I think I must have called at the wrong flat."

"Who were you looking for?"

"Miss Erith."

"No, this is right. Come on in."

I followed him inside, down a short corridor and then into a bright but small sitting room filled with clutter. Three free-standing mahogany bookcases were crammed with old hardback books and a few battered paperbacks, an ancient stereo system (dating from the 1970s, I would say, or maybe even the 1960s) with a whole lot of vinyl records and cassettes ranged around it (no CDs), at least a dozen pot plants and a number of pictures on the walls, most of which even I recognised as reproductions of Old Masters. There were two armchairs placed opposite each other, and in one of them sat an elderly figure who I took to be Miss Erith. I guessed that she was at least ten years older than the man who had let me into the flat, although there was a liveliness in her eyes which belied her physical frailty. She was wearing brown slacks and a navy-blue cardigan over her blouse, but the left sleeve was rolled up and, judging from the equipment on the table beside her, she was in the process of having her blood pressure taken.

When she saw me, her body gave a visible jolt and she almost jumped out of her chair in astonishment. "Good grief," she said. "It's Harold!"

"Don't get up," I said. "I'm not Harold. My name's Max."

She stared at me more closely. "Well," she said, "thank God for that. I thought I was going mad for a minute. You do look like him, though."

"I'm his son," I told her.

"His *son*?" She looked me up and down, as if this information made it even more difficult to accept the reality of my sudden appearance—or indeed my existence. "Well," she continued, mostly to herself, "Harold's son. Who'd have thought it? Max, did you say your name was?"

"That's right."

"Your father isn't with you?"

"No."

"Is he still alive?"

"Yes, he is. He's very well, actually." With one thing and another, I seemed to have reduced her to speechlessness. To fill the silence, I said: "I was just passing through the area, so I thought . . . well, I thought it was about time someone checked up on the flat." Still no response. "I'm on my way to Scotland. To the Shetland Isles."

At this point, Miss Erith's companion stepped forward and held out his hand.

"Allow me to introduce myself. I'm Doctor Hameed."

"Pleased to meet you, Doctor," I said, shaking his hand. "Maxwell Sim."

"Maxwell. The pleasure is all mine. Call me Mumtaz, please. Margaret, why don't I make a pot of tea for your guest?"

"Yes, of course. Of course." She slowly emerged from the daze into which my presence had thrown her. "Yes, where are my manners? Sit down, please, and have some tea. Would you like some tea?"

"That would be lovely. But shouldn't you finish . . . ?" I gestured at the blood-pressure monitor on the table.

"Oh, we can do that afterwards. Come on, this is a special occasion."

"Very good," Mumtaz said. "I'll make a pot for all of us."

When he had disappeared on this errand, Miss Erith explained: "Mumtaz used to be my GP, until he retired. But he still comes and sees me every couple of weeks, completely off his own bat. He gives me a quick MOT, and then we drive out somewhere for lunch. Nice of him, isn't it?"

"Very."

"You see, if there were more people around like him, we wouldn't be in the state we are now."

It wasn't clear to me exactly what she meant by this remark, so I let it pass.

"I haven't seen your father," Miss Erith continued, "for more than twenty years. Nineteen eighty-seven, it was, when he left. He'd only been here a year or so. I was just getting excited about the idea of having him for a neighbour when he buggered off to Australia, without so much as a by-your-leave."

"I know," I said. "It was a bit of a surprise for me, as well."

"Well, I'm not sure I was surprised, exactly. Not in retrospect, anyway. It never struck me as being a very sensible thing to do, coming back here to his home town after his wife had died and everything. What he really needed was a fresh start. Still, I was very disappointed. He was good company, and we're not exactly spoiled for that around here, I can tell you. He never wrote or anything. Never got back in touch. Miserable sod. How old would he be now, seventy-something? He's still in good shape, did you say?"

"Yes. I saw him in Sydney last month. That was when he asked me to call in here. He wants me to find some . . . some items from the flat. Trouble is, I can't seem to get in. I think I was given the wrong key."

"Don't worry, I've got one somewhere. I still go in there every so often, to check the post. You know, it's very irresponsible of him to leave that flat empty for so long. It could have been squatted by now. In fact, it should have been, really. If it had been anybody else I would've reported him to the housing association."

Mumtaz now returned with a tray loaded with teacups, saucers and a plate full of biscuits. I fetched another chair from the corner of the room and offered him the armchair he must have been using before. Soon we were all settled again.

"You never knew Mr. Sim, did you?" Miss Erith asked him. "From the flat across the corridor."

"No, I never had the pleasure," said the doctor. "A little before my time."

"Max has come to collect some of his things," said Miss Erith. "Though I don't know what, exactly, because there isn't much in there."

"I was told something about some postcards," I said.

"Ah! Of course! Well, I've got those, unless there've been any others in the last three weeks."

She began to rise effortfully to her feet, but Mumtaz tried to stop her. "Please, Margaret, don't exert yourself."

"Give over," she said, brushing him away. "I'm not a cripple yet, you know. Now hang on, they're in the spare room somewhere . . ."

While she was away, Mumtaz poured me some tea and handed me the cup, smiling in a confiding sort of way. "She has plenty of spirit, Margaret—still plenty of spirit. Mind you, her body's not in such bad shape either. Would you have guessed that she's seventy-nine? You should get her to tell you the story of her life. Fascinating. She was born on the canals, you know. Her father used to keep a famous shop for canal people, a few miles north from here at Weston. All that trade and traffic is gone now, of course. But just imagine! Imagine the changes she must have seen in her lifetime. Someone should fetch a tape recorder and keep her story for posterity. In fact, that's what I should be doing. I've mentioned it to her, of course, but she's too modest. 'Oh, nobody wants to hear about a boring old lady like me,' she'll say. But stories like hers need to be remembered, don't you think? Otherwise, England has forgotten its own past, and once that happens, we're in trouble, aren't we? Even more trouble than we're in at the moment."

Another enigmatic remark; but before I had time to think about it, Miss Erith re-entered the room, saying, "I'm sorry they're not in a box or anything," and dragging a large black bin liner behind her.

"What the . . ." I said, opening the bag and peering inside.

"You see, I never sorted them, or anything like that," said Miss Erith, "because I had no idea whether your father was ever coming back or not. And he specifically told me not to forward anything."

The bag was full to the brim with picture postcards. I reached inside and pulled out a handful at random. They were nearly all from places in the Far East—Tokyo, Palau, Singapore—and each had my father's address written neatly in block capitals on the right-hand side, while the other half was filled to the very edges with cramped, intense handwriting. And they all bore the same signature: "Roger."

"Wait a minute," I said. "This is beginning to ring a bell."

And yes, it was true: I remembered, now, that similar postcards used to arrive at the family home in Birmingham every so often. They would be scooped up from the doormat along with the rest of the post, either by me or my mother, and placed without comment on my father's desk in the dining room, for him to read when he returned home from work in the evening. Like everything else that took place in our uncommunicative household, this practice was hardly ever discussed or even remarked upon. Although I did recall saying to my mother, at least once, "Who is Roger, anyway?" to which she had simply replied, "I think he was some old friend of your father's." And that had been the end of it.

"I've seen this handwriting before," I went on. "And always on postcards like this. All through the seventies, my dad used to get these."

"They come about once a month, generally," said Miss Erith. "He doesn't get anything else. A bit of junk mail sometimes."

"I'll take them away with me," I said. "Is that all right?"

"Of course it is. Oh, and the key's over there, while I remember. In the fruit bowl on top of the bookcase."

I got up to retrieve the key and, while I was on my feet, said: "I'll just pop across and look for the other stuff, I think. Shouldn't take a minute or two."

To tell the truth, I was dreading going into the flat and wanted to get it over with as soon as possible. So I left Miss Erith and Dr. Hameed drinking their tea and stepped back into the gloom of the corridor. And this time my father's door unlocked easily.

Have you ever been inside a place that has not been lived in for more than twenty years? If not, you will find it difficult to understand what it feels like. Just then I tapped out a couple of sentences, but decided to delete them again because they didn't seem to do justice to the atmosphere in there: I used words like "cold," "sparsely furnished" and "eerie," but somehow that's not enough. There's another word I could have used, of course. Perhaps rather a melodramatic word. "Dead." Does that seem over-the-top to you? Well, never mind—it may be a little blunt, but still, this is exactly what my father's flat felt like: like a place that belonged to someone who had died a long time ago.

After I'd been in there for about two minutes, I couldn't wait to get out.

There were two bedrooms. One contained a single bed (with mattress but no linen), while the other—much smaller—was dominated by a desk and a large self-assembly bookcase made of artificial wood. Thick dust everywhere—that goes without saying. There were about a dozen books on the shelves—all the ones my father hadn't wanted to take to Australia with him—and a few papers and items of stationery in the desk drawers. The precious ring binder was sitting on the third shelf of the bookcase and was easy to recognise. It was pale blue, and on the spine my father had stuck on a label which read *Two Duets: A Verse Cycle and a Memoir.* You could tell he had stuck the label down with double-sided sellotape, because the paper had faded and now you could clearly see the two strips of sellotape coming through underneath.

I plucked down the binder and carried it with me into the kitchen. Here there was a French window leading out onto a little balcony, and with a bit of effort I managed to turn the latch-key and push it open. It was good to get out into the fresh air. From up here I could see traffic circling endlessly, purposelessly, on the orbital road, and beyond that rural Staffordshire stretched out towards the horizon in grey waves of gentle, unremarkable countryside. A light but persistent drizzle had started to fall. I could see the A5192 ribboning away into the distance and suddenly felt a strong desire to be driving on that road, back towards the motorway, just me and Emma again, heading north to Kendal, where this evening (God, this was such a wonderful prospect, until now I had barely allowed myself to contemplate it) I would actually be seeing Caroline and Lucy for the first time in months. Perhaps the most important evening of my life, in some ways. Certainly a chance to prove—once and for all—that I was not going to repeat my father's mistakes; that I was capable of having a relationship with my daughter based on something more than mutual toleration and the prolonged accident of sharing the same living space. I was *not* (I intoned the words to myself, in silence but fervently) going to end up like this. My memorial was not going to be an empty, unloved, unlived-in apartment on the forgotten outskirts of a Midlands city.

Now full of resolve, I went back into the kitchen, locked the French window, took one more pitying look around the sitting room as I passed through it and then left the flat for good, locking the door behind me. I felt a strange, irrational flood of relief, as if I'd just had a narrow escape from the jaws of some fate so imprisoning and nightmarish that it couldn't even be defined.

"Mumtaz and I were just trying to decide where we should go to lunch," Miss Erith said, once I rejoined them and took a welcome sip of my still-warm tea. "We can't just go to any old place, you see. I don't know what he thinks about it, but it's a date, as far as I'm concerned, and a girl expects to be taken somewhere special." She glanced at the blue ring binder on my lap. "So, did you find what you were looking for?"

"Yep. I think these are some of Dad's poems and things. Apparently he's lost the other copy and now this is the only one." I glanced through the pages and saw there were two sections, one in verse, the other in prose. "Don't know why it's so important. I suppose I'd better hang on to it. Weird title," I added, looking at the first page. *"Two Duets."*

"Hmm, I see," said Miss Erith. "A quarter of Eliot."

"Eliot?"

"T. S. Eliot. You've heard of him, haven't you?"

"Of course I have," I said, defensively. Then added, just to make sure I was thinking of the right person, "He wrote the lyrics for *Cats*, didn't he?"

"His most famous poems are the *Four Quartets*," she said. "Have you never read them?"

I shook my head. "What are they about?"

She laughed. "You'd have to read them to find that out! Oh, they're about time, and memory, things like that. And they're all themed around the four elements—air, earth, fire and water. Your father was a great admirer of Eliot's. We used to argue about him all the time. Not my cup of tea, you see. Not my thing at all. He was an anti-Semite, apart from anything else, and you can't forgive something like that, can you? At least I can't. But that sort of thing wouldn't have bothered your father. He's got no interest in politics, has he?"

"Well . . ." I had never really thought about this, I must say. And besides, I wasn't very interested in politics either. "We never really talk about stuff like that. Our relationship is sort of based on . . . other things."

Miss Erith was closing her eyes, now. I wondered at first whether she was about to nod off, but it seemed instead that this was an attempt at recollection.

"The point is," she said, "that I'm an old lefty, and always will be. Ever since I started reading George Orwell and E. P. Thompson and people like that. Whereas your father had no political awareness at all. That's why it's probably a good thing that we never went on our trip together, because we were going into it for completely different reasons."

"You were planning a trip?" I asked politely, hoping this wasn't going to trigger a long reminiscence.

"There was a book called *Narrowboat*. Quite a famous book in its day. Rolt was the author's name—Tom Rolt. I've still got it on the bookshelf over there. He and his wife bought this narrowboat back in the thirties and lived on it for a few months, going up and down the canals. Then he wrote all about it and he published this book in the 1940s, and the amazing thing about it is that it mentions my father's shop—because I grew up on the canals, you know, and my father used to have a shop at Weston, where all the barges used to stop every day. He sold everything: every kind of rope and line you could think of, every kind of food, all sorts of tobacco, and then lamps, crockery, saucepans, clothes—you name it. And shelves and shelves of sweets for the children, of course. Such an Aladdin's cave it was! And the boats used to be stopping all the time, we got to know all the canal folk—it was a different world, a secret world, with its own codes and rules. Just a tiny little shop, the front room of a thatched cottage in a row of other cottages, and I must have served behind the counter from when I was about eight or nine years old. Dad would have been amazed to know his shop was mentioned in this famous book but of course he didn't read books like that—or any sort of book, really—so he never knew anything about it. And I didn't find out until years later. I left home when I was sixteen, you see, to be with this man—a bargeman he was, naturally—and a year later I'd had my first baby and we left the canals and started living not far from here, in Tamworth. But we never got married—that was a bit of a scandal, I can tell you—and a couple of years later we had another baby and then this man left me. Well, I booted him out, if you must know, because he was a dead loss, really, never got a job or anything, used to spend all his time down at the pub or chasing other women, and after a while I decided he was more trouble than he was worth. So there I was, in the early 1950s, living all by myself in a poky little flat with two small children, and the only thing I could do to stop myself from going crazy was to start reading. Of course I'd hardly had any education to speak of, but the Workers' Educational Association was very strong in those days and I used to go to lectures and meetings and all sorts of things. And actually I did manage to go to university in the end, but that was when I was almost forty so that's another story entirely. Anyway, that was how I started reading books and I can't remember how old I was when I read *Narrowboat* but I know that my mum and dad were both dead by then because I would have loved to tell them that their shop was mentioned in the book and I never did."

While she was pausing for breath, Mumtaz said: "Do try to keep to the point, Margaret. You were supposed to be telling us something about Max's father. Now none of us can remember what you were talking about."

She gave him a pointed stare. "Well, *I* can remember. The thing was that Harold and I made this plan, you see, that we were going to hire a narrowboat ourselves for a few weeks and follow the same route this man Rolt and his wife had taken. We were going to do it in 1989, exactly fifty years after they'd set off. The idea was that we'd visit all the same places and see how things had changed in the meantime. Well, that was *my* idea, anyway. All Harold wanted to do, I'm sure, was sit on the roof of the boat looking at the clouds and daydreaming and writing poems. But for me, you see, the point about Tom Rolt's book, and *this*"—she fixed Mumtaz with another stare—

"is why I'm telling you about it, is that it's not just a book about canals at all. It's one of the most amazing books about England ever written. Rolt was a very interesting man—a man with very strong beliefs—and although I daresay he was a bit of a Tory in his politics he was also into green issues years before the term had been invented. And do you know what he saw—way back in 1939? He saw a country that was *already* quite happily allowing itself to be killed off by the power of the big corporations."

Mumtaz rolled his eyes and gave a comically theatrical sigh. "Oh, I see. Now I get it. Watch this carefully, Maxwell," he said, holding up a finger in warning, "because you are about to see a woman climbing on board her hobbyhorse, and once that happens, you are never going to be able to get her off again. We are going to be here for the rest of the morning and most of the afternoon, I tell you."

"It's not a hobbyhorse," Miss Erith insisted, "and I'm not going to climb on board it. All I'm saying is that, if you read that book, you'll understand a bit more of what's going on in this country, and how long it's been happening. What big business is doing to it. It's not a recent thing at all. It's been going on for years—centuries, even. Everything that gives a community its own identity—the local shops, the local pubs—it's all being taken away and replaced by this bland, soulless, corporate—"

"What she's really saying," Mumtaz explained to me with a weary smile, "is that we've been trying to think of a nearby pub where we can go for our lunch, and she doesn't like any of them anymore."

"No, I don't," said Miss Erith. "And do you know why? Because they're all the bloody same! They've all been taken over by the big chains and now they play the same music and serve the same beer and the same food and—"

"And they're full of young people," Mumtaz interrupted.

"Young people enjoying themselves—that's what irks you! Young people who like it that way."

"They like it that way because they don't know any other!" Miss Erith said, her voice suddenly rising to an angry pitch. The good-humoured, bantering aspect of their conversation seemed to evaporate in an instant. "Mumtaz knows very well what I mean." She had turned to look at me directly, now, and I was amazed to see that there were tears in her eyes. "I'm saying that the England I used to love doesn't exist anymore."

A long silence followed, while these words were allowed to hang in the air.

Miss Erith sat forward and drank the remains of her tea, not saying anything more, looking straight ahead of her.

I looked down at my father's ring binder, wondering if this would be a good moment to make my excuses and leave.

Mumtaz sighed and scratched his head. He was the first one to speak.

"You're right, Margaret, absolutely right. Things have changed a lot, even since I've been here. It's a different place now. Better in some ways, worse in others."

"Better!" she echoed, scornfully.

"Anyway," he said, rising to his feet, "I think we should try the Plough and Harrow again. It will be nice to get out into the countryside, and the piped music isn't too loud, and the food is good." He turned to me and said, kindly, "Why don't you join us, Maxwell? We'd be glad to have your company."

I stood up as well. "That's really nice of you," I said. "But I think I'd better get going. I've got a long journey ahead of me."

"You're going to Scotland, I think you said?"

"That's right. About as far as you can go—up to the Shetland Isles."

"Marvellous. What an adventure. And what takes you there, might I ask? Is it business, or pleasure?"

The simplest answer to this, it seemed, was to reach inside the pocket of my jacket and fetch out another of the toothbrush samples I'd been carrying around with me since yesterday. I'd given my two IP 009s to Mr. and Mrs. Byrne, and all the others were still in the boot of the Prius, so what I handed over to Mumtaz was the nice, plain, elegant model that Trevor had shown to me first of all—the ID 003, made of sustainable pine, with the boar's-hair bristles and the non-detachable head.

"I represent a company that markets and distributes these," I explained, surprised to find how proud I was to be saying it.

Mumtaz took the brush from me and whistled admiringly through his teeth. "Wow," he said, running his fingers along the shaft, "this is a beauty. A *real* beauty. You know, I might even enjoy cleaning my teeth if I had one of these, instead of it being a chore. And you are going to sell some of these in Shetland?"

"That's the plan."

"Well," he said, giving the toothbrush back to me, "you will have no difficulty, that's for sure. Margaret! Margaret, did you hear any of that?"

But Miss Erith was still in a kind of daze. She turned towards us slowly, almost as if she had forgotten that we were in the flat with her at all. Her eyes remained rheumy and unfocused. "Mmm?"

"Maxwell was telling us that he's going to Shetland to sell toothbrushes. Beautiful, wooden toothbrushes."

"Wooden?" she said, her concentration gradually appearing to return.

"Perhaps this idea will . . . appeal to you," I said hesitantly, trying hard to find the right words. "My company, you see, is not a big corporation. In fact we're fighting against the big corporations. We're a small company, and whenever we can, we commission our brushes from other small companies. This beautiful brush was made in Lincolnshire, by local craftsmen—part of a family business."

"Really?" she said. "May I see?"

I passed her the brush, and she turned it over in her hands, slowly, reverently, again and again, as if she had never seen such a wondrous object in all her seventy-nine years. When she gave it back to me—unless I was imagining it—her eyes had cleared, and were shining at me with a new, rejuvenated light.

"You can . . . You can have that if you like."

"Really?" Unexpectedly, she pulled back her top lip to reveal teeth which were yellowing but otherwise complete, strong and healthy. "These are all mine, you know. I clean them three times a day."

"Here you are, then. Please, take it."

Perhaps I'm being fanciful now. Perhaps my memory of that day is playing tricks on me. But as that exquisite toothbrush was passed back from my hand to hers, in the rapt silence of Miss Erith's flat high above the city of Lichfield, with Dr. Mumtaz Hameed looking on, smiling benignly, I felt what was taking place was almost religious. That we were doing something—what's the word? Something you might almost describe as—yes, I know . . . sacramental.

There, I told you I was being fanciful. It was definitely time to say my farewells and get back to the car. Back to Emma, the motorway and reality.

15

I had a late lunch at a place called the Caffè Ritazza at Knutsford Services. I'd driven slowly from Lichfield, trying to conserve petrol, and it was after 2:30 by the time I arrived there. The café (or should that be caffè?) was on the first floor, quite close to the bridge connecting the two halves of the service station, so I was able to get a small table near the windows and watch the traffic going by. While I sat there, eating and watching the traffic, I thought about Dr. Hameed and Miss Erith driving to their country pub, enjoying a nice lunch together and lamenting the slow death of the England they both remembered. I wasn't sure whether I agreed with them about that. I supported the ethos of Guest Toothbrushes, of course, but all the same—speaking personally—I really like the way you can drive into almost any city nowadays and be sure of finding the same shops and the same bars and the same restaurants. People need consistency in their lives, don't they? Consistency, continuity, things like that. Otherwise everything just gets too chaotic and difficult. Supposing you drive into a strange town—Northampton, say—and it's full of restaurants whose names you don't recognise. So you have to take a punt on one, just on the basis of what the menu looks like and what you can see through the window. Well, what if it's shit? Isn't it better to know you can go to any random town in the country and find the nearest Pizza Express and have an American Hot with extra black olives? To know exactly what you're getting? I think so. Maybe I should have gone for lunch with them and argued this point. In fact, why hadn't I done that? It wasn't true, as I had told Dr. Hameed, that I was pushed for time. Actually, I had at least two hours to spare. But again—just like last night, when Mr. and Mrs. Byrne had asked me to stay to dinner—I had fought shy of the chance to have a face-to-face meal with someone. When was I going to get over this? When would I find it easy to have a normal conversation again? As it happened, I'd attempted one just now, with the girl in Caffè Ritazza who had served me my lunch. She gave me a strange look when I asked for a tomato and mozzarella panino, so I launched into my explanation of how panini was actually a plural word and it was grammatically incorrect to ask for one, single panini. I'd recently become quite obsessed with this (and by the fact that no shops seemed to serve toasted sandwiches anymore, only panini—even in Knutsford, for God's sake). The idea was that it might trigger some lighthearted banter between us, perhaps about the way that England was slowly becoming more European, or declining standards in education or something, but her initial response was an expression so hostile and suspicious that I thought she was going to call Security. Eventually she did say something, but even then her only comment was "I call them paninis," and that was the end of it. She obviously wasn't the bantering type.

It was quite relaxing and hypnotic, sitting there watching the traffic going by under the motorway-services bridge. It reminded me again of my friend Stuart, and how he'd had to stop driving because he was freaked out by the idea that millions of traffic accidents were only averted every day by a matter of inches or seconds. Watching the northbound traffic on the M6, you could see his point. Nobody seemed to think anything of taking life-threatening risks just to shave a couple of minutes off their journey. I started to count the number of times people pulled out without indicating, or overtook on the inside lane, or tailgated someone remorselessly, or cut in on another car without giving it enough space. After counting over a hundred such incidents, I suddenly realised I'd been sitting there for more than an hour and that it was time to finish driving up to Kendal.

—*Proceed on the current motorway*, Emma said, for the eighth or ninth time.

I didn't mind the repetition. I still liked just hearing the sound of her voice. I wasn't feeling very talkative myself, so every few minutes I would throw out some casual remark to her—"Crossing the Manchester Ship Canal now, look," or "Those must be the Pennines over to the east"—and then press the "map" button on the steering wheel to elicit her reply. The rest of the time, I preferred to be alone with my thoughts.

I thought about Lucy, first of all. Why did people have children in the first place? Was it a selfish act, or supremely unselfish? Or was it just a primal biological instinct that couldn't be rationalised or analysed? I couldn't remember Caroline and I discussing whether to have children or not. To tell the truth, our sex life had never been very lively anyway, and after a couple of years' marriage we just reached a tacit agreement that we would stop using contraception. Conceiving Lucy had been an impulse, not a decision. And yet, as soon as she was born, life without her became unimaginable. My own theory—or one of them—was that once you started to hit middle age, you became so jaded and unsurprised by life that you had to have a child in order to provide yourself with a new set of eyes through which to view things, to make them seem fresh and exciting again. When Lucy was small, the whole world to her was like a giant theme park, and for a while that was how I'd seen it too. Just taking her to the toilet in a restaurant became a voyage of discovery. Even now, for instance, when I saw all those trucks overtaking me (I was in the inside lane, with the cruise control stuck at sixty-two miles per hour), I felt a pang of longing to have the seven- or eight-year-old Lucy with me again, to play the game we always used to play on motorway journeys where you had to guess which country the truck was from by looking at the writing on the side and trying to identify the names of the foreign cities. A game at which she had been surprisingly—

"Oh, shit!" I shouted out loud.

—*Proceed on the current motorway*, said Emma.

"I haven't got her a present!"

And it was true: the morning's adventure in Lichfield had driven paternal obligations clean out of my mind. But I couldn't possibly turn up empty-handed. I would have to come off at the next service station, in about eight miles' time.

Once I'd parked the car and dashed inside, I looked around frantically, but at first I could see very little that might impress her. There was the usual shop selling mobile-phone accessories, but somehow I didn't think she would be too excited to be presented with an in-car charger or a Bluetooth headset. (Which reminded me: I really needed to get the headset on my car working as soon as possible, maybe tonight.) Probably my best bet was W. H. Smith, but even there . . . Would she get much use out of fold-up garden chairs, even if they were on sale at two for ten pounds? There were plenty of cuddly toys, but even I could see they looked horrendously cheap and ugly. A continental power adaptor, suitable for both northern and southern European countries, was practical if hardly likely to bring a grateful sparkle to a young girl's eyes. What about a colouring pad? They had plenty of those, and she was keen on art, as I knew from the school pictures she'd until recently been in the habit of sending me. They had pens to match, as well. Surely that would be fine. All children liked drawing, didn't they?

I went over to pay, didn't attempt to engage in any banter with the terrifyingly bored-looking guy in a turban sitting behind the till, and was back on the motorway within a few minutes.

—*In two miles, exit left, towards South Lakes*, Emma said, before very long.

The countryside by now was rugged and interesting. Brown heritage signs had started to appear, reminding me that the delights of Blackpool were mine for the sampling, a few miles off to the west, and hinting subtly that the nearby Historic City of Lancaster was well worth a short detour. We were emphatically in the North, at last, having left Middle England far behind.

—*In one mile, exit left, towards South Lakes.*

"God, I'm nervous, Emma. I won't try to hide it from you. Well, I can't really hide anything from you, can I? You know everything there is to know about me. You're the all-seeing eye."

—*Next exit left, towards South Lakes. Then a quarter of a mile later, heading slightly left at the roundabout.*

"I don't know why I'm so nervous, though. Caroline's been quite friendly recently on the phone. I suppose the problem is that it's not friendliness I want. That's not enough. In a way, it hurts even more when she's nice to me."

—*Heading slightly left at the roundabout, take first exit.*

"And I really hope Lucy hasn't changed too much. She's always been an affectionate girl. We were never as awkward together—nothing like as awkward—as Caroline makes out in that rotten story of hers. Lucy's simple, uncomplicated. You'll like her—I know you will."

—*Proceed on the current road.*

Dusk was falling as we drove along the A684 together. We passed a roadside café which consisted of little more than a Portakabin with a flag of St. George flying above it, and numerous brown heritage signs inviting us to visit the World of Beatrix Potter, which would have to wait till another day. Soon enough, through the rain and the encroaching dark, the lights of Kendal flickered up ahead.

"Hello, Max," said Caroline.

On the doorstep, she leaned forward, put an arm around me, and kissed me on the cheek. I held the kiss for as long as I thought I could get away with, breathing in her scent, hugging the contours of the body I had once known so well.

"Ooh—is that your car?" she said, breaking free and wandering down the front garden path to get a closer look. "Very nice. You don't see many of those round here."

"It's the company's, actually," I said.

She nodded her approval. "Impressive. You must be coming up in the world."

The rain had stopped now, more or less. I turned to get a closer look at the front of the house. It was small, *bijou*, semidetached and built of local stone. I suddenly wished with all my heart that I was staying the night here and not at the local Travelodge, where I was already checked in. But no such invitation had been forthcoming.

"Brr. Let's get out of this cold," Caroline said, and led me inside.

"Nice haircut, by the way," I said, risking a compliment as I followed her into the kitchen. For years, her hair had been a disaster area. She'd never known what to do with it; it was always not quite long, not quite short, not quite curly, not quite straight, not quite blonde, not quite brown. But now somebody had given it a serious going-over, and she looked more stylish than I'd ever seen her. Brown with blonde highlights—such an obvious choice, when I thought about it. Following her retreating back, I could see she had lost quite a bit of weight, too—a stone, maybe even a stone and a half. She was wearing a tight cashmere top and skinny jeans that hugged the curve of her hips and buttocks. She looked terrific, a good ten years younger than when I'd last seen her. She could easily have passed for someone in her mid-thirties. I felt flabby, old and unfit by comparison.

"I'll put the kettle on," she said.

"Great." I'd been hoping that she might offer me a glass of wine or something, but it was going to be tea, apparently. "Where's Lucy?"

"She's upstairs. Beautifying herself. She'll be down in a minute."

"Great."

In the car, I'd been building up a mental image of Lucy rushing down the stairs to throw herself into her dad's arms. Seems I was wrong about that as well. In fact, the warmest welcome I got was from the little brown Dachshund puppy who ran over from the other side of the kitchen, yelping at me and trying his best to jump up as high as my knees.

I caught him in the middle of one of his jumps and held him to my chest. "So you're Rochester, are you?" I asked, stroking his head as he nuzzled against me eagerly. "What a cute little thing you are, eh?"

"How did you know he was called Rochester?" Caroline asked, putting my cup of tea down on the kitchen table next to me.

"Pardon?"

"How did you know he was called Rochester? We only got him a couple of weeks ago."

This, of course, was a stupid mistake: something Caroline had mentioned to me in my guise as Liz Hammond. In the circumstances, only one lie was available to me. "Oh, I heard it from Lucy. She told me in an e-mail."

"Really? I didn't know Lucy had been e-mailing you."

"Well, you don't know everything, do you?"

"No, that's true." She scraped the two used tea bags off a saucer into the compost bin. "I don't even know what you're doing up here. Did you say you were on your way to Scotland?"

"That's right. Shetland, actually."

"Selling toothbrushes?"

"Sort of."

"You've moved on a bit, then. I thought you'd never leave that job."

"Well, I suppose you need to get a kick up the arse every so often. Which is exactly what you gave me. When you and Lucy went, it . . . well, it brought a few things into focus, shall we say."

Caroline looked down into her teacup. "I know I hurt you."

I looked down into mine. "You were within your rights."

We said no more on the subject.

"Where are you taking her tonight?" Caroline asked, more brightly.

"I booked that Chinese in the centre of town," I said. Lucy had always liked Chinese food.

"It's supposed to be good. We haven't tried it yet."

"I'll let you know."

We were distracted at this point by the arrival in the kitchen of a tall, willowy teenage girl, with dark tousled hair, slightly too much make-up, the obligatory surly pout and a seductive womanly figure insinuated beneath her sprayed-on jeans and midriff-revealing stripey top. It took me two or three seconds to realise that this was my daughter.

She came over and kissed me brusquely. "Hi, Dad."

"Lucy? You look . . ." I struggled for the right word, then decided there wasn't one. "You look—wow. You look amazing."

I could see that since coming here, my daughter had transformed herself. If her mother seemed to have lost ten years, Lucy seemed to have gained at least four or five. She was unrecognisable as the little girl I had last seen (could I think of this again? I had never once tried to picture the scene since it happened. It was too painful to contemplate, and human beings have mechanisms for dealing with that kind of thing—*the mind has fuses*) on that terrible Saturday morning when Lucy and Caroline had driven away in a rented transit van, all their possessions packed away in the back, Cumbria-bound, both of them staring ahead in resolute silence, glassy-eyed, not returning my final wave . . .

There: I had thought of it again, at least. And now, as I realised how much Lucy seemed to have changed since that day, it was with a dawning sense of dread that I reached for the present on the kitchen table and handed it over to her, unwrapped, still in its plastic carrier bag.

The memory of her response still pains me, even now. I cringe whenever I think of it. Opening the plastic bag and seeing the colouring book and the felt-tip pens, she did a momentary, barely noticeable double-take, then said, "Thanks, Dad," and gave me a hug; her eyes flickered briefly over to Caroline's, and they exchanged a glance—a tiny, slightly amused, despairing glance that said, far more eloquently than if they had put it into words, "*Poor old Dad: he doesn't have a clue, does he?*"

I looked away and said, for no other reason than to fill the silence, "Come on out and have a look at my car before we go and eat. It's got a built-in SatNav and everything."

As if that would impress her.

Lucy told me she didn't like Chinese food anymore, because it was full of monosodium glutamate, so we went to an Italian restaurant in the same street instead. I noticed apprehensively that it wasn't part of a chain, which of course meant a leap into the unknown. Lucy ordered a vegetable lasagne—apparently she was a vegetarian now—and I resisted the temptation to go for a meat-feast pizza and had mushroom risotto. It sounded pretty boring, but I didn't want to upset her or seem insensitive towards her convictions. Maybe if I smothered it with spoonfuls of Parmesan cheese it wouldn't taste too bad.

"Well then," I began. "What's it been like, moving up north?"

"Good," said Lucy.

I waited for her to elaborate. She didn't.

"The house looks nice," I ventured. "Do you like it?"

"Yeah," she said. "It's fine."

I hoped she might expand on this. She didn't.

"And school?" I said. "Have you made lots of new friends?"

"Yeah," she said. "A few."

I hoped she would continue, but instead there was an electronic tinkle from somewhere inside her handbag. She took out a BlackBerry and glanced at the screen. Her face lit up, she laughed out loud and immediately began tapping something on to the keyboard. I poured myself more wine and dipped a chunk of bread into the saucer of olive oil while she attended to this.

"Is that your mother's BlackBerry?" I asked, when it looked as though she had finished.

"No. I've had one for ages."

"Oh. Who was it?" I asked, gesturing at the little screen.

"Just someone I know."

A silence fell between us, and I felt a mounting sense of frustration. Was this what it had come to, my relationship with my own daughter? Was this all she had to say to me? For God's sake, we had lived together for twelve years: lived together in conditions of absolute intimacy. I had changed her nappies, I had bathed her, I had played with her, read to her, and sometimes, when she got scared in the middle of the night, she had climbed into my bed and snuggled up against me. And now— after living apart for little more than six months—we were behaving towards each other almost as if we were strangers. How was this possible?

I didn't know. All I knew was that I wasn't going to give up on this evening, not just yet. I would get her to start having a conversation with me if it was the last thing I did.

"It must seem very different," I began, "living—"

At which point my own mobile phone started playing its little melody, announcing that a text message had arrived. I picked up the phone and held it at arm's length (with my eyesight going, I have to do things like this nowadays). The message was from Lindsay.

"Read it if you want," said Lucy. "I don't mind."

I opened the message: *Hi there, you must be at sea by now hope its all going well get in touch when you can L*

It wasn't the most effusive message in the world, but I'd

been waiting for some contact—any contact—with Lindsay for a day and a half now, so I read it with a relief I couldn't begin to disguise. Almost immediately, I put the phone back on the table as nonchalantly as I could, but this didn't fool Lucy for a second.

"Nice message?" she asked.

"It was from Lindsay," I said. Lucy's eyes showed that she wasn't satisfied with this answer, so I added: "Business colleague of mine."

She nodded. "I see." Then, biting off the top of a breadstick, she asked: "I'm never sure about that name—is it a man's name, or a woman's?"

"I think it can be both," I said. "In this case, it's a woman."

"Aren't you going to reply?" she asked.

She picked up her BlackBerry, and I picked up my phone.

"This won't take a minute," I promised.

"No worries."

Actually it took much longer than a minute. I'm not very quick at sending text messages, and I wasn't sure what to say. Eventually I settled on: *Not got as far as the ferry yet. Still in Kendal, taking lovely daughter out to dinner. Really sorry my progress has been so rubbish—don't give up on me!*

By the time I had sent this, Lucy seemed to have sent and received about four messages. We both put our phones down, slightly reluctantly, and smiled at each other.

"So," I said, "it must feel very different—"

The waiter arrived with our food. The table was pretty small and it took him a while to find space for everything. Then there was the palaver of grinding the black pepper and sprinkling the cheese, all of which he turned into quite a performance. Before he finished, another message from Lindsay had come through: *Max, enjoy the ride and dont worry about progress or lack of it, always remember its only a bit of fun x*

I smiled to myself as I put down the phone, and Lucy noticed that I was smiling, but she didn't say anything.

After trying my first mouthful of risotto—which didn't seem to taste of anything at all—I took the opportunity to ask a question. "You do a lot of texting, don't you, Luce?"

"Not really," she said. "I maybe send about twenty or thirty a day."

"Well, that seems like a lot to me. An awful lot. What does it mean when somebody puts an x at the end of a text message?"

She began to look mildly interested. "Is this from your business colleague again?" she asked.

"Yes."

"Let me see."

I passed her the phone, and after reading the message she handed it back to me.

"Hard to say," she admitted. "Depends on what kind of person she is, really."

"Is there no real . . . etiquette to this sort of thing?"

I was pleased with this question, I must say. I was pretty sure that I'd at last hit on a topic we could bond over. If Lucy was texting at the rate of about twenty or thirty messages a day, she ought to be able to talk about it for hours.

"Well, there isn't really, like, an etiquette," she answered. I was disappointed to hear that her tone of voice sounded bored, even disdainful. "You know, it's just a little kiss at the end of a message. It probably doesn't mean anything. In fact, how am I even having this conversation with my own dad? This is too . . . sad for words. This is lame, Dad. It's a kiss, that's all. Take it any way you want." She fell silent and picked at her lasagne.

"OK, I'm sorry, love," I said, after a short, unhappy interval. "I was just trying to find something to chat about, that's all."

"That's all right. I'm sorry too. I didn't want to sound

mean." She sipped her Diet Coke. "Why didn't Mum come out with us tonight, anyway? Are you two not even talking to each other?"

"Of course we're talking to each other. I don't know why she didn't want to come. I think she said she had something on."

"Oh, yeah. Tuesday night. That's writers' night."

"Writers' night?"

"She goes to this writing group. They write stories and stuff and read them out to each other."

Great. So right at this very moment Caroline was wowing an enraptured audience with the hilarious story of Max, Lucy and the nettle pit. She'd probably just got to the bit where I had no idea why the grass was green. I could already hear their smug, appreciative laughter, as clearly as if they were right here in the restaurant with us.

"She's serious about this writing business, then, is she?" I asked.

"I think so. The thing is . . ." She smiled, now, and looked almost conspiratorial. "You see, there's this bloke who goes to the writers' group as well, and I'm beginning to think that she—"

Beginning to think that she what? I could guess, but would never know for certain, because at that moment her BlackBerry started tinkling again.

"Hang on," she said. "I have to look at this."

The message made her scream with laughter, whatever it was. "It's from Ariana," she told me, as if this explained everything. "She's photoshopped this picture—look." She held the screen up to me. It showed a picture of a perfectly ordinary-looking girl.

"Very good," I said. What else was I supposed to say?

"No, but she's put Monica's head onto Jess's body."

"Ah, OK. That's clever."

Lucy started writing her reply, and in the meantime I took out my phone and began tapping out another message to Lindsay. It was probably for the best that I never got around to sending it. So, what stopped me? It was the look on the face of a woman sitting at the table next to ours, and I don't know quite how to describe it. All I can say is that she took in the scene at our table—a weary, middle-aged father taking his daughter out for dinner, the two of them sitting opposite each other with nothing to say, one sending a text, the other playing with her BlackBerry—and she responded with a toe-curling mixture of amusement and sympathy, all contained in that one glance. And in that instant an image came to my mind, again, of the Chinese woman and her daughter sitting opposite each other at that restaurant in Sydney Harbour, laughing together and playing cards. The connection between them. The pleasure in each other's company. The love and closeness. All the things that Lucy and I seemed not to have. All the things I had never been taught how to create between us, by my sad fuck-up of a father.

I sent one more text message that night. Not to Lindsay, though. In fact you'll never guess who I sent it to—so I'll tell you. I sent it to Poppy's uncle, Clive.

I dropped Lucy back home at about 9:30. Caroline wasn't back yet. Lucy took me inside and made me a cup of coffee and sat talking to me (after a fashion) in the kitchen for half an hour or so. When it became obvious that Caroline wasn't exactly rushing home to see me, I decided to call it a day and got back into the car and drove to my Travelodge, which was about ten minutes out of town.

So much for my family reunion, then.

Back in the hotel room, although I was tired, I knew I was too agitated to go straight to sleep. There was nothing on TV so I got Clive's DVD of *Deep Water* out of my suitcase and slotted it into my laptop. I had a weird notion that watching it might somehow cheer me up. You know the cliché "There's always someone worse off than yourself"? Well, in my case, I figured it would be hard to find that someone right now. But there was always a chance it could be Donald Crowhurst.

It was a powerful film. Over the last week, before setting out on this journey, I had been reading *The Strange Voyage of Donald Crowhurst*. I was about halfway through, which was pretty good going for me. The book was really detailed and well researched, but the film took you much further into the story, into the whole atmosphere. It opened with images of enormous waves heaving in the wind-tossed night, and immediately you got a sense of how lonely and scared Crowhurst must have been out there, putting himself at the mercy of the elements; just looking at it made me feel cold and seasick. Then there were shots of the man himself, taken late in his voyage, that showed him toughened and hardened by it: a cruel-looking moustache on his upper lip, his eyes by now guarded and wary. After a few more of these, accompanied by unnerving, portentous music, we flashed back to a scene which at once gave me a shock of recognition: the approach to the harbour at Plymouth, lined with cheering crowds that had turned out to witness the homecoming of Francis Chichester following his solo voyage. (A scene I could still remember watching on TV with my mother, one Sunday evening back in the spring of 1967.) Next up, you got introduced to all the major players in the story: Crowhurst himself; his wife and family; his main competitors, Robin Knox-Johnston and Bernard Moitessier; his sponsor, Stanley Best; and—perhaps most memorably of all—his press agent, Rodney Hallworth. Hallworth was described as a "Dickensian figure," and the description certainly seemed to fit this imposing, fleshy presence, whose avuncular manner barely concealed the clear streak of cynicism and ruthlessness running just beneath the surface. "Many people who do great things are often, as personalities, rather dull," he was heard to declare, blithely. "The press agent's job is to get hold of the package, which could be as dull as an old tin box, and then you've got to dress it up—make it a bit Christmassy—so that it appears attractive." Crowhurst, I supposed, was the "old tin box" in this scenario, and it would be Hallworth's endeavours to exaggerate his qualities, to "dress him up," that would be largely responsible for creating the impossible situation that edged him on towards madness. The film went on to chronicle this process in sympathetic but unsparing detail. You saw the chaos that accompanied his departure from Teignmouth, and how apprehensive he looked when caught off-guard by the camera. (It was at this point, I thought, that his resemblance to my father was most pronounced.) And then, as the voyage progressed, the focus gradually began to shift from the challenging practicalities of sailing single-handed to Crowhurst's diaries, his logbooks, his disturbed scribblings, his disintegrating state of mind. The lingering close-up on his final statement—*"IT IS THE MERCY"*—was especially chilling. When the film was over I felt shaken and drained.

By now it was after midnight. Despite this, I decided to send Clive a message: *Hi there, just watched the Crowhurst film. Absolutely amazing! Thanks so much for lending it to me. Still on my way to Shetland—not there yet.*

I went into the bathroom to brush my teeth. A few minutes later I fell into bed and I was almost asleep when my phone started to sing its familiar tune. Clive had texted me back already: *Glad you enjoyed it! Have a safe crossing and look forward to hearing about your exploits when you get back. X*

I looked at this message—or rather, that final "X"—in some puzzlement. Why was Clive, of all people, sending me a virtual kiss? Coming from Lindsay, I could just about understand it, but *Clive*? I had never, ever in my life received a text message from another man that ended in a kiss. The idea of Trevor, for instance, putting a kiss at the end of one of his texts or e-mails was unthinkable. So what was Clive playing at? I wished that it hadn't been too late to contact Lucy, to ask for her opinion about this. She might at least be able to tell me whether it was normal or not.

Thinking about it made me uncomfortable. At last I started to sink into sleep, but the Crowhurst documentary had left queasy, unsettling images stamped upon my mind. They were still there, swimming before me, as my breathing began to settle. The fall and rise of the waves . . . Crowhurst's face, reminding me more strongly than ever, tonight, of my father's . . . the fall and rise of the waves . . . Rodney Hallworth and his "old tin box" . . . the fall and rise of the waves, and where had I heard that expression before? . . . Rodney Hallworth . . . Lindsay Ashworth . . . the fall and rise . . . Rodney Hallworth . . . Lindsay Ashworth . . . the fall and rise . . . the fall and rise . . .

KENDAL-BRAEMAR

16

"OK, Emma, it's all starting to become clear now. It's all falling into place."

—*Proceed on the current road.*

"I don't know how it's happened, but I seem to be turning into Donald Crowhurst. That's who I'm about to become. Call it fate, call it predestination, call it whatever you like, but it looks like I have no choice in the matter. It's going to happen whether I like it or not."

—*In three-quarters of a mile, right turn.*

We had left Kendal about ten minutes ago and were now driving along the A6 in the direction of Penrith. The weather had taken a turn for the worse, the windscreen now splattered with heavy drops of something between rain and sleet. The road was climbing steadily in a series of curves through wild, verdant countryside.

"Here I am, after all, driving a car meant to be new and innovative and a radical step forward in design—just like Crowhurst's trimaran. It's a sort of modern version of the *Teignmouth Electron*, and I'm at the helm."

As we turned off the A6 towards Junction 39 of the M6, on our left were the vast chimneys of the Corus limestone works, hidden away at the bottom of a long, somehow intimidating private road which gave it the look of a secret military installation. A few minutes later, at the motorway junction, Emma noted:

—Heading left at the roundabout, take first exit.

"And just think who the other characters in his story were. Rodney Hallworth, Stanley Best—do those names remind you of anyone? It all makes sense."

—Exit coming up.

"So what's going on? Have I become sort of . . . possessed by him, or am I just going mad? And if I'm going mad, does that really change anything? Because that could be all part and parcel of me turning into him, couldn't it? What do you think, Emma? What's your advice?"

—Proceed on the current motorway.

Well, yes, that was sensible enough, I suppose. There seemed to be little else I could do, at any rate.

It was getting on for 12:30. After a long bath and a late breakfast at the Travelodge, I had driven back into Kendal and wandered around the town for a little while, trying to enjoy the experience of being in a different part of the country, and to shake off the unaccountable feeling of strangeness, of *foreignness*, that had been creeping up on me for the last couple of days, ever since leaving Watford. I had spent three weeks in Sydney and never noticed this sensation, so why did it now seem as though every new English town that I found myself in was slightly more unreal than the last? Perhaps it had something to do with my growing Crowhurst fixation. I was beginning to feel disconnected from myself: I sometimes had the sense I was standing outside my own body, looking down on it, and even that morning in Kendal there was a moment when it seemed as though I was looking down on the High Street from above and watching myself walking along it with all the other shoppers, like extras in a perfectly composed shot from a film, with these hundreds of insectlike people in the foreground and the huge sweep of the hills forming a distant, painted-in, not-quite-believable backdrop.

Late in the morning I saw Caroline again. She wasn't expecting me, but I decided to surprise her. I knew she was working as the manager of one of the charity shops in the High Street, so I dropped in unannounced, not expecting much more than a curt rebuff but in fact finding myself welcomed far more warmly than I might have hoped. She made me some coffee and took me into the back office and we talked for half an hour or more—mainly about Lucy—and this morning Caroline seemed warm, and kind, and interested in what I was doing, and when I left it wasn't because she wanted me to but because I needed to. Because having her being nice to me like this just made me want to be with her more than ever, and I knew that could never happen again; and in that case the only thing to do was to get out and move on.

—*Proceed on the current motorway.*

Now we were somewhere between Junctions 41 and 42, heading north, and the farther north we went, the thinner the traffic seemed to get. We were averaging sixty-eight miles to the gallon, because here it was easy to drive at a comfortable fifty-five miles per hour without people tailgating you and flashing their lights to make you hurry up. And oddly, despite the fact that it would have been safer to drive fast here than it would a hundred miles south, there weren't so many cars exceeding the speed limit. Everybody seemed more relaxed. Are there statistics to show that drivers in the north of England consume less petrol than their southern counterparts? It wouldn't surprise me at all.

—*Proceed on the current motorway.*

There's not much you can do when you're driving for hours at a moderate speed, other than to notice the few distractions that the motorway throws up—a yellow police notice reporting a "Possible Homicide," exit signs pointing to Penrith, Keswick, Carlisle, a big blue sign saying "Welcome to Scotland / Fàilte gu Alba," a large pine forest planted on a hillside in the shape of a "T," with the shadows of dark rain clouds drifting across it—and to let your thoughts start drifting. It's funny how, when you do that, memories pop into your head, things that you'd forgotten or perhaps suppressed for forty years or more. Today, it was thinking about Francis Chichester that did it. I could remember watching the TV coverage of his homecoming with my mother, but not if my father had been there. And then it came back to me: something odd had happened that night. My father *had* been watching television with us, at first, but then the doorbell rang and he went to answer it, and a few seconds later this strange man came into our house. I say "strange" not just because Mum and I didn't recognise him but because he was . . . well, strange. He was wearing a fancy wide-brimmed hat, for one thing, and the kind of clothes people might have been wearing in Carnaby Street in 1967 but that certainly had never been seen within fifty miles of Rubery. He had a thin, reddish beard, too—that's the only other thing I can picture about him. He didn't come into the living room, and I saw no more of him than the glimpse I caught through the open living room door as Dad led him towards the back of the house. The two of them went into the dining room and started talking while Mum and I carried on watching television. The man must have left after I'd been put to bed, because I don't remember him leaving at all. In fact, as I say, I had forgotten all about his bizarre, unexpected appearance in our house until this very moment, when the memory of it came back to me vividly as I drove with Emma across the border into Scotland and the M6 shaded into the A74(M). And the question I immediately asked myself was this: who could it possibly have been other than the mysterious "Roger," who had sent my father monthly post-cards from the Far East all through the 1970s, and apparently continued to do so even now? I had never been told the visitor's name—of that I was certain; but I was equally certain that it could only have been Roger.

—*Proceed on the current motorway.*

I held on to this peculiar memory for a few moments but found that it was quickly supplanted by more random thoughts. The miles slipped by as we travelled farther into Scotland, and I continued to drive in an almost dreamlike state, miraculously failing to collide with any other cars. At least ten minutes must have gone by before I snapped out of it and realised, with a start, what it was that I'd just been thinking about.

I had been trying to work out the square root of minus one. This wouldn't do at all.

Another solitary lunchtime, another motorway service station, another panino—this time, mushroom and prosciutto with a green-leaf salad.

Abington Services. Welcome Break. I can't help it, I like these places. I feel at home in them. I liked the dark-wood chairs and the light-wood tables, the Habitat look. Very 1990s. I liked the two enormous yucca plants sitting between the tables. I liked the windswept decking area outside, the folded-up sun umbrellas flapping in today's wet breeze. I liked how in the midst of this spectacular rural landscape someone had contrived to create a little oasis of urban ordinariness. I liked the look of pleased expectancy on people's faces as they carried their trays of pizza and fish-and-chips away from the counter of Coffee Primo, confident they were about to tuck into something special. This was my sort of place. The sort of place where I belonged.

Nonetheless, my feeling of slight, palpable unease wouldn't

shift. Was it because I was nervous about seeing Alison? I could always phone her and call it off, although I'd still miss that day's ferry from Aberdeen, however fast I drove from here. But anyway, that wasn't it. Something else was bothering me. Perhaps the weight of all these resurfacing memories.

After I'd finished eating, I booted up my laptop and inserted the little gadget that connected me to the mobile broadband network. I checked my e-mails, and then Facebook. Nothing. As I turned the laptop off I noticed the battery was almost empty.

Feeling guilty that I had barely used it so far, I took the digital video camera outside and shot some footage of the service station and the surrounding mountains. Only about thirty seconds' worth. As before, when I'd taken some film of my father's apartment block in Lichfield, I could sense this wasn't at all what Lindsay would be wanting, that it would probably never make the final cut.

There are also delays on the northbound side of the M6—the problem is a stranded lorry between Junctions 31 and 31A, it was in Lane 3, and there are queues back to Junction 29. Stranded lorry in the roadworks on the M1, northbound after Junction 27 north of Leicester—that's now been recovered. But our problems continue on the M1, which is blocked southbound at Junction 11, which is at Luton— being diverted via the sliproads, queues there, though. Thanks to Mike and Fiona for this one—those folks say it's back to Junction 14, which is Milton Keynes, loads of traffic using the A5 into Dunstable which is now very heavy on that southbound side. Northbound the M1 was closed for a while, to allow an air ambulance to land—it has now landed and taken off, so that road is fully open again. There was a vehicle blocking the M25, Junctions 18 and 17, that's anti-

*clockwise from Chorleywood to Rickmansworth. That's all been
cleared. It's left quite a long delay, in roughly the usual place, but it
seems heavier today—this is anti-clockwise from Junction 23, which
is the A1(M) to Watford at Junction 19. There's also an accident
which has just been picked up from the M25 anti-clockwise from
Junction 5, which is the M26 turn. At Cambridge, there's an accident on the northbound A11, it's closed northbound at Papworth
Everard, that's north of the A428 at Caxton Gibbet . . .*

"Sorry about that, Emma," I said, turning the radio off.
"It's not that I'm getting bored of listening to you, it's just
that—you know, sometimes a man needs a change of scene,
some different company."

—In three-quarters of a mile, slight left turn.

"I knew you'd understand," I said gratefully. Emma's voice
was gracious and calming after the traffic announcer's strident,
hectoring monologue.

Edinburgh was now just a few miles away. According to
the car's information screen, we had travelled only 410 miles
since setting off from Reading two days earlier, but hearing
all those familiar names—Rickmansworth, Chorleywood and
(of course) Watford—made it feel as though we were about
to arrive at a place that was unimaginably remote. Darkness
had already closed in and we were a part of a long line of
cars threading steadily along the A702, a funeral cortège of
tail-lights and occasional brake-lights as far as the eye could
see. A few minutes ago we had passed a sign saying "Welcome to Scottish Borders," and now we passed another saying
"Welcome to Midlothian." It was nice to know that we were
welcome. I wondered if I would be made equally welcome at
Alison's house.

Soon we had crossed the ring road and were driving into
the outer suburbs. Alison lived in an area of Edinburgh known

as the Grange, which I had already guessed would turn out to be quite wealthy. I didn't know what her husband did for a living, exactly, only that he ran a large, successful company with offices in many different parts of the world and spent a lot of his time travelling. All the same, I was surprised when Emma continued to guide me—as though she had known this city all her life—into ever wider, quieter, more sequestered and exclusive streets. Most of the sandstone properties here seemed to be more like mansions than houses. And Alison's, when we pulled up outside it, was by no means the smallest.

—*You have arrived at your destination*, said Emma, betraying no sense of triumph or boastfulness: just quiet satisfaction in a job well done. *The route guidance is now finished.*

17

I never expected to be single at the age of forty-eight. But now that it had happened, and it was obvious Caroline had no intention of coming back to me, I realised I was faced with a very specific problem. Sooner or later, if I didn't want to end up a lonely old man, I was going to have to find myself another partner. The trouble was, younger women (such as Poppy) apparently weren't going to look at me, and I didn't find older women attractive.

Perhaps at this stage I should define "older women." I've been thinking about this, and I reckon an "older woman" is one who's older than your mother was when you were a teenager. Say that you start getting *really* sexually preoccupied—to the point of not being able to think about anything else—at the age of sixteen. (I know it's younger than that for kids nowadays, by all accounts. The Western world is so sexualised that most boys are probably at it by the time they're fourteen or so. And I read in the paper the other day about a woman who was a grandmother at the age of twenty-six. But my generation was different. We were the last of the late developers.) OK, so when I was sixteen, my mother was thirty-seven, and I can tell you now that she appeared *ancient*. It would never have *occurred* to me that she might have had a romantic life, or an internal life, let alone a sex life (except with my father: and now I wasn't even sure about that, if Alison's essay was anything to go by). Sexually and emotionally, she was a non-person, as far as I was concerned. She was there to provide for my physical and emotional needs. I know it sounds shocking, put like that, but teenagers are selfish and self-absorbed, and that was how I saw her. And even now, at forty-eight, I find it hard to come round to the idea that women of my mother's age—OK, then, women of *my* age—can be regarded as sexual beings. Of course this is illogical. Of course this is *wrong*. But I can't help it, and I'm only trying to be honest about it. This, after all, was why I was so mortified on the night of Poppy's dinner party, when I realised that she had only invited me along to meet her mother.

All of which, I suppose, is by way of explaining my feelings when I pressed the electronic security buzzer at Alison's house and she opened the door to me. The last time I had seen her was more than fifteen years ago. And what burned most strongly in my memory was almost twenty years before that, when she was seventeen and my pervy father had taken that photograph of her wearing a tiny orange bikini. And now here she was, standing before me again: as stylish, confident, good-looking and elegant as ever. And fifty years of age. Quite a bit older than my mother had been when I was sixteen and we all went to the Lake District together. Older, for that matter, than my mother had been when she died.

"Max!" she said. "How gorgeous to see you."

She offered me her cheek, and I kissed it. The skin was soft and powdery. I breathed in a distinct but not unpleasant scent, somewhere between honey and rosewater.

"It's lovely to see you too," I said. "You haven't changed a bit." (Isn't this what people are supposed to say, whether it's true or not?)

"What a bit of luck that you should be passing by. And Mum said you were on your way to Shetland, is that true?"

"Yes, that's right."

"How thrilling! Well, come on in!"

She led me through the hallway and into what I took to be one of two or three downstairs sitting rooms. Somehow it managed to combine minimalism and opulence at the same time. There were modern paintings on the walls, thick velvet curtains drawn against the unfriendly night, and different areas of the room were subtly illuminated by hidden spotlights. A large L-shaped sofa with deep, comfortable cushions was arranged around a glass coffee table tastefully strewn with books and magazines. In the hearth, a cheerful fire was burning. I assumed it was a real fire until Alison said, "Is it too hot for you? I'll turn it down if you like."

"No, no. It's perfect. I love a good fire."

I regretted those words as soon as they came out of my mouth. Did she remember the fiasco of that fire in Coniston? Or was I only even thinking of it because of the essay I'd read two days ago? Impossible to tell. Her expression gave nothing away.

"Well then, get yourself good and warm. It's pretty nasty out there, isn't it? They say it might snow later tonight. Can I get you a drink? I'm going to have a G&T."

"Sounds great. Same for me, please," I said, forgetting that I was supposed to be driving us both to the restaurant in a minute.

When Alison returned with the drinks, we sat down on different sides of the L-shaped sofa.

"Nice room," I said, stupidly. "Nice house, actually."

"It is nice," she agreed. "But it's far too big. I've been rattling around in it by myself all week. It's ridiculous, really."

"Aren't the boys here?"

"Both at school. Boarding."

"What about Philip?"

"Away in Malaysia. Possibly back tonight. Possibly not."
She took a breath. "Goodness, Max, you're looking . . . what's
the word?"

"I don't know," I said. "What *is* the word?"

"Well . . . troubled, I suppose. You look a bit troubled."

"I'm quite tired," I said. "I've been on the road for three
days."

"Yes," said Alison. "Yes, that must be it."

"It's been a funny old year," I added. "Did your mother tell
you that Caroline had left me?"

"Yes, she did." Alison reached out and laid a hand on my
knee. "Poor Max. You can tell me all about it over dinner."

While Alison was upstairs making some last-minute adjust-
ments to her appearance, I went outside to get her box full
of papers. It was fiercely cold now, and tiny snowflakes were
beginning to spiral ominously in the night air. When I stepped
back into the hallway with the cardboard box, she looked at me
incredulously.

"What on earth's that?"

"These are yours. Your mum and dad asked me to bring
them up."

"I don't want them."

"Neither do they."

"Well, what are they?"

"University stuff, I think. Where shall I put the box?"

"Oh, just leave it there." She tutted. "They're dreadful.
Fancy making you bring it all the way up here."

She swaddled herself in a fake fur coat and entered a four-
digit security code on some gizmo on the wall before stepping
outside and closing the door behind us. The ground underfoot

was a little slippery already, so she took my arm as we walked to the car. It was nice to have her leaning against me. The texture of her fur coat was strangely comforting.

"Ooh, lovely—a Prius," she said. "Philip and I have been thinking of getting one of these."

I was about to tell her that it was actually the company's, but then thought better of it. For some reason I liked the idea of her thinking I owned it.

The car glided in its usual silent manner through these quiet, dark, secretive streets. The houses seemed massive and imposing, and there were few lights on in any of the windows. We had only been driving for a minute or two and already had passed two police cars—one of them patrolling the streets slowly, the other parked at a kerbside. I mentioned this to Alison and she explained: "There are a lot of concerns about crime round here. You know, this area is full of millionaires—bankers, mostly—and there's a lot of anger directed at these people at the moment. Just along the road there . . ."

She began telling me about some multi-millionaire financial wizard who lived in this street and had been brought in to run one of the major banks but had somehow managed to reduce its assets to nothing while simultaneously walking off with a fortune in personal bonuses and pension payments, though I wasn't listening very carefully. I had already programmed tomorrow's destination into the SatNav, so Emma now seemed to think I was heading to Aberdeen and was directing me accordingly.

—*In two hundred yards, left turn*, she said.

"Hold your horses," I told her. "That's where we're going tomorrow."

"Pardon?" said Alison.

To my embarrassment, I realised that I'd interrupted her

while she was in mid-flow about this recent financial scandal. For a moment, in fact, while Emma was talking to me, I'd almost forgotten that Alison was there.

"Who were you talking to just then?" she asked.

"I'm sorry?"

"It just didn't sound as though you were talking to me, that's all."

"Of course I was talking to you. Who else would I be talking to?"

"I don't know." She gave me a slightly worried, suspicious glance. "Your SatNav?"

"My SatNav? Why would I be talking to my SatNav? That would be a crazy thing to do."

"Yes, it would."

We dropped the subject and drove on to the restaurant.

It was a welcoming, intimate sort of place, located not far from the castle. The snow had more or less petered out when we arrived, but we were still glad to hurry out of the cold into that cosy interior, with its vaulted ceilings and bare stone walls. There were lots of little alcoves where pairs of diners could eat and talk to each other in relative privacy, and our table was in one of these. The waiter seemed to know Alison and was notably attentive and courteous while seating us. After scanning the list of intriguing, locally sourced dishes on the menu, Alison chose a goat's-cheese salad for her starter, while I went for smoked duck. To accompany these, she ordered a French Chardonnay priced at £42.50. Luckily Alison had already offered to pay for the meal. I knew I would have been pushing my luck too far if I'd tried to claim it on expenses.

"So your husband's in the Far East?" I prompted as we sipped the wine, which tasted to me much like the sort you can buy for five pounds at Tesco or Morrisons. "What's he doing out there?"

"Oh, visiting suppliers, I think," said Alison, vaguely. "He has to travel more and more these days. Actually he's on his way back from Australia."

"I've just got back from Australia myself."

"Really? What were you doing there?"

"Visiting my father."

"Oh, of course. I'd forgotten that was where he ended up. How did you find him?"

"He's . . . fine. In good shape."

"No, I mean how did you get on with him? Because my memory is—and this may be wrong—that you were never that close to your father."

I didn't really want to talk about this, to be honest. What I really wanted to do was to get everything out in the open, to blurt out something along the lines of how sorry I was that thirty years ago she'd caught my father having a wank over a picture of her that she'd never wanted him to take in the first place. But somehow it was difficult to find the right words. Perhaps fortuitously, I was rescued at that moment by the ringing of my mobile phone. I looked at the screen and saw that the caller was Lindsay Ashworth.

"I'd better take this," I said.

"Of course."

Alison began to pour us both some more wine. I pressed the answer button on my telephone.

"Hi," I said.

"Ahoy there!" said Lindsay—loudly and somewhat unexpectedly. "Avast, me hearties! Splice the mainbrace and hoist the topsail! How are you coping with life on the jolly old ocean waves, you salty old seadog, you?"

"Excuse me?"

There was a pause. "Max, is that you?"

"Yes."

"Well, what's it like on the boat, then? What's your cabin like?"

"I'm not on the boat. I'm in Edinburgh."

There was a longer, more shocked silence. Also, a noticeable change in Lindsay's tone of voice. "You're *where*?"

"I'm still in Edinburgh."

"What are you doing in Edinburgh?"

"I'm having dinner with an old friend."

"Max," she said, and now I could definitely hear an edge of anger, "what are you *playing* at? You're supposed to be going to the bloody Shetland Isles!"

"I know that. I'm going tomorrow."

"Tomorrow? Trevor and David got to their destinations yesterday. Tony went there and came back in one day!"

"I know that, but you told me there was no hurry."

"Not hurrying is one thing, Max. That doesn't mean you have to treat this journey as an excuse to wander through the country at the firm's expense visiting everybody you know on Facebook."

There was something strange going on here. Why was she suddenly giving me such a hard time? Two days ago she had been supportive and affectionate. Had something changed in the meantime?

"Lindsay, are you OK? Is everything all right? Because I think you're being a bit . . . well, I think you're overreacting a bit."

There was a pause at the other end of the line. Then she

sighed. "Everything's fine, Max. Everything's fine. Just make sure you get there, and do what you have to do, and then get back. OK? Just get on with it."

"Of course. I'll be on the ferry at five o'clock tomorrow. No question."

"Good. That's what I want to hear." She seemed to be on the point of saying goodbye, but asked me one more question: "How's the video diary coming along?"

I hadn't shot anything, needless to say, apart from that footage of my father's block of flats in Lichfield and the service station at Abington. "Fantastic. Well, of course I've mainly been saving it for the boat journey, and the islands themselves. But what I've got so far is pretty good as well."

"Great. I knew I could rely on you, Max."

"Where are you?" I asked. For some reason I had the sense that she wasn't calling from home.

"I'm in the office. Just having a bit of a conference with Alan. Yeah, working late. We've got a few things to . . . iron out."

On that slightly enigmatic note, she hung up. As I put my phone away, I noticed that a little warning sign had come up on the screen to tell me that the battery was almost empty. Better recharge it tonight. Meanwhile, Alison gave me a questioning look as she delicately placed a sliver of beetroot between her teeth.

"That was Lindsay," I explained. "From the head office. Keeping tabs on my progress."

"Or lack of it," said Alison.

I smiled. "Well, there've been quite a few delays so far," I admitted. "Yesterday I saw Caroline again. For the first time since she . . . walked out."

"And how was that?"

For once the right word came easily. "Painful."

For the second time that evening, Alison reached out and touched me, this time laying her hand gently on mine.

"Poor Max. Shall we talk about it? I mean, about why she left? I'd heard a few things, but I don't know if they're true."

"What have you heard? Who from?"

"From Chris, mainly. He said that when they went on holiday with you a few years ago, things were . . . well, a bit tense."

"That's true. It wasn't a very successful holiday. In fact all sorts of things went wrong. Joe had this nasty accident, and—"

"I know. Chris told me all about it."

"Somehow I think he blamed me for it. At any rate, we haven't spoken to each other since."

"I know. He told me." Her voice became lower, more earnest. "Look, Max, can't you and Caroline patch things up? Everyone goes through difficult times."

"Do they?"

"Of course they do. Philip and I are going through one now."

"Really? In what way?"

"Oh, he's always travelling. He barely talks to me when he's here. Can't stop thinking about work. But business is everything with him, I knew that when I married him. That was part of the deal, and I suppose, looking at things from a purely material point of view, I've done very nicely out of it. You know, you have to make compromises. You sometimes have to . . . settle for things. Everybody does it. Couldn't you and Caroline see that? I mean—it's not as if either of you was unfaithful or anything, is it?"

"No, that's true. If that's all it had been about, things would probably have been easier."

"So what *was* it about?"

I took a sip of wine—actually, more of a gulp—while I wondered how to put this. "There was one thing she told me, not long before she left. She said the problem was me. My own attitude, towards myself. She said I didn't *like* myself enough. And that if *I* didn't like myself, other people would find it difficult to like me as well. She said it created a negative energy."

Before Alison had a chance to reply, our main courses arrived. Her fillet of John Dory looked pale and delicate next to my slab of blood-red venison. We ordered another bottle of wine.

"I won't be able to drive after this," I said.

"Take a taxi," said Alison. "You could probably do with a break from driving, after the last couple of days."

"True."

"Why exactly *are* you driving to Shetland, anyway?" she asked.

And so I began telling her about Trevor, and Guest Toothbrushes, and Lindsay Ashworth. I told her about Lindsay's "We Reach Furthest" campaign and the two prizes we were supposed to be competing for. Then I got sidetracked and told her about my detour to Lichfield to see my father's flat, how eerie and desolate it had felt; about Miss Erith, her fascinating stories and her sadness at the passing of the old ways of life; her weird, solemn, almost inexpressible gratitude when I had made her a gift of one of my toothbrushes. I told her, too, about the bin liner full of postcards from my father's mysterious friend Roger, which was now in the boot of my car, and the blue ring binder full of my father's poems and other bits of writing. Then I told her about driving on from Lichfield and stopping in Kendal to see Lucy and Caroline, and how I'd planned to get the ferry from Aberdeen the next day, until her parents had persuaded me to come to Edinburgh instead.

"Well, Max," she said, holding my gaze for a few moments. "I'm glad you came, whatever the reason. It's been too long since we saw each other—even if it's only happened because they steamrollered us into it."

I smiled back, uncertain where this was leading. Rather than responding to everything I had just told her about my journey, it felt as though Alison was getting ready to move the conversation into a different gear altogether.

But then she seemed to think better of it. She arranged her knife and fork neatly on her plate and said, "We're a strange generation, aren't we?"

"How do you mean?"

"I mean that we've never really grown up. We're still tied to our parents in a way that would have seemed inconceivable to people born in the 1930s or 1940s. I'm fifty now, for God's sake, and still feel I have to ask my mother's . . . *permission*, half the time, just to live my life how I want to. Somehow I still haven't managed to get out from under my parents' shadow. Do you feel the same?"

I nodded, and Alison went on:

"Just the other day I was listening to a programme on the radio. It was about the Young British Artists. They'd got three or four of them together and they were all reminiscing about the first shows they'd done together—those first shows at the Saatchi Gallery, back in the late nineties. And not only did none of them have anything interesting to say about their own work, but the main thing they talked about—apart from the fact that they'd all been shagging each other—was how 'shocking' it had been, and how worried they were about what their parents were going to say when they saw it. 'What did your mum say when she saw that painting?' one of them kept being asked. And I thought, you know, maybe I'm wrong, but I'm sure that when Picasso painted *Guernica*, with its graphic depictions of the horrors of modern warfare, the main thing going through his mind wasn't what his mum was going to say when she saw it. I kind of suspect he'd got beyond that some time ago."

"Yes—I've been thinking the same thing," I said, eagerly. "Take Donald Crowhurst: he already had four kids when he set out to sail around the world, even though he was only thirty-six. You're right, people were so . . . so *grown-up* in those days."

"What days?" Alison asked; and I realised, of course, that she had no idea who Donald Crowhurst was.

Perhaps it was a bad idea to start telling her the story. Or rather, it would have been a good idea if I could have stuck to it. But before long, I was no longer telling her about Crowhurst's doomed round-the-world voyage but explaining all the parallels I'd started to see between his situation and mine, and how strongly I was coming to identify with him. And although she didn't seem to understand more than about half of what I was saying, I did notice that she was starting to look even more worried than before.

"What's the matter?" I said. "Why are you looking at me like that?"

"This man Crowhurst," said Alison. "He set out to sail around the world even though he was totally unequipped for it. He realised he couldn't manage it, so he decided to fake the whole thing, and then realised he couldn't go through with that, either, so he went mad and committed suicide—is that right?"

"More or less."

"And now you're starting to identify with this person, are you?"

"A bit, yes." All at once I had the distinct feeling that I was stretched out on a psychiatrist's couch. "Look, I'm not going mad, if that's what you're getting at."

"Don't be silly. It's just that you're clearly tired, you've been spending a lot of time alone, you've even started talking to your SatNav, and tomorrow you're heading off to one of the remotest areas in the country. Can you blame me for hearing a few alarm bells?"

"I'm fine. Really."

"It may have been a long time ago, Max, but I did once qualify as a psychotherapist."

"Yes, I'm well aware of that."

"So I *know* something about what you're going through. I know about depression."

"Well—thank you for your concern."

"Where are you staying tonight?"

"I don't know. I was going to find the nearest Travelodge."

"Absolutely not. Come back home with me. You can sleep in one of the spare rooms."

"So what are you doing, exactly—putting me on suicide watch?"

Alison sighed. "I just think you need a good night's sleep, and a late start in the morning, and maybe a few home comforts along the way."

I tried vainly to think of objections, but all I could come up with was: "My suitcase is in the car."

"Fine. We'll go to the car, get your suitcase, and take a cab back to my place. Nothing could be simpler."

And, put like that, it did sound the most sensible thing to do.

———

In the cab, an unexpected thing happened. We were sitting side by side in the back, a decent number of inches between us, when Alison edged up closer to me, leaned against me, and rested her head on my shoulder.

"Hold me, Max," she whispered.

I put my arm around her. The cab rattled over North Bridge, past the railway station.

"I can still see what you're doing here," I said.

"Mmm?"

"This is some technique you were taught, isn't it, as part of your training? You've wounded my ego, by making me feel as though I need help. Now you're trying to build it up again, by making me feel strong and protective."

She looked up at me. Her eyes glinted teasingly in the dark. Her slightly dishevelled auburn hair would have been close enough to stroke, had I wanted to.

"Nothing of the sort," she said. "It's just that I'm really pleased to see you, and I don't see anything wrong with two old friends, who've known each other since they were kids, giving each other a friendly hug."

It felt like more than a friendly hug to me, but I didn't say so.

"I wonder if Philip will be back," she murmured.

"You're expecting him tonight, aren't you?"

"If he sticks to his schedule, yes."

"Will he mind that I'm here?"

"No. Why should he?"

"Do you miss him when he's away?"

"I get very lonely. I'm not sure that's the same as missing him."

Suddenly, and rather to my own surprise, it occurred to me that it would be nice if Alison's husband didn't come home tonight. I held her a little closer than before, and she nestled comfortably against me. I let my lips brush against her hair and breathed in its warm, inviting scent.

Was it actually going to happen, more than thirty years after it should have happened? Was I going to sleep with Alison at last? Was I being offered one final, redeeming chance? Part of me yearned for this resolution; another part of me started to panic, to look around for excuses. And it wasn't necessary to look very far.

Of course—Alison was married. Married with children. If I wasn't careful, I was about to play the most contemptible role of all: that of homebreaker. For all I knew, this guy Philip might be the nicest, gentlest, most decent man on earth. Utterly devoted to his wife. He would be crushed, devastated, if anyone were to come between them. So what if he spent too much time at work? That didn't make him a bad husband, or a bad father. In fact it made him a good husband and a good father, because his motivation, obviously, was to provide the best possible standard of living for his beloved family, now and in the future. And here I was, planning to turn this paragon of fatherly pride and marital loyalty into a cuckold!

I withdrew my arm from Alison's shoulder and sat up straight. She looked across at me curiously, then sat up as well, tidying her hair and re-establishing those decent inches of space between us. We were almost home, in any case.

Once inside, she took off her coat and led me into the kitchen.

"Do you want a coffee?" she said. "Or something stronger?" When I hesitated, she announced: "I'm having a Scotch."

"Perfect," I said. "I'll have one too."

As she fetched the bottle of Laphroaig and poured the golden liquid into two glasses, I kept glancing across at her and noticing that, for a woman of fifty, she was really in good shape.

She and Caroline made me feel ashamed of myself. When I got home, I would have to start going to the gym. And improving my diet. At the moment I seemed to live off nothing but crisps, biscuits, chocolate and, of course, panini. No wonder I had no muscle tone and a spare tyre. I was a disgrace.

"Cheers," she said, coming towards me with the drinks. We clinked glasses, and drank, and then there was a long moment of expectancy, both of us standing there, in the middle of the kitchen, waiting for something to happen. It was my first opportunity to make a decisive move. I missed it.

Sensing this, Alison turned away, with an air of mild disappointment, and noticed that the wall-mounted telephone was blinking at her.

"One message," she said. "I wonder if that's Philip."

Of course it would be! Philip would be calling from the airport to say that his flight had landed fifteen minutes ago, he was just waiting for his luggage to come round on the carousel and would be home within the half hour. Phoning to say that he had missed her like crazy and was counting the minutes.

She pressed the button, and we both listened to the message.

"Hello, darling," said her husband's voice. "Look, I'm really sorry about this, but the chaps in Thailand are playing silly buggers and now I'm going to have to hop across to Bangkok to see them. With any luck I can get a direct flight from there and it should only set me back a couple of days so I should be back with you on Friday. Does that sound OK? Really sorry, sweetheart. I'll bring you back something nice and try to make it up to you. All right? Take care, darling. See you Friday."

After that, the message ran on for a few seconds. Philip wasn't speaking anymore, though. In fact, it was hard to know why he hadn't hung up more promptly, unless he was particu-

larly anxious that there should be no chance of his wife failing
to notice the ambient noise of the airport in the background
and the sing-song voice of the announcer over the PA system: *"Welcome to Singapore. Passengers in transit are respectfully
reminded that it is forbidden to smoke anywhere inside the terminal
building. We thank you for your cooperation and wish you a pleasant
onward journey."*

18

And so the only remaining obstacle had been removed at last.

There was a beautiful logic, I suppose, to what happened next, as if we had both always known that it would happen one day; as if it were pre-determined. Even so, I'm surprised to find that I can't remember it in any detail. You always expect the defining, most precious experiences in your life to be stamped indelibly on the memory, yet for some reason these often seem to be the first ones to fade and blur. So I'm afraid I couldn't tell you much about the next few hours, even if I wanted to. I forget, for instance, the look that Alison gave me just before putting down her glass and kissing me on the mouth for the first time. (Yes, it was left to her to make that move, in the end.) I forget precisely how it felt when she took me by the hand and led me towards the staircase. I forget the sway of her back and the curve of her body as I followed her up the stairs. I forget how the initial coldness of the unused bedroom turned to warmth as she took me in her arms and clasped me against her. I forget how it felt, after so many long, long years, to have another human body in blissful, loving contact with mine: clothes intervening at first but soon discarded. I forget, now, the texture of her skin, the faint, familiar smell—the smell of homecoming—when my lips touched the back of her neck, the softness of her breasts as I cupped and then kissed them tenderly. I forget the hours that followed, the slow, inevitable rhythms of our lovemaking, how we ebbed and flowed between love and sleep, love and sleep. How we finally woke up in each other's arms, incredulous to find ourselves together—together and inseparable—in the blue light of a wintry Edinburgh dawn. I forget it all. I forget it all.

As for what followed . . .

But listen—you know the end of this story. Or at least, now that it's finished, now that Alison and I are together, and happy, now that the whole nightmare of what came before is over and done with, then the story has served its purpose. No need to carry on spilling words on to paper. If we all lived in a state of perfect happiness—no conflicts, no tensions, no neuroses, anxieties, unresolved issues, monstrous personal or political injustices, none of that rubbish—then all the people who run to stories for consolation all the time, they wouldn't need to do that anymore, would they? They wouldn't need art at all. Which is why I don't need it, and neither do you, from this point on: you don't need to read about the plans Alison and I made that morning, you don't need to hear any of the boring practical details about her separation and divorce, or how we moved into a house in Morningside together a few months later, or how long it took me to get used to having two teenage stepsons, how wary and mistrustful they were of me at first until we took them on our first holiday as a family, to Corsica, and somehow it all got resolved, the resentment and bad feeling seeming to evaporate under the Mediterranean sun, and . . .

Well. As I say, you don't need to know any of that. None of it is true, in any case.

19

No, none of it is true, but you know what? I think I'm finally beginning to get the hang of this writing business. In fact, I might even follow in Caroline's footsteps and make another attempt to get that Watford writers' group started up. I reckon some bits of that last chapter were every bit as good as her effort about our holiday in Ireland. Did you like how, when I was describing the sexy bits, I started every sentence with "I forget"? That's good writing, that is. It took me quite a while to come up with that idea.

And I did enjoy it, I must say. I never knew that making things up could be so satisfying. I did enjoy my little fantasy about Alison, and our night of passion, and our subsequent life together. For a while there it almost felt that I was back in her house, back in her bedroom, that it was really happening, instead of the awful, miserable, predictable fucking truth, which was this:

That I stood there like a block of marble while she did her best to come on to me.

That she eventually gave up, and went upstairs with the words, "I've got a feeling I'm wasting my time here, but just in case, Max, I'm going to leave my bedroom door open."

That I finished my glass of whisky and about ten minutes later went into the hallway where I'd left my suitcase.

That I realised I didn't know which bedroom I was supposed to be sleeping in, so I went into the sitting room and sat down on the L-shaped sofa and stayed there for a long while with my head in my hands.

That I finally decided I might as well crash out on the sofa and flipped open my suitcase to look for my sponge bag but found myself taking out my father's blue ring binder instead.

That I glanced through the poems but as usual couldn't understand a word of them.

That I stared for some time at the title page of the second section, *The Rising Sun: A Memoir,* knowing that I wasn't going to like what I found in there.

That I heard the sounds of Alison padding about upstairs, getting ready for bed.

That I waited for the sounds to stop, and then drank some more whisky, and then waited another ten or fifteen minutes, and then went upstairs to use the bathroom, and then listened outside her open bedroom door to her soft, regular, sleepy breathing which I could hear quite clearly in the almost-silence of the house, and then tiptoed back downstairs and picked up the ring binder and stared at the title page again.

That the last thing I can remember is hearing a car drive by in the snow-dusted street outside, breaking the stillness of the night.

And that I then started to read.

AIR

June 1987

Last week I was obliged to visit the Strand, in central London, to complete the final paperwork for my departure to Australia; and now, in a few days' time, I shall be leaving this country at last—perhaps never to return. In the meantime, my trip to London has stirred up some very potent memories, which I feel compelled to set down on paper before I leave.

It did not take as long as I'd expected to complete the formalities at Australia House. After which, finding myself with most of an afternoon to spare, I decided to take a walk into the City. For old times' sake, if nothing else. I had brought my camera with me—my trusted Kodak Retina Reflex IV, bought in the 1960s, which has never taken a bad picture yet—and wanted to make a permanent record of those places which had once been so familiar to me—if any trace of them still remained.

As I made my way in blazing sunshine down Fleet Street, up Ludgate Hill, through the long shadow cast by St. Paul's Cathedral and along Cheapside until I could glimpse the massive portico of the Bank of England itself, I realised that it was almost thirty years since I had last walked these streets. Twenty-seven years, to be precise. Everything had changed, in the meantime. Everything. The old City of London, which had been the centre of my universe for a few intense, troubling months towards the fag-end of the 1950s, had witnessed a revolution which even in those far-off days had been considered long overdue. A revolution in architecture, in fashion and now, finally—or so one read in the newspapers—in working practices. All the fine, arrogant old buildings were still there—the Guildhall and the Mansion House, the Royal Exchange and St. Mary-le-Bow—but wedged in amongst them were dozens of new tower blocks, some dating from the benighted 1960s, others only a couple of years old, vaulting, sleek and glittery, like the decade we were now enjoying. The men (there were still not very many women) all wore suits, but sharper, more aggressive suits than the ones I remembered, and there wasn't a single bowler hat to be seen. As for the working practices . . . well, nearly all of the trading was done on screens now, if reports were to be believed. The face-to-face meetings, the chummy handshakes on the Stock Exchange floor, were consigned to the past. No more deals adumbrated over port and cigars at the Gresham Club; no more business gossip swapped in well-bred undertones at the George and Vulture. Traders apparently took lunch at their desks these days—cellophane-wrapped sandwiches brought in at silly prices by outside caterers—and never lifted their glazed eyes from the screens where figures flickered their ceaseless announcements of profit and loss, from early morning to late at night. What role could I possibly have played, as an ignorant twenty-one-year-old, in this frantic and impatient new world?

Yes, I had been only twenty-one when I first came to London. In the last few weeks of 1958, this was. I had not been to university, and for two years had tucked myself away in the tedious anonymity of a filing clerk's job in Lichfield, but some dormant mutinous impulse—my youthful horror, I suppose, at the thought of being stifled like this forever—had finally propelled me away from the safety of my home town and my parents' house and sent me to London—to seek my fortune, as the cliché would have it. Or, if not my fortune, something even more elusive and intangible—my vocation, my destiny. For I had—without telling my family, nor would I have told my friends, if I'd had any—started writing. Writing! Such presumption, if my parents had known about it, would not have been tolerated. My father would have mocked me mercilessly, especially if he were to discover that my instincts inclined me towards poetry: and not just poetry but, worse still, "modern" poetry—that apparently formless, apparently meaningless cultural aberration that was hated above all other things by the middle-brow lower classes. Lichfield, the birthplace of Samuel Johnson, was certainly no place for an aspiring poet in the 1950s; whereas, if rumours were to be believed, London was awash with poets. I envisaged long, wine-fuelled conversations with fellow poets in the bed-sitting rooms of South London suburbs; heady evenings spent in Soho pubs listening to poetry readings in an atmosphere thick with Bohemianism and cigarette smoke. I imagined a life for myself in which I could make the momentous declaration "I am a poet" without attracting incredulity or ridicule.

I have a long story to set down, so I must move it forward. Easily enough, I found a room in a shared house near Highgate Cemetery, and—through the classified advertisements in the *London Evening News*—a temporary job as messenger boy for the stockbroking firm of Walter, Davis & Warren. Their offices were in Telegraph Street, and a large part of my job involved carrying mail by hand to and from the central clearing point for Stock Exchange Member firms in Blossoms Inn:

a system which allowed for all settlement transfers and cheques to be delivered within the same day. (Such a thing would not be necessary now, of course, with faxes and electronic transfers.) I was allowed one hour for lunch, between 1 and 2 p.m., and most days I would take it at Hill's, an old-fashioned City restaurant near Liverpool Street Station, where—if you didn't mind the green-tiled walls that made it look somewhat like a public lavatory—you could dine on steak and kidney pudding, mashed potatoes and apple crumble for something in the region of half a crown.

Dining alone is a problematic activity. I had no friends in the City, or indeed anywhere in London, and no one to talk to over lunch. Most days, therefore, I would take a book with me—usually a slim volume of contemporary verse, more than likely borrowed from the library in Highgate. The restaurant would be crowded, and you might find yourself sharing a table for six with five strangers. One day, early in January 1959, I looked up from my book—it was Eliot's *Four Quartets*—and found a bearded man of about my own age staring at me intently. His fork was poised over a plate of liver and onions, but instead of eating he fixed his eyes on me and declaimed, in a loud and perfectly modulated voice:

> *Time present and time past*
> *Are both perhaps present in time future,*
> *And time future contained in time past.*
> *If all time is eternally present*
> *All time is unredeemable.*

The other diners at our table looked across at both of us in some puzzlement. One of them may even have tutted. To speak to a stranger in such a loud voice, in a public place, and to make use of such peculiar phraseology, was no doubt considered a grave breach of City protocol. For my own part, I was dumbstruck.

"Tell me, do you consider Mr. Eliot to be a genius," my new acquaintance continued, in an insolent tone, "or a fraud and a humbug of the first water?"

"I . . . I don't know," I stumbled. "Or at least . . . well"—more boldly, now—"that is to say, in my view . . . for what my view is worth . . . I consider him . . . the greatest living poet. In the English language, that is."

"Good. I'm pleased to find myself sitting opposite a man of taste and refinement."

The man held out his hand, and I shook it. Then he introduced himself: his name was Roger Anstruther. We talked a little more about Eliot, touching also, I seem to remember, on the work of Auden and Frost, though what I recall best about that first conversation was not its substance, but the strange sort of electric thrill which coursed through me in the presence of this singular and overbearing man. His hair had a slightly reddish tint, his beard was thin and closely trimmed, and although the sobriety of his suit marked him out unmistakably as a working denizen of the Square Mile, a yellow handkerchief with pale blue polka dots protruded from his top pocket in a manner that suggested some idiosyncratic sense of personal style—if not actual foppishness.

Abruptly, at a quarter to two, he rose to his feet and looked at his watch. "Well then," he said. "They are playing Fauré at the Wigmore Hall tonight. The Quartet in E-Minor among other works. I have booked two tickets for the front row, where I intend to lose myself in delicious mists of French introspection. Here is the other ticket. We shall meet at the Cock and Lion, a few doors along the street, at seven o'clock. If you get there first, mine will be a large gin and tonic, with ice. Goodbye."

He shook my hand again, draped a long, black cashmere overcoat over his shoulders, and was gone with a flourish. I gazed after him in shocked silence. But when the shock had receded, my predominant emotion was a throbbing, delirious happiness.

Roger Anstruther was, it goes without saying, completely unlike any other man I had ever met in my short, circumscribed life.

Music was his passion and, although he did not perform, his knowledge of the classical repertoire, from the baroque period to the present day, was flawless and comprehensive. But he could also discourse, with absolute authority, on any other branch of the arts. Architecture, painting, drama, the novel— there seemed to be nothing he hadn't read, seen, heard and thought about. And yet he was only one year older than me. How had he acquired so much knowledge and experience—and *confidence*, of course—in such a short span of time? The discrepancies between us (magnified as they were by Roger's grandiloquent, teacherly, sometimes arrogant, sometimes downright bullying manner) could only make me feel more insular, provincial and poorly educated than I had felt before.

So, at any rate, began what I consider to have been my real education. From now on, Roger and I would go out together almost every night. Orchestral concerts at the Royal Festival Hall; experimental theatre in Soho and Bloomsbury; the National Gallery; Kenwood House; poetry readings in windowless basements or the upstairs rooms of shabby Hampstead pubs. And when we could find nothing of that sort to interest us, we would simply walk—walk through the mazy, empty back streets of London long into the night, while he pointed out strange architectural features, quirky buildings, forgotten landmarks with some recondite fragment of history attached to them. Once again, his knowledge seemed inexhaustible. He was enthusiastic, opinionated, fascinating, indefatigable and infuriating, in equal measure. He could be frivolous and loveable; he could also be impatient and cruel. He dominated me completely. It was a relationship which (at first) suited both of our needs perfectly.

Many of our evenings together started directly after work, in a pub called the Rising Sun in Cloth Fair, close to Smithfield Market. I would usually get there first, shortly after five o'clock, and buy Roger his gin and tonic while waiting for him to arrive. I had discovered that he worked on the Stock Exchange floor, but not in as exalted a capacity as I might have imagined. He was what used to be known as a "Blue Button"—someone at the very lowest level of the trading hierarchy. Essentially he was, like me, an errand boy, although he was certainly closer to the centre of things than I would ever be. The men who actually traded in shares on the Exchange floor were known as jobbers: they were not allowed to deal directly with members of the public, so they took their orders from the brokers, many of whom had little offices (or "boxes") on the periphery of the floor. The Blue Buttons were intermediaries between the brokers and the jobbers: they carried messages, relayed instructions and were generally required, during trading hours, to do whatever their jobber instructed them to, however trivial or eccentric. I couldn't help thinking that for someone of Roger's preternatural intelligence (as I thought of it) and lofty ambition, this job was rather on the demeaning side.

"Well, I won't be at it for long," he told me one evening

as we sat over our drinks in the Rising Sun, a fug building up inside while flurries of snow continued to swirl along Cloth Fair in the January wind. "My disillusionment with the world of high finance is more or less complete."

These were grand words, you might think, for a man of twenty-two. But this was the tone in which Roger always expressed himself.

"I always knew that the Stock Market would be a frightful place," he continued. "But I'd also noticed that the people who worked there—while they invariably seemed to be dreadful bores—never gave the impression of being short of money. Of course, for a lot of them, it's all inherited from Mummy and Daddy. Most of the brokers have been to Eton—and half the jobbers as well—and we all know that kind of education doesn't come cheap. But still, they're making a show of opening the place up to grammar-school boys like me, and I reckoned that if I at least got a sense of how large amounts of cash tend to be traded back and forth, then surely some of it would come my way eventually. But I think I was being naive. And besides, I don't have the temperament for it. I don't love money enough to want to spend my whole life thinking about it. That's where I differ from Crispin, you see."

Crispin Lambert was, I knew, the name of the jobber for whom (or with whom, as Roger preferred to phrase it) he had been assigned to work.

"How do you get on with him?" I asked.

"Oh, well enough," he said. "He's decent, I suppose, by the wretched standards of this place. But he's just a typical product of the system, really. Charm personified, on the surface. If you ever meet him, you'll think he's the friendliest fellow you've ever set eyes upon. But that's just a mask for his fundamental ruthlessness. He loves money more than anything else, and he wants money, and he'll use any means at his disposal to get it. That's what I mean when I say these people are all such bores. For me, money is a means to an end. I'd use it to travel. To see the world in style. I'd like to be able to afford good seats at the opera. I'd like to own a Picasso or two. But for Crispin and his ilk, money *is* the end. Their aspirations stop there. Well, I'm sorry, but to me that's just a tedious view of the world. Shallow. Superficial. Nothing to it. I mean, what actually goes on inside the heads of people like that? Where's their inner life?"

"Doesn't he have, you know . . . pastimes? Hobbies, recreations?"

"He's a fiend for the horses," Roger admitted. "Studies the form assiduously. Knows the name of every trainer at every stable in the country. But I'm not sure it gives him any *pleasure*. He simply bets to win. It's all about the money again, you see."

As it happened, I did meet Crispin Lambert a few weeks later, by which time various subtle but disquieting shifts had taken place in my relationship with Roger. For one thing, I'd had my first experience of his facility—one might almost call it a relish—for creating embarrassing situations. We had attended a production of *Titus Andronicus* where the entire play was performed in modern dress and set in the offices of a local council building in Stockton-on-Tees. This innovation had been greeted with some approval from the newspaper reviewers, but Roger was noticeably unimpressed. Twenty minutes into the performance, he stood up and declared, at the top of his voice: "I see that we are being bamboozled, ladies and gentlemen, by talentless oafs. These cretins are dragging our greatest playwright through the mire, and I will not stand for it a moment longer. Anyone who wishes to join me in making a swift exodus to the nearest pub is more than welcome. Come, Harold." On this occasion he was wearing—as was often his way—a black, silk-lined cape which he swirled around himself in the most effective and compelling gesture before stumbling out over the legs of the other audience members in his row, dragging me after him while everyone (including the actors) looked on in outraged astonishment. To me, prone as I was to an attitude of deference and self-effacement whatever the circumstances, this was frankly a mortifying experience. My cheeks flamed under the knowledge that hundreds of pairs of eyes were fixed on us, whereas Roger, I'm sure, savoured the moment. He liked nothing more than to be the centre of attention. Afterwards, as we were sitting in the pub, he laughed heartily. "Someone had to show those idiots up for what they were," he said. "Everyone else would just have sat there like a flock of hypnotised sheep." Then, observing that I was upset and embarrassed by the whole episode, he began to chide me for my timidity. "Harold, you lack spirit," he said. "You are too cowed by inhibitions, which make you afraid not only to speak your own mind but even to look inside and find out what's really in it. Your sort will do anything to preserve the status quo. With that sort of attitude, I'm afraid, you will never amount to anything."

This sentiment was to be expressed several times during our friendship. It next happened after I had made the mistake of showing Roger some of my own poetry, an act of presumption on my part which led to a most painful evening together—the first time I ever spent with Roger when for a while I really believed I hated him, and wished him dead. As usual, we were in the Rising Sun, where we had been sitting for more than an hour and a half, while he lectured me on ancient British pagan rituals (the latest field to have attracted his fickle, quicksilver interest) without alluding once to the precious manuscript I had put into his hands two days earlier in an anonymous A4 manila envelope. Finally, during a brief interlude in his mono-

logue, my patience deserted me and my curiosity would wait
no longer.

"Have you read them?" I blurted out.

He hesitated, swirling the gin around in his glass. "Oh
yes," he said at last. "Oh yes, I've read them all right."

The subsequent pause seemed to go on forever.

"Well? What did you think?"

"I thought . . . I thought it probably best, on the whole, if I
didn't say anything."

"I see," I said—not seeing at all, but feeling very wounded
all the same. "Didn't you have any criticisms to make?"

"Oh, Harold, what would be the point?" Roger sighed
heavily. "You have no poetry *in* you, that's the problem. No
poetry in your soul. The soul of a poet is a floating, airy thing.
You are earthbound. Of the earth."

He regarded me almost kindly as he said this, and clasped
me by the hand. It was an extraordinary moment: our first
instance of real physical contact, I believe (after seeing each
other for so many weeks!), which sent such a pulse of exhilaration through my body that I could almost feel the blood
tingling through it, as if a circuit had been completed at last.
And yet, at the same time, I felt an absolute revulsion: my
fury at his rejection, at the sheer contempt in which he clearly
held my attempts at verse, was so strong that I could not speak,
and withdrew my hand sharply after only a second or two had
gone by.

"I'll get some more drinks," he said, rising to his feet. And
I was sure I could glimpse an almost daemonic smile in his eye
as he looked back over his shoulder at me and carelessly asked:
"Same again?"

———

I was in thrall to Roger. However cruel he was to me, I could not escape him. I had made very few other friends in London, and besides, his personality was so much stronger than mine that I accepted even his severest criticisms of me and believed them to be well founded. We continued with our schemes of pleasure and self-improvement. But he didn't take me by the hand again, not for quite a while.

A recurrent feature of our conversations was our plan to take a long trip together, at some unspecified time, through France and Germany and thence down to Italy, to visit Florence, Rome and Naples, and to view the splendours of the ancient world. Like all of Roger's schemes, it was grandiose. He would never contemplate a quick journey there and back by rail. There were many places he wanted to see en route; and he even began to talk about returning along the Italian and French rivieras, with a possible detour to Spain. The whole excursion, he said, if carried out properly, would take a number of months and cost several hundred pounds. And so the main obstacle facing us was both entirely predictable and seemingly intractable: a serious lack of funds.

The germ of a solution presented itself, however, early one evening in March as we were making our way towards the bar of the Mermaid Theatre, where we were intending to have a drink and perhaps see the performance afterwards. As we strolled together down Carter Lane, we passed a tall City gent in his pin-striped suit and bowler hat walking in the other direction. Roger stopped in his tracks and looked after him as he ambled by.

"That's Crispin," he said. "Come on, let's go and have a word. I'll introduce you to him."

"Will he be pleased to see us?" I asked, somewhat nervously.

"Horrified, I should think. That'll be half the fun."

Crispin had disappeared through the door of a pub which also, I noticed, went by the name of the Rising Sun, despite being less than a mile from our regular haunt in Cloth Fair. We found him standing at the bar, bent in deep thought over the pages of the *Sporting Life*.

"Good evening, Mr. Lambert," said Roger, in a deferential tone I had never heard him use before.

"Roger!" He looked up, thoroughly startled. "Good gracious. I didn't know this was one of your watering holes."

"One of many, Mr. Lambert, one of many. Allow me to introduce my friend, Harold Sim."

"Charmed, I'm sure," he said, extending a lukewarm handshake. He hesitated, waiting for us to move away. But we stayed where we were. "Well . . . ," he said, after an awkward silence, "I suppose you gentlemen will be wanting a drink?"

Once we'd had a few drinks together, Crispin Lambert turned out to be amiable enough, not that I took a very active role in the conversation. He and Roger soon fell to discussing their work on the Stock Exchange floor, and I found myself lost in a thicket of financial jargon of which I had not the least understanding. My mind drifted off and I began thinking of other things. Some lines of a sonnet occurred to me and I wrote them down in my notebook. I took no further notice of my companions, in fact, until several minutes later, when I realised that Roger was addressing me directly.

"Well," he said, "that sounds an interesting proposition. What do you say, Harold—shall we pool our resources and give it a try?"

I knew that they had been discussing, among other things, the prospects of a particular horse running in the 3:30 at Newmarket that Saturday, so I assumed at first that Roger was suggesting a bet. But it turned out to be rather more complicated than that.

"Mr. Lambert has already placed his bet," he explained, holding up a crumpled piece of paper with a bookmaker's scrawl across it. "This is the betting slip, and what he is proposing is that he sells *us* the right to buy it from him in the future. What he wants to sell us, in effect, is an option on the bet."

"An option?"

"Yes. You see, he's really being very decent about it. He's placed five pounds on a horse called Red Runner to win, at odds of 6 to 1. Now, you and I can't afford that kind of stake, obviously. But what he's suggesting is that we pay him one pound now for the right to buy the betting slip from him for twenty pounds—*after* the race has been run."

"Twenty pounds? But we don't have twenty pounds."

"Well, we'll just have to borrow it. You see, at that point we can't lose. We only have to buy the slip off him if the horse has won—by which time it will be worth thirty pounds. So even if we buy it for twenty, plus the original pound we've paid for the option, then we've made nine pounds profit. And the only thing we're risking is our original one pound."

"I still don't get it. Why don't we just place a bet ourselves?"

"Because this way we stand to make more money. If we just bet one pound at 6 to 1, we'd only make five pounds profit. As opposed to making almost twice as much."

"It's what we call leverage," Mr. Lambert explained.

My head was still swimming. "But surely this means you will be out of pocket yourself?"

Mr. Lambert smiled. "You leave me to worry about that."

"Believe me," said Roger, "he wouldn't be doing it if he stood to lose any money on the deal. I'm sure he's thought it through."

"Precisely," said Crispin. "The fact is that I already have

another each-way bet on this race, with a different book-maker. So really, you understand, I have nothing to lose by this arrangement, and might even gain by it. In fact, everybody gains by it."

"So come on, Harold—what do you say? We stand to make nine pounds. That would make a good start to our European fund."

"True."

"Well then, stump up the money, there's a good chap."

I wasn't too happy about being the sole contributor—this had not, as I understood it, been part of the arrangement—but it seemed Roger only had five shillings with him at the time. I handed Mr. Lambert a crisp, green one-pound note—not by any means an inconsiderable sum, for me, in those days. In return, he scribbled some words on a sheet of paper torn from his pocket book, signed the document, and passed it over to my friend.

"There," he said. "Now it's all strictly legal. Let's settle up on Monday morning, and hope for a satisfactory outcome all round." With that he drained his glass and took his leave, waving a cheery goodbye from the door of the pub as he did so.

Roger smiled and clapped me on the back. "Well, today was our lucky day," he said. "Another round?"

"I'm not sure about this," I said, frowning into the remains of my beer. "There has to be a catch. And anyway, nine pounds isn't going to get us to Naples and back."

"True," said Roger, "very true. But we've made a good start. And besides, I've thought of something else. I'll go up and see my sister at the weekend."

"How will that help?" I asked.

"She's filthy rich, that's how. Married the boss of a big

chemical engineering firm a couple of years ago. I shall pop up there on Saturday afternoon, play the part of the devoted younger brother to the hilt, stay the night, and ask her for a little loan in the morning."

"A loan?"

"Or an advance—that's how I shall put it. An advance on the fabulous book I shall write about the archaeological sites of Northern and Southern Europe. I shall invite her to invest in the brilliance of her brother. How does that sound? These people like to talk of investments."

Roger's enthusiasm was infectious sometimes, there was no denying that. "It sounds just fine," I said, and by way of celebration he stood me a whisky chaser with my next pint of beer.

When I saw Roger at Hill's Restaurant on Monday lunchtime, he brought good news and bad. Red Runner had come in first, which meant that we could exercise our option on Crispin's betting slip and collect the winnings—thirty pounds on his five-pound stake, less the twenty pounds we owed him and the one pound for the option, leaving us nine pounds in profit. Very satisfactory. Less satisfactory, on the other hand, was the outcome of Roger's approaches to his sister.

"Let this be a warning to you, Harold," he said gravely, "that women are not to be trusted, or relied upon. In fact, one should not even take the slightest notice of the selfish, small-minded creatures. Harriet showed not the least interest in our expedition, or in the book which I told her might come out of it. Her horizons are simply too . . . *limited* to take in the importance of what we're proposing to do. She focuses entirely on her own tiny, trivial, domestic concerns."

"Such as?"

"Oh, this baby she's going to have. It was all she could talk about."

"Ah. Well, I can see how that might seem—"

"Harriet's always been like this, you know. I'd forgotten what she was like. I'd forgotten how much I hated her."

"When is the baby due?" I asked, rather shocked by his language.

"I wasn't going to flatter her sense of self-importance by asking her questions like that. Come on, let's get some fresh air."

We left the tiled gloom of the restaurant behind us and spent the rest of our lunch hour in the pleasant green space of Finsbury Circus, a short walk away. It was now early in March, and just about warm enough to sit outside reading a book in the weak sunshine. I had with me a copy of *The Hawk in the Rain*, the first collection of Ted Hughes, then a little-known poet. Roger was reading his well-thumbed edition of *Witchcraft Today*, by Gerald Gardner. This sensational volume had been published about five years earlier and had attracted considerable attention, especially in the popular Sunday newspapers which liked to titillate their readers with the notion that modern witches' covens existed the length and breadth of suburban England, where sex orgies and acts of naked devil-worship regularly took place behind respectable closed doors. Roger dismissed these reports as lurid fantasies and insisted, on the contrary, that Mr. Gardner's book was one of the most important publications of recent times: he maintained that it had uncovered a vital, authentic spiritual heritage which stretched far back into the pre-Roman era and provided a valuable counter-tradition to the repressive authoritarianism of the Christian Church. Mr. Gardner's name for this alternative religion was "Wicca," and its main characteristic was that it involved the worship of two gods, or rather a god and a goddess, represented respectively by the sun and the moon. Not being much inclined towards religious belief of any sort, I tended not to listen too closely when Roger was expounding on this theme, although I do remember what he said to me that afternoon in Finsbury Circus. "You should pay attention to this, Harold, if you're serious about wanting to write. The Goddess is where all poetic inspiration comes from. Read Robert Graves if you don't believe me. You'd better keep on the right side of her. Unfortunately"—he put the book down and lay back on the grass, his head resting on folded hands— "she absolutely disapproves of homosexuality, and has terrible punishments in store for those who practise it. Bad news for the likes of us."

I said nothing, but a shiver of protest went through me when I heard this remark, which was thrown out casually, as if merely the statement of an obvious truth. I knew Roger sometimes took pleasure in being foolishly provocative. It was also this afternoon, I remember, that he first mentioned his intention to place a malediction on his sister.

Meanwhile, Roger did not neglect the more material side of our affairs. Over the next few weeks, he came to a series of further financial arrangements with Crispin Lambert and his numerous bookmakers, each one more ambitious and elaborate than the last. I heard talk of each-way bets, four-folds and accumulators. Then we were on to any-to-come bets, fives-pots, pontoons and sequential multiples. Each one of these bets was recorded on a betting slip: Crispin would calculate what this slip might be worth if the race had the desired outcome, and would then sell us an option to buy the slip off him when the result was announced. Somehow—I presumed because

Roger and Crispin were accurate in their calculations, and in their study of the horses' form—we seemed to make a profit every time, and everybody came out of it a winner. Soon we became bolder, and the agreements we signed no longer gave us the *option* of purchasing Crispin's betting slips when the race was over, but imposed on us the *obligation* to do so. We chose to do this because the terms he offered us were more favourable, even though the risk involved (on our side) was much greater. Steadily, however, our travelling fund grew larger and larger. Roger became increasingly excited about the prospect of giving up our jobs and embarking on this voyage, until he could barely talk about anything else: it became his absolute obsession. The cultural pleasures on offer in London seemed to have palled, as far as he was concerned, and we rarely went to concerts or the theatre anymore. Instead, if we were not poring over maps of Pompeii and drawings of ancient German burial mounds, he preferred to stay indoors and study his growing library of volumes on witchcraft and paganism. And somehow, subtly, indefinably, although our trip was still talked about as very much a shared endeavour, I felt the closeness between us beginning to slip away, was more and more conscious that I had somehow disappointed him, failed to meet his expectations, and this realisation upset me deeply.

Then, one day in the middle of the week, he came to me with a proposal which caused me some alarm.

"I was with Crispin most of last night," he said, "in the Rising Sun. He's a very decent fellow, I think. He really wants to help us raise the money for this trip. Anyway, last night we worked out a way we could do it—all in one fell swoop. By Saturday evening, the money could be ours. We could hand in our notice next week and be on the train to Dover within a fortnight. What do you say?"

Naturally, I said that it all sounded wonderful. But I was less enthusiastic when he told me what he had in mind.

The proposal, in fact, was for one single, gigantic bet—or rather, a phenomenally complex spread of bets—to be placed with five bookmakers on Saturday's races. I cannot remember the details now (not surprisingly, since I could never really understand them then), but among the different terms being floated were "single stakes about," "round robin," "vice versa," "the flag," and "full-cover multiples." As before, it was Crispin who had chosen the horses, calculated the odds, placed the bets, and bundled the whole package up into one financial instrument—the usual signed piece of paper, taken from his pocket book—which he was now offering to sell to us for . . .

"For *how much*?" I said to Roger, incredulous.

"I know it sounds a lot—but the winnings will be *five times* that, Harold. Five times!"

"But that's the whole of our fund. Everything we've saved up so far. All the sacrifices we've made to put that money together . . . Supposing we lose it all?"

"We can't lose it all. That's the beauty of it. If we were just to place that money in a single bet, like most punters would do, then of course we'd be taking a huge risk. But the system Crispin and I have worked out is much cleverer than that. It's flawless—look." He handed me a sheet of foolscap paper, on which were written a series of calculations and mathematical formulae far too complicated for me (or any other averagely intelligent being) to comprehend.

"But if this system worked," I objected, "everyone would be doing it."

"If they had the brains to work it out, yes."

"What are you saying? That you've found a way of making money out of nothing? Out of air?"

Roger smiled a proud, secretive smile as he took the paper back. "I've told you this before," he said. "You, Harold, are earthbound. You need to develop a more spiritual outlook. Don't become one of those lesser mortals who inhabits the material world. The world where people spend their lives making things and then buying and selling and using and consuming them. The world of objects. That's for the hoi polloi, not the likes of you and me. We're above all that. We're alchemists."

It was when Roger began to talk like this, I'm ashamed to say, that I found him most irresistible—even when I knew I was being controlled and manipulated. It was with a sinking heart, all the same, that I agreed to hand over our entire fund (and rather more) to Crispin in return for his promise to sell us, in a few days' time, the betting slips which both he and Roger assured me would by then be worth a fortune. A sinking heart, and a hollow, nervous feeling in the pit of my stomach.

"Will you telephone me on Saturday?" I asked. "To let me know the outcome—not that it's in any doubt, of course."

"Telephone you? Why on earth would I do that? You'll be with me, surely."

"I was planning to visit my parents," I explained. "It is the Easter weekend, after all."

"Oh, don't talk such nonsense," he said, with an impatient wave of his hand. "Haven't you learned anything from me in the last few months? Must you always run for cover to the safety of those silly bourgeois, Christian values that your family drummed into you from an early age? These Christian festivals are just a sham—a pale shadow of the real thing. You're coming with me this weekend to discover what Easter is *really* about."

"Coming with you? Where?"

"To Stonehenge, of course. We'll drive down late on Saturday night. We have to be there before dawn—that's when the ceremony will begin."

He went on to explain, carefully, as if to an imbecile child, that the Christian story of the resurrection of the Lord Jesus Christ was in fact nothing more than a corruption of much older and more powerful myths concerning the rising of the sun following the vernal equinox. Even the word "Easter" and its German equivalent, *Ostern*, came from a common origin— *Eostur* or *Ostar*—which to the Norsemen meant the season of the rising sun, the season of new life. And so, at dawn on Sunday, hundreds of pagan worshippers would gather within the great circle of stones outside Salisbury to pay their homage to the Sun God.

"And you and I, my dear Harold, will most certainly be among them. Come to my place on Saturday evening—we'll have a little supper—and then some friends will pick us up in their car at about two. We should be there in plenty of time."

"Friends?" I asked. "What friends?"

"Oh, just some people I know," he said enigmatically. Roger liked to keep the different areas of his life strictly compartmentalised, and if he was about to introduce me to some of his fellow pagans, I knew I was expected to regard this as a special privilege.

"Remember," he said, just before we parted, "the Sun God is the masculine god. That's what we will be going there to worship—the spirit of manhood, the essence of maleness. I shall," he added, with a challenging gleam in his eye, "take it very amiss if you choose not to come."

I told him I would think about it, and left in a state of genuine indecision.

————

Writing all of this down, at almost thirty years' distance, it seems incredible to me now that I should have been so in thrall to Roger Anstruther and his arrogant, domineering personality. But remember, whoever you are, reading these pages, that I was callow, I was unsure of myself, I was a young man alone in a big, frightening city, and in Roger I felt that I had met someone who—how shall I put this?—*confirmed* something about myself. Something I had always suspected—always known, even, in the very remotest depths of my being—but which I had been too frightened (too cowardly, he would say) to acknowledge. I was still, at that tender age, hungry to unravel the mysteries of life. At first I had thought the answers lay in poetry, but now Roger was beginning to open up a different, even more alluring world to me—a world of shadows, portents, symbols, riddles and coincidences. Was it coincidence, for example, that all our schemes seemed to be coming to fruition on the eve of the festival of the Rising Sun, when this was the very name of the pub where we'd had all our earliest and most significant conversations? Questions like this nagged at my youthful, impressionable mind and made me feel that perhaps I was now on the verge of some revelation, some momentous breakthrough which would resolve all difficulties and set me free from the bonds which I felt had been restraining me all my life.

It was for these reasons—reasons which might seem feeble and even frivolous to an unsympathetic reader (forgive me, Max, if that is you!)—that I chose not to return to my parents' home at the weekend. Instead, on Saturday evening I set out on the long walk which led from my shared house in Highgate to Roger's rented bed-sitting room in a decrepit Notting Hill terrace.

———

When I arrived, he was sitting at his desk. I could see at once that something was wrong. His face was deathly pale, and his hands were trembling as he sat hunched over pages and pages of densely scribbled figures, to which he was adding further calculations in pencil, in a state of such ferocious concentration that he barely looked up to register my arrival.

"What's happened?" I asked.

"Don't interrupt," he answered curtly, and began whispering some more numbers under his breath while scrawling ever more frantically on the paper.

"Roger, you look dreadful," I persisted. "Is it . . . ?" Of course, I knew what it was. I felt suddenly faint, and sat down heavily on his bed in the corner of the room. "Don't tell me it's the wager. Did it go wrong?"

"Completely wrong," he said in a trembling voice, crumpling up one of the sheets of paper, tossing it aside and starting on a new one. "Utterly wrong."

"Well . . . what does that mean?" I asked.

"Mean? What does it *mean*?" He glared at me in fury. "It means that we've lost everything. It means that on Monday morning I have to give Crispin the lot."

"But you told me that wasn't possible."

"It wasn't. Or at least it shouldn't have been."

"How did it happen, then? Didn't the right horses win?"

"Almost, yes. But one of the races ended in a dead heat and that threw the whole thing out. We hadn't allowed for that."

"I thought you'd allowed for everything."

"Will you just *be quiet* for a minute, Harold?" He seized the sheet of paper and waved it at me. "Can't you see what I'm trying to do? I'm trying to make sense of it all."

He seemed, however, more or less to have given up on this

attempt: instead of making any more calculations, he simply sat there, sucking on his pencil and looking at the pages of arithmetic with sightless, unfocused eyes.

"But Roger," I began, gently, "Crispin is your friend, after all. He won't hold us to this, will he?"

At these words, after a short pause in which to digest them, Roger leaped up and began to pace the room. "Are you a half-wit?" he barked after a minute or two. "Don't you understand *anything*? We signed a piece of paper. The City has a code of conduct for this sort of thing. *Dictum meum pactum*—'My word is my bond.' He's going to take everything he can off us, you fool! Down to the last farthing. He's in this up to his neck as well, you know. He will have lost a fortune today. An absolute bloody fortune. So he's not going to let us wriggle out of this one."

There was a longer silence, during which I took in the enormity of what he was telling me, and its consequences: all our plans come to nothing, and ahead of me the prospect of weeks, or months, not merely of poverty but of debt, for Roger had persuaded me to commit to this ludicrous wager even more money than I actually had to my credit in a bank account. And when my mind began to dwell on that fact, I started to feel towards him something which, until now, I had never allowed myself: pure, boiling, seething indignation.

"No, *you're* the half-wit," I said to him—in a measured tone, at first: but when he looked across at me in disbelief, my voice started to rise. "You *idiot*, Roger! How could you have done this? More to the point, how can I have been so trusting? Why did I listen to you? Why have I let you treat me like this for months, doing everything at your behest, running around at your beck and call as if I were your mistress? I was so impressed by you, so in *awe* of you, and . . . now *this*!

You didn't know what you were doing. You didn't even know what you were talking about. You're a fraud, that's what you are. What our American cousins would call a phoney. And here I've been hanging on your every word, believing everything you tell me—giving away half of my favourite books because you despise the authors, throwing away most of my own poems because you treated them with such . . . cold, calculated disdain. And yet you're a fraud, pure and simple! To think that I listened to you, that I took you seriously! When you weren't making a spectacle of us both in the theatre, you were telling me the Christian faith was bunkum and we should all be sacrificing goats in the middle of a stone circle instead—you even told me you were going to put a curse on your sister, for pity's sake! Well, who do you think you are, exactly? A guru, a magician? A cross between Leavis, Midas and Gandalf? I'm afraid it won't wash anymore, Roger—it just won't wash. You've dazzled me for long enough. The truth is, I can see through you now. My eyes have been opened. I suppose I should be grateful for that, at least—although it's been a heavy price to pay, a very heavy price. Well, one lives and learns."

I picked up my coat from the bed and started putting it on again, intending to leave; but I was halted by Roger's next words, spoken in a low, insistent, chilling monotone.

"I did put a curse on my sister," he said.

I paused, with my arm halfway into a sleeve. "Pardon?"

By way of reply, Roger walked over to the mantelpiece and picked up a letter. It was written on two sheets of blue notepaper, folded in half. He handed it to me, and stood over me while I read it.

It was from his mother. I can't remember much of what it said, but the thrust was to let Roger know that his sister was distraught, having lost her baby in a miscarriage a few days earlier.

"So?" I handed back the letter, then finished putting my coat on.

"I did that," he said.

I looked at him for a moment, to see if he was being serious. Apparently, he was. "Don't be ludicrous," I said, and made for the door.

Roger grabbed me by the arm, pulling me back.

"It's true, I tell you. That was what I asked her for."

"Asked her? Asked *who*?"

"The Goddess."

I was in no mood to hear this. Whether what he said was true or not (or, perhaps more to the point, whether he believed it or not), I wanted to leave. "Enjoy your festival tomorrow morning," I said. "I'm going home."

I tried to shake myself free from his grip, but it became tighter. I looked into his eyes and was amazed to see there were tears welling up in them.

"Don't go, Harold," he said. "Please don't go."

Before I really knew what was happening, he had drawn me closer, and was kissing me on the mouth. I tried to pull away but his embrace was stronger than I would have thought possible.

"So much," he was whispering, as the bristles of his beard brushed coarsely against my lips, "so much we haven't done. So much still to do . . ."

I could feel his erection growing against my own crotch. With one final return of strength, I wrenched myself free and pushed him away with all the force I could muster. In fact it was enough to throw him off his feet and into the fireplace, where he knocked over the electric fire (fortunately unlit) and ended up half-sitting, half-lying, and rubbing his head where it had inadvertently cracked against the Victorian tiling. It crossed my mind for a moment that I might actually have caused him some injury, but such was my fury that, instead of rushing to his aid, I fumbled with the latch on his door, pulled it open as quickly as I could, and was gone without bothering to close it, without so much as a backward glance.

There is not much more to tell.

I did not see Roger again for more than a year after that. A short, businesslike note arrived from him on the Monday morning, informing me that Crispin Lambert was demanding the payment of a large sum of money. I scraped the sum together (borrowing most of it from my parents) and sent it off to him as soon as I could. After that, things went very quiet. I heard that Roger had left his jobbing firm and no longer worked on the Exchange floor, but I had no idea what had become of him. Of course I was curious, but I suppressed that curiosity. I began to see that he was a dangerous person. And I began to feel that there was danger, too, in the feelings he had almost managed to arouse in me. I wanted nothing further to do with them. The period of my life that I now entered into was safe if colourless. I had been genuinely fond of Roger, and found that life without him was flat, lacking in piquancy. A new secretary joined the firm of Walter, Davis & Warren in the autumn. Her name was Barbara. She came from Birmingham, and she was blonde, busty and pretty. I made overtures towards her. She responded encouragingly. We began to see each other out of office hours. We commenced upon a low-key, chaste and uneventful courtship. I took her to the cinema, I took her to the theatre, I took her to the concert hall. One night early in the summer of 1960 I took her to hear Prokofiev's *Romeo and Juliet* Suite being performed at the Albert Hall, in the hope that its grand romantic climaxes would stir in both of our breasts some corresponding passion for each other. It failed to do so. In the interval, she said she would rather I didn't take her to classical music concerts anymore, that she preferred Cliff Richard and Tommy Steele. She told me this while we were finishing our drinks at the bar—mine a half pint of bitter, hers a Dubonnet and lemon—after which, she went to the ladies', and I looked across to the other end of the bar to see Roger staring at me. He was alone, and his face wore a satisfied, knowing smile. He raised his glass to me. I finished my beer and left, without returning the gesture.

The next morning, a note arrived for me at work. It said:

> *There is still time for me to rescue you.*
> *The Rising Sun, 9 p.m. tonight.*

He was right, of course. I could no longer fight what I knew to be my destiny. I could no longer tell myself lies about my own nature. When I turned my footsteps in the direction of the Rising Sun that night, it was with one fixed intention: to do whatever it was that Roger Anstruther asked of me.

I arrived rather early, at twenty to nine, and ordered a double whisky in order to steady my nerves. I drank it quickly and ordered another. The second drink lasted for at least half an hour, at the end of which time I looked at my watch and realised Roger was late. I ordered a pint of bitter and took out my notebook, thinking that it would help me to compose myself if I occupied the time in writing. The pub was busy. Another half an hour went by.

It was only then that I began to see the obvious explanation for Roger's lateness. Could he possibly have been referring to the other Rising Sun? Strange though it may seem, the thought had not occurred to me until this moment. To me, the Rising Sun in Cloth Fair would always be *our* pub: it was where we'd had our first drink together, and where all our most tender and meaningful encounters had subsequently taken place. As for the other one in Carter Lane, I'd only been there once— the evening when Roger introduced me to Crispin Lambert. It had no special significance or resonance for me at all; but I was aware that Roger had returned there many times, usually to meet Crispin and to confer about their elaborate bets. Had I made a silly, humiliating mistake by assuming that his conversations with me would loom far more impressively in his memory than those sessions with Crispin? Was he sitting there now, waiting for me, just as I was sitting here waiting for him?

I delayed another quarter of an hour, and then decided it was worth taking a chance. I could walk from one pub to the other, if I hurried, and have a good chance of finding him there. I would cut down West Smithfield, then Giltspur Street, and then straight down past the Old Bailey and into Carter Lane via Blackfriars Lane. It ought to be safe enough. The only danger—a very remote one—was that Roger might have the same thought, leave the Rising Sun at the same time, and come to find me via a different route: up Creed Lane, for instance, then Ave Maria Lane, Warwick Lane, King Edward Street, Little Britain and Bartholomew Close. But this was surely a risk worth taking.

I drained my glass and left the pub, then half-walked, half-ran through the empty streets until the welcoming lights of the Rising Sun were visible in Carter Lane. Short of breath—partly from making such haste, but mainly from anxiety that this crucial evening was dissolving into chaos—I threw open the doors of the pub and rushed inside. There were few people in either the snug or the lounge bar, and Roger, I could see at once, was not among them. A young barman was collecting glasses from the unoccupied tables.

"Has a young man been in here?" I demanded. "Early twenties, red hair, beard, quite possibly wearing a cape?"

"Mr. Anstruther? Yes, he was here. He left about two minutes ago."

I let slip a torrent of swear words at this news, much to the barman's consternation. Then, leaving the pub even more hastily than I'd entered it, I stood for a moment in the street, looking left and right. It seemed likely that Roger might have hurried over to the pub I had just left, so breaking into a sprint I retraced my steps and was back in the Rising Sun in three or four minutes flat.

"Are you looking for your friend?" the barman said, as soon as I appeared. "Because he was in here a moment ago, asking after you."

"No!" I shouted, putting my head in my hands and tearing at my hair. This was too horrific to contemplate. "Which way did he go?"

"Up towards Middle Street, I think," said the barman.

But I never found him. I ran outside and spent the next twenty or thirty minutes searching for Roger, calling out his name as I scoured every street within a few hundred yards of Smithfield Market. But he was nowhere to be seen. He was gone.

There was only one last chance. I remembered there used to be a pay phone in the communal hallway of the Notting Hill house where he had his bed-sit. I called the number (which I still knew by heart) and waited what seemed like an age for someone to answer, my nervous breath steaming up the windows of the telephone box. But it was no use. It was more than a year since I had last used this number, and when a stranger's voice finally answered, it was to tell me that Roger no longer lived at this address. After a few seconds' silence, during which I struggled to regain my power of speech, I thanked the anonymous voice, slowly replaced the receiver, and leaned my forehead against the wall of the telephone box.

So, it was over. Everything was over. Cold, paralysing despair took me in its grasp.

What was I to do now?

I am not sure, in retrospect, how I managed to find myself in the street outside Barbara's flat in Tooting. Did I get there by bus? Did I take the tube? I can't remember. That interval of time has been wiped from my memory. It must have been late at night when I arrived, however, for I do remember that I could get no answer from her doorbell, and had to wake her by throwing pebbles at her third-floor window.

She was not especially pleased to see me. She was extremely sleepy, and I was extremely drunk. Somehow we managed, nonetheless, to fall into an embrace. The lovemaking that followed was breathless, fumbled and quickly finished. Neither of us, I believe, really knew what we were doing, or why. "You always remember the first time," they say, but I would have to take issue with that. The whole episode passed, for me, in a kind of haze. What I do remember is lying next to Barbara in bed for the next couple of hours. Neither of us slept, at first. I was staring at the ceiling, trying to make sense of the evening's events through the alcoholic fog that clouded my brain. I do not know what Barbara was thinking. At one point I glanced across at her and saw tears glistening on her cheeks. At four o'clock in the morning I sneaked out from beneath her bedclothes, left her flat without saying goodbye and walked back to Highgate through the silent London streets.

I did not go into work that day. My hangover was too severe, for one thing, and for another I shied away from the prospect of seeing Barbara again. The meeting would surely be too painful and awkward. And it turned out, of course, that she felt exactly the same way. Later that week she handed in her notice, and on the Friday afternoon she was given a small, subdued leaving party which I did not attend. I was told by colleagues that she had decided to return home to Birmingham. I had no reason to think I would ever see her again.

Three months later, I received a letter from Barbara's father. He told me Barbara was pregnant and that she believed me to be responsible. It was clear from the letter that he expected me to do what was still considered, in those days, to be the decent thing.

And so, six weeks later, we were married.

We lived for a few months in her parents' house, near the Cadbury factory in Bournville, but it was not a satisfactory arrangement. I secured a post as assistant librarian at a local technical college, and before too long we had scraped together the money to rent a small flat in Northfield. Our first and only child, Max, was born in February 1961. It would be another five years before we could raise enough money to put down a deposit on a house of our own: at which point we moved to Rubery, to an anonymous, pebbledashed, three-bedroom house, in a characterless street of similar houses not far from the municipal golf course at the foot of the Lickey Hills.

We would live here for most of the next two decades; and it was also here, in the spring of 1967, that I saw Roger Anstruther for the last time.

How he found my address, I cannot say. All I know is that he appeared on my doorstep early one Sunday evening in May. In the City, Roger had always cut a distinctive figure. That evening, materialising without warning in the Birmingham suburbs, dressed as before in a long black cape but with the addition of a matching fedora tipped stylishly on his head, he seemed positively outlandish. When I first saw him, I was too surprised to speak. I simply beckoned him inside.

I led him into our back room, known to myself, Barbara and Max as the "dining room," although we hardly ever took our meals there. There was no gin and tonic to offer Roger, so he had to make do with sweet sherry instead. Barbara joined us for a while, but she had no idea who this exotic stranger was (I had never mentioned Roger to her) and it was clear that she was uneasy in his presence. After a while, she went next door to the living room, to watch television with Max. It was the day, I remember, of Francis Chichester's return to Plymouth after his triumphant round-the-world voyage, and all three of us had been watching the live television coverage. Even while I was talking to Roger, I could hear the cheering of the crowds through the thin dividing wall, and the stentorian voice of the BBC commentator.

There was some difficult small talk between us at first, but in his usual forthright manner, Roger wasted little time in announcing the point of his visit. He was leaving the country. England, he gave me to understand, no longer had anything to offer him. In the years since I had known him, he had converted to Buddhism, and now wished to travel in the Far East. He was going to start in Bangkok, where he had been offered a job teaching English to the local students. But before departing, he said, there were some "ghosts" from his past which he felt needed to be "laid to rest."

Taking this to be a reference to myself, I told him, rather indignantly, that I did not consider myself to be a ghost, but a living being, composed of flesh and blood.

"And this," said Roger, looking around at our dining room, with its neat array of ornaments, the "best" china put out for display on the dresser, the cheap framed landscapes on the wall, "you consider this 'living,' do you?"

I did not answer. Fortunately, it was the only remark Roger made that evening which implied a criticism of the life I had chosen for myself. For the most part, his mood appeared to be conciliatory. He stayed for little more than an hour, having to catch a train back to London Euston in time to pack for his departure the next day. He asked me if I forgave him for the way he had behaved towards me. I told him (not entirely truthfully) that I rarely thought about it, but that, when I did, it was not with any malice or reproach. He told me he was glad to hear this, and asked if he could write to me, occasionally, from Bangkok. I told him that he could, if he so desired.

The first postcard from Roger arrived about a month later. Over the years it was followed by many others, at wildly irregular intervals, from places as diverse as Hanoi, Beijing, Mandalay, Chittagong, Singapore, Seoul, Tokyo, Manila, T'ai-Pei, Bali, Jakarta, Tibet—anywhere you care to name. He never seemed to stay in the same place for more than a few months. Sometimes he appeared to be working, sometimes just travelling, driven on by that perpetual spirit of restless enquiry that seemed to be an essential part of his nature. Occasionally—very occasionally—I would reply, but I was wary of Roger, always, and careful never to reveal too much about myself or my life. I would simply write a few lines giving him the bare outline of recent events—that Max had passed five of his O-Levels, for instance, or that I'd had a poem accepted for publication in a small local magazine, or that Barbara had died of breast cancer at the age of forty-six.

Last year, some months after Barbara died and Max left home for good, I moved back to my home city of Lichfield. On this occasion I sent out change-of-address cards to only a few select friends: but Roger was one of them, so I suppose that at some level I must have liked feeling we were still in touch with one another. But I wonder now whether it was the right thing to do. If there was really any point.

And now, in fact, I have reached a decision: no more.

In a few days' time I shall leave for Australia, and for the start—God willing—of a new life. And no, this time I will not tell Roger where I have gone. It is time to forget all that, surely: to make a clean, and long overdue, break with the past. Writing all of this down at long last, after so many years, has been a lengthy but also a refreshing and even purgative process. Max can read this one day, if he so chooses, and learn the truth about his father and mother. I hope it will not upset him too much. Meanwhile, I must try to learn something from this protracted incursion to the past. I must take some inspiration, if not from my memories of Roger or of Crispin Lambert (whose jobbing firm, I notice from the newspapers, has just been acquired for a small fortune by a leading clearing bank), then from my visit to the Square Mile itself—that labyrinth of ancient, history-laden streets dedicated to the single-minded accumulation of money. Mired in the past for far too long, the City of London has recently been in the process of reinventing itself. It has proved that such a reinvention is possible, and for that I salute it. From now on I shall endeavour to do the same thing, in a more modest way; and hope that I might even find some small measure of personal happiness as a result.

20

"So, tell me, Emma—how long have we known each other now?"

—*Proceed on the current road.*

"Can't remember? Well, amazingly, it's less than three days."

—*In two hundred yards, left turn.*

"I know, it feels longer than that, doesn't it? I feel I've known you for years now. Which is why I feel I can say something to you. Pay you a little compliment, if that's all right. I mean, the last thing I want to do is to embarrass you—"

—*In one hundred yards, left turn.*

"—but what I wanted to say, really, was this. I just wanted to say that there's one thing I really like about you. One thing about you that I've never encountered in any other woman. Can you guess what it is?"

—*Left turn coming up.*

"It's the way . . . well, it's the way you never judge people. That's a very rare quality, you know, in a woman. Or a man, for that matter. There's nothing judgemental about you at all."

—*Proceed for about three miles on the current road.*

"You see, I know I'm behaving badly. I know I shouldn't have done what I did, and I shouldn't be doing what I'm doing now. But you're not going to give me a hard time about it, are you? You know that I've got my reasons. You know there are extenuating circumstances."

—*Proceed for about two miles on the current road.*

"It doesn't look good, I realise, walking out of Alison's house at five o'clock in the morning without saying thank you, without saying goodbye. Not only do I walk out, but I raid her drinks cabinet while I'm at it. Now, I know Alison and her husband are stinking rich, and they're not going to miss a couple of bottles of whisky. Not just any old whisky, admittedly, but two very expensive single malts. Well, that isn't my fault. I don't care what the bloody stuff tastes like, if they'd had Bell's or Johnnie Walker in the cupboard I would have been just as happy to take those. Still, as a matter of principle—even leaving aside the cost—I can see that I shouldn't have done it. As I said, none of this looks particularly good. So there I am, dragging my suitcase along the street at five o'clock in the morning, a stolen bottle of whisky bulging out of a jacket pocket on either side, two coppers in a parked police car glaring at me suspiciously as I walk by, and somehow . . . *somehow* I make it back into the centre of town, where I manage to find you again. What time would that have been? I lose track of time. Can you remember?"

—*Proceed for about one mile on the current road.*

"I mean, there were other things that happened in between. I'm pretty sure of that. There was a lot of walking around. There was that homeless guy in the doorway who followed me down the street and kept asking 'Are you all right, pal?' And I sat on a bench for a while. Quite a long while, actually. It was high up somewhere, near a park, looking down over Princes Street and Princes Street Gardens and the whole city. The classic tourist view. It was still dark when I sat on that bench, and light when I got up and left. The snow was falling again, by that stage. Not settling, though. Just falling. Still hasn't started to settle."

—Heading right at the roundabout, take third exit.

"It was a relief to get back to you again, I must say. I was pretty cold by then. Took a few sips of the Laphroaig to warm myself up before we got going, which I know is really a bad—"

—Exit coming up.

"Whoa! Thank you—nearly missed that one. Wasn't concentrating. Sorry. And don't pip your horn at me, you rude, impatient bastard, just because there's someone who doesn't know the roads around here as well as you do. We're not all bloody natives, you know. Now, where was I?"

—Proceed on the current road.

"Oh, never mind, I can't remember. Let's just enjoy the scenery. You know, I don't think I've ever driven over the Forth Bridge before. This must be the farthest north I've ever been. That's a bit stupid, isn't it? Forty-eight years old and never been north of Edinburgh. I should make a list, a list of all the things I ought to do before I get to fifty. Bungee-jumping. Hang-gliding. Reading one of those godawful books that Caroline always said would be good for me. *Anna Karenina. The Mill on the Floss.* Finding someone else to marry, going to bed with them, learning not to be scared of intimacy again, not being lonely anymore—*shut up, shut up, shut up*—or sailing single-handed round the world in a trimaran . . ."

—Proceed on the current road.

"Ah, Donald, you never stood a chance, really, did you? You stood no more chance of sailing round the world than I do of getting to Unst tomorrow and turning up at that shop with a box full of toothbrushes. Who are we trying to fool, eh? Who are we trying to kid? Ourselves, probably. Yes, that's right. We have to fool the rest of the world at some point as well, but that's not the difficult part—the difficult part's convincing ourselves, isn't it? Isn't that right, Donald, me old mucker? Me old shipmate? Eh?"

—Proceed on the current road.

"Sorry, Emma, it's you I should be talking to, isn't it? Were you beginning to feel left out? Or perhaps you're beginning to get worried, hearing me chat away to someone who died forty years ago, someone I've never even met. That's not right, is it? That's not healthy. Anyone would think I'd been drinking too much whisky before getting behind the wheel of this lovely car. I don't believe in ghosts, and neither do you. Of course you don't. You're nothing if not rational, are you? A pure reasoning machine, you are. You don't have a body, or a soul, just a mind, a beautiful mind, and that's how I like it. What use would I have for someone with a body and a soul? What use would someone with a body and a soul have for someone like me? No, we're made for each other, Emma, you and me. We're like those 'cosmic beings' that Crowhurst thought everyone was going to turn into. Disembodied. Too good for the physical world. In fact we're so well suited that there's something I have to ask you. Will you marry me? Go on—I'm serious. Gays and lesbians can get married nowadays, so why shouldn't we? Where's the harm in that? I thought we were all supposed to be liberal and tolerant and inclusive in this country. Go on, what do you say? Marry me. Come live with me and be my wife. What's your answer?"

—Proceed on the current motorway.

"Oh, we're on a motorway now, are we? When did that happen? I hadn't even noticed. So which motorway would that be, exactly? The M90. I see. And where are we heading towards on the M90? Perth, apparently. Perth, followed by Dundee, followed by Forfar. Forfar! Now there's a name. There's a name to conjure with. Makes me think of football results. Didn't the guy who used to read the football results on the BBC say that was the most difficult one to get right? *East Fife 4, Forfar 5*, or something like that? In fact everywhere around here makes me think of football results. Cowdenbeath. Dunfermline. Arbroath. I'd no idea where any of these places were before today, but God those names take me back. Saturday-afternoon telly. *Final Score*. What time was that on? 4:40, I think. Yes, that would be about right. Kick-off at three o'clock, game over at 4:45. Then the results would start coming up on that little automatic typewriter thing. What did they call it? The teleprinter or something. God, 1960s technology! We've come a long way since then. How old would I have been when I started watching that—seven or eight? I bet every eight-year-old boy in the country was doing the same thing, sitting in his front room at teatime on a Saturday afternoon, glued to the telly. I wonder how many of them had their fathers with them at the time? Did my father sit down and watch it with me? Well, come on, Emma, what do you think? Take a wild guess. Of course he didn't, the miserable fucking bastard. He was too busy sitting next door in the dining room reading T. S. Eliot and his *String Quartets*. Or planning when he was going to have his next wank."

—*Come on, Max, have a bit of sympathy for your father.*

"What the . . . Did you just answer me back?"

—*Proceed on the current motorway.*

"OK, I'm turning you off for a bit now. I think you're getting too big for your boots."

"Better off without her, for the time being. Till I need her again, anyway. Not much chance of getting lost at the moment. What do I want to go to Aberdeen for, anyway? There's no

318 • THE TERRIBLE PRIVACY OF MAXWELL SIM

way I'm getting on a ferry this afternoon. Look at this weather, for one thing. What I should really do is go back to Alison. Turn round at the next junction, go straight back to her house and apologise. Poor woman. Pig of a husband cheating on her. What would she say if I turned up looking like this? She'd understand. Trained psychotherapist, after all. Shoulder to cry on. That's what I need, really. Someone to talk to about . . . all this. All this stuff. Everything that's come out in the last couple of weeks. Bit too much to cope with, really. Bit much to take in all at once. We all need somebody to talk to. How did you think you were ever going to manage it, Donald? Nine months at sea, was it? Ten, something like that? With no human company at all, just a radio transmitter that barely worked. Unimaginable. And, of course, you didn't manage it in the end. Was that what tipped you over the edge, finally—the loneliness? The terrible privacy, as Clive called it? I'm not surprised. Nobody could be expected to handle solitude like that, and why should you be any different? You're human like the rest of them. But you should've turned back when you had the chance. When you first realised that the boat was never going to make it. I don't know, though, maybe things were already too far gone by then. Perhaps what you should have done, that day, when you realised the mess you'd got yourself into, instead of putting it all down on paper and trying to work out the way forward yourself . . . perhaps you should have used the radio, made contact with your wife somehow. I bet she would have told you to turn round and come back.

"Would've, should've, could've.

"Still, you know—for me, it isn't too late. I should phone someone now, shouldn't I, while I still have the chance? I need to talk this stuff over. Who shall I phone? Lindsay, Caroline, Alison? What do you think? Poppy, even?

"Lindsay, I suppose. She'll have the most practical take on it. Yeah—Lindsay. She's the one. Let's go for it.

"Ha! Battery's dead. Run down completely. I saw it was getting pretty low last night. Meant to charge it when I got to Alison's. Maybe I can find somewhere to charge it later.

"Anyway, it's out of action for now—just like your radio transmitter, at the time when you needed it most.

"There'll be call boxes at the next service station, I suppose.

"Oh, fuck it. It wouldn't have made any difference anyway."

—In one mile, heading left at the roundabout, take first exit.

"Ah, welcome back."

—In one mile, heading left at the roundabout, take first exit.

"I heard you the first time."

—In one mile, heading left at the roundabout, take first exit.

"All right, there's no need to nag. If there's one thing I can't stand, it's a nagging woman."

—In a quarter of a mile, heading left at the roundabout, take first exit.

"I'm sorry, Emma. I didn't mean to jump down your throat. Not feeling my best, to be honest. Haven't eaten since last night. Driving around the outskirts of Dundee while pissed—not a good look. On top of that, trying to come to terms with the fact that my whole . . . existence, apparently, is nothing more than a horrific mistake on the part of my parents, and my father in particular."

—Heading left at the roundabout, take first exit.

"So—thanks, Dad, for clearing that up. Just in case there was the slightest chance I might ever start feeling good about myself. Not that it was ever going to be very likely, in the near future, but it's good to know you've knocked it on the head anyway. Just when I was starting to feel that my life couldn't get any more disappointing, I now learn that I never should've had one in the first place. So, there's something new to put on my gravestone: 'Here lies Maxwell Sim, the most unnecessary person ever born.'"

—Straight on at the roundabout, take second exit.

"Is that how I'll have to think of myself, then, for the rest of my life? A non-person? The square root of minus one?"

—Next right.

"Or is this somebody's subtle way of telling Maxwell Sim that he isn't wanted anymore? That perhaps it's time for him to disappear?"

—Straight on at the roundabout, take second exit.

"OK, I need to think about this. Leave me alone for a while, will you, Emma? Just give me a little space?"

"Now then."

—Proceed for about one mile on the current road.

"I think the time is fast approaching. The time when . . . the time when . . ."

—In a quarter of a mile, heading straight on at the roundabout, take second exit.

"The time when I have to give up on this pretence—"

—Heading straight on at the roundabout, take second exit.

"—and accept what's happening to me. Which means that right now, exactly at 12:09 p.m. on Thursday, March the fifth, 2009, forty miles south of Aberdeen, proceeding north on the A90 at forty-seven miles per hour, I am going to leave this road and abandon this journey . . . So I shall *not* go straight on at this roundabout, Emma, I shall go *left* at this roundabout, following the signs to Edzell. Now, what do you think of that?"

—In two hundred yards, make a U-turn.

"Ha! Is that the best you can do? Oh no, Emma, there won't be any U-turns, not from now on. I'm not going to follow your directions anymore, and I'll tell you why. Because I don't want to go to Aberdeen and get on the ferry. And in fact the logic of this situation dictates that I *can't* go to Aberdeen and get on the ferry. Do you know why? *BECAUSE I AM NOT MAXWELL SIM ANYMORE. I AM DONALD CROWHURST,* and I have to follow in his path and repeat his mistakes. He didn't sail around the world at all, and I won't be sailing to the Shetland Isles either. He decided to fake his voyage and I'm going to fake mine, and I don't care how many satellites there are in the sky trained on me right now, from this moment onwards nobody knows where I am, I have disappeared, disappeared into the darkness of this approaching snowstorm, and I will hide out here, drifting in the mid-Atlantic for as long as it takes, until the time is right, until the time is right for me to emerge again, in triumph, and present myself to the world."

—In two hundred yards, make a U-turn.

"Nope. No can do. This is it, baby. The parting of the ways."

—In three-quarters of a mile, slight right turn.

"Oh, something just occurred to me."

—Slight right turn coming up.

"It might have been a good idea to put some petrol in the car back in Brechin. So far we've done . . . 527 miles since we left Reading, and I haven't filled up once. There can't be much more left."

—Next right.

"Still trying to get me back to Aberdeen, then? I thought I told you we've abandoned that idea. Left turn here, I think."

—*In two hundred yards, make a U-turn.*

"You don't give up, do you? Give into it, Emma. Surrender. There's something fantastic about just giving up. The sense of . . . release is incredible. I can remember when I first discovered that, actually. It was on that holiday to Coniston, with Chris and his family. One day we decided that we were going to climb up the Old Man of Coniston, all of us, and then about halfway up Chris and I got ahead of the others and it turned into a kind of race between us. And before we knew what was happening, we were *running* up this bloody great hill, or mountain or whatever it is. And then pretty soon Chris got ahead and it became obvious that he was much fitter than me—well, that should've been pretty obvious all along, really—and then he was more or less out of sight but I kept sort of plodding on, out of breath, tripping over all these rocks, with this terrible stitch in my side and thinking I was going to have a heart attack at any minute. And after a few more minutes of this, I thought, What is the *point*, what is the bloody *point* of carrying on like this? So I just flopped down by the side of the path and let him get on with it. I knew what I was capable of, you see. I knew I couldn't compete with Chris. Never could, never would. And to accept that—to accept *myself* for what I was—was such a relief. Soon I was caught up by the others who were walking along behind—Mr. and Mrs. Byrne, and Mum and Dad, and Alison—and they stopped and I remember Mr. Byrne asking if I was just going to sit there, if I wasn't even going to try. And I told him I was perfectly happy sitting there while Chris ran on to the summit and everyone else followed him. I'd given up and I was happy about it, and for the next hour or more I just sat there enjoying the view. Knowing that I'd found my level and I'd never rise above it."

—*Proceed on the current road.*

"I think that might have been a deer we just passed. Did you see it? In the woods."

—*We need to talk about Chris.*

"Yes, you're right. We do need to talk about Chris. We need to talk about a lot of things, Chris being one of them. But before we do that, I'm going to pull over into this lay-by here and have another drop of whisky, and then a little snooze, if that's all right by you. Because suddenly, Emma, I feel tired. Incredibly tired. And I would hate for us to have an accident. I'd never forgive myself if anything happened to you."

—*We need to talk about Chris.*

"Mmm?"

—*I said, We need to talk about Chris.*

"Shit! What time is it? Three o'clock! Bloody hell.

"Where did all this snow come from?

"And what happened to all the whisky? I didn't drink all that, did I? Well, now I'll have to open the other bottle . . .

"Oh God, my head . . .

"Right. Let's get started. Not much visibility this afternoon, I must say. And so dark! Feels like it's night time already."

—*Proceed on the current road.*

"OK. Will do. Now, what was it you wanted to talk about?"

—*Chris.*

"OK. We can do that. Was there anything in particular you wanted to discuss?"

—*Yes. The photograph.*

"The photograph? You'll have to be more specific. I'm not with you."

—*Proceed on the current road.*

"Which photograph did you have in mind?"

—*The folded photograph.*

"Ah, you mean the one of Alison? In her bikini?"

—*Why did he fold it?*

"Pardon?"

—*Why did your father fold the photograph?*

"I thought we'd established that. Because he was turned on by the picture of Alison, and that was the only half he wanted to look at."

—*Are you sure?*

"Of course. What other explanation is there?"

—*In one mile, right turn.*

"Come on, Emma, what are you getting at?"

—*In half a mile, right turn.*

"No, that takes us back on the road to Aberdeen, and I've already told you I'm not going to Aberdeen. Today or any other day."

—*You know.*

"I know? I know what? Do you mind not being so cryptic?"

—*You know why your father folded the photograph.*

"Can we change the subject?"

—*Right turn coming up.*

"Left turn, I think you'll find."

—*You know.*

"Will you *shut up* about that, Emma! Will you stop talking about it?"

—*Say it, Max. Say it.*

"Fuck off."

—*Don't cry. Don't cry, Max. Just tell the truth.*

"I'm not crying."

—*You can say it.*

"Why are you *doing* this to me? Why are you putting me through this?"

—*Was it really Alison's picture he wanted?*

"Of course it wasn't. Oh, God. Oh, Dad! You miserable . . .You miserable man. Why didn't I see? Why didn't any of us see? It was Chris, wasn't it? You had a thing for Chris. All those years. Your best friend's son. Couldn't take your eyes off him. Even now—even *now* you still think about him. Even in Australia you were asking after him all the time. And not just Chris, probably. Probably other people as well. Friends of mine? Friends of Mum's? Who knows? You bottled it up, Dad. You bottled it up all that time, for years and years. In fact I think you're still bottling it up now. Your sad little secret. The thing you could never admit, to Mum or to me or to anybody else."

—*In two hundred yards, make a U-turn.*

"So sad. So very, very sad."

—*Make a U-turn. Then, proceed for about three miles on the current road.*

"Video diary, Day Four.

"Well, doubtless you'll want to know how I've been getting on.

"I'm pleased to report that I'm well on my way to Shetland. Well on my way. Of course it's a bit too dark outside for you to see exactly where I am, but my guess would be . . . my guess would be somewhere off the west coast of Africa. Yesterday we certainly passed by Madeira, on the starboard side, and today I can see, over on the port side, a looming mass of glowering rock and earth which I think must be one of the Canary Islands. Either that or, quite possibly, the Cairngorms, because unless I'm very much mistaken we're now on the B976, heading in a westerly direction, away from Aberdeen and into the mountains. Let me just check that with my trusty navigator."

—*In three hundred yards, make a U-turn.*

"Ha, ha! Yes, she's been saying that for some time. That's Emma, there, my trusty—as I said—my trusty navigator, who has been disagreeing with me today over the route we should take. She seems to think that at this rate we have no possibility of rounding the Cape of Good Hope before Christmas, which means bad weather in the Roaring Forties, although I have to say the weather here is pretty bad already. Thick, spiralling snowflakes, as you can see outside the car, and a howling wind—can you hear it?—that makes it pretty difficult to steer a straight course at the moment. Not helped by the fact that the driver—that is to say, the captain—has been drinking pretty steadily for the last, well, the last fifteen hours or so. Nothing like a bit of ship's rum, I always say, to cheer you up in stormy weather! Anyway, the road's getting pretty—pretty winding and treacherous around here. I'm sticking to a steady twenty miles an hour or so and supplies—petrol supplies, that is—are pretty low, and, whoops, here comes a big bend, didn't see that one coming, and if you're wondering what that sound was, it was the sound of the camera sliding off the dashboard and on to the floor, which is why you currently have a good view of my left foot.

"OK. Cut."

"Emma?

"Emma, are you still there?"

—Yes, I'm still here.

"You haven't said anything for a while."

—I'm still here. What is it?

"Shall we stop soon? I'm getting tired again."

—Proceed on the current road.

"OK. Whatever you say. Is this a good time to talk, though?"

—In three hundred yards, make a U-turn.

"Don't you ever give up? I wanted to talk to you about my dad, and Roger."

—Proceed on the current road.

"I've been thinking about it, and maybe it's not such a sad story. You know, in a way they loved each other. I mean, Roger sounds a bit of a bully, and a bit of a prick, but I think he really cared for my father. And that means that at least *somebody* really cared for him once. I'm not sure that Mum ever did, you see. If you think about it, Roger and my dad were just unlucky. And it was Crispin Lambert who screwed things up for them, most of all. If it wasn't for *him* and his stupid schemes, things might have turned out all right. Although I don't know whether my father would ever really have had the nerve to come out, to admit to himself that he was . . . the person he was. But the path he chose for himself was much harder, in fact. Deceiving himself, deceiving everybody close to him, for a whole lifetime. That's what Crowhurst was considering, too, isn't it? Must be why he reminded me of Dad . . .

"Emma?"

—Proceed on the current road.

—Proceed on the current road.

"It's all very well saying that now. I can't proceed any farther on the current road. Look—it's closed. The police have closed it. They've put a gate across it.

"Where the hell are we, anyway? Didn't we just pass a town?

"Let's have a look. Yes, there we are. That's us—that little red arrow on the screen, come to a dead halt. That's you and me, that is. But look, if we just go back a while, there's a tiny road to the west that'll by-pass this gate and bring us back on to the main road. Then we've got to climb up this mountain, over the top and down the other side. No worries.

"Thing is, I'm not sure we've got enough petrol. That warning light's been flashing for a while now. Still, never mind, eh? What's the worst that can happen to us? We've got our whisky, we've got each other—let's make a night of it. What do you say?"

—*It's up to you, Max. Completely up to you.*

"Good girl. Come on, then.

> *"The wheels on the bus go round and round,*
> *Round and round, round and round,*
> *The wheels on the bus go round and round, all day long.*
> *The wipers on the bus go swish swish swish,*
> *Swish swish swish, swish swish swish,*
> *The wipers on the bus go swish swish swish, all day long.*

"Do you know that song, Emma? You must do. You can join in if you like. Come on, sing along. It's good to have a bit of a sing-song when you're in dire straits. Keeps your spirits up.

> *"The horn on the bus goes beep beep beep,*
> *Beep beep beep, beep beep beep,*
> *The horn on the bus goes beep beep beep, all day long.*

"What's the matter, don't you know the words? I used to sing this with Lucy all the time. Know it off by heart. I wonder if she still remembers them? We used to sing it in bed, first thing in the morning. At the weekends, Caroline would get up and have the first shower and I'd stay in bed and then Lucy would jump in with me and sit on my stomach and we'd sing this song."

—*I don't know the words.*

"Well, the next verse goes like this:

> "*The children on the bus go up and down,*
> *Up and down, up and down,*
> *The children on the bus go up and down, all day long.*

"Then:

> "*The babies on the bus go wah wah wah,*
> *Wah wah wah, wah wah wah,*
> *The babies on the bus go wah wah wah, all day . . .*

"You know what? I don't think we're going to make it up this hill. The car's not built for this kind of driving. It's not gripping properly on the ice. And did you hear that splutter? That sounds to me like a car that's running out of gas. So close, as well! If we could just get to the top then we could probably freewheel all the way down the other side. But sadly . . . I don't think we're going to make it.

"Nope. We're out of luck.

"Stuck. Stranded.

"Quiet, isn't it?"

—*Very quiet.*

"You know where we are, don't you?"

—Where are we, Max?

"The doldrums, of course. We're in the doldrums, just like Donald Crowhurst when his radio finally packed in. He had a broken radio, I've got a dead mobile."

—But Max, there's something I want you to remember. Something very important. You're not Donald Crowhurst. You're Maxwell Sim.

"No, you don't understand. You still don't get it. Everything that happened to him is happening to me. It's happening now."

—We're in the Cairngorms. Not the Sargasso Sea.

"Close your eyes and we could be anywhere."

—The inside of his cabin was hot. Here it's cold.

"Well, that's easily fixed. I'll put the heating on full blast."

—If you do that, Max, the battery will soon be flat.

"I don't care. And Crowhurst was naked, wasn't he? Didn't he spend a lot of his last few weeks naked?"

—Max, please don't do that. Control yourself.

"What's the matter, have you never seen a naked man before? No, I suppose you haven't."

—Max, stop it. Put that shirt back on. And turn the heating down. It's already getting too hot in here. You'll waste the battery.

"Here come the trousers. Look away now if you don't want to get a shock. There! Now we're all comfy and cosy. No secrets between us. How about a wee dram, at this point? Talisker, we've got, twenty-five years old, courtesy of Alison and Philip. You won't join me? Well, I can't say I blame you. Very wise. I've had enough of this stuff already today, but if we're going to get through a whole night on this mountainside . . ."

"What? What happened? Where am I?

"Emma?"

—*I'm here, Max.*

"Did I fall asleep?"

—*Yes, you did. For more than an hour.*

"Really? Shit, I was hoping it would be longer than that. God, it's hot in here."

—*The heater's been on all this time. I told you not to keep it on so high. Now there's hardly any power in the battery. You know what that means, don't you, Max?*

"No, what does that mean?"

—*It means that I'll be going soon. I'm fading away.*

"Oh, no! Not that, Emma! Not you as well. Don't leave me, please."

—*Soon I'll be gone. Just a few more minutes.*

"I'll turn the heating down. I'll turn it off completely."

—*No, Max, it's too late. We have to say goodbye to each other.*

"But Emma, I can't do without you. You've been . . . every-thing to me, these last few days. Without you . . . Without you, I can't go on."

—*It has to be this way.*

"No! You can't go! I *need* you."

—*Don't cry, Max. We've had some good times together. Now it's run its course. Accept it, if you can. We have just a few more minutes together.*

"I can't accept it. No."

—*Is there anything you want to tell me in that time?*

"What? What do you mean?"

—*Is there perhaps something you want to tell me, before I go?*

"I don't understand."

—*I think there's something you ought to tell me. Your little secret. Something you never told Caroline. Something that involves Chris.*

"Chris?"

—Yes. Now you know what I'm talking about, don't you?

"You mean . . ."

—Yes?

"You mean what happened in Ireland? The nettle pit?"

—That's it. Come on, now, Max. You'll feel better if you tell someone.

"Oh God . . . oh God . . . How did you know about that?"

—Just say it out loud. Just tell me what happened. Tell me what happened to poor little Joe. What you did to him.

"Fuck . . . fuck . . . *fuck*."

—That's all right. Cry if you want to. Let it all out.

"You want the truth?"

—Of course I want the truth. The truth is always beautiful.

"But the truth is, Emma . . . The truth is . . . Oh God. The truth is, I hated him. Isn't that a terrible thing to say? Just a little boy. Just a happy, curious, lively little boy. I hated him for being so happy. I hated him for having Chris as a father. For having two sisters to play with. I hated him for everything he had . . . that I'd never had. All the things Dad had never given me . . ."

—Cry if you want to.

"I never realised, you see. I never realised how much hate I had in me. I never realised that I could hate a *child* like that."

—Let the tears come, Max. It'll do you good. So what happened? What did you do?

"I can't say it."

—Yes you can. You can say it, Max. He was playing on the rope, wasn't he? He was swinging over the nettle pit.

"Yes."

—And then he swung over to the edge, and tried to get off, and what did you do then?

"I can't say it."

—*Yes, you can say it. You can, Max. I know what happened. You pushed him.*

"I . . ."

—*Is that what happened? You pushed him back in? Did you push him, Max?*

"Yes. Yes, I did. He knew, too. He *knew* it was me. He told his father. Chris couldn't believe him, not at first, but in the end I think he did. And that's why they all left. That's why Chris has never spoken to me since."

—*Cry if you want to. But it's better if you tell someone.*

"I couldn't help it. I wanted to hurt him. I so wanted to hurt him. I never would've believed I could want to hurt someone so much. And he was just eight years old. Eight years. *Fuck.* I'm a bad man. I'm a horrible man. I shouldn't have told you that, should I? Do you hate me now, Emma? Can you ever forgive me, or like me again?"

—*I'm the only person you could have told, Max. Because I don't judge—remember? I'm glad you told me. It was right that you told me. In the end, you had to tell somebody. But the battery's almost finished now. I'm going to have to say goodbye. I'm going to have to leave you, Max.*

"Emma, don't go."

—*I have to. I'm going to leave you at the mercy of the elements. The snow will fall on you. The darkness will cover you. The elements have reduced you to this. Now they control you.*

"Don't you have anything else to say to me? Because I've got something I want to say to you. Something I've been meaning to say for ages."

—*All right, then. One more thing. You go first.*

"OK. Here it is. I love you, Emma. I really do. I've been meaning to say it for days, but I never dared. Never had the nerve. But now it's out. I love you. Always have. Ever since I first heard your voice."

—*Goodbye then, Max.*

"But . . . what were you going to say to me?"

—*In three hundred yards, make a U-turn.*

"Emma, *please* don't go. Don't leave me alone. Don't leave me alone here, *please*.

"Emma? Emma?"

FAIRLIGHT BEACH

21

When I saw the Chinese woman and her daughter playing cards together at their restaurant table, the water and the lights of Sydney Harbour shimmering behind them, I knew it would not be long now, not long at all, before I found what I'd been looking for.

It was 11 April 2009: the second Saturday of the month.

I got to the restaurant at seven o'clock, and they arrived three-quarters of an hour later. They didn't seem to have changed a bit since I'd last seen them, on Valentine's Day. They were just the same. I think the little girl might even have been wearing the same dress. And everything they did together at their table was just the same as well. First of all they ate a big meal together—a surprisingly big meal, four courses each, in fact—and then the waiter cleared their plates and dishes away and brought some hot chocolate for the little girl and some coffee for her mother and then the Chinese woman took out her pack of cards, and they started to play. Once again, I couldn't tell exactly what game they were playing. It wasn't a proper grown-up card game, but neither was it a childish one like snap. Whatever it was, they found it entirely absorbing. Once the game started, they seemed to exist in a little cocoon of intimacy, oblivious to the presence of the other diners. The restaurant terrace was not quite as busy as it had been the last time, partly because that had been Valentine's Day, of course, but also because Sydney now had a noticeably cooler and more autumnal feel to it and a lot of people had chosen to eat inside. I was even getting a little chilly myself, but still, I was glad the Chinese woman and her daughter had chosen to stay out on the terrace, because that meant I could see them again just how I remembered them, with the water and the lights of Sydney Harbour shimmering in the background. I tried to watch them unobtrusively, just the occasional glance in their direction, not staring openly or anything like that. I didn't want to make them feel uncomfortable.

At first I was simply glad to see them. I was happy to savour the overwhelming sense of rightness and calm that came over me once I saw them walk onto the restaurant terrace. After all, even though the waiter had assured me, not so long ago, that they came to this restaurant regularly on the second Saturday of every month, I'd still not quite been able to bring myself to believe they would be here tonight. So my initial reaction had been one of relief, pure and simple. This was rapidly succeeded, all the same, by a growing sense of anxiety. The fact was, even after thinking about it for hours, I hadn't yet come up with an appropriate way of introducing myself to them. A tired old line like "Excuse me, but haven't I seen you somewhere before?" would get me nowhere. On the other hand, if I said that the prospect of meeting them had been one of my main incentives for flying over from London, halfway around the world, it would probably freak them out. Was there anything I could tell them that might steer a middle ground between these two approaches? Perhaps if I were to tell them the truth: that I had first seen them at this restaurant two months ago, and ever since then they had become, for me, a sort of totem, a symbol of everything that a real relationship between two human beings should be, at a time when people seemed to be losing the ability to connect with one another, even as technology created more and more ways in which it ought to be possible . . . Well, I was going to get bogged down if I pursued that line of argument too far, but I still reckoned that—with a bit of luck, if the right words managed to come to me somehow—this might just about be feasible. And I had better hurry up, if I wanted any chance of speaking to them this evening. It was getting late, and the little girl was beginning to look tired, and any minute now they would probably be leaving. Already their card game seemed to be over and they were talking and laughing together again, having a friendly little quarrel about something or other while the Chinese woman looked around to see where the waiter was, presumably to ask for the bill.

So—this was it. My heart pounding, I was just on the point of rising out of my seat and walking over to their table when something stopped me. Some*one*, I should say. For just at that moment, quite unexpectedly, my father walked out onto the restaurant terrace and came over to my table.

Yes, my father. At that moment, the last person I was expecting to see. He was supposed to be in Melbourne with Roger Anstruther.

All right, I admit that I've left out some important parts of the story. It's probably time to do a little back-tracking.

It was Saturday afternoon when I finally woke up in the hospital ward in Aberdeen. I woke up to find that two people were sitting by my bedside: Trevor Paige and Lindsay Ashworth. They had come to bring me home.

The next day, Trevor and I travelled back to London together, by train. Lindsay drove down in the Prius. On the train, Trevor told me the news about Guest Toothbrushes:

they had been forced into liquidation on Thursday morning, after the bank had refused to extend their lines of credit any further. The announcement had been made round about the time I was skirting the edges of Dundee, but nobody from the firm had been able to make contact with me. All ten members of staff had been made redundant, and the project to launch the new range at the British Dental Trade Association fair had, of course, been aborted. All of Lindsay's plans had come to nothing.

Back in Watford, it took me a few days to recover from my journey. I spent most of the next week in bed. Plenty of people came to visit me, I must say. Not just Trevor and Lindsay, but even Alan Guest himself, which I thought was a nice touch. He seemed to feel quite guilty about how my part in the campaign had turned out, almost as if it was his personal responsibility. I told him that he should have no worries on that score. Poppy came to see me twice, bringing her uncle with her the second time. And at the weekend things got even better, when I was lucky enough to witness a true miracle in the form of a visit from Caroline and Lucy. They didn't stay the night or anything like that, but even so: it was the first time they had been down to Watford since our separation, and Caroline promised me that it wouldn't be the last.

As soon as I felt well enough, I contacted my old employers and made another appointment to see Helen, the Occupational Health Officer. I told her I had reconsidered my position at the department store, and that if there was any possibility that my old job might still be open, I would like to start working there again. Helen seemed taken aback by this request, and then told me she would have to consult with the personnel department, and would get back within a few days. She kept her word. They had already taken on another After-Sales Customer Liaison

Officer, she said, but she would e-mail me a list of the vacancies currently available in other parts of the store, and she assured me that any application I might make for one of these posts would be looked upon favourably. The list arrived, and after some deliberation I applied for a job in soft furnishings. I'm pleased to say that I got the job, and agreed to start work there on Monday, 20 April.

In the meantime I'd made a resolution, and now realised that I didn't have long to carry it out. One morning I sat down at the kitchen table with the plastic bin liner full of Roger Anstruther's picture postcards. I tipped them all on to the table and began sorting through them. I wanted to put them in chronological order, first of all. It wasn't easy, because not all of them were dated, and of those which were undated, many had postmarks which were now illegible. A certain amount of guesswork was involved. After a few hours, however, I had made enough progress to be able to sketch out a rough map of his itinerary over the last few years. Since January 2006 he had travelled down from Southern China through Myanmar, Thailand, Cambodia and Indonesia, and had then spent almost a year on the island of Peleliu, about six hundred miles west of the Philippines. This was about as remote a spot as anyone could possibly find, and the thought that Roger might have settled there, at least for the time being, made my scheme look even more fantastic and impractical than it had seemed in the first place. My plan was . . . Well, have you guessed it by now? Of course my plan was to effect some sort of reconciliation between Roger Anstruther and my father. To contact Roger and suggest that he and my father meet again: in person, that is, not by e-mail or over the telephone. However, now that I considered the geographical distance between them, this idea began to appear ridiculous. They were in the same hemisphere, admittedly, but that was about it. And yet . . . the more I thought about my plan, the more it started to feel like not some idle fantasy but a necessity. My father and Roger's story *had* to end this way. In my very bones I felt there was something more than chance operating here—that their reunion was also their destiny, and that bringing it about was the task I had been born to perform. Does that sound to you, after the disastrous end to my journey, as though I had not fully recovered my wits? Well then, just consider this. There were still a couple of dozen unsorted postcards in the bin liner at this point, and when I took them out I discovered that although most of them seemed to date from the early 1990s, there was one that was much more recent. It bore a picture of the waterfront at Adelaide . . . and it was dated January 2009.

Roger was now in Australia. He and my father were living less than a thousand miles apart. Breathlessly, I read and reread the message on the back of the postcard.

> *Got tired of living in the back of beyond at last. Have started yearning for some Western comforts again. Also occurred to me—though this is a morbid thought—that I should start looking for somewhere to end my days. So, here I am, for the next few months at least. My boarding house marked with an arrow—must have had a nice view of the bay, in days gone by, but all the new condos seem to have put paid to that . . .*

Now, tell me—does that not seem like destiny to you?

Often, as I'd come to realise over the last few weeks, the Internet is something that puts up barriers between people as much as it connects them. But there are also times when it can be an uncomplicated blessing. In a matter of hours, I had used Google Earth to locate the stretch of Adelaide waterfront on

Roger's postcard, identified his boarding house and established its name and address, then sent an e-mail to the owners asking if they had anyone staying there by his name. Their reply arrived the next morning, and it was just the one I'd been hoping for.

So I had already found Roger Anstruther.

I flew out to Australia on 4 April. It was going to be a short trip this time, little more than a week: not even long enough to get over my jet lag properly. I couldn't really afford it, either—not without getting even further into debt. But it had to be done. At first I didn't plan to tell my father that I was coming. I thought it would be better to surprise him. Then I realised this was silly—people didn't just fly across to the other side of the world, at considerable expense, on the off chance of seeing their fathers. Supposing he'd gone off somewhere? Supposing he had decided to take a couple of weeks' holiday? So, the night before I was due to fly, I tried phoning him, and I couldn't get through. There was no reply from his home number, nor from his mobile. Then I started to panic. Maybe something had happened to him. Maybe he was lying dead on the kitchen floor of his new apartment. Now I would *have* to fly out to see him.

Naturally, when I turned up at his apartment thirty-six hours later and rang the doorbell, he came and answered it in a couple of seconds.

"What are you doing here?" he said.

"I've come to see you. Why didn't you answer the phone?"

"Have you been calling? There's something wrong with it. I've managed to mute the ring tone, I don't know how. Now I can't hear it when somebody calls me."

"What about your mobile?"

"The battery ran down and I can't find the charger. You didn't fly all the way out here because of that, did you?"

I was still standing on the doorstep. "Can I come in?"

I think my father was genuinely touched that I'd taken the trouble to come and see him so soon after my last visit. Touched and astounded. For most of the week we didn't do anything special, but there was an easiness and even (dare I say this?) a closeness between us that was new to both of us. I gave him back the precious blue ring binder I had retrieved from Lichfield and told him I had read his memoir, *The Rising Sun*, but apart from that we didn't discuss it. Not for a while, at any rate. Nor did I mention that more than half of the space in my suitcase was occupied by layer upon layer of Roger Anstruther's postcards. Instead, I bided my time, and we passed the first days of my visit in various low-key domestic ways. My father had been in this apartment for three months now but it still wasn't furnished properly, so we spent some time going round furniture stores buying chairs and cupboards and a spare bed. Also, he had a television that was about twenty years old and barely worked, so one day we went out and got him a nice new flat-screen TV and a DVD player. He complained about this and said he now had nothing to play all his old VHS tapes on and the remote controls were too small and he was bound to lose them, but basically I think he was pleased, not just about the TV but about everything else as well. We were already getting on much better than the last time I'd visited.

Friday night came around and I still hadn't told him what I had planned for the next day. We ordered a Chinese takeaway and opened a nice bottle of New Zealand Shiraz and then, while he was cutting up the quarter of crispy duck and taking the little pancakes out from their cellophane wrapper, I went into the next room.

When I came back I said, "Dad, I've got something for you." I put a Qantas ticket on the table between us.

"What's that?" he said.

I said, "It's a plane ticket."

He picked it up and looked at it. "This is a ticket for Melbourne," he said.

"That's right."

"For tomorrow."

"Yes, for tomorrow."

He put it down again. "Well, what's going on?"

"You're going to Melbourne tomorrow," I said.

"Why would I want to go to Melbourne?"

"Because . . . because someone will be there tomorrow who I think you ought to see."

He looked at me without comprehension. I realised that I had made it sound like I wanted him to consult a specialist doctor or something.

"Well—who?"

"Roger," I said.

"Roger?"

"Roger Anstruther."

My father stopped cutting up the duck into small, flaky pieces and sat down at the table. "You've been in touch with Roger? How?"

"I tracked him down."

"How?"

"The clue was on the last postcard he sent you. I found it in Lichfield."

"He's still writing to me?"

"Yes. He's never stopped writing. I've got about two hundred postcards from him upstairs, in my suitcase."

My father scratched his head. "He wants to see me?"

"Yes."

"Did you speak to him?"

"Yes."

"How did he sound?"

"He sounded . . . keen to see you."

"He's living in Melbourne now?"

I shook my head. "Adelaide. We chose Melbourne because it was a good halfway point."

My father picked up the ticket again and looked at the time of the flight, although he didn't seem to be taking any of the details in. "So it sounds like this is all arranged."

"If you want to go through with it."

"Where are we supposed to be meeting?"

"In the tea rooms of the Botanical Gardens," I said, "at three o'clock tomorrow afternoon."

He put the ticket down and picked up his knife and fork and resumed work on the duck, his brow furrowed in thought. For a long time after that he said no more on the subject. My father, I'm beginning to realise, has a genius for silence.

That night, all the same, it was obvious he was highly agitated. I handed over the bundles of postcards and when I went to bed I left him sitting at the kitchen table, reading through them methodically. At three o'clock in the morning, still jet-lagged, I woke up and saw there was a light coming from beneath his bedroom door. I could hear the creak of the floorboards as he paced up and down. I suspect that neither of us slept for the rest of the night.

I was the first one to use the kitchen the next morning. While I was in there making coffee at about seven o'clock, my father came in and said abruptly: "You didn't get me a return ticket."

"No."

"Why not?"

"I didn't know how long you'd want to stay. I thought that kind of depended on how things panned out. You'll have to buy the return half yourself."

"I can't afford to buy a plane ticket from Melbourne to Sydney."

"I'll reimburse you."

When I said this, he did something . . . well, he did something that I found quite extraordinary. If you were lucky enough to have had a reasonably normal relationship with your own parents, you might find it hard to understand just how extraordinary this was, to me. First of all, he said, "Thank you, Max." Then he said, "You didn't have to do this for me, you know." But that's not the strange thing. The strange thing was that while he was saying this, he came over to where I was pouring boiling water onto the coffee grains in my mug, and he put his hand on my shoulder. He touched me.

I was forty-eight years old. It was the first time I could remember him ever doing anything like that. I turned round and our eyes met, very briefly. But the moment was too uncomfortable, for both of us, so we soon looked away.

"What are you going to do with yourself today?" he asked me.

"No great plans," I said. "Except that tonight I have to go to this restaurant. I'm hoping to meet somebody there myself."

I told him it was the same restaurant where we'd failed to have dinner together at the end of my last visit. And I also told him a little bit about the Chinese woman and her daughter.

"You know this woman?" he asked, as I handed him a mug of instant coffee.

"No, not exactly. But"—this felt like a bizarre thing to be saying, but I ploughed ahead—"in a way it does feel like we know each other. That I've known her a long time."

"I see," he said, doubtfully. "Is she married? Does she have a boyfriend?"

"I don't think so. I'm pretty sure she's a single mother."

"And tonight you're going to talk to her, is that the idea?"

"That's the idea."

"Well, good luck," he said.

"And you, Dad," I said. "It's a big day for both of us."

We clinked our mugs together and drank to the success of our prospective encounters.

About half an hour later, just before he left, I reminded my father that I'd found the charger for his mobile phone and charged it fully and left it on top of the bookcase in the living room.

"Don't forget to take it, will you!" I called while he was in his bedroom, cramming a few things into an overnight bag.

"Don't worry," he called back. "I've already got it. I've got it right here."

And, stupidly, I believed him.

And now here he was: back in Sydney, little more than twelve hours later, taking his seat opposite me on the restaurant terrace while the water and the lights of Sydney Harbour shimmered behind us. Apart from the Chinese woman and her daughter, we were the only people left out here. A cool breeze was blowing in off the water. It ruffled my father's hair, and as it did so I thought he was lucky to still have a full head of hair at his age. Thinking about this, I ran a hand through my own hair, which was almost entirely grey now but—like my father's—still full and thick, and I reflected that I had probably inherited his hair and should be grateful for that because a lot of men my age were already practically bald. I looked at my father while thinking these thoughts and realised that I was like him in many ways—the colour of my eyes, the line of my chin, how we both liked to swirl our drinks around in our glasses before drinking them. And for the first time, this knowledge felt welcome, a good thing, and it gave me a warm feeling in the pit of my stomach: like a kind of homecoming.

"I was hoping I'd find you here," he said. "Have you finished eating? Will you join me in a drink? Because, believe me, I feel like a drink."

I told him that I would certainly join him in a drink, so he called the waiter over and asked for two large amarettos (except that he called them "amaretti").

"So, how did it go?" I asked, although I could see already that something must have gone wrong. "How did it go with Roger? Did you manage to recognise him after all these years?"

The waiter brought our drinks over (that was another thing I liked about this restaurant—fantastic service) and then went to the other table to settle up the bill with the Chinese woman and her daughter.

My father swirled his amaretto around in the glass before taking a long sip. "Whose idea was it that we should meet in the tea rooms at the Botanical Gardens?" he asked. "Was that your idea, or Roger's?"

"That was my idea," I said. "Why, was there something wrong with it? Don't tell me they were closed for renovation or something."

"No. No, there was nothing wrong with the idea, really. Those gardens are beautiful. I'm just surprised you were the one to choose them, because I didn't think you'd ever been to Melbourne."

"I haven't," I admitted. "Actually, I've got a Facebook friend who lives in Melbourne, so I asked him to suggest somewhere. So I suppose it was actually his idea, not mine."

"Ah. All right, then. Well, that's fine."

I could sense that it wasn't fine. That something about it wasn't fine at all. "But?" I prompted.

"Well . . ." My father took another sip while he thought carefully about his words. "Well, it was a lovely idea, Max, but there's just one problem."

"Yes?"

He leaned forward, and said: *"There are two different tea rooms at the Botanical Gardens in Melbourne."*

I had been just about to take a sip of amaretto. I lowered the glass slowly.

"What?"

"There are two different tea rooms. At opposite ends of the gardens. One is up at the main entrance, opposite the big war memorial, the other one's down by the ornamental lake. I went to the one down by the lake."

"And Roger?" I said, although I was barely able to speak.

"Well, it seems he went to the other one."

The full absurdity, the full horror of it was dawning on me. "You missed each other?"

My father nodded.

"But . . . I gave him your mobile number. And I put his number into your phone. Didn't he try to call you?"

"Yes. Fourteen times. As I found out when I got home. Here." He took his mobile out of his jacket pocket and showed me the little message on the screen: "14 missed calls."

"So why didn't you answer?"

"I didn't have my phone with me."

"You *didn't*? Dad—you . . . idiot. I *asked* if you had your phone with you. And you said you did. I asked you that this morning."

"I thought I'd got it with me, but I hadn't. I had this

instead." He took something out of his other jacket pocket and laid it on the table between us. It was the remote control for his new flat-screen TV. "You've got to admit," he said, positioning it next to his mobile on the table, "they do look similar."

It was true. They did. "So . . . so what happened?"

"Well, I got to the tea room at about ten to three, and I sat there for about half an hour or so, and then it occurred to me that Roger was late. So I checked my phone to see if he'd maybe called and I hadn't heard it, and that was when I realised I'd brought the remote control with me by mistake. Well, I didn't panic, because at that point, as far as I knew, there was only one tea room at the Botanical Gardens, and I was sitting in it. So I waited there for another twenty minutes, and when a girl came over to clear my tea things away, I said, 'Incidentally, if you told someone that you were going to meet them at the tea room of the Botanical Gardens, is this where you'd come?' And she smiled at me and said, 'Of course it is,' but then just as she was leaving, she turned round and said, 'Oh—unless you meant the other one, that is.'"

We both swirled our amaretti around in our glasses and took another drink. Both glasses were almost empty.

"So then I knew exactly what had happened. And I asked the girl how long it would take to walk from one place to the other and she said about ten or fifteen minutes (she could see that I wasn't exactly in the first flush of youth), and I asked her whether there was more than one path and she said there were several different paths. So I thought Roger surely would realise what had happened as well, and that it would be best to stay put for a little while. So I sat there for another fifteen minutes and then started to panic, because I probably could've asked someone in my tea room to phone the people in the other one and ask if they could see if there was anyone like Roger there.

But anyway, I didn't think of that, I just got up and left my table and walked over to the other tea room. Which actually took me more like twenty-five minutes, because I can't walk so fast these days and I kept getting lost. In any case, when I got there, Roger was gone."

"Had he been there in the first place?"

"Oh yes. The man serving behind the counter described him to me."

"But you haven't seen Roger for forty years."

My father smiled. "I know. But it was Roger he was describing. Some things you don't forget."

"So then what happened?"

"So then I . . ." My father was about to launch into a further narration, but seemed to have lost the will. "Oh, Max," he said. "Do you really need to know? What about another drink?"

We ordered two more amaretti from the waiter: at which point I realised the Chinese woman and her daughter were no longer sitting at their table.

"Oh no—they've gone," I said, my heart sinking. I'd been so distracted by my father's story that I hadn't even noticed they were leaving.

"Who's gone?"

"The woman and her daughter. The ones I wanted to speak to."

"Didn't you manage to speak to them?"

"No."

"I assumed you'd spoken to them already."

"I was just about to speak to them when you turned up. And now they've gone."

Distraught, I stood up from the table to get a better look around me and spotted them about a hundred yards away, walking hand in hand back towards Circular Quay. For a moment

I actually contemplated running after them. I had come all the way from London to speak to this woman, after all. In fact I would probably have left the terrace and sprinted off in pursuit if it hadn't been for my father's restraining hand on my arm.

"Sit down," he said. "You can talk to them tomorrow."

"What do you mean, tomorrow?" I said, angry with him now. "They've *gone*, do you hear me? They've gone and there's absolutely no chance of finding them again, unless I come back here in a month's time."

"You can talk to them tomorrow," my father repeated. "I know where they'll be."

Our second round of amaretti arrived. These were on the house, the waiter told us. We thanked him, and my father continued: "If you mean the woman and the little girl who were sitting in the corner of the terrace there"—I nodded, breathless with the fear that he was about to tease me with some sort of false hope—"I overheard them talking when I arrived. The girl was asking if she could go swimming tomorrow, and her mother said that she could if the weather was nice, and the girl said she wanted to go to Fairlight Beach."

"Fairlight Beach? Where's that?"

"Fairlight's a little suburb over towards Manly. There's a sheltered beach there with a natural swimming pool. So that's where they'll be tomorrow, by the sound of it."

"If the weather's nice."

"If the weather's nice."

"What's the weather forecast?"

"Rain," said my father, sipping his amaretto. "But they usually get it wrong."

"Did they say what time they were going?"

"No," said my father. "I suppose you'll have to get there pretty early if you want to be sure of seeing them."

I contemplated this possibility. My flight back to London was leaving at about ten o'clock the following night, and I had no definite plans for the rest of the day. The thought of spending hours and hours sitting on some beach looking out for the Chinese woman and her daughter was slightly daunting, however. But what choice did I have? My need to speak to her had become all-consuming—even if it meant only exchanging a few words. The thought of going back to London without making some kind of connection with her was insupportable.

"Well," I said with a sigh, "I suppose that's what I'll have to do then."

"Don't worry, Max—everything will be fine."

I looked at him in surprise. I was definitely seeing some new sides of my father this week. It wasn't like him to be reassuring. "You seem very . . . calm, considering what you've been through today," I said.

"Well, what can you do?" he said. "Some things, Max . . . some things just aren't meant to be. It's more than forty years since I last saw Roger. It's fifty years since we did the things I wrote about in that memoir. I've survived without him all that time. Sure, I was pretty cut up when we managed to miss each other again today. A dreadful sense of history repeating itself, as you can imagine. But then . . . Then I walked back to the tea room—the one I'd gone to first, down by the ornamental lake. And I sat there for a while, ordered a beer and thought, Well, if he comes, he comes, and if he doesn't, he doesn't. And he didn't. It was a beautiful afternoon. It's much warmer in Melbourne than it is here. I sat there, and drank my beer, and listened to all the exotic bird noises, and looked at the palm trees and the date trees . . . I had a lovely time, actually. They have a magnificent bald cypress there, just by the ornamental lake. A

Mexican bald cypress. In fact I wrote a poem about it. 'Taxodia-ceae,' I called it. Here—have a look."

He handed me his black moleskin notebook and I attempted to read the little eight-line poem he'd written in there this afternoon. Trying to decipher his handwriting was bad enough: as for the poem itself, as usual I couldn't make head nor tail of it.

"Great," I said, handing the notebook back, and struggled to think of something else to say. "You should really get these poems of yours published."

"Oh, I'm just an amateur, I know that."

"Did Roger leave any messages on your phone?" I asked, still hoping to salvage something from today's debacle.

"I've no idea," my father said. "I don't know how to retrieve messages, and I don't really want to hear them if he did."

"Really?" I said. "After all these years, you have no . . . curiosity?"

"Max," my father said, leaning forward and resting his hands on mine. Another unprecedented gesture. "You did an amazing thing for me today. I'll never forget that. Not because I really wanted to see Roger again, but because it shows that you accept me. You accept me for what I am."

"Better late than never," I said, with a quiet, regretful laugh.

"What do you think of my apartment?" my father asked after a short pause, during which he withdrew his hands from mine.

"Well, it's . . . OK, I suppose. Needs a bit of work, maybe, to make it more homey."

"Hideous, isn't it? I'm going to give notice."

"And move? Where to?"

"I think it's about time I came home, really. That flat in Lichfield's just going to waste, after all. It would make far more sense for me to live there. If you get worried about me again—or I get worried about you, for that matter—it makes life much easier if I'm three hours' drive up the motorway, doesn't it? Rather than a twenty-four-hour flight."

And yes, I agreed: it would make far more sense if he lived in Lichfield rather than Sydney. So we spent the rest of the evening talking about that: not about Roger Anstruther, or the Chinese woman and her daughter. Instead I told my father about Miss Erith and how she had called him a miserable sod for going away and not telling her when he was going to come back, and how friendly she was with Dr. Hameed, and how she had railed against the takeover of England by the big corporations. And he agreed it would be nice to see her again. And somehow, I'm not quite sure how—talking about his original move to Lichfield, I suppose, as a reaction to my mother's death—we ended up talking about my mother. Talking about my mother, after all these years! Before tonight, I don't think either of us had mentioned her name to the other since her funeral. And now, for the first time, I saw my father's eyes fill with tears, real tears, as he started talking about their years of married life together, what a lousy husband he felt he had been, what a shitty time he had given her, what a useless hand she had been dealt by God or fate or whatever it was—dying at the age of forty-six, when all she'd known up to that point was the joylessness of being married to a man consumed with self-hatred, a man who had no idea how to relate to her, or even to his son, a man who knew nothing except how to bottle up his emotions and repress his desires . . .

My father only started to compose himself again when he realised the waiter was standing over us.

"Gentlemen," the waiter said, "we'll be closing in a few minutes."

"Fair enough," I answered.

"Before then . . . perhaps two more amaretti?"

When he brought the drinks, my father and I clinked glasses again and drank a toast in memory of my mother.

"She meant everything to me," I said. "I never told her that, you know. I should have done. I hope she understood, somehow or other, just how much I loved her."

I looked across at Dad, wondering if he was going to say something similar. Had he loved her too? Surely he must have, in his own way, to have stayed with her all that time. But he said nothing, just smiled back at me sadly.

The waiter had begun to stack chairs on the tables around us. We were both tired and ready for bed.

"Well, anyway—let's look to the future. At the very least, we should do something about Mum's gravestone. All it says is 'Barbara Sim, 1939–1985.' We really ought to come up with something better than that."

"You're right," my father said. "That's the first thing we'll do."

I had a moment of inspiration. "I know—what about those lines from *Four Quartets*? Those really nice ones, about time past being contained in time present."

My father considered this. "Not bad. Not bad at all."

But I could tell that he wasn't convinced. "Have you got a better idea?"

"Not really. But the trouble is, your mother couldn't stand poetry. She would have hated to have T. S. Eliot on her gravestone."

"All right, then. What did she like?"

"Oh, I don't know. She liked Tommy Steele, Cliff Richard . . ."

"OK, let's go with Cliff. A few lines from one of his songs."

" 'Living Doll' . . . ," mused my father, and shook his head. "Not very appropriate for a gravestone, really."

"What about 'Devil Woman'? Maybe not."

" 'Congratulations'? I don't think so."

" 'We're all going on a summer holiday'?"

"No, those don't work as epitaphs. None of them."

Our eyes met again, and suddenly we burst out laughing—then continued to swirl the two glasses of amaretto around in our hands before drinking them down to the last drop.

22

Donald Crowhurst started to contemplate the insoluble mystery of the square root of minus one and before long found himself entering a "dark tunnel" from which he was never to emerge. Most of us, thankfully, are luckier than that. Few people are able to avoid those tunnels altogether, but usually something brings us out the other side. The one I was in . . . well, it actually turned out to be longer and darker than I could ever have imagined. I realise now that I had been lost in it for most of my life. But the important thing is that I escaped in the end, and when I did finally step out into the sunlight, blinking and rubbing my eyes, it was to find myself at a place in Sydney called Fairlight Beach.

I arrived there at nine o'clock in the morning, having taken one of the earliest ferries from Circular Quay to Manly. From Manly Wharf to Fairlight was a walk of perhaps fifteen minutes. The skies were grey and puffy with rainclouds, but despite this there was a moist, dense heat in the air. It was certainly warm enough to go swimming. The dozens of joggers I passed on the coastal walk from the wharf to the beach were covered in sweat. I'd imagined that I would be conspicuous, that I would have the place to myself and would cut a suspicious-looking figure sitting above the beach all alone, but no: there was a continual flow of passers-by. Not just the joggers but the dog walkers and the sightseers and people who were just out for a morning stroll, wandering down to the shops to buy their Sunday papers. I felt at home here, felt myself to be part of a community that was genial and relaxed and accepting.

Three hours, though, is a long time to sit by yourself on a bench overlooking the sea, waiting anxiously for someone to appear. I'd picked up a copy of the *Sun-Herald* on the way, but that only kept me occupied for about an hour. The only other item I'd thought to bring was a small bottle of water, and I didn't drink too much of that in case it made me want to go to the toilet. The view was spectacular: at the edge of the sandy beach there was a saltwater swimming pool built into the rock, an iridescent rectangle of blue-green water, and beyond that the sea, calm and grey this morning, stretched out towards the horizon, dotted with yachts, and then farther still, well off in the distance, implied rather than glimpsed, lay the gorgeous immensity of Sydney itself. You would have thought it was impossible to get tired of this view. Perhaps on another occasion, when I wasn't looking out so hungrily for the arrival of the Chinese woman and her daughter, I could have been happy to spend the whole day sitting on that bench looking out over the beach and the water. But today, this prospect quickly began to lose its charm.

Anyway, I don't want to make you wait for as long as I did. They came. They came shortly after midday. The Chinese woman, her daughter and another little girl of about the same age. A friend of the daughter's, obviously. Blonde and Caucasian. The three of them walked right past my bench and then down onto the beach, where the Chinese woman spread out a picnic rug on the sand and the two little girls immediately undressed down to their swimming costumes and ran off towards the rocks to play. The Chinese woman—who was wearing a white T-shirt and navy-blue slacks, flared at the ankle—sat on the rug and poured herself something hot to drink from a thermos flask while looking out towards the opposite side of the bay.

So, here was my chance. The moment had come at last. But could I really do it? Could I really walk over to a complete stranger, a single woman who had come for an afternoon at the beach with her little daughter and her friend, and break into her world, invade her privacy, with some clumsy phrase like "Excuse me—you don't know me, but . . ."?

I was just preparing to admit to myself that I couldn't go through with it after all when there was a sudden scream of pain and distress from the direction of the swimming pool.

I looked up. It was the little Chinese girl's friend. She had slipped and fallen. She'd been standing right on the edge of the swimming pool, balancing on the stone wall, where she lost her balance and fell over the edge into the sea. Instinctively, I ran to her aid. Coming from a different direction, from the beach where she'd laid out her picnic rug on the sand, the Chinese woman was running towards her too, and we both reached the same spot at the same moment.

"Jenny!" she called. "Jenny, are you all right?"

The water here was quite shallow, and Jenny was standing upright now, in floods of tears. The drop from the wall to the sea was about four feet, too high for her to climb, so the first thing to do was to pull her back up towards us.

I held out my arms. "Here you are," I said, "hold on to me. I'll pull you up."

The little blonde girl seized both of my hands and I lifted her easily back on to the edge of the pool. We could see now that her left shin and ankle were grazed where she'd fallen against the rocky sea floor. They were bleeding slightly. She flung herself into the Chinese woman's arms and cried there for a few moments, and then all four of us made our way around the edge of the pool and back towards the picnic rug.

"Thank you, thank you so much," the Chinese woman was saying. She was even more beautiful now that I could see her close up.

"Is there anything I can do?" I said.

"I think she'll be fine. She just needs to be cleaned down and—"

"We're not going home, are we, Mum?" her daughter said.

"I don't know, honey, that depends on what Jennifer wants. Jennifer, do you want to go back home to your mother?"

Jennifer shook her head.

When we reached the rug, Jennifer lay down and we had a good look at her leg. One of the scratches was pretty big. The Chinese woman took some Kleenex out of a box in her picnic basket, and I poured water from my water bottle over the wound, and together we cleaned it and mopped away the blood. Then she rummaged through the basket again and I heard her whispering to herself, "No Band-Aids! How could I not have brought any Band-Aids!"

And I remembered passing a pharmacy on the way to the beach, so I said: "I'll go and get some."

"No—please—really—it's too much to ask."

"Not at all. There's a shop just up the road from here. She really needs to have something to cover up those scratches. Otherwise she's not going to be able to go in the water all day."

"Really, I don't think—"

But I didn't listen to her protests, and before she had finished making them I set off on my errand. I was there and back in less than ten minutes. Once I'd returned, and handed over the Band-Aids, I felt there wasn't much else to offer by way of help. The scratches were covered over quickly enough, and the two little girls—who seemed to have polished off most of their picnic while I'd been away—had fully regained their high spirits. Now they were ready to rush off to the swimming pool again.

Before they were allowed to go, the Chinese woman stood up and pulled her daughter's hair back into a tight ponytail, securing it with a hair-tie. "Now, don't get into the water until your food's digested," she said. "And please be careful this time."

"We will."

"And what about saying thank you to the nice gentleman, for all his help?"

"Thank you," they chorused dutifully.

"Don't mention it," I said. But they were already gone.

We stood there for a little while, the two of us, me and the Chinese woman, in confused silence. Neither of us knew what to say.

"Really," I managed, in the end, "I'm just glad that I happened to be here. I mean, I'm sure you would've been all right by yourselves, but . . ."

She looked at me with a frown and said, "I'm not usually very good with accents—but yours is English, right?"

"It is, yes."

"So are you just visiting? Have you been in Sydney for long?"

"Just a week," I said. "I came to see my father. Bit of family business to sort out. Now that it's done, I'm heading back to London. Tonight, as it happens."

On hearing this, she held out her hand stiffly, formally. "Well, thank you very much for your help, Mr. . . . er—"

"Sim," I said, taking her hand and shaking it. "Maxwell Sim."

"Thank you, Mr. Sim. Before you go, there was one thing I wanted to ask you—if I may."

"Of course."

"Well, I was just curious, really. I was just curious to know whether it was purely coincidence that we were eating at the same restaurant last night."

"Ah," I said. My game, it seemed, was up.

"And also two months ago, if I'm not mistaken."

"Two months ago," I repeated. "Yes, that's correct."

"Are you following me, then, Mr. Sim? Should I be calling the police?"

I didn't know what to say. Her eyes now had quite a glint in them, but it was a glint of defiance rather than alarm. "I did come here," I said carefully, "because I knew I'd find you. And I wanted to find you because there's a question I'd like to ask you. Something I need to know that only you can tell me. That's all."

"That's all? Well then, we'd better have the question."

"Right. The question." Oh well, I might as well blurt it out. "Are you married? Do you have a boyfriend? Does your daughter have a father?"

The Chinese woman smiled tightly and looked away. "I see," she said. Then, turning back towards me: "Yes, Mr. Sim, I am married. Happily married, as I believe the saying is."

"Ah. Right." Immediately it felt as though a huge chasm of disappointment had opened up in front of me, and all I wanted to do now was to throw myself in. "In that case," I said, "I think I'd better go. I'm very sorry if I . . . disturbed you in any way. It was extremely—"

"Please," said the Chinese woman. "Don't go. You haven't disturbed me at all. In fact you've been more than helpful. And what you've done is—well, quite romantic, from one point of view. If you've come out here just to see me, then the least I can do is to offer you something. A cup of tea, perhaps?"

"That's very kind of you, but—"

"Please, Maxwell, sit down. May I call you Maxwell?"

"Yes, of course."

She sat down on the rug and motioned for me to join her—which I did, with a certain sense of embarrassment.

"My name is Lian. My daughter's name is Yanmei. Her schoolfriend's name you already know. Will you take your tea with lemon? I'm afraid I didn't bring any milk."

"I'll just have it . . . as it comes, actually. Whatever's easiest."

Lian poured black tea into two plastic cups and handed one of them to me. I thanked her, and we drank in silence for a moment or two. Then I said, "If I can offer you some sort of explanation—"

"Please do."

"The truth is that when I saw you and Yanmei having dinner together at that restaurant two months ago, it made a profound impression on me."

"Really? In what way?"

"I'd never seen anything quite like the . . . intimacy I saw between the two of you. I saw that intimacy and I felt the lack of it in my own life, and I started to hope—to fantasise, actually—that I might be able to share in it."

Lian gave another of her tight but captivating smiles. She looked down into her teacup and said, "Well, those dinners we have together are very special to us. We go there on the second Saturday of every month. Once a month, you see, my husband, Peter, has to go to Dubai. The working week there starts on a Sunday morning. So he catches a flight from Sydney at ten past nine the evening before. Yanmei and I go to the airport to see him off, and then she's always a little downcast, because she loves her father so much and misses him when he's away. So, as a special treat, I take her to that restaurant. Twelve times a year, without fail, be it summer or winter. Children need patterns; they need routine. Well, so do grown-ups, actually. Going to that restaurant is one of the constants in our life."

"I love," I began, feeling that I now had nothing to lose, by speaking my mind as clearly as possible, "—I love how you play cards together. It's as if the rest of the world doesn't exist. And Yanmei is just like a miniature version of you." I glanced across to where she was poised on the edge of the swimming pool, summoning up the courage for a dive. "She sounds the same, her movements are the same, she looks just like you."

"Really?" said Lian. "You think there's a physical resemblance?"

"Of course."

"But you know," she said, "Yanmei is not my biological daughter."

"She isn't?"

"No. Peter and I adopted her three years ago. In fact, we don't even have the same nationality. I come from Hong Kong, originally. Yanmei is from China—a city called Shen-yang, in Liaoning province. So perhaps the resemblance between us is only in your head. Perhaps it's something you wanted to see."

"Maybe," I said, sipping my tea and looking across the bay. I was disturbed by this information, for some reason. Knowing that there was no blood relationship between Lian and Yanmei somehow changed my fantasy about them. "You have no children of your own, then?"

"No. It was a great sadness in our lives, for a while. But now we have Yanmei, so . . ."

"She was an orphan?"

"Yes. Her mother died a few years ago, when she was only three. A horrible death, I'm afraid. You know, the working conditions in some of those factories are beyond belief. The things those workers put up with so that we in the West can have our cut-price goods. Yanmei's mother was working fifteen or sixteen hours a day in her factory, handling molten plastic all the time, full of toxic chemicals. No proper precautions—no masks or anything. She died of cancer. Cancer of the brain."

"How awful," I said. It was a weak enough phrase, but the best I could manage. "What was the factory making?"

"Toothbrushes, I believe."

I looked across at Lian sharply when she said this. Had I heard correctly? "Toothbrushes?"

"Yes—cheap plastic toothbrushes. You look surprised. Is that so surprising?"

I was speechless, in fact.

"Do toothbrushes have some sort of special significance for you?"

Gradually, I started to find my voice again. "Yes, they do. A very special significance. More than that. What you've just told me, the story of Yanmei's mother . . . well, I find it astonishing. Incredible."

"There is nothing incredible about it at all. These things are happening all the time, in the developing world and elsewhere. Unfortunately, we tend to blind ourselves to them."

"No, I mean that what I find incredible is its . . . its personal significance. The significance to me, personally."

"Oh, I see. But could you perhaps explain this significance?"

I took a deep breath, then shook my head. "It would take . . . I'm afraid it would take a very long time. You see, in a weird sort of way, everything that's happened to me in the last few weeks is connected to Yanmei and her mother. But I'd have to tell you the whole story to make you understand that, and I'm sure you'd find it very boring."

"But now you have to tell me. Look." She gestured over at Yanmei and Jennifer, who were happily splashing from one side of the pool to the other. "The girls are enjoying themselves. They won't want to leave for at least an hour. I didn't bring anything to read. So tell me your story. I want to hear it, however long and boring it is. What else am I going to do?"

And so I began telling her about all the things that had happened to me since I had seen her and Yanmei sitting at the restaurant overlooking Sydney Harbour on Valentine's Day. It was difficult to know how to begin, and I think at first I was just confusing her. I started off by talking about Alan Guest and all the ideals and ambitions he'd tried to realise with his little toothbrush company. I was thinking that if my recent experiences had taught me anything, it was about the cruelty of the world, that we still lived in an age when even the most well-meaning and innovative organisation could be brought to its knees by more powerful forces. But then I thought that perhaps this wasn't the meaning of the story at all, and that maybe what I had really learned (or started to learn) was something about myself, about my own nature and my own problems. So I was trying to flip backwards and forwards between these two ideas, and Lian was getting more and more bewildered, and at that point she told me to start again and just tell the story from the beginning, exactly as it had happened. And when I started doing that, what I found myself telling her didn't feel much like a proper story at all anymore, just a series of random, unconnected episodes, encounters, mainly, with strange and unexpected people who had all done something, in small ways, to change the course of my life over the last few weeks. It had begun with Lian herself, of course, and Yanmei. But then there had been . . . well, first there had been the man at the airline check-in desk in Sydney who had upgraded me to Premium Economy class for no particular reason. Then there had been poor old Charlie Hayward, who had had a heart attack while sitting next to me on the flight to Singapore. Then there was Poppy, with her secret recording device and her story about Donald Crowhurst. Then there was the man in the park in Watford who stole my mobile phone and came back afterwards to ask me for directions. Then there was Trevor Paige and Lindsay Ashworth taking me out for a drink at the Park Inn and asking me to join their sales team. Then the dinner at Poppy's mother's house, where I met Poppy's mother and her obnoxious friend Richard and the only person who had really been friendly to me was her uncle Clive. Then my meeting with Alan Guest himself, the day I set off from his office on the first stage of my journey to Scotland. And then Mr. and Mrs. Byrne, Chris's parents, and then Miss Erith and Dr. Hameed, high up in that apartment block on the edges of Lichfield, and then Caroline and Lucy, and our failed dinner together in Kendal, and then Alison Byrne inviting me to sleep with her in Edinburgh, when I'd run away with her whisky bottles and got into my car at dawn and driven off into the Scottish mountains by myself. In fact the only person I didn't mention once in all of this was Emma, because it embarrassed me now to admit that I'd started talking to my SatNav, and I thought Lian might think less of me if she knew.

As I was telling her about all these encounters, Lian lay back on the picnic rug, put her hands behind her head, and closed her eyes. She didn't say anything, and she didn't ask me any questions; she didn't interrupt me once, even though

I was talking for a long time, and then when I had finished she didn't make any comment, her silence actually making me suspect that she might have fallen asleep. But no, she hadn't fallen asleep. She was just thinking very deeply about what I had told her, and eventually she raised herself onto her elbows and looked at me.

"Well, Maxwell," she said, "now it begins to make sense."

"Now what begins to make sense?"

"Now I can see why you looked so different last night, from the man who'd come to that restaurant two months ago."

"Really?" I said. "You saw a change in me?"

"Of course. That first time, you scared me slightly. I thought I had never seen anyone look so lonely and depressed. But last night—and today—you look . . . well, you look calmer, at least. You look like a man who is almost at peace with himself."

"Almost," I repeated.

"Almost."

"Mum!" Yanmei came running over, with Jennifer not far behind. "What time is it? It isn't time to go yet, is it?"

"Yes, I'm afraid so. Jennifer's mother will be expecting us soon. And don't look so disappointed. Unless I'm much mistaken, she said something about an Easter-egg hunt . . ."

The girls' faces brightened at once.

"OK," said Jennifer. "But one more swim first!"

They ran off laughing in the direction of the pool.

"Five minutes!" Lian called after them. She turned back to me, and saw that I was lost in thought once again.

"Sorry," I said, snapping out of it. "I hadn't even realised that it was Easter Sunday today. The festival of the Rising Sun . . ."

"The rising sun?" said Lian, puzzled.

"Isn't that how Easter began? It's supposed to be a time for new dawns, fresh starts."

Now she smiled at me, and said gently, in a tone of apology, "And you thought I was going to be your fresh start. Me and Yanmei. Well, I'm sorry, Maxwell, but . . . you're going to have to look elsewhere."

"I know."

"In any case . . ."

"Yes?" I said. There was something tantalising, even a little unsettling, about how she'd trailed off, as if she didn't quite dare to say whatever she'd been about to say.

"In any case," she continued, after a moment, "this thing that you're looking for—this intimacy . . . You wouldn't have found it with us."

"Is that what you think? How can you be so sure?"

Lian picked up my plastic cup from the sand and tipped it over, shaking out the last droplets of tea. Then she carefully screwed the cup onto the top of the thermos flask. Her movements were slow and mechanical, suggesting that her thoughts—her real thoughts—were elsewhere.

"This girl Poppy," she said at last. "She interests me. Out of all the people you met on your journey, there is something very special about her. She was the one who understood you the best, I think."

"Yes, but Poppy made it very clear that we could only be friends, nothing more."

"Of course. And yet . . . when she invited you for dinner at her mother's house, didn't you think that was an extraordinary gesture on her part?"

"Extraordinary? In what way?"

"Well, it was generous of her. Also hopeful. And also rather . . . perceptive."

"Yes," I said, a little impatiently, "but as I explained, I didn't get on with her mother, if that was the idea. I didn't find her attractive."

"You think Poppy was trying to make a match between you and her mother?"

"Of course. She told me as much."

"But there was someone else at the party that night."

"Someone else?"

"Someone else."

Who was she talking about? "No there wasn't," I said. "There was a young couple—about twenty years younger than me—and then there was her uncle, Clive. That's all."

Lian gazed at me steadily. Another smile began to spread across her face, but she managed to suppress it when she saw my growing look of outrage.

"I'm sorry," she said. "I spoke out of turn." She hastily crammed the remaining picnic things into her basket, then stood up. "I'd better go and collect my girls."

Still shocked into silence, I rose to my feet as well and took her hand again, unthinkingly, when she offered it to me.

"Goodbye, Maxwell Sim," she said. "And try not to be angry with the people who think they know you better than you know yourself. They mean well." She turned and began to walk away.

I hesitated for a few seconds and then hurried after her, running to catch up. "Lian!" I called.

She wheeled around. "Yes?"

Now out of control—without stopping to think about what I was doing—I seized her, clasping her in my arms and hugging her fiercely. I held on to her so tightly that she couldn't move. Could hardly breathe, I expect. I held her like that for . . . I don't know how long for. Until my own body shook, convulsively, with a single, gigantic sob, and I put my mouth against her hair and wept and whispered into it: "It's hard. Really hard. I know I've got to face it, but it's the hardest thing I've ever . . ."

I felt her palm against my chest, pushing me away, gently at first, then more forcefully. I eased myself away from her and took a step back, then wiped my eyes and looked away: ashamed; shipwrecked; bereft.

"I think you're almost there, now, Maxwell," she said. "You're almost there."

She touched me on the arm and again turned and walked away, back towards the pool, calling for her daughter.

I stayed on the beach until sunset.

It was interesting to watch the changing colours of the sky. I had never done that before. The greyness turned slowly to silver as the clouds began to fracture and let through some glimpses of the dying sun. Before long they were tinged by a more golden glow, then they began to break away and drift even farther apart as the light itself softened and faded until the sky became gradually streaked with the palest of reds and blues. People continued to come and go on the beach. Nobody was using the swimming pool anymore. The long day was finally closing.

Already I missed Lian. I hated the thought that I would never see her again. I missed my father as well. I should really have gone back to see him—I only had a few more hours left in Australia, after all—but something was stopping me. Something was paralysing me. There was no urgency about talking to him anyhow, now that I knew he'd be coming back to live in England. We would soon be having plenty of times together, plenty of good times.

374 • THE TERRIBLE PRIVACY OF MAXWELL SIM

I couldn't sit here forever. I would miss my plane if I didn't leave soon. But I knew there was something I needed to do first.

I needed to talk to someone. I needed to talk to someone really, really urgently—more urgently, even, than when I'd been driving drunk around the Cairngorms in a raging blizzard and my mobile phone had run out of battery.

Today, of course, my phone was fully charged. What was stopping me, then?

I was like little Yanmei, standing poised on the edge of the swimming pool, summoning up the courage for a dive. But knowing that once it was done, once I had found that courage, there was the coolness of the water to look forward to, the long-delayed sense of release, of freedom . . .

Almost there, now, Max. Almost there.

What time was it in London? The time difference had gone haywire in the last couple of weeks. Britain had put its clocks forward by an hour for the summer, and Australia had just put its clocks back by an hour for the winter, or was it the other way round? Something like that, anyway. So if it was five o'clock in Sydney, it was . . . pretty early in the morning in London. Too early to call someone? Difficult to say. The timing of this call was neither here nor there, in any case. Either this call was going to be welcome, or it wasn't.

I took out my phone and scrolled through the memory until I reached Clive's name. Then I took a deep breath and pressed the call button.

The phone rang for what seemed like aeons. He wasn't going to answer. But finally he did.

"Hello?" I said. "Hello, Clive?"

"Yes, this is Clive. Good God—is that Max, by any chance?"

"Yes, it is. Did I wake you up?"

"You did, actually, but never mind. Doesn't matter a bit. It's just lovely to hear from you."

Now, tell me if I'm repeating myself . . . but have I ever mentioned that the first thing I find attractive in someone, nine times out of ten, is his voice?

I stayed on the beach until sunset.

(Stop me if you've had enough of this by now.)

I watched the changing colours of the sky.

(You don't have to read any more if you don't want to. The story is over.)

I telephoned Clive and knew that everything was going to be all right.

(It's been a long haul, I know. Thanks to all the people who have stayed with me. Really, I appreciate it. And I admire your stamina, I must say. Most impressive.)

And then . . .

And then a group of people arrived at the beach. A family group. They hadn't come from Manly Wharf, but along a coastal path in the opposite direction, from the west, and there were seven of them altogether. A husband and wife and their two daughters—they were easy enough to spot—whereas the others, well, that was harder to say. Grandparents, maybe? Aunts, uncles, family friends? I couldn't be sure. The two girls were very pale, and they were wearing floaty summer dresses over their swimming costumes. The younger one seemed to be about eight, the older one twelve or thirteen—close to Lucy's age. They ran straight down to the water's edge and began splashing and paddling in the shallows. Their mother, who had long, blonde hair, went down to keep an eye on them, while their father stayed on the path above the beach and walked along it slowly, looking dreamy and preoccupied. He had grey hair—bordering on white—and was wearing a light-brown jacket over a white T-shirt that gave away rather too much of his middle-age spread. The whole ensemble made him look a bit like a caffè latte, served in a tall glass with a slight bulge in the middle.

There were free benches on either side of mine, but to my surprise he ignored those and sat down right beside me. At any other time I might have resented the intrusion, but by now my mood was relaxed, expansive and hopeful: it had begun to feel that anything that happened to me from now on could only be for the best. And besides, I thought I could detect a certain kindness and benevolence in the deep-blue eyes of this affable stranger. So, if he wanted to engage me in conversation, I was ready for it.

"Evening," I said.

"Evening," he repeated back at me, and added: "How's it going?"

It was one of those meaningless questions that normally don't require a proper response. Today, however, I decided to defy social convention and take it seriously.

"Well, since you ask, it's going pretty well," I told him. "It's been a draining couple of days, in some respects, but at the end of it all . . . I have to say I'm feeling good. Very good."

"Excellent. Just what I wanted to hear."

"You're from England too, right?"

"Ha! The accent's a giveaway, isn't it? Yes, we're over here for three weeks. My wife's from Australia originally. Catching up with some of her relatives."

"That's your wife down there?" I asked, indicating the

pretty blonde woman standing on the rocks with the two pale little girls.

"It is, yes."

I looked at the man more closely.

"This may sound a weird thing to ask," I said, "but would I be right in thinking we've met somewhere before?"

"Do you know, I was just thinking the same thing. I believe we have. In fact, I'm sure of it. I can even remember where."

"Well," I said, "there you have the advantage over me. Please don't take it personally, but the thing is, I've met so many different people over the last few weeks—"

"That's all right. I understand," the man answered. "In any case, it's a bit misleading to say that we actually met. Our paths crossed—that would be more accurate. We didn't speak to each other."

"Where was it, then?"

"You really don't remember?"

"I'm afraid not."

"It was at Heathrow airport, nearly two months ago. You were sitting in one of the cafés trying to drink a cappuccino, only it was so hot that you could barely touch it. I was sitting at the next table, getting ready to go to Moscow."

"That's right! Your wife and daughters were there as well."

"They'd come to see me off."

Yes, I remembered it clearly now. This was one encounter I'd failed to mention to Lian when I was telling her the story of my last few weeks. I could recall eavesdropping on the family's conversation and being slightly baffled by it.

"Why *did* you have to go to Moscow?" I asked. "I did happen to overhear some of what you were saying at the time, and I think you mentioned something about . . . interviews?"

"That's right. It was a publicity trip. I'm a writer, you see."

"Ah—a writer. That would explain it." It occurred to me that Caroline, had she been here, would have been excited to meet a genuine writer. I can't say I was very thrilled. "Should I have heard of you?" I asked.

He laughed. "No, of course not."

"What sort of books do you write?"

"Novels, mostly. Fiction."

"Ah, I don't read much fiction. Are you working on something at the moment?"

"Just finishing one, since you ask. Getting very close to the end now."

I nodded in what I hoped was an encouraging way. Then we fell silent.

"One thing I've always wondered about writers," I said. "Where do you get your ideas from?"

He looked at me in some surprise. I suppose it was quite possible that he'd never been asked this question before.

"Hmm—that's a tricky one," he said. "You know, it's really very difficult to generalise . . ."

"Well, what about this book you're just finishing?"

"Where did I get the idea for that, do you mean?"

"Yes, if you like."

"Well now, let me see." He leaned back on the bench and looked at the sky. "It becomes quite hard to remember in any detail, but . . . yes, that was it! Yes, I can tell you exactly where I got the idea."

"Please do."

"Well, two years ago—Easter 2007, that is—I came to Australia with my family for another visit, and we were eating out one night at this restaurant overlooking Sydney Harbour, and I happened to see this Chinese woman and her little daughter having a card game together at their table."

I stared at him.

"And I don't know why," he continued, "but there was something so touching about them—there seemed to be such an intimacy, such a connection between them, that I wondered what it would feel like to be a lonely man eating at that restaurant all by yourself, and to be offered this little glimpse into their world and to want to be a part of it."

I tried to stop him, but he was in full flow by now.

"And then, on that same trip, I'd arranged to meet Ian—my old friend Ian from Warwick University, who teaches at the ANU in Canberra now—I'd arranged to meet him in the tea rooms at the Botanical Gardens in Melbourne, but I hadn't realised that there were *two* tea rooms at the Botanical Gardens in Melbourne, so we almost missed each other. And I think it was the combination of those two ideas that got me started writing the book. That's usually how it works. A couple of ideas like that, sort of . . . rubbing up against each other." He turned to look at me. I no longer felt like interrupting him, having all but lost (not for the first time that day) my power of speech. "Does any of this sound at all familiar?"

My throat was dry.

"I think I'm beginning to get the picture," I said, finally.

"So how does it feel," he asked, "to be part of someone else's story?"

"I'm . . . not sure," I answered, choosing my words with care. "It's going to take some getting used to, I think." Then, with a sinking feeling, already knowing what the answer would be, I asked, "Does this book of yours involve toothbrushes, by any chance? And Donald Crowhurst?"

"Funnily enough," said the writer, "it involves both of those things. I wanted the story to revolve around a household object—one that people use every day, without really thinking about the political or environmental implications. Well, I had trouble coming up with anything suitable, and in the end, it was actually my wife who suggested toothbrushes. And shortly after that I was having coffee in London with my friend Laura, who's an art critic, and she started telling me about these works by Tacita Dean that were inspired by the Donald Crowhurst story, and she also put me on to this brilliant book about him by Nicholas Tomalin and Ron Hall. So you see, what generally happens—to answer your original question—is that I get all sorts of different ideas, from all sorts of different places, and then, when I start putting them together, other things start to emerge. People, to be precise. Characters. Or in this particular instance"—he looked directly at me—"*you.*"

Suddenly I felt like the hero of a low-rent spy movie, just when he realises that he's walked straight into the trap set for him by the villain.

"I see. So that's . . . me, is it?" I said, playing for time as much as anything else. "I'm just a by-product of your ideas, is that right? Well, I have to say that doesn't do wonders for my self-esteem."

"Look at it this way," he answered. "It's no worse than discovering that you exist only because there are two pubs close to each other in London called the Rising Sun, is it? Or knowing, for that matter, that you exist only because of some random, billion-to-one collision between one of your father's sperm and one of your mother's eggs? Really, Max, I'd say that your existence has *more* meaning than most people's."

The writer's tone when he was telling me all this was hard to gauge. Was he trying to be nice to me, or was he just playing with me like a cat plays with a mouse before making the final, deadly pounce?

I looked across the beach. His daughters had slipped out

of their dresses and were now taking turns jumping into the swimming pool and climbing out again. Set against the sweep of the bay, and the ever-changing pinks and golds of the sunset's dying embers, it was a ravishing scene. It seemed days, weeks, even years since Yanmei and her friend had been swimming in there. My whole conversation with Lian already seemed to belong to a different time altogether.

"You see, I worked out your itinerary in some detail," said the writer—rather boastfully, I thought. "Starting with Valentine's Day 2009. And then, when I realised that you'd have to arrive at Heathrow two days later, and when I remembered I'd actually been there myself that very same morning, going off to do some readings in Moscow, I thought it would be nice if I could look in on you—while we were both passing through, as it were. You know, just to check if things were going OK. I do feel quite responsible for you, after all."

"And Fairlight Beach, in Sydney?" I was getting a pretty good idea of how his devious mind worked by now. "I'm guessing you really were here on Easter Sunday with your family—is that right?"

"Of course. I mean, just look at this place. It's so lovely, isn't it, at this time of year, and in this light? Such a sad, beautiful spot. I knew as soon as I saw it that the last scene in the book would have to be here."

My heart sank when I heard these words. They sounded like a death knell.

"The last scene?" I said. "You're really that close to finishing, are you?"

"I think I am, yes. So—have you enjoyed it? I mean, have you enjoyed being part of it? How was it for you, Max?"

"I'm not sure 'enjoyed' is really the word I would use," I said. "It's been . . . an experience, that's for sure. I suppose I've learned a thing or two along the way."

"That was the whole idea."

What a smug thing to say! I was beginning to suspect that beneath his courteous exterior, this guy was full of nothing but conceit and self-admiration.

"Don't you think it's rather an undignified thing to do," I said, definitely trying to rattle him now, "making up stories for a living? Let's face it, you're no spring chicken anymore. What about writing something more serious? History, or science, something like that?"

"Well, that's a very interesting point," the writer said, sitting back on the bench and looking as though he was about to start addressing a seminar. "Because you're absolutely correct that the kind of thing I write, from a literal point of view, isn't objectively 'true.' But what I like to think is that there's another kind of truth, a more universal—erm, excuse me, where do you think you're going?"

I'd thought that while he was rabbiting on like this, it might be a good opportunity for me to sneak away. My plane left at ten o'clock, after all, and I would have to check in a good two hours before then.

"Well, I have to go now, you see. I've got a plane to catch."

The writer stood up and blocked my path.

"I don't think you understand, Max. You're not going anywhere."

Just at that moment, his wife came by and spoke a few words to him.

"Could you go and get the girls out of the pool? Daddy's looking a bit tired, and I think we should get home."

"Yes, in a minute," he answered impatiently.

"Talking to your imaginary friends again, are you?" she said with an undertone of scorn, then headed off towards the swimming pool herself.

He turned back to me.

"Like I said, Max—I'm sorry, but you're not going anywhere."

"But I have to catch that plane," I said, my voice starting to shake now. "I've got to get back to London tomorrow. I'm having dinner with Clive in the evening. And then my dad's going to come back to live in Lichfield and everything. We were going to do something about Mum's gravestone."

"But the story's finished, Max," he said.

I looked into his eyes, and they no longer seemed kind. It was like looking into the eyes of a serial killer.

"It can't have finished," I protested. "I still don't know how it ends."

"Well, that's easy," said the writer. "I can tell you exactly how it ends." He gave me one last smile—a smile that was both apologetic and ruthless—and clicked his fingers. "Like this."

Acknowledgements

Parts of this novel were written during a stay at the Villa Hellebosch in Flanders, funded by the Flemish government under the Residences in Flanders scheme administered by Het Beschrijf in Brussels.

I'd like to express personal thanks to my kind and attentive host at the villa, Alexandra Cool; also to Ilke Froyen, Sigrid Bousset and Paul Buekenhout; and to James Cañón for his excellent company during my stay.

"The Nettle Pit" first appeared as part of the collection *Ox-Tales: Earth*, published by Profile Books in support of Oxfam. Many thanks to Mark Ellingham at Profile and Tom Childs at Oxfam for their inspiration and encouragement.

www.jonathancoewriter.com

THE HOUSE OF SLEEP

Like a surreal and highly caffeinated version of *The Big Chill*, this novel follows four students who knew each other in college in the eighties. Sarah is a narcoleptic who has dreams so vivid she mistakes them for real events. Robert has his life changed forever by the misunderstandings that arise from her condition. Terry spends his wakeful nights fueling his obsession with movies. And an increasingly unstable doctor, Gregory, sees sleep as a life-shortening disease which he must eradicate. But after ten years of fretful slumber and dreams gone bad, the four reunite in their college town to confront their disorders. In a Gothic cliffside manor being used as a clinic for sleep disorders, they discover that neither love, nor lunacy, nor obsession ever rests.

Fiction

THE RAIN BEFORE IT FALLS

As a young girl, Rosamond is sent to Shropshire to escape the Blitz. Here, in the countryside, she forms a close bond with her cousin, Beatrix, a young woman haunted by anger and resentment. Sixty years later, just before her death, she records these memories on cassettes, addressing them to a distant cousin—a near stranger—named Imogen. As Gill, her beloved niece, listens to these tapes, a heart-stopping family saga is revealed. In this masterful portrait of three generations of women Jonathan Coe exposes the profound reserves of hope and loss within the lives of ordinary women.

Fiction

THE ROTTERS' CLUB

Birmingham, England, c. 1973: industrial strikes, bad pop music, corrosive class warfare, adolescent angst, IRA bombings, four friends. A class clown who stoops very low for a laugh; a confused artist enthralled by guitar rock; an earnest radical with socialist leanings; and a quiet dreamer obsessed with poetry, God, and the prettiest girl in the school. As the world appears to self-destruct around them, they hold together to navigate the choppy waters of a decidedly ambiguous decade.

Fiction

THE CLOSED CIRCLE

The characters of *The Rotter's Club*—Jonathan Coe's beloved novel of adolescence in the 1970s—have bartered their innocence for the vengeance of middle age in this incisive portrait of cool Britannia at the Millennium. "Immensely satisfying. . . . Coe is a witty writer with a talent for social satire that singes characters without burning away their humanity" (*The Washington Post Book World*).

Fiction

THE WINSHAW LEGACY

This shamelessly entertaining novel introduces readers to what may be the most powerful family in England—and is certainly the vilest. When mad Aunt Tabitha Winshaw engages Michael Owen to write a history of the Winshaw family, he uncovers a trail of backstabbing and deceit that leads from World War II to the wholesale plunder of the 1980s. Michael implicates Winshaw bankers, politicians, and media princesses, but he also discovers unnerving truths about himself. For ensuing events bear an uncanny resemblance to a film that has haunted Michael since his childhood, a film whose gory denouement will be eerily repeated one rain-drenched night in the Winshaws' crumbling mansion.

Fiction